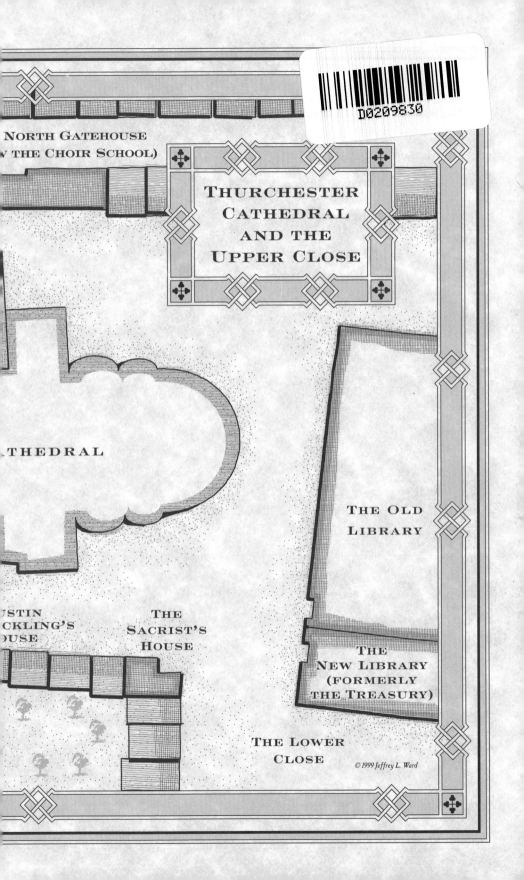

NORTH GATEHOUSE
(NOW THE CHOIR SCHOOL)

THURCHESTER
CATHEDRAL
AND THE
UPPER CLOSE

CATHEDRAL

THE OLD
LIBRARY

AUSTIN
HUCKLING'S
HOUSE

THE
SACRIST'S
HOUSE

THE
NEW LIBRARY
(FORMERLY
THE TREASURY)

THE LOWER
CLOSE

© 1999 Jeffrey L. Ward

BASALT REGIONAL LIBRARY DISTRICT

99 Midland Avenue
Basalt CO 81621
927-4311

F PAL
Palliser, Charles, 1947-
The unburied.
$25.00

ALSO BY CHARLES PALLISER

The Quincunx

The Sensationist

Betrayals

THE
UNBURIED

Charles Palliser

FARRAR, STRAUS AND GIROUX

New York

Farrar, Straus and Giroux
19 Union Square West, New York 10003

Copyright © 1999 by Charles Palliser
Printed in the United States of America
Designed by Abby Kagan
First published in 1999 by Phoenix House in the United Kingdom
First American edition published in 1999 by Farrar, Straus and Giroux

Library of Congress Cataloging-in-Publication Data
Palliser, Charles, 1947–
    The unburied / Charles Palliser. — 1st American ed.
        p.   cm.
    ISBN 0-374-28035-5 (alk. paper)
    I. Title.
PR6066.A43U5   1999
823´.914—dc21   99-14740

To E.R.

Acknowledgements

I am grateful to the following for reading and offering advice on the novel during its period of gestation: Helen Ash, James Buxton, Jane Dorner, Mary Dove, Roger Elliott, Lorna Gibb, John Hands, Tom Holland, Hunter Steele and Janet Todd.

Contents

❖

Editor's *Foreword*

✤

FEW BOOKS IN RECENT TIMES have created as much controversy as *The Thurchester Mystery* when it was published three years ago. I have sat many times in the houses of friends in the town and watched families, bitterly divided by conflicting theories, quarrel fiercely about it. My opinion has, inevitably, been sought but I have always refused to be drawn. Although the case appeared at the time to have been resolved, rumours continued to circulate and the allegations against even the most respectable individuals involved became more and more grotesque as the decades passed. With the publication of the present work, however, all argument should end for the account which forms the bulk of the book now in your hands has offered an entirely new perspective on Miss Napier's discoveries.

The circumstances in which the Courtine Account became available are described in my 'Afterword', where I also explain the reasons why, before that document could be unsealed, I had to undertake a journey to Geneva. That was eight months ago—the earliest moment at which the situation on the Continent made it possible to travel again—albeit with great difficulty. My journey was slow and uncomfortable and it was not until two days after leaving my house that I reached my destination.

The taxi from the station brought me to a big house on the shore of the lake surrounded by a park dotted with gloomy pine-trees—looking all the more ominous as the sky darkened at the approach of a storm. In my rusty French I instructed the driver to wait.

Although the servant who opened the door made it clear that she recognized my name, I was not sure if I would be admitted. I had written a few days earlier from England to say that I would come at precisely that hour and hoped it would be convenient, but I had not given time for a reply. I was optimistic, however, for my letter had been written in terms carefully calculated to gain me admission.

The servant showed me into the hall and asked me to take a seat and then vanished. The house was cold and I reflected that fuel was in short supply here as in England. It occurred to me that that must be why some of the trees in the park had been felled. As I gazed out at the desolate scene, the light slowly ebbed from the sky over the grey expanse of water. I waited for forty minutes and had almost abandoned hope when the woman reappeared and led me through a door and up an imposing flight of stairs. She ushered me into a huge room at the end of which was a vast window whose curtains were drawn back to display the louring sky and the dark surface of the lake. To one side of the window stood a black grand piano—its lid lowered. On the other side—placed to achieve the greatest dramatic effect—a figure was seated in a high-backed chair. I moved forward like an audience taking its seat and as if on cue there was a flash of lightning across the sky.

The servant lighted a lamp beside her mistress and picked up a tray on which were the remains of tea. The old lady waved me to a seat and for a moment or two I was able to study her features while she watched the servant at work: the high nose and bright blue eyes set in an intelligent and mistrustful face. When the servant had withdrawn I began to make conversation, saying that it was gracious of her to admit me, a stranger.

She interrupted me as if I had not been speaking: 'Have you and I ever met?'

Her voice was surprisingly firm for a woman in her early nineties, and also remarkably deep—though I had expected that. Her question put me on the spot. I had hoped to coax and flatter her into saying what I wanted to hear, but I now saw that I would have to adopt a different strategy.

'No, not exactly. But I saw you once, many years ago.'

'Under what circumstances?'

'It was in Thurchester.'

She looked at me with close scrutiny and I saw no sign of unease. 'You are mistaken. That is quite impossible.'

'I saw you the day you gave the performance of your life.'

She smiled thinly. 'I know that wretched little theatre in the High Street. I once knew it very well indeed. But I never appeared there myself.'

'I did not say I saw you there.'

She gazed at me narrowly: 'You must have been born twenty years after I gave up the stage.'

'The stage, yes.' Seeing her expression of surprise I added: 'You will understand when I give you what I have brought.'

My heart was pounding as I said the words. I so much wanted proof. I needed her to say something that would convince me that she was the woman I had been seeking. I don't mean legal proof for I had that already. The succession of property transactions and changes of residence from country to country, which I had managed to follow through the decades, had already satisfied the relevant requirements. But that had not appeased my need to know that it really was she. I had to hear from her lips something that would connect the woman before me with that figure which, though only briefly glimpsed, had come to haunt my memory.

It was clear that she did not like that remark and, as if to bring our encounter to a speedy conclusion, she said: 'You stated in your letter that you have property of mine.'

'Which I wished to place personally in the rightful owner's hands in order to vindicate an ancient injustice.'

She nodded. 'Those were your words. What is it? Do you expect to be paid for it?'

'Not with money. And I have no intention of bargaining. The property belongs to you.' I realized that, more precipitately than I should have, I had reached the main point of my journey. I hesitated a moment and then added: 'To you and your son.'

Her head jerked up involuntarily and she looked at me for the first time with naked interest and, it seemed to me, anger. A moment later the mask was back in place. I went on as matter-of-factly as I could: 'I have tried to find him since I would have preferred not to have bothered you with this matter. I have made extensive efforts to contact him but my endeavours have been unavailing. If you tell me how to reach him, I will cease to trouble you and conclude my business with your heir.'

'My heir?' She uttered the words in what seemed to me a tone of mocking raillery.

'I assume that your son is your heir?'

'I am not responsible for your assumptions.'

'Whether he is your heir or not, this matter concerns him as much as yourself.' When she made no response I put the brutal question: 'Will you tell me if he is still alive?'

I could discern no reaction. After a moment she said: 'Kindly give me whatever it is you say is mine.'

I rose from my seat and pulled an envelope from my pocket with a certain theatricality of my own, and held it out to her.

She seized it and tore it open. There is a common belief that the very old have reached a stage in which they are gradually detaching themselves from the world of self and emotions and greed. I saw no evidence that she was withdrawing from life; and on the contrary, as I watched her eagerly ripping open the envelope, I felt that I had achieved at least part of my purpose: I understood things about motives and scruples that I had not grasped before.

'What are these? What does this mean?'

She dropped the contents of the package contemptuously onto a small table beside her chair.

'They are the keys to a mystery,' I could not prevent myself from replying. 'Won't you take them?'

'I have no idea of what you are referring to.'

'You don't recognize them?'

'Why should I?'

'They are the keys to a house in Thurchester. A house you know very well.' She turned her gaze upon me with mild curiosity, but that was all the emotion she showed. I tried to prompt her: 'I rescued them as they were about to be lost for ever.' When she still failed to speak I added: 'That day—I mean the day which changed your life as dramatically as it affected mine—I followed you from the back-door of the house. You didn't notice me, or if you did, you thought me no danger.'

When I finished speaking she did not answer. For perhaps a minute we sat in silence. Then she tugged at a bell-pull beside her chair. Almost immediately the servant, who must have been waiting outside the door, entered. The old lady said in good French: 'This gentleman is leaving. Will you show him out.'

'Does your servant understand English?' I asked. She made no response and merely stared out of the window. 'I need to find your son. What name does he use?'

Now at last she turned to look at me and it was with an expression of such blank and incurious hostility that I knew my questions would never be answered.

I stood up.

'Your journey has been unprofitable,' the old lady said. 'But you cannot blame me for that.'

'It has not been without profit. It was enlightenment more than anything that I sought.'

She gave no sign that my remark interested her.

I went on: 'Meeting you has enabled me to comprehend things that have puzzled me for more than four decades.'

I made my way towards the door and had almost reached it when she called out: 'Mr Barthram. You have forgotten your keys.'

I turned and walked towards her. 'I have not forgotten them. I assure you, I have never forgotten them for a single day of my life. They are yours and it is with an indescribable sense of relief that I leave them with you.' I halted about ten paces away. 'Do you remember the name Perkins?' She remained impassive.

I did not realize how menacing I must have seemed until the servant said in a terrified voice: 'Shall I go for Pierre, Madame?'

The old lady impatiently gestured to her to be silent without taking her eyes from me.

'Do you ever think about a young man called Eddy Perkins?' I repeated.

To my astonishment, she smiled. 'I imagine that you do. Why has it taken you so long?' She nodded at the little table. 'If you had made more timely use of these, the whole thing would have been understood even by the most obtuse. Were you too timid?'

'I was a child,' I answered.

'When I was a child I was frightened of nothing. Or perhaps it would be truer to say that if I was frightened, it didn't inhibit me from doing what I wanted. That's the difference, isn't it, between those who go through their lives merely repeating their lines and those who invent their role as they act it?'

'You were good at that.'

'I was magnificent.'

'Are you confessing?'

'Confessing? My dear man, I'm boasting. The greatest actors can create a human being before the very eyes of spectators—not show them something fabricated beforehand like a puppet. To go out onto the stage and become the character at a moment of crisis and speak without knowing what you are going to say until the words come out! To court that danger and to triumph, that is the great adventure that life offers. The incomparable adventure. Don't you see that?'

'I've never acted.'

'I'm not talking about just acting. I'm talking about being alive. Otherwise you're dead without the dignity of burial.'

'You regret nothing?'

'Only that I am now dying.'

There was nothing to be gained by asking her again about Perkins, who died because he lacked the imagination to live anywhere but in the present moment. I turned and left the room.

My trip turned out to have been worthwhile in a more concrete way. As my train made its slow and necessarily roundabout progress towards the coast, the names of Flemish towns and villages which had acquired a hideous familiarity in England in the last four years began to appear on the signboards. I thought of the grieving mothers of so many of my pupils for whom I had been unable to find words of comfort. And then there came into my memory the old woman's involuntary start at the word 'son', and as I pictured her, I saw the black piano with its lid lowered and at that moment an idea about how I might proceed came to me.

The death of the old lady just two months ago removed the last obstacle to publication of the document which follows. As a preface to it I need only say that this comment was written on the outside of the envelope which contained it—written as a consequence of my own intervention, though I did not know that until many years later: *I have just learned that I was wrong about the role of Ormonde who I now know was dead many years before the events recounted here. Nevertheless, I will let this stand as a true record of what I witnessed and the conclusions I later drew from my experiences—wrong though some of them must have been. E.C.*

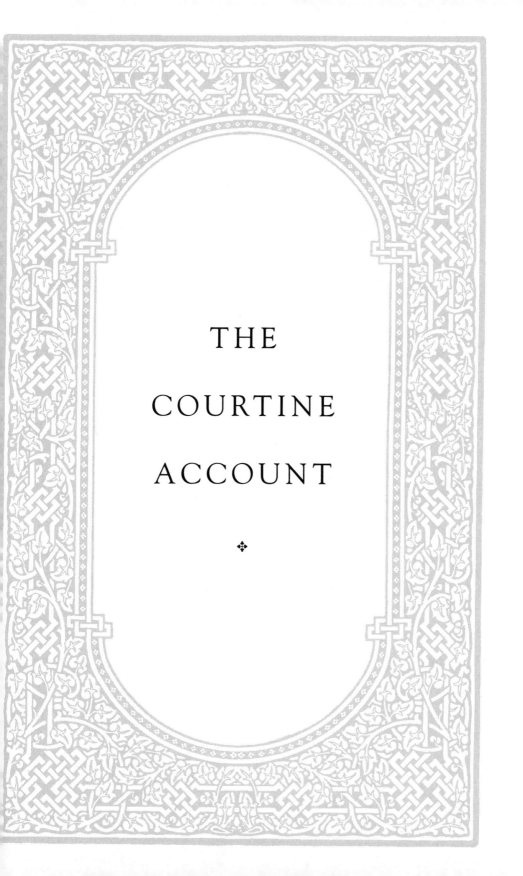

THE

COURTINE

ACCOUNT

❖

Tuesday Evening

✢

WHILE MY MEMORY IS FRESH I am going to describe exactly what I saw and heard on the occasion, less than a week past, when I encountered a man who was walking about just like you and me—despite the inconvenience of having been brutally done to death.

My visit began inauspiciously. Because of the weather, which for two days had draped a cloak of freezing fog upon the southern half of the country, the train was delayed and I missed a connection. By the time I reached my destination—two hours late—I had been travelling for several hours through a premature night. As I sat alone in the ill-lit carriage, holding a book in front of me but making little attempt to read, I gazed out at the shrouded landscape that grew increasingly unfamiliar and indistinct as the dusk fell and the fog thickened. Gradually the impression took hold of me that the train was bearing me not forwards but backwards—carrying me out of my own life and time and into the past.

Suddenly I was recalled to myself when, with an abrupt jerk, the train began to slow down and, after a series of shudders, came to a halt in a darkness that was barely mitigated by the dim lights from the carriages. We were so far behind the timetable that I had no idea if this was my station. As I stood at the door trying to see a signboard in the liverish yellow glow of a distant gas-lamp, I heard a window further along the train being lowered and a fellow-passenger call out to ask if we had reached the terminus. A voice from somewhere along the platform replied in the negative, saying that this was the last stop before the end of the line and naming my destination.

I took my bag from the rack and descended with only two or three other travellers. They passed from my sight while I stood for a few moments on the platform, shocked by the cold and stamping my feet and clasping my arms about me as I tried to breathe the foul air in which the acrid smell of hard frost was mingled with the smoke of the town's thousands of coal-fires.

Austin had told me that he would be unable to meet me at the station because his duties would detain him, and that I should therefore go straight to the house. I had preferred that, since it had occurred to me that I might not recognize him and it would be better to encounter him at his own door. I could not decide if the prospect of finding that he had changed was more or less disturbing than discovering that he had not. I believe, however, that what I was really afraid of was not so much the changes I would find in him as seeing in the face of my old friend the transformation which the years had wrought upon myself.

The train whistled and shunted out of the station leaving me gasping at the soot-laden smoke it had belched forth—a dark, bowels-of-the-earth mineral smell. Darkness fell again and all that was visible now was a flaring gas-jet above what must be the gate from the platform. I directed myself towards it and at the barrier a railway employee, muffled up with a scarf across his face, took my ticket with one of his gloved hands.

When I passed out to the forecourt I found that my fellow-passengers had vanished like phantoms. There was only one cab waiting and I engaged it. The face that the driver turned to me had a bulbous nose and hanging lower lip which, together with the stench of sour beer on his breath, inspired little confidence. I gave the address and we lurched into motion.

Although the town was unfamiliar to me I knew that the station was about a mile from the centre. Through the little window of the swaying vehicle I could see almost nothing, though I could hear that there were few other vehicles on the road. In three or four minutes we started going up a slight rise and I guessed that we were ascending the hill at the summit of which the Romans had built their fortress to guard the ancient crossroads.

On both sides of the road were rows of cottages in several of whose lighted windows I caught sight of families sitting down for their evening meal. Though my welcome so far was cold, I told myself that at least I would not be spending the week in College with the dreary remnant of my unmarried colleagues who had not been invited anywhere.

The cab slowed as the hill grew steeper and I realized, with surprise, that my heart was beating faster. I had often wondered what sort of a hand my old friend had made of his life. As undergraduates we had talked much of the stir we would make out in the great world—both of us passionate about our studies and ambitious for recognition. Did he regret the way his life had turned out? Was he happy in this remote little town? Had he found other compensations? From time to time I had heard rumours about his way of life from our common acquaintance, though I gave them little credit. I had speculated often about him and when I had received his invitation—so surprising after such a long estrangement—I had not been able to resist.

The carriage breasted the rise, and as the wheels began to clatter over the cobbles, our speed increased. Now there were street-lamps whose misty haloes cast scant light in the thick fog and I could see that although we appeared to be in the High Street, there was little traffic in the carriageway and few foot-passengers on the pavements. As the hooves of the cab-horse rang out in the silent street, we might have been travelling through a sacked city deserted after a siege. Then, without warning, I was thrown from side to side as the vehicle made a succession of sharp turns and passed through a great arch—the clattering hooves echoing around me. I thought the driver had brought me to an inn by mistake but at that moment I heard—I might almost say I was stunned by—the heavy thud of a great bell. It struck four more times—each chime seeming to overtake the last like ripples spreading outwards through the fog—and I realized that I was right underneath the Cathedral and that in the near-darkness of the fog we had come upon it without my being aware.

The cab swung round sharply for the last time and drew up. A few yards away was a porch—the south door of the transept. In the flaring light of a gas-mantle I saw a stack of bricks and some wooden slats, covered by a tarred cloth.

'Are they working on the Cathedral?' I asked the driver as I descended.

'Aren't they always?' he answered.

As I was paying the fare the door of the nearest house opened and a figure came hurrying towards me.

'Old fellow, how glad I am to see you,' said a youthful voice that I remembered so well I shivered. The voice was the same but I saw before me a stranger, a middle-aged man with lined cheeks and a high forehead from which the thin greying hair was receding. Austin seized me and hugged me, and as I felt how slight his frame was, I remembered that un-English impulsiveness and emotionalism of his that I had always envied and been a little afraid of.

'Thank you for coming,' he said, one hand patting my back as we embraced. 'God bless you. God bless you.'

At his words I felt a profound regret for what had happened. It could not have been foreseen during the period of our friendship that we would be parted for so long—parted by an estrangement that had come about because he had been implicated in the most painful experience of my life. Afterwards it was I who had written to him in a gesture intended to show that I wanted our friendship to survive. It was only when he had failed to respond that I had begun to wonder if he felt guilt for the part he had played and then to speculate more and more about what role exactly he had been assigned or had taken upon himself. Despite that, I wrote him a short note that first Christmas and every subsequent one, and after a few years he had begun to do the same—more briefly—and had continued to do so about every two or three years.

I heard news of him through common acquaintances, though less and less often as they lost touch or went abroad or died. And then a month ago—long after I had assumed that the embers of our friendship had turned to ashes—I had received a letter inviting me to visit him—indeed, urging me to do so in the warmest terms—on any date of my own choosing since he never went away, provided only that I had 'the patience to endure the company of the dull and crotchety old fellow I've become'. At first I had wondered if blowing on those embers now would revive or extinguish them, but I had an idea of why he might have decided to invite me and so I had written back to say that I would come with pleasure and that it fortunately happened that I was anxious to survey and measure the ancient earthworks at Woodbury Castle just outside the town. I said that I would come early in the new year on my way back from my niece and that I would give him as much warning as possible. (In the event, I had altered my plans and had been able to give him only a few days' notice.)

Behind me I heard the cab turning in the narrow way between the houses and the Cathedral.

Austin drew back, still holding me by both arms, so that for the first time I could see him, though only in the feeble light cast by the gas-mantle some fifteen yards away. There was the old Austin smiling at me. The same brightness in his large black eyes, the same boyish eagerness. He was smiling and yet, for all his apparent pleasure at seeing me again, I thought there was something evasive, something shadowed in his gaze that did not quite meet mine. Was he thinking what I was thinking: What have the years done to you? What have they given you to match the bright youthfulness they have taken?

'Dear Austin, you're looking very well.'

'All the better for seeing you,' he said. 'Come in, my dear old friend.'

He seized my bag and winced theatrically at its weight. I tried to take it from him but he drew it away too quickly for me so that for a moment we were a couple of playful undergraduates again. 'What on earth is in it? Books, I suppose?'

'And Christmas gifts for my niece's children. Though one of them is for you.'

'Oh, capital! I love being given presents,' he exclaimed. He carried the bag ahead of me to the door where he thrust out an arm to invite me to enter before him.

I peered up at the building. 'What a pretty old house,' I said. In fact, as I spoke the words I perceived that the house was quaint rather than pretty. It was tall and narrow and the casement windows and doors were so manifestly out of alignment with each other and with the ground that, squashed between two bigger houses, it looked like a drunken man being held up under the armpits by his companions.

'It comes with the post. It's regarded as a benefit, but I often think I should be paid more for living in it. The best houses are in the Lower Close.'

Meanwhile the cab-driver had effected his awkward manoeuvre and I heard the vehicle roll away. As I passed over the threshold I went down a couple of steps, for the level of the cobbled court outside had risen over the centuries. In the dark little hall I found myself facing a staircase—indeed, the house was all stairs, for it was of an ancient construction with only two rooms on each floor. When

I had removed my greatcoat and hat, Austin led me into his front-parlour. I could see that the kitchen was the little room beyond it. The front-parlour—or dining-room as he called it, and it was apparent from the table laid for two that this was where he ate—was cold, though there was a newly-lit fire burning. In the light of the gas-lamp I could see Austin clearly at last. His nose was redder than I remembered it, and though his skin was still as pale as paper, it was now coarse and wrinkled. He was as slender as he had been as a young man. (I cannot say the same in my own case, I fear.) Oddly, he was taller than I remembered. Seeing my scrutiny he smiled and I did the same. Then he turned away and began to tidy up as if he had made no preparations for my arrival.

All the while he asked me questions about my journey and I responded with enquiries about the house and its position and its amenities. I seated myself in one of the two old chairs at the table. The furniture was shabby and broken down, with a greasy shine upon the fabric. The old panelling was blackened by a couple of centuries of candle-flames and on the bare boards there was only a threadbare Turkey carpet. Absurdly, I felt my heart thumping. The place was so mean, almost squalid. I thought of my own comfortable apartments and the college servants who kept everything clean and neat.

Austin poured me a glass of madeira-wine from a decanter which stood on a side-table. As he handed it to me, the smell of the place suddenly struck me—thick, heavy, intimate. Holding the glass, I drew breath with difficulty through my nostrils. I shut my eyes and thought of the Cathedral so near, of bones and flesh rotting beneath the stones, of what might be beneath this house which was in the shadow of the great building. The smell was sweet, obscene, like a rotting corpse pressing down upon me, holding me in a clammy, slippery embrace, and suddenly I believed I was going to be violently ill. I managed to sip a little of the wine and somehow to turn my thoughts elsewhere and the moment passed. I looked up and saw that Austin was watching me curiously and I forced a smile and then we toasted each other and my arrival.

What could we talk about after so long? It seemed absurd to engage in the trivial chatter of mere acquaintances—the weather, the journey, the proximity of the house to the Cathedral and the various amenities and inconveniences thereof. Yet that is what we did. And all the while, I was scrutinizing him and wondering how the passage of time had changed him. And I supposed he was looking at me with the same questions. Could we fall back into the boyish intercourse that we had enjoyed or, much more to be hoped, could we find a new mature note of friendship? Or would we flail uneasily between the old and now inappropriate manner and a new realization that we had little in common?

'How good it is to see you,' I said when there was a pause.

He smiled at me and his smile stayed even as he lifted his glass to his mouth and drank.

I felt I was smiling idiotically back at him. Simply for something to say, I blurted out: 'How long it must be since we last saw each other!' As soon as the words were uttered I wished them recalled. How strange that when one has resolved not to speak of a particular subject it should be the very first thing one brings up.

As if the remark awakened no memories, he put down his glass and made a show of counting on his fingers. 'Twenty years.'

'Longer. Twenty-two. Nearly twenty-two.'

He shook his head with a smile.

I hadn't intended to raise the subject at all, but now that I had, I wanted us to remember it correctly. Then I would say no more about it. 'You came to the station at Great Yarmouth to see me off. To see us off. I have always remembered my last sight of you on the platform as the train drew out.'

He gazed at me as if with nothing more than polite curiosity. 'How strange. My recollection is that you and I returned to London alone.'

'Absolutely not. I can see you standing there and waving good-bye. The date was July the twenty-eighth and it was twenty-two years ago come the summer.'

'You must be right. You're the one who knows about the past.'

'It's very hard to know the truth about the past, Austin. But the events of that summer are, I assure you, engraved upon my memory.'

I had spoken with more emotion than I had intended. As I drank, the glass clattered against my teeth. I was suddenly terrified that he would utter one of the two names that were never to be mentioned between us. I lowered the glass, trying to keep my hand steady.

'We won't argue about it. It isn't worth it.' Then he smiled and said: 'But now to the future. You can stay until Saturday?'

'With pleasure. But I will have to leave early in the morning since it is Christmas Eve and I am expected at my niece's in the afternoon.'

'And that is where?'

'Exeter, as I mentioned in my letter.'

'Yes, of course. Well, that is agreed. We will meet in the evenings, but I'm afraid I shall be working during the day.'

'And I have things to do myself that will keep me occupied most of the day.'

'So you wrote. I hope this wretched cold and fog won't hamper your work too much.'

I smiled. It was an odd thing to say, but Austin had always had an elfin sense of humour. I had written to him only a few days earlier to ask if it would be convenient if I were to alter our arrangement and come at such short notice and he had replied that he would be delighted. What had prompted me to bring forward the visit was this. When I had received the invitation from Austin, I had remembered that my College Library had the uncatalogued papers of an antiquarian called Pepperdine who, I recalled, had visited the town shortly after the Restoration, and so I had decided to look at them. While doing so, I had come across a letter which—as I had explained to Austin—suggested that a long-standing scholarly controversy relating to my beloved Alfredian period might be resolved by the discovery of a certain document in the Library of the Dean and Chapter. I was so anxious to begin my researches that I had changed my plans and decided to visit Austin on my way to Exeter rather than on the journey back in the new year.

'After your long journey,' he went on, 'I thought you'd like to stay in tonight, and I'll cook our supper.'

'As you did in the old days,' I exclaimed. 'Do you not recall? When we lodged in Sidney Street, we used to take turns to grill chops?'

Memories flooded back and I found myself quite misty-eyed.

Austin nodded.

'Do you remember your "chops St Lawrence" as you called them? Burnt to a crisp like the poor saint? You called your dinners an *auto-da-fé* for you said more faith was required to eat them than the wretched victims of the Inquisition ever needed.'

He smiled but it seemed to be at my own nostalgia rather than at the memories I was evoking. 'I have lamb-cutlets and capers ready. I have had enough practice in the intervening years to be able to promise no acts of martyrdom in the eating of them.'

It was odd to think of Austin keeping house for himself. I remembered how slovenly he had been—crumbs always scattered on the floor of his rooms in college, his clothes thrown over a chair, cups and plates rarely washed. The room I was in now was not very much tidier than that.

'I will show you your room,' Austin said. 'I expect you will want to wash while I am cooking.'

'Do I have time to look at the Cathedral? I need to stretch my legs after a long day on the train.'

'Supper will not be ready for about half an hour.'

'Won't the Cathedral be locked by now?'

'Not tonight.'

'Good. I'm looking forward to seeing the ambulatory.'

Austin appeared surprised, even startled. 'I thought you had never been here before?'

'But, my dear fellow, I know the Cathedral intimately from written accounts and illustrations. It has one of the finest ambulatories in England.'

'Has it?' he asked absently.

'It is altogether a remarkable building, and almost completely intact.' Remembering what I had seen as I arrived and how uninformatively the cab-driver had answered my question, I asked: 'But is work being done on it now?'

He smiled. 'Oh, you've brought up the great issue that has divided the town more bitterly than anything in its history.'

'At least since the Siege.' I laughed. 'Don't forget that.'

'They are indeed working on it, which is why you'll be able to get in so late.'

'What is being done? Not some of that so-called restoration work?'

'They are merely working on the organ.'

'Even so, that can do considerable damage.'

'Hardly likely. And it will immensely improve the organ. They are introducing steam-power to blow it and carrying the action down from the old console to a new gallery.'

I could not help shaking my head in dismay. 'Quite unnecessary. It will sound no better.'

'On the contrary. It is also being tuned to equal temperament and extensively improved. At present it has a short compass and no clarion or cremona.'

I was surprised by his expertise, although I remembered that he sang and had some skill on the flute. 'I didn't know you played the organ?'

'I don't,' he said sharply. 'I have been told so by those who understand these things.'

'Once you start to interfere with an old building you never know where it will end. The introduction of steam-power for ecclesiastical organs in the last thirty years has led to extensive demolition.'

'Well,' Austin said with that odd smile I now recalled which always seemed intended only for himself, 'if they find work that needs to be done to keep the building practical for modern-day needs, they must do it. It's not a mummy to be preserved in a glass case in a museum.' I was about to reply when he sprang up: 'I must show you to your room.'

He had always been quick and active—ready to leap to his feet and hurry out of the house on some hare-brained idea. And his mind was just as quick—though perhaps a little too hasty and easily bored. Mine was possibly a little slower but much more tenacious and prepared to burrow deeper into things—perhaps precisely because it did not grasp them as readily as Austin's. So it was not surprising that I, not he, had become the scholar although he had shown great brilliance in his field of study.

And so now he seized my bag and hurried out of the room leaving me to follow him. In the hall, he snatched up a candlestick and lit it from the mantle, explaining that there was gas laid only on the ground floor. Then he bounded up the stairs while I laboured after him in near-darkness. He waited for me on the half-landing, where a grandfather clock barely left room for both of us. We climbed the last few stairs and he pushed open a door and showed me the cosy little room at the back which he used as his study. The larger room at the front was his drawing-room—as he expressed it with a self-mocking smile.

We climbed the next flight of the queer old stairs where bare dusty boards replaced the threadbare carpet lower down. Austin showed me into the front-bedroom, saying: 'I hope you won't be troubled by the blessed bells.'

'I'm used to them,' I said. 'I should be, after more than thirty years.' With the ceiling slanting down over half of it, the little room was like a ship's cabin—an effect enhanced by the sloping floors and tiny window.

He left me to unpack and wash. The room seemed not to have been used for some time and smelt musty. I opened the little case-ment window and the rasping, smoky air blew in. The Cathedral loomed up out of the fog giving the illusion of being in motion as the mist swirled about it. There was no sound from the Close. I shut the window against the cold. The small looking-glass above the wash-stand was clouded and even when I had rubbed at it with my handkerchief, the image remained shadowy. Beside the stand lay a leather dressing-case with the initials 'A.F.' which I remem-bered from our college days. It looked hardly any older than when I had last seen it. As I unpacked my bag and washed, I reflected on how Austin had changed. He had always had a theatrical side but it seemed to me that it was accentuated now—almost as if for a purpose. I wondered once again if he had invited me in order to make amends for what had happened twenty-two years ago and asked myself how I could convey to him, without our having to rake over the past, that I did not blame him for what had occurred.

When I came down ten minutes later I went into the kitchen and found Austin chopping onions. He looked me up and down with a mysterious smile and after a few seconds he said: 'Where's my gift?'

'How foolish of me. I took it out of my bag and put it on the bed in order to remember it. I'll go up and get it.'

'Fetch it later. Go to the Cathedral now. Supper will be ready in twenty minutes.'

I did as he suggested. When I was out in the Close a moment or two later I saw a couple of people hurrying away from the doorway in the south transept which was almost opposite Austin's house. Evensong had presumably just finished. I entered, letting the heavy door swing shut behind me before I raised my eyes and looked ahead, anxious to savour the excitement I always felt when I entered an ancient edifice that was new to me.

As if they had been waiting for my entrance, the unaccompanied voices of the choir suddenly rose—the pure trebles of the boys soaring above the deeper tones of the men in an image of harmony between idealism and reality. The voices were muted and I had no idea where the choristers were. I was surprised to find them singing so late.

The great building was almost dark and it was cold—colder, it seemed, than the Close. There was the smell of stale incense and I remembered that the Dean was of the High Church tendency. Keeping my gaze lowered, I advanced across the flagstones which were so worn down in the centre that I fancied I was walking across a series of shallow soup-bowls. When I reached the centre I turned and raised my head so that the vast length of the nave suddenly fell away in front of me with the thick columns rising like a stone grove whose trunks gradually turned like branches into the delicate tracery of the roof. Far away the great sheets of uneven glass of the rose-window at the western end, like a dark lake under a clouded moon, caught the gleams of the gas-lights. The few lamps only threw into relief the vastness of the soaring arches. When I had gorged my sight, I leant my head back and looked up at the vault high above me. I smelt fresh wood and I thought of how, seven hundred and fifty years ago, the heavy beams and huge blocks of stone were lifted through that space a hundred and twenty feet into the air. How strange to think of this ancient building as once having been startlingly new, rising shockingly above the low roofs of the town. How miraculous that so much had survived the civil wars of Henry VI's reign, the demolition of the Abbey in the Dissolution and the bombardment during the Siege of 1643.

The voices died away and there was silence. I turned and my gaze fell on an utter monstrosity: a huge and hideous new organ-gallery thrusting itself forward in the transept. With its gleaming pipes, polished ivory and shining ebony it resembled nothing so much as a huge cuckoo-clock from some feverish nightmare.

And now another outrage: I became aware of harsh raised voices whose source, in that echoing, muffled space, it was impossible to discern. When I had ascended the steps of the chancel I noticed lights in the furthest corner. There were more shouts and then the musical ring of spades on stone, all of which the vast building seemed to receive and slowly absorb as it had absorbed the joys and the anguish of men and women for nearly eight hundred years. I turned the corner of the stalls and found three men working—or, rather, two working and one directing them—their breath visible in the light of two lanterns one of which was standing on the floor while another was perched insolently on a bishop's tomb.

The labourers, who had taken up a number of the great paving-stones, were young and beardless, but the older man who was supervising them had a piratical appearance with a great black beard and an angry, swaggering manner. But I was more intrigued by a tall old fellow in a black cassock who was watching. He was certainly seventy and very possibly older than the century and, with great pouched bags under his eyes and deep lines around his sunken cheeks, he looked like a man to whom a terrible wrong had been done and who had spent decades brooding upon it. His great height and smooth hairless skull made him resemble some part of the Cathedral itself that had come to life or—rather—taken on some small degree of animation. His almost perfectly horizontal mouth was fixed in an expression of disapproval.

I approached and said to him: 'Would you be good enough to tell me what they are doing?'

He shook his head: 'A deal of mischief, sir.'

'Are you a verger?'

'Head-verger and have been these twenty-five years,' he answered with melancholy pride, stiffening his back as he spoke.

'And my father and grandfather before me. And all three of us singing-boys in our time.'

'Really? That's a remarkable dynasty. And the next generation?'

His face darkened: 'My son cares nought for it. It's a sad thing when your own child turns his back on the thing you've given your life to. Do you know what I mean, sir?'

'I can imagine. Though I have no children myself.'

'I'm very sorry to hear that, sir,' he said earnestly. 'That must be a sorrow to your wife and yourself, if you'll pardon me for saying so.'

'I have no wife either.' I added: 'I once had a wife. I . . . that is to say.' I broke off.

'Then I'm sorry for that, too. I can't have much longer on this earth, sir, but it's a great comfort to me to know that I shall leave three fine grandchildren behind me. Three grandchildren and twelve great-grandchildren.'

'That is indeed a cause for congratulation. Now will you be good enough to tell me what is going forward here? If you've worked here all these years, you must know the building well.'

'I know every corner of her, sir. And it pains me to see them hack her open like this.'

'Why are they doing it?'

'It's that blessed organ. They've built a new console in the transept. You must have noticed that dreadful new-fangled thing that's more like a traction-engine than an organ. And now they're laying down the pipes for it.'

'They're not going to take up all that length of paving, are they?' I asked, indicating it with my arm.

'They are indeed. They don't know what they might not be raking up. Nor they don't care.'

'But what's wrong with the original console? As far as I recall it's a beautiful piece of work from the early seventeenth century.'

'That it is, sir. But it wasn't good enough, it seems. Not for His

Nibs who had to play it—and that's more important than us that hears it, seemingly. Or us that will have to see that Babylonish monstrosity every day of our lives.'

'You are speaking of the organist?'

He went on without noticing my question: 'For some of the canons wanted the organ to be big and loud and to be right out here where the congregation could see it and would join in the singing, and them on the other side wanted to keep the old one because it sounds so well with the choir and doesn't drown out the voices the way this one will.'

'Such disputes between Ritualists and Evangelists have divided every Chapter in the country,' I said.

'How right you are, sir. We didn't have none of that when I was a boy. Then you was a good Christian and worshipped in the Cathedral or you was Chapel or a Papist and that's all there was. Now the Chapel and the Papists is all in the Church and fighting each other about vestments and candles and incense and processions. To my way of thinking, these new ways are all mummery and play-acting and not a respectful way of worshipping the Almighty at all.'

'But now it's the Low Church canons who are getting their way with the organ?'

'Aye, for he seems to have most of them in his pocket. And so, no matter what it costs or what damage it does, he has to get the organ he wants.'

I assumed he was still referring to the organist. 'Didn't the other canons oppose it?'

'Dr Locard tried but they were too many for him. Just as they seem to be in this new to-do over the school.'

I knew who Dr Locard was. 'What is the matter at the school?' I asked, wondering whether some crisis had arisen there that affected Austin and, if so, whether it could be the clue to why he had suddenly invited me. He had been impulsive and self-indulgent and took little thought for the future and it might have led him into difficulties now as it had in the past.

The old verger seemed to realize that he was being indiscreet and muttered, 'They're going to decide about it at the next Chapter meeting. I don't know much more than that.'

'When is the next meeting? The canons should consider stopping these works.'

'Thursday morning.'

'That will be too late!'

I turned and hurried down the stairs and across the Choir to where the men were working.

'Are you the foreman?' I asked the bearded man.

He looked at me curiously. 'I am.'

The men stopped and listened.

'You can't put the pipes through there, my good fellow.'

'I can't, can't I?'

I didn't like his manner at all. 'You'll do some serious damage.'

'I do what I'm told,' he said.

'Wait,' I began. 'Allow me to . . .'

'I take my orders from Mr Bulmer and Dr Sisterson and nobody else,' he interrupted me, and then signalled to his men to go back to work. They exchanged grins of amusement at my expense and one of them swung his pickaxe again.

I returned to the verger. 'If they have to do it, they should take the pipes round another way where they will do less harm.'

'You're right. But how do you know that, sir? With respect, I don't believe I've ever seen you in here before.'

'I've never been. But I've made a study of the construction of cathedrals and I've read a great deal about this one.'

'Where do you think they should put the pipes, sir?'

'I'm not sure. Could I go up to the organ-loft? The old one? I can see better from up there.'

'You're very welcome, sir.'

'It will not inconvenience you?' I asked. 'You're not about to lock up?'

'Not the least bit in the world, sir. We usually lock up after Evensong but tonight—and tomorrow night—the men will be working until eight or nine and I'll have to stay until they've finished to secure the transept door behind them. That's always the last to be locked.'

'Why are they working so late?'

'They need to get it finished for Friday. There's to be a grand service of re-dedication for the organ in the afternoon and the Bishop himself is going to officiate. That's why the choir has been practising so late.'

He picked up the lantern from the tomb and made his way in front of me across the presbytery to a small door just behind the choir-stalls. To my dismay, many of the ancient oaken panels had been removed and some were laid across the door. 'I won't go up myself, sir. It's awkward with my rheumatic joints. Can you squeeze past them panels? They took them off to work on the console.'

'But they are putting them back?'

'Oh yes, thank the good Lord. But they quite blocked that door for a couple of weeks.'

He handed me the lantern and I climbed the stair and found myself in the organ-loft from which I had a good view of the Choir and Presbytery and could see how potentially damaging was the work that was being done. I could also see a much less dangerous way of doing it.

Just as I was about to descend, I saw a figure approaching the old verger from the direction of the chancel. It was a small and youngish man whose prematurely bald head was gleaming as it caught the lights.

When I rejoined the old man a moment or two later I found him talking to the newcomer as they watched the men at work.

'This is Dr Sisterson, the Sacrist,' the old verger said to me.

With a friendly smile the young man held out a hand. He gave an impression of extreme domestication and I had the odd fancy that his wife had washed him and wrapped him up like a precious parcel before sending him out. I told him who I was and, since his office gave him responsibility for the building, explained why I was so alarmed by what the workmen were doing.

'I believe you are right,' he said. 'Unfortunately, Bulmer, the Surveyor of the Fabric, is away for a few days on urgent family business. I myself had reservations about the advisability of this way of effecting the work and suspected that the foreman had misunderstood his instructions.' With a smile at me he said: 'You have confirmed my fears.'

I indicated the alternative route for the pipes which I had spied from the organ-loft. 'They should go along here and just under this tomb,' I said, indicating a handsome piece of sculpted bas-relief on a large slab of marble high up on the wall. It dated from the early seventeenth century and portrayed in profile two lines of kneeling figures inlaid in basalt—the men facing the women and each series diminishing in size from adults to children. It was the more prominent for not being flush with the wall but projecting from it by several inches.

'Memorial not tomb,' Dr Sisterson murmured. 'The Burgoyne memorial. It has rather an interesting history. I mention it because I have just come from a reception being given by my colleague, Dr Sheldrick, to mark the publication of the first fascicle of his history . . .' He broke off suddenly. 'I beg your pardon. That cannot possibly be of any interest to you.'

I shook my head. 'On the contrary. I am myself a historian.'

He smiled. 'Then I understand your concern for preserving the testimony of the past.'

'And the gentleman knows a great deal about these old buildings,' the head-verger said.

'I'm sure he knows more than I do, Gazzard,' Dr Sisterson said, with a chuckle. He moved back and stood for a few moments with his head on one side, examining my proposal.

Then he stepped forward and said to the foreman: 'I have decided to follow this gentleman's advice. We will take the pipes through this way.'

As he was explaining in more detail I saw the bearded man glaring at me over his shoulder, but when Dr Sisterson had made his wishes clear he reluctantly instructed his men on the change.

Feeling rather pleased with myself, I took leave of my two companions and walked on round the ambulatory—which was as magnificent as I had expected—and then down the other side of the chancel, encountering nobody but a young man in a cassock whom I took to be another verger.

I went into one of the side-chapels and knelt down. As a child I had been devout. Then I had decided I was a sceptic and at Cambridge I had called myself an atheist. I don't know if I really was but I do know that a few years later, in the worst crisis of my life, I found I could not pray. The Cathedral had no spiritual meaning for me. It was a beautiful monument to a vast, wonderful mistake. I respected the moralist of Galilee—or whoever had composed his teachings—but I could not believe that he was the son of God.

Tuesday Night

✛

A S I WAS PASSING A HOUSE in the Close a few minutes later, I saw on the curtains the shadows cast by the lamps of figures moving about inside the room. That must be where the reception that Dr Sisterson had mentioned was taking place. It occurred to me that Austin had probably been invited, but had had to decline because of my arrival. While I was removing my hat and coat in Austin's hall, I smelt frying meat. I found my host in the kitchen holding a skillet over the flame with one hand and a glass of wine with the other. There were two opened bottles of claret standing on the little sideboard and I noticed that one of them was only half full.

'Do you cook for yourself often?' I asked with a smile as he poured me a glass. I was trying to imagine his life here.

'Are you wondering how much practice I've had?' he answered with a laugh. Then with mock solemnity he added: 'I can reassure you: my emoluments do not permit me to dine out very often. Has your walk given you an appetite?'

'It's as I feared,' I said. 'They're vandalizing it.'

'They're only putting down pipes!' he exclaimed and turned the frying chops over vigorously.

'That's how it starts. I remember what happened at Chichester a few years ago. They demolished the pulpitum to lay gas-pipes for heating and so weakened the structure that the crossing-tower collapsed.'

'Taking up a few flagstones is hardly going to bring the building down.'

'It's always risky to disturb the piers and, as the old verger said, they neither know nor care what the consequences of their actions might be.'

'So you met Gazzard? He's a cheerful old soul, isn't he? I suspect he's not really worried about the building. What he's afraid of is rousing the Cathedral ghost. The vergers are all terrified of it.'

'A building as old as that must have several.'

'This is the most famous and most feared. The Treasurer's ghost. William Burgoyne. Did you notice the family memorial?'

'I did, though it was too dark to see it properly.'

'It's a handsome piece of work. In fact, it plays an important role in the ghost's story.'

'What form does the haunting take?'

'What does any competent ghost do? He walks—I should say, stalks—about the Cathedral and the Close at night, frightening people.'

I laughed. 'Does he carry his head under his arm?'

'I believe he displays it in its customary position.'

'And what great wrong is it that keeps him from his grave at night? For there is always some terrible injustice at issue.'

'The greatest of wrongs, for he was murdered, and his murderer was not brought to justice. I will tell you the story after supper. No, don't say anything. You have absolutely no choice in the matter for at this season of the year such tales are prescribed. If I don't frighten you into a state of terror and send you to bed quaking, I shall consider myself a poor host.'

'Then I shall play the perfect guest and sit spellbound and frozen with horror.'

He smiled and announced that supper was ready, and handed me a number of plates and dishes to take into the dining-room.

We sat down at the little table—in truth, a card-table hastily covered in a rather grubby cloth to hide its green blushes—and made a good supper: devilled lamb-cutlets with capers and roasted turnips followed by a delicious quince-tart which Austin told me— in case I imagined he had prepared it himself and conceived an in- flated view of his culinary skills—he had purchased from the bakery. We both drank freely of the claret—Austin far more than I did. The room was still very close—with the smell of the gas, the food, the coal and something else that was not quite nice—but I had no recurrence of my earlier qualm.

As we ate, Austin oscillated between outbursts of light-hearted chatter and periods of taciturnity when he seemed lost in his own thoughts. I tried to talk of the interests we had once shared but he seemed incurious, and I remembered with a pang the boyish pas- sion with which we had sat up late talking about Plato. I attempted to get him to talk about the town—the school and the little com- munity around the Cathedral—but he evaded my questions.

I found that he did not want to talk about the past, either. It was as if he had forgotten it. When I alluded to people or incidents from the former time, he seemed uninterested. I talked of our fel- lows at Cambridge and what had become of them, and he smiled and nodded and when I prompted him he told me news of those with whom he had remained in touch but I had not. I told him of my work on Alfred and my interest in his heroic resistance to the invading heathen, and he nodded as if he was not paying much at- tention. Altogether, his manner made me all the more puzzled about his reasons for renewing our acquaintance.

At last he stood up: 'We will take our dessert upstairs and . . .'

'Stop!' I said, raising a hand. 'I heard the street-door. Someone has come in.' I was sure I had heard the click of the lock.

'Nonsense,' he said impatiently. 'You probably heard the stairs creaking. This is an old house and it mutters to itself like a dotard. As I was saying, we will go upstairs and I will tell you the story of the restless Canon.'

'But tell me your own story first!' I cried. I hadn't meant to be so frank but the wine—although I had not drunk very much—made me less restrained than usual. For two decades he had dwelt in this town grinding out his mathematics for the benefit of the loutish sons of prosperous linen-drapers, apothecaries and farmers. I had often contemplated his narrow, weary life and wondered whether he thought of me and of how different things might have been.

He looked at me strangely.

'The story of your life, I mean. The tale of your days here.'

'I have no story,' he said shortly. 'I have been quietly working here at my duties. There is no more to tell.'

'Is that all you can say of twenty years and more?'

'What is there to say? I have my friends, some of whom you will meet. Some of my fellows at the school—bachelors like myself—are close friends and I also have acquaintances in the town. Altogether we're a raffish, slovenly crew of men who sit in public-houses too long because we have nobody waiting for us to come home. And I move in more genteel circles, for I have been taken up as a kind of pet by some of the wives of the canons and the masters.'

I smiled. 'And have you never thought of marrying?'

He glanced at me with a smile. 'Oh, who would marry me? I wasn't much of a catch when I was a young fellow and I'm less of one now.'

I dared not ask more because I didn't want him to think I was merely curious. I thought of the delicacy with which he had avoided asking me any questions about my life, since we had lost touch, that might wound. It had occurred to me that he had asked me to come because he needed my advice or help on some matter and from what I had just heard in the Cathedral, I believed I had

an inkling of what it might be. I would at least give him the opportunity to unburden himself: 'Is everything all right at the school?'

'Why do you ask?'

'Oh, just that I heard there is some dispute there.'

He stared at me with sudden intensity. 'What do you mean?
Who could have told you that?'

I wished I hadn't spoken. 'The old man—the verger—mentioned some sort of difficulty there.'

'Gazzard? Why on earth do you imagine he knows anything
about it?' He glared at me. 'It might be better if people paid attention to their own business. Gazzard is a gossiping old woman. Just
like most of the canons. They spend their time inventing malicious
lies about each other. And about anyone else unfortunate enough
to have dealings with them.'

'What sort of lies?' I asked.

'I'm sure you can imagine.' He turned away and I could see that
he was bored with the topic and I remembered how irritated he
used to become at my habit of worrying at a subject in an effort to
make it yield new perspectives. For Austin a fact was a fact and
that was all there was to be said about it. He stood up. 'We will go
upstairs. I've lit a fire.'

As we passed through the hall I noticed a package propped
against the wall opposite the door of the room. I was sure it had not
been there earlier.

Austin picked it up. 'How did that get there?' I asked.

'What do you mean?' he replied quickly. 'I left it there before
supper to remind myself to carry it upstairs.'

We ascended without further conversation and found a cheerful
blaze in the sitting-room. While I seated myself before the fire,
Austin put the package on the floor beside the other chair and
lighted candles. Then he opened a bottle of rather good port and
filled two glasses.

It was like old times and made me think so vividly of what might have been that I was prompted to ask: 'Do you remember how, when we were undergraduates, we talked of one day being fellows of the same college?'

He shook his head. 'Did we?'

'How inspired we were by the idea of devoting ourselves to the life of the mind.'

He smiled sarcastically. 'I take it you believe that is possible only within a Cambridge—or just conceivably an Oxford—college?'

'Not at all. For example, I'm sure the canons are intelligent men . . .'

'The canons!' he interrupted. 'I have as little as possible to do with them. They are men of very limited capacities, almost without exception. That's why they are obsessed, most of them, by the out-ward forms—incense, vestments, candles and processions. The Church is full of men like that, just as the universities are. Men with no emotional life who are intellectually daring—which is easy enough—but emotionally timid.'

'I've heard that the Chapter suffers particularly acutely from the usual conflicts between the Ritualists and the Evangelicals,' I said, carefully avoiding Gazzard's name.

'That's what lies behind the argument about work on the Cathedral,' he said with a nod. 'For some people it is nothing but a beautiful old shell and they want to preserve it unchanged because for them it has no significance beyond its material being.'

I smiled to hide my irritation. 'Is anyone who loves old churches to be regarded as an infidel?'

'I'm talking of all those in this age who have made a religion out of things peripheral to, or other than, Christianity: music, history, art, literature.'

He spoke with such resentment that, although the last thing I wanted was to be drawn into an argument, I felt I had to explain my position. 'Speaking for myself, I would say that I've retained the moral meaning of works of art like the Cathedral but separated it from the baggage of superstition.'

He had slumped sideways in the chair so that his legs were dangling over one arm—a habit of his that I suddenly recalled from our youth—and he now stared at me fiercely and rather ludicrously from this undignified position. He slowly repeated my words: 'The baggage of superstition. You and your like are the purveyors of baggage. What you have done is to put together a jumble of beliefs to produce a new form of superstition that is much more dangerous than anything in Christianity. And of less use. It won't help you with the great issues: loss, the death of those you love, the imminence of your own death.'

'Is that what religion should be? A comforting fiction? I'd rather choose the truth—like the Roman Stoics or my beloved Anglo-Saxons before they were Christianized—however harsh it might be.'

'There's nothing harsher than Christianity.'

'Are you a believer now, Austin? You used not to be.'

'You're talking of twenty years past,' he said irritably. 'Don't you think some things might have changed in the world outside the confines of a Cambridge college?'

This was a change indeed. We had both been Shelleyan free-thinkers, like the most advanced among the thinking undergraduates of our generation. How passionately we had denounced religion as organized humbug. I had not changed and, in fact, my experience as a historian had deepened my conviction that religion was a conspiracy of the powerful against the rest. But my views had mellowed so that I now pitied rather than raged against those who were believers.

'And anyway, I was a believer when I was at the University,' he went on bitterly. 'It was the desire to avoid being mocked by you and your circle that led me to pretend to be an agnostic.'

Austin had arrived as a Tractarian of a very dandyish kind—I believe he was trying to annoy his father who was a Low Church vicar of modest birth and small fortune—but had quickly announced himself to be an unbeliever. Had I converted him without even realizing it? Had he been so malleable? If I had influenced him, it had not been because I was more intelligent but because I knew more clearly what I believed and wanted. Austin had had a kind of laziness which let him drift, giving in much more readily than I to the temptation to self-indulgence. It was that aspect of his personality that had allowed him to fall under the influence of the man who had done me so much harm.

'As undergraduates we used to talk glibly of Christianity as superstition,' Austin said. 'A superstition which had all but evaporated in the light of rationalism and whose final disappearance we confidently predicted. But now I understand that it is the other way around: that without faith, all you have is superstition. Fear of the dark, of ghosts, of the realm of death which continues to frighten us, whatever we believe. We need stories to stop us being frightened. You've created your comforting myths and fictions from history—like your idea of King Arthur.'

'King Arthur? What are you talking about?'

'Didn't you just tell me you are writing about King Arthur?'

'Good heavens, no. I spoke of King Alfred.'

'King Arthur or King Alfred. No matter. I may have confused them but the point is the same. You are creating your own stories to console you.'

'In contradistinction to Arthur, Alfred is a well-attested historical figure,' I protested indignantly. 'Unlike your Jesus of Nazareth. Much as I respect the moral system associated with his name.'

'Respect the moral system associated with his name!' Austin repeated. 'What I'm talking about is faith, belief, acceptance of the absolute reality of salvation and damnation. You—and others of our generation—lost your faith because you decided that science can explain everything. I believed that myself for a while but I came to understand that reason and faith are not in conflict. They are different orders of reality. Although I understand that now, when I was younger I shared your error. I know now that because there is darkness, there is light. That because there is death, there is life. Because there is evil, there is goodness. Because there is damnation, there is redemption.'

'Because there is bacon there are eggs!' I could not prevent myself from exclaiming. 'What poppycock!'

Austin merely gazed at me coldly with his large black eyes, as if it was not worth the trouble of putting me right.

'I'm sorry,' I said. 'I should not have spoken like that. But you believe that because you want to think that you are saved. You've fallen into the trap we always used to denounce. You've been taken in by the lure of eternal life and all that nonsense.'

'What do you know of my beliefs?' he said softly.

I realized suddenly something that I had half-known since my arrival—that he was a complete stranger to me. And then I felt even more disconcertingly that even the Austin I had believed I had known twenty-five years ago I had not really known. The man who was now gazing at me with such contempt had been in some sense present *in potentia* within the youth I had known, and I had perceived nothing of it.

There was a long silence. Outside, the thick fog was like a clammy comforter wrapping the Close and the Cathedral in a tight but chilly embrace. Austin drank, still watching me over the top of his glass. To avoid his gaze I, too, sipped my wine. He put the glass down on the floor and shifted into a different position. 'You were to hear the story of the ghost.'

He spoke pleasantly, as if we had not just a moment earlier been on the edge of an open rupture. I responded to his changed mood.

'Indeed, I should like that.'

Only two days later it came to seem very significant that Austin should have told me the story of a murder within the ancient Liberty of the Cathedral Close, but at the time it seemed a way to revive the cosy intimacy of the old days. After a moment he began to speak: 'During the last couple of centuries people have frequently seen a tall black-clad figure moving silently around the Cathedral and the Close.'

I nodded, but he said: 'You look sceptical, but there is physical proof for at least part of the story. That, at least, is something which you can see with your own eyes and even touch if, like Doubting Thomas, you accept only that as evidence, for it is written in stone and is not fifty yards from where we are now.'

'What is it?'

'All in due time. About two hundred and fifty years ago, William Burgoyne was the Foundation's Canon-Treasurer. If you were to open that window—please don't since it's far too cold!—and peer out to your left, you would just catch a glimpse of what was at that time the Treasurer's House. It is now called the New Deanery, though it is no longer that, either. Although not quite as large as the Deanery of that period, and certainly not a third the size of the Bishop's Palace, it was by far the handsomest house in the Close. Burgoyne's predecessor had refurbished it from the proceeds of robbing the Foundation, for the post of Treasurer was highly lucrative for a man who was prepared to take advantage of it. Burgoyne never yielded to that temptation nor countenanced it in others. It was precisely because of his probity that he made a powerful enemy. This was an ambitious canon of about the same age as Burgoyne called Freeth, Launcelot Freeth, who was the Sub-Dean. A man deeply mired in materialism.'

'I know who he was!' I exclaimed.

'Oh, do you?' Austin said. 'Well, be quiet for now and listen. Until Burgoyne arrived, Freeth had effectively had unbridled power because of the old Dean's incapacity. He ruled the Chapter in alliance with a canon called Hollingrake, the Librarian—a clever scholar but another greedy and unscrupulous man. You can imagine how much they resented the newcomer.'

'I must tell you, Austin,' I could not resist putting in, 'that I have recently discovered an entirely new account of the Freeth affair.'

'How interesting,' Austin said perfunctorily. 'But let me continue with my story and then you can tell me yours. Otherwise we'll both lose the thread. There was something else apart from personal dislike between Burgoyne and Freeth. Burgoyne was a godly and unworldly man who devoted his life to prayer while Freeth was ambitious for power, cared nothing for learning and was only interested in advancing his own material interests.'

'Wait a minute.' I could not prevent myself from interrupting. 'I have discovered an account by an eyewitness which suggests that it was Freeth's love of books that led him into being embroiled with the soldiers on that fateful day.'

'I don't believe that,' said Austin. 'It happened because of his cowardly attempt to flee.'

'Not according to my witness,' I objected. 'He maintained . . .'

'Tell me when I have finished my own story. It's complicated enough without your interruptions.' He paused in schoolmasterly fashion before continuing: 'The canons of that time were lazy and greedy—how little has changed!—and had not only allowed the Cathedral to fall into disrepair but were neglecting their many educational and charitable responsibilities in the town. Burgoyne attempted to change all that. He wanted to repair and reopen the Cathedral to make it once again a centre of worship for the whole town, and to restore the schools and hospitals. To raise money he tried to reduce those of the Cathedral's functions which were in his opinion not essential, and in doing so he offended entrenched interests and made himself even more enemies among the canons. Things came to a head when there was a row over some Foundation property that Burgoyne wanted to sell in order to raise money. Freeth produced an ancient document which prevented him from doing this—though the document was later revealed to be a forgery. Burgoyne suspected it and that should have served as a warning of just how unscrupulous his antagonist was prepared to be. He persevered, however, and, in the end, he got his way and raised most of the money he needed. He appeared to have triumphed, but there was a price to pay. In some mysterious way that was probably connected with all of this scheming and plotting, he came into possession of an appalling secret, a secret so terrible that brooding upon it changed him from a man of reclusive and regular habits to an insomniac who spent his nights in the ruined Cathedral or pacing about the Close.'

'I assume you are going to tell me what it was?'

'Indeed I am not, for Burgoyne took it to the grave with him. But whatever it was, it transformed the dignified and respectable cleric into a man in mental torment. It was a very dangerous secret.'

'Are you saying that he was murdered to prevent him revealing it?'

'So it appears. He was found in the Cathedral early one morning, crushed beneath scaffolding which had been erected to carry out the repairs he had forced upon his colleagues.'

'As if he were being punished for his success?'

'And further evidence for believing that he was murdered is the fact that the Cathedral Mason, a man called Gambrill, disappeared the same night and was never seen again. He, too, had fallen out with Burgoyne. But another possible explanation for his disappearance and the Canon's death is that both men were killed by Gambrill's deputy, a young journeyman. That was the gossip in the town for many years afterwards.'

'What motive could the deputy have had?'

'There was some ancient enmity between his family and Gambrill. But let me tell you about the ghost since this is a ghost-story. Burgoyne's funeral service in the Cathedral was disrupted by horrid moanings so that some of those in attendance became so frightened that they fled. Thereafter and for many years the ghost of Burgoyne haunted the Cathedral and heart-rending groans are often heard coming from the memorial—particularly when the wind is high. That is the ghost which old Gazzard fears has been roused by the recent building-works. And that is the end of the story I promised you.'

'I don't call that a story,' I grumbled. 'There are far too many loose ends.'

'I told you there is a clue—although a somewhat enigmatic one.'

'Does it cast any light on the secret Burgoyne learnt? Or suggest who murdered him?'

'That depends on the interpretation. On the morning after the murder, an inscription was found on the wall of Burgoyne's house, the New Deanery of our own day. It had apparently been carved during the night—an astonishing feat in so short a time and by the light of a lantern.'

'What did it say?'

'I can't recall the exact words, so I will leave you to read it for yourself.'

'That's very irritating of you, Austin. I have half a mind to go out now and read it this very minute.'

'Don't be silly. You can't trample all over someone's property in the middle of the night.'

'Who lives in the house now? Is it one of the canons?'

'It's in private hands. The owner is an elderly gentleman. Wait until daylight and then you can read the inscription through the gate without even going into the yard.'

'I can't stand peering into a stranger's yard in broad daylight.'

'The owner's habits are very regular. Go between four o'clock and half past and I can promise you there will be nobody there.'

'I wonder if there are any written sources for that story,' I mused.

'I suppose they would be in the Dean and Chapter's Library. I could ask the Librarian when I see him tomorrow.'

Austin glanced at me quickly. 'You're seeing Locard? Why ever should you do that?'

'Because of my work.'

'Your work? What has he to do with that?'

'Why, everything!' I smiled. 'I am relying on him to point my researches in the most promising direction.'

'I thought you were going to tramp about over those blessed Roman earthworks out along the Winchester road? What has that to do with Locard?'

'The barrows around Woodbury Castle, you mean? They're probably not Roman, though that was believed until fairly recently. In fact, they are either . . .'

'But, for heaven's sake, the point is: aren't you going to be working on them?'

'That was my intention when I first wrote to you. You know, they have never been properly surveyed? Consequently, we have no idea if they date from the time before the Romans or were built by them or by the Anglo-Saxons. My own . . .'

'But you have changed your mind?'

'Didn't I tell you in my last letter that a much more exciting prospect has come up? Why, I believe I could not have made it clear that I was referring to something entirely different. Of course! That's why you talked about the weather interfering with my work! I believed you were joking.' I laughed. Austin, however, asked irritably:

'What are you talking about?'

'I learnt very recently that there might be a manuscript somewhere in the Library whose discovery would settle once and for all a fascinating and very important controversy.'

Austin rose and went to the fire. Then, turning his back to me, he reached for something on the mantelpiece and started stuffing a pipe. I had never seen him smoke before.

I went on: 'I have been preparing a monograph on Grimbald's *Life of Alfred the Great*, properly called *De Vita Gestibusque Alfredi Regis*. Do you know of it?'

'I don't believe I do,' he muttered.

'Grimbald was a cleric who was a contemporary of Alfred and there is a reference to him in Asser's much better known *Life of Alfred the Great*. His account is a fascinating work which brings that remarkable king most movingly to life. You're wondering why it is not as well-known as Asser's?'

'I imagine you're going to tell me.'

'The answer is that its authenticity has never been accepted. But I hope to establish that it is genuine and to write my own biography of Alfred drawing upon it. It will be a work which, in all modesty, will transform our view of the ninth century for there is much wonderful material in Grimbald which historians have not made use of . . .'

'Because they think it's fraudulent,' Austin interrupted.

'Some of them do, perhaps because their own self-serving cynicism is reproached by the portrait of the king that Grimbald offers. You see, his account confirms how extraordinarily brave and resourceful and learned Alfred was, and what a generous and much-loved man. For example, it tells us a great deal about his friendship with the great scholar-saint, Wulflac.'

'Wulflac?'

'He was the king's tutor when he was a boy and was with him at some of the worst crises of his life. There's a scene in Grimbald when the king and he discuss the role of kingship the night before the crucial battle of Ashdown. And there's a fascinating chapter in which Alfred—guided by Grimbald—visits the boys studying at the abbey here at Thurchester. And above all, Grimbald's work is the sole source for our knowledge of Wulflac's martyrdom.'

Seeing his blank expression I said: 'You don't know the story?' He shook his head. 'The account of his capture by the Danes?'

'I don't know what you're talking about,' he said almost irritably.

'Then I will tell you. I believed every English schoolboy learnt that wonderful story.'

'I know about the blessed cakes.'

I laughed. 'A very late and confused tradition. But the story of Wulflac's martyrdom is a true account and a very moving one. I remember it well but I'll bring down Grimbald's text in case I've forgotten any details.'

'That wouldn't do,' he said, shaking his head.

I hurried to my bedroom and picked up the book from the side-table, noticing that lying beside it was my somewhat ill-judged gift for Austin which had been very beautifully wrapped by the young lady in the shop. I brought them both down and as I reached the landing was surprised to meet Austin coming up the stairs. As we entered the room I handed the gift to him and he thanked me and placed it beside his chair before sitting down again. My present now lay just where the package had been and, wondering what Austin had done with it, I glanced around the room. I could not see it on the shelves or on the small table by the window. Perhaps he had put it in the armoire. Or had he taken it downstairs again? But why should he have done that?

'I'll open it later,' Austin said. 'Half the fun of a present is the anticipation.'

I nodded, but since I now knew that the gift was highly inappropriate, I could not share his pleasure.

I seated myself and found the right section of the book. 'You've told me a story set in Thurchester and now I will tell you one. As you know, the town was Alfred's capital and the castle was his most important stronghold.'

Austin turned slowly towards me, the pipe projecting rather ludicrously from his mouth.

'As a boy Alfred revealed a passion for learning which was most unusual at that time. It was all the more admirable in a young prince who was expected to devote himself to mastering the arts of war. Alfred did that, too, and remarkably well. But he also learnt to read, which was not customary for members of aristocratic or royal families—especially for a prince whose father was the hard-pressed king of a little backwater on the edge of European civilization, which is what Wessex was at that time. Years later, as an adult, he learnt Latin, too. Perhaps it was because he believed that he was not likely to become king since he had a number of older brothers, that he was able to indulge his passion for knowledge. Grimbald describes how Alfred's father sent for a certain young monk from Saxony to become the boy's tutor. That was Wulflac who was one of the most learned men in the whole of Western Europe at that bleak time. As it turned out, each of Alfred's elder brothers was killed fighting the Danes and at a very early age he did become king—just in time to face the most serious threat his kingdom had ever confronted. A huge Danish invading force had landed in 865 with the intention of conquering and settling the whole of England. Alfred defended his kingdom with intelligence and courage, managing to hold together the faint-hearted among the English who wanted to submit and pay tribute rather than to fight.

'By 892 Alfred had been king for nearly thirty years and had fought a long struggle to preserve his kingdom against the Danes. His old friend and tutor, Wulflac, was now Bishop of Thurchester. Although Alfred had defended Wessex successfully, the Danes were now occupying much of the north and east of England. Then in the early summer the Danes sent a huge invading army into Wessex to loot and destroy everything in its path. News of this reached Alfred while he was here in the town with his council—the witan. Grimbald writes:

The king held a counsel of war and it was decided that, although this would mean a delay of several weeks, the ealdormen would return to their shires in order to levy troops. Afterwards the king's young chaplain secretly took the king aside and warned him that his trusted nephew, Beorghtnoth, in alliance with other thegns, was plotting with Olaf, the leader of the Danes, to kill him and become king. Alfred, though he trusted his chaplain absolutely, refused to credit such a terrible thing about his nephew. In the midst of this, news arrived that the Danes had laid siege to Exeter, and Alfred, accompanied by most of his thegns including Beorghtnoth, set off for that city leaving Wulflac in charge of the town. The king was riding his half-wild stallion, Wederstepa or 'Storm-Treader', which none but he could mount and which was tended by a faithful stable-boy. And he took with him the royal treasury—three great iron-bound coffers containing the gold, silver and precious stones—which the Danes were so eager to obtain.

'I won't read the next sections but just explain that, unfortunately, the chaplain was right about the king's nephew. (And, by the way, the references to that young priest are rather interesting and I have a little theory about them.) Beorghtnoth had entered into a secret agreement with Olaf and the attack on Exeter was intended to lure the king away from Thurchester. By the time Alfred left his capital, the Danes had already divided their army at Exeter: the smaller part remained near that city in order to delay the king's return while the larger, led by Olaf himself, hastened towards Thurchester by a route that led them in a wide circle to the north. Since Thurchester was now only lightly defended, they captured it very easily. So when Alfred arrived at Exeter he found that the Danes had abandoned the city. He hurried back to Thurchester but found that the Danes had taken the town and, to his utmost dismay, that they were holding Wulflac hostage. I'll read the next section.'

At these words Austin sighed gently. 'No, really,' I said. 'You'll see that it's crucial:

Olaf sent a message telling Alfred that he would kill Wulflac unless the greater part of the gold and silver was surrendered to him and unless the king further agreed, binding himself by a solemn mass, to live at peace with the Danes. When Alfred replied that he had left his treasury in Exeter and that he would send some of his army to bring it, Olaf agreed to wait for ten days but said that if the gold was not handed over by dawn on that day, Wulflac would die. Now the truth was that Alfred had the treasury with him but had said that it was in Exeter in order to stall for time because the fresh levies should arrive within nine or ten days. In the witan, however, Beorghtnoth, supported by those among the thegns who wanted him to betray Alfred to the enemy, argued that the king should surrender the treasury. The king was in an agonizing dilemma and in order to resolve the situation he proposed a sudden and daring attack upon the town. The thegns refused to countenance this proposal, however, and insisted on waiting for the fresh levies to arrive. The days passed and the new troops did not appear. Finally, on the ninth day, Alfred told the witan that he would surrender himself in order to save his former tutor's life. They were horrified—except for Beorghtnoth and his allies who were secretly delighted—and they argued with Alfred that the survival of the kingdom depended on his remaining in command. Alfred went to his private chamber and, accompanied only by his young chaplain, began praying to God to tell him what was the right course of action.

'As Grimbald describes it, this is an astonishing moment. It's one of the first glimpses of the inner life of an individual since the end of Roman civilization. And of course it's a classic dilemma: the ties of love in opposition to those of duty. By the way, I wonder if you've spotted the evidence for that hypothesis of mine?'

Austin made no response. 'Grimbald goes on:

> The king asked the priest for his advice and the young man, deeply moved by this mark of the king's respect for him and alarmed by what he suspected of Beorghtnoth's treachery, urged him to hand over the gold. After that he could attack the Danes as soon as his fresh levies arrived. The king objected that that would require him to break his solemn undertaking which would be a grievous offence to God. The young priest replied that no promise made to a heathen could be considered binding in the sight of God.

'You know, that is very shrewd advice. It makes sense both militarily and politically. And theologically the chaplain was right, too. But Alfred was obviously bound by the pre-Christian Anglo-Saxons' code of morality for the text goes on:

> Alfred, however, insisted that his sense of honour would not permit him to behave thus. And so, after three hours of prayer and discussion, the king emerged to announce to the witan that he had decided that it was his duty to negotiate in person with the enemy and, if necessary, to offer himself as a hostage in place of the bishop. The thegns were furious and now it was the most loyal among them who shouted loudest that they would not allow him to do such a thing. Beorghtnoth spoke up and offered to go to Olaf in order to try to find a solution to the crisis and Alfred trustingly agreed to this. And so Beorghtnoth went to Olaf not in order to help, but to betray, his uncle. He told the Danish leader that since Alfred had his gold with him and was waiting for reinforcements, Olaf

should force the king to settle the matter quickly. Now Wulflac was brought in with his two chaplains and Beorghtnoth, conducting himself with hateful duplicity, commiserated with him. The learned bishop, however, himself had a secret design—though one that was wholly honourable and benign—and this was to convey to Alfred a message which only he would understand. So the bishop said to Beorghtnoth: *Tell your uncle to be comforted and to think this very night of what the learned Pliny wrote: A man who is truly wise will find even in a moment of darkness a light that obscures the sun; while the foolish man will be dazzled by nothing more than the mere dawn. It is a passage that he will remember well.* He made the unlettered nephew repeat this message until he had it perfectly. This was the scholar's secret design: because of his profound knowledge of the heavens and the movements of the stars therein, Wulflac knew that there was to be an eclipse of the sun at dawn on the very next day. And because he and the king had recently been reading together the works of Pliny in which those phenomena are described, he was sure that Alfred would understand. Unfortunately, however, Beorghtnoth guessed that he was trying to convey some hidden meaning and decided that he would say nothing to his uncle of the bishop's message. So when he returned to the camp of the English he told Alfred and the witan merely that he had been unsuccessful in his attempt to negotiate with the Danes.

Meanwhile, acting on Beorghtnoth's advice, Olaf gave orders that Wulflac be suspended from the West Gate of the city-walls in the sight of the besieging army. When Alfred saw this, he was filled with anger and grief and announced that he was determined to give himself up in return for the bishop. The thegns—joined by the hypocritical Beorghtnoth and his fellow-conspirators—pleaded with him in tears not to do so, arguing that it was certain that the Danes would kill him if he did. But Alfred answered that he was now using his authority to designate his heir and was choosing his nephew who, he was sure, would make a fine king if he himself were to die. Then the most loyal of the thegns, seeing that he was determined, went to the length of trying to thwart him by physically preventing him from leaving his private quarters.

The king, however, in the hours of darkness before dawn on this, the tenth day and the one on which Wulflac was to be killed, disguised himself as one of his own servants and managed to escape. Unrecognized, he made his way to where the army's horses were stabled and found his own mount— the fierce Wederstepa, which nobody but he could ride. The horse resisted being saddled and mounted, but as soon as the king was astride, it recognized its master and grew still. Because of the noise the stallion had made, the young stable-boy was roused from sleep and as soon as he saw the horse's gentle demeanour he knew that Alfred was the stranger in the saddle.

'Incidentally,' I said, 'I don't know if you're familiar with that painting by Landseer in the National Gallery on the subject?'

'Landseer?' He smiled. 'What is it called? "The King at Bay"?'

I saw instantly that this was a joke and laughed. 'No, this is Edwin's brother, Charles Landseer. The painting is called "King Alfred being recognized by his devoted stable-lad". It's very moving. In the foreground the king, with an expression of mingled guilt and affection beautifully caught on his noble features, is turning his head away from the cry of startled recognition that has just come from the lips of the handsome boy who gazes at him with awe and devotion.'

He removed the pipe and smiled. 'Indeed? I'll make a point of seeing it next time I'm up in Town.' He seemed to be making some private allusion which was lost upon me.

'Anyway, back to Grimbald:

The boy seized the horse's bridle and shouted until the rest of the household came running. The thegns were so moved by the king's courage and determination that they now agreed to make an assault on the town without waiting for reinforcements. So the troops were quickly woken, mustered and drawn up facing the walls. The bishop could be seen still hanging above the main gate, and it was clear that he was close to death. Shortly before dawn the English army assembled and waited for the king's signal to attack. At that moment the sun, which had just risen over Woodbury Downs, began to be swallowed up by a black shadow and the land grew darker and darker until within the space of a minute, complete darkness fell and a cold wind sprang up. Flames seemed to shoot out from the sun which was now hidden behind the disc of the moon. The horses neighed in terror and birds flocked together and wheeled about the skies in confusion, unsure if it was time to roost or not. This was something that nobody then living had ever seen and everybody imagined that it signified the end of the world. Only Alfred knew that this was an eclipse; and so he rode up and down the lines shouting to his men that the sun would return within a minute or two. But his explanation came too late and his troops fell into a state of complete panic. The Danes were overcome by the same terror and Olaf, who was standing atop the main gate, believing that Wulflac had summoned the darkness up by the use of magic, ordered that the ropes which were holding him be cut. The scholar plummeted to his death just as the darkness began to lift. Shamefully, the Danes then threw the martyr's body into a well beside the Old Minster—

now known throughout Christendom as St Wulflac's Well. Alfred's horror and grief may be imagined. And although he managed to regain command of most of his scattered army, there was now no possibility of launching an attack on the town with frightened soldiers, especially now that the element of surprise had been lost.

Fortunately, however, the new levies arrived the next day and Alfred immediately led an assault on the town and recaptured it, inflicting utter defeat on the enemy. At a mass in the Old Minster Olaf and his family and thegns were baptized and took the sacrament, and then he and Alfred exchanged rich gifts. With the capture of the town the treachery of Beorghtnoth was discovered for one of Wulflac's chaplains, a man called Cathlac, revealed how the martyred bishop had tried to convey a message to the king about the eclipse. Beorghtnoth proved his treachery by fleeing to the Danelaw. Wulflac's body was recovered from the well and buried in the Old Minster in a black stone coffin lined with lead and embellished with sculptures depicting . . . [et cetera, et cetera]. The body was washed and anointed and covered in a cloth of fine . . .

'I don't think that's particularly interesting.

The Old Minster had been looted by the Danes and now that its buildings were being repaired, a curious incident occurred. Cathlac found an old document hidden in a wall which had been laid open by the ravages of the Danes. This was a charter under which an earlier king of Wessex a hundred years before had granted certain rights to the Abbey. Alfred accepted the validity of the charter and confirmed these rights henceforth in perpetuity, further endowing the see as a tribute to his martyred friend and teacher. And from that time forth miracles began to occur in association with St Wulflac and in particular with the well into which his body had been thrown. For it was found that loathsome sores were healed by water from the well, trees that were nourished with water from the well bore fruit in the depths of the winter . . .

'There's rather a lot more of this and it's not frightfully interesting—nor particularly convincing—so I'll stop there.'

I was very moved by the story—as I always am when I think of the life of that extraordinary man, the English scholar-king who saved the nation from extinction. 'Can you guess what my hypothesis is about the young chaplain?' I asked.

Austin shook his head.

'Did you notice that he is the only character about whose private thoughts and feelings we are informed? In that scene when Alfred is praying, Grimbald writes that he was "deeply moved by this mark of the king's respect for him and alarmed by what he suspected of Beorghtnoth's treachery". I believe the young chaplain was none other than Grimbald himself.'

Austin pursed his lips. 'That would explain why he is allowed to give such wise advice.'

I laughed. 'That's very cynical. But you're right and that supports my theory which I recently published in a paper for the *Proceedings of the English Historical Society*.'

'How authentic is that story?' Austin asked. 'To me it sounds no more so than the famous cakes.'

'There are a few difficulties,' I admitted.

'What about Wulflac predicting an eclipse?'

'Yes, that raises some awkward questions. The astronomical knowledge that would have permitted that had been lost centuries earlier—at the collapse of Alexandrian civilization, in fact. But the writings of Ptolemy and Pliny were certainly known in England at that time, and so Wulflac and Alfred could well have understood what an eclipse was when one occurred.'

'Was there an eclipse at that time? Is it possible to establish that?'

'There is not known to have been one at precisely that moment. That is one reason why many scholars have refused to accept the authenticity of the *Life*.'

'Believing that it was forged? By whom and why?'

'Well, it survived in only one manuscript with the addition of a preface by Leofranc who described there how he had ordered it to be copied and distributed so that everyone should know how wise and learned King Alfred was.'

'Does the manuscript itself provide any clues?'

'Unfortunately it was destroyed in 1643 when the Library here was ransacked. So all we have is a very inadequate edition of the Leofranc recension published by the antiquarian, Parker, in 1574.'

'Why would anyone have bothered to forge it?'

'I don't believe anybody did, though I am prepared to concede that Grimbald's original text was altered and added to by Leofranc. He certainly added that material at the end describing the finding of an old charter that enriched the abbey, and he probably added the account of the miracles in order to make the abbey a centre of pilgrimage.'

'In that case, perhaps he forged the whole thing?'

'That's what a rogue who disgraces the name of scholar—a man called Scuttard—suggested about three months ago when he published a paper in the same journal attacking my own in the most violent terms. He argued that Leofranc forged the whole of it by plagiarizing and cobbling together other texts.'

'You keep talking about this Leofranc as if he were living next door. Who was he, for heaven's sake?'

'Do you really not know? He was the bishop who created the cult of the martyred saint, Wulflac, here in Thurchester. Scuttard argues that he did so in order to raise money to demolish the Anglo-Saxon Minster and build the Cathedral . . .'

'I noticed that Grimbald refers to "the Old Minster" which suggests that the account was composed after it had been replaced. And that was not until twelve-something, was it?'

'It was at the beginning of the twelfth century, Austin.'

'Sorry. I get the elevens and the twelves and the thirteens a bit confused. The medieval period is nothing but monks and battles to me until you get to Henry VIII and his wives.'

I shuddered and went on: 'The manuscript published by Parker was copied in about 1120, so that fits Leofranc's dates. But you're right that that is one of the pieces of evidence Scuttard used. And he argued that the whole enterprise that Leofranc carried out—elevating Wulflac's Well and his tomb into a shrine which became an object of pilgrimage throughout the Middle Ages—was based on this forgery.'

'Scuttard argues that Wulflac was not martyred?'

I nodded. 'He goes much further: he actually argues that he never existed. And it's true that there is no reference to his existence apart from Grimbald's *Life*. But one of my objections to Scuttard in my riposte last month was to ask why, in that case, did Leofranc not forge a life of Wulflac rather than of Alfred?'

'I suppose that what he did was much more sophisticated. Writing a life of Alfred in which St Wulflac is shown to play a significant role smuggles the martyr into existence much more effectively.'

'That is exactly what Scuttard has replied,' I acknowledged gloomily. 'And if that is accepted, then some of his other outrageous suggestions are given plausibility. Above all, his absurd and horrible idea that Alfred did not defeat the Danes but was actually defeated by them, paid them Danegeld and became their vassal.'

Austin studied my face dispassionately. 'Does it really matter?'

'I don't like to see a man using bogus scholarship to boost his career. That paper of his has made him the leading contender for the new Chair of History at Oxford. But if I can find what I'm looking for, the original version of Grimbald which I believe the antiquarian Pepperdine saw in 1663, then I can destroy his argument and prove that Grimbald's *Life* is genuine.'

'Who was the most likely candidate until Scuttard published his paper?'

I felt myself blushing. 'I hadn't decided whether or not to let my name go forward, if that's what you mean.'

'Did Scuttard attack you because he saw you as a possible rival?'

'Without a shadow of doubt.'

'So finding the manuscript would hugely help your chances?'

I was struck by the malice in his tone and I wondered if he felt bitter because, despite his brilliance, he had gained a disappointing degree and had had to abandon hopes of a fellowship. His lack of success was at least partly due to his refusal to work at the things he was not interested in—though other factors were also responsible.

'I'm not sure that I would want the Chair. A life of quiet scholarship and teaching is all I desire and I have that already. The respect and even affection of my pupils mean more to me than the title of "professor".'

Austin smiled to himself in the most irritating way. 'Suppose you find the manuscript but it disproves your argument?'

To change the subject, I said: 'Why don't you open your gift, Austin?'

He picked it up. 'I'd almost forgotten about it.' He removed the paper with great delicacy and held the book in front of him. 'Thank you,' he said.

In some embarrassment, I said: 'I understand it's a formidable contribution to the debate about chronology.'

'It was kind of you to think of it. I'm sure it's a very intelligent piece of work.'

He made a pretence of being interested, opening and looking at it.

'The author is a Fellow of Colchester which for you and me must be the strongest recommendation anyone could have. And he is, indeed, a brilliant man in his field. I know you will disagree, but he argues that the evidence from geology pushes the date of the Creation back to millions of years ago. I understand that . . .'

'I suppose it's because of this blessed manuscript that you've arranged to see Locard?' he interrupted me.

'I assume you know him?'

'Oh yes, I know him. I know him for a cold-hearted, ambitious and dry-as-dust pedant. He is one of those men for whom the shell is more important than the content, the form than the substance. He is one of those men who have stood on the edge of life, too frightened to dip more than a toe in the water.'

'I don't mind how dry Dr Locard keeps his feet so long as he knows his business,' I said with a smile.

'He might know his business as a scholar but he certainly does not know it as a churchman. Beneath all the accoutrements of a Ritualist, he's as devoid of faith as the author of this.' He tapped the book. 'Like so many in our age, he has abandoned the centre of our religion and fled to the trappings. But all of these scientific hypotheses about apes and fossils and galaxies are irrelevant. The fact that everything can be explained by one theory—the rationalistic-scientific as it might be termed—does not mean that there is not a larger theory to which it is subordinate.'

'Oh, you mean that God put the fossils there when he made the world one Monday morning in 4004 BC just in order to test our faith, as some of your distinguished co-religionists have argued?'

'No, I do not mean that. If you would do me the courtesy of attempting to follow my argument, you might grasp the point I'm making.'

I felt in his cruel words all the frustration of a clever man who knows he has thrown away his opportunities.

There was a moment of silence. 'I hope you haven't made an enemy of Dr Locard,' I said, remembering what old Gazzard had said. 'He's obviously a powerful man.'

'Powerful? Why, what could he do to me?' he said, throwing the book down on the floor beside him.

'At worst, I imagine he could have you dismissed from your post.'

'Yes, in worldly terms he is powerful, if that is what you mean.'

'How would you live if you lost your situation?'

'Very poorly. I have no resources and no friends who could help me. But do you think I would regret the loss of my post—teaching lumpen youths in this vicious little town? I long to return to Italy. You remember I was there once?'

'But, Austin, how would you live? Even in Italy you would need some sort of income.'

'You reduce everything to money and jobs. Don't you see that none of that really matters? Not ultimately.'

'Then what does matter?' I asked.

He gazed at me with an unfathomable expression and when at last I realized that he didn't intend to answer I said: 'Do you mean that all that is important is the fate of your soul?'

I meant to keep from my tone any note of sarcasm as I pronounced those last words. But Austin smiled bitterly. 'You accused me just now of believing in "eternal life and all that nonsense".'

'I apologize. I momentarily forgot myself. It is quite contrary to my principles to ridicule the beliefs of another.'

'However ridiculous?' he asked with the merest hint of irony.

'Historically, most men in most societies have believed in the survival of the soul after death. In believing in a heavenly reward you have at least the weight of opinion on your side.'

He held up a hand to stop me. 'I haven't made myself clear. I do believe in good and evil and redemption and damnation. I accept them utterly and without question. They are as real to me as the chair I am sitting on. More real. You say I'm taken in by the idea of eternal life, but I tell you, damnation is more real and convincing to me than salvation. And certainly more probable.'

Just as I believed I was close to understanding him, comprehension was snatched away. 'Why do you say that?'

He held my gaze until I looked away. 'Let me ask you the question you just put to me: What does matter? What ultimately matters to you?'

I found it hard to answer. 'I suppose scholarship. Truth. Humanity.' I broke off. 'Oh for God's sake, Austin, that's a question for undergraduates. What matters is trying to live decently. Trying to do one's best. I mean, trying to behave with respect and understanding towards other people. And finding some degree of intellectual fulfilment, social sustenance and aesthetic pleasure.'

'There you have the difference between us. Let me put this to you. Suppose you had to describe your life as if it were a journey, then what would you say about it?'

'I don't understand.'

'I am suggesting that for you life is a slow progress across a wide plain—you can see the land ahead and behind for many miles.'

'I understand. And you don't see your life in such terms?'

He smiled. 'Hardly. For me, life is a dangerous quest through thick mist and darkness along a narrow ridge with a steep drop on either side. At moments the mist and the darkness lift and I see the giddying drop on either side of me, but I also see the peak towards which I am making my way.'

'My life is not without its moments of unexpected excitement. For example, when I found the reference to the possibility of the Library here having that manuscript . . .'

'I'm not talking about manuscripts,' Austin interrupted. 'What about passion?'

I smiled in irritation. 'At our age, Austin . . .'

'At our age! What nonsense. You sound like an old man.'

'Austin, we're no longer young. We're both nearly fifty.'

'Fifty! That's no age at all. We have several decades of life before us.'

'Be that as it may, I think I've had enough passion for one lifetime.'

'I assume that you are referring to . . . ?'

'Don't speak of it, Austin. Really, I have no wish to rake it up.'

'And since then?'

'Since then?'

'It's been more than twenty years. Did everything but your professional life end at that moment?'

'My professional life—which you seem to dismiss as insignificant—has been rich and rewarding. I have my pupils, my colleagues, my scholarly papers and my books. I believe I am a respected member of my college and of my profession. I think I can say that many of the young men I teach even feel a degree of affection for me as I do towards them.'

'You talk of it as if it is in the past. Have you no desire for that Chair or are you perfectly content to see that man—Scuttard, is it?—carry it away?'

'I've told you, I won't stoop to obtain it. And it would be a risk.'

'A risk?'

'If I were known to have sought it and failed, I would be somewhat humiliated.'

'That's what you call a risk?'

'I don't need a Chair. My professional life is already very full without it.'

'Very well.' He leaned back. 'Have you never thought of marrying again?'

'I am still married,' I said shortly. He looked at me severely and I added: 'At least, so far as I know.'

'As far as you know. Well, I can tell you . . .'

'I don't wish to know. I've told you I have no wish to discuss that.'

'Did your passional life end twenty years ago? Have you never developed tender feelings for anyone else since then?' His tone was impatient rather than affectionate.

'How could I? I'm not free to do so. And besides, as I've just said, I've had enough passion for one lifetime.' In the face of his silent scrutiny I said, absurdly: 'I'm perfectly happy as I am.'

'Happiness,' he said softly, 'is much more than merely the absence of misery.'

'That may be, but I dare not risk again the misery I endured twenty years ago. I will settle for the absence of pain.'

'How can you say that? The only thing in life that matters is passion. The only thing.'

Many responses rose to my lips—that what we call passion is often nothing more than a childish love of excitement, of wanting to be the centre of attention—but they died there as I looked at his face. There was such intensity there, such concentration. I turned my gaze away. What on earth was he referring to? What was the passion which animated his life? Who was its object? It was strange to connect a man of his age and mine with the notion of passion. And yet perhaps he was right. Certainly he was if he was talking about love. But the word Austin had used was not 'love'.

'What do you mean by passion?' I asked.

'Do you need to ask? I mean that we don't exist in and for ourselves but only in as much as we are re-created in the imagination of another person—by entering that person's life as fully as possible. I mean, entering it imaginatively, intellectually, physically and emotionally with all the conflicts that that makes inevitable.'

'I don't believe that. I believe we are absolutely alone. What you describe is a temporary condition of obsession.' I smiled. 'Temporary, even if in some cases it lasts a lifetime.'

'We're alone if we choose to be so.'

I disagreed but I would not respond. I was curious now. 'Is this abstraction that you call passion so different from love, from affection?'

He seemed to reflect for a moment before saying: 'Let me put it like this. Passion is what is at issue if the person you feel about in this way asks you to do something that goes beyond all moral bounds and you agree to do it.'

'You mean something like lying or stealing?'

He smiled. 'Yes, if you like. Or perhaps something worse, if you can imagine it.'

'I can't conceive of doing that.'

'No. Can't you?'

After a moment I asked: 'Am I to assume, then, that there is at this moment some object of your passion?'

He nodded without speaking.

'I'm intrigued,' I said, pausing to allow him to say more if he chose. He remained silent. Who could she be, the mysterious person with whom he was in love? Could this be related to his reason for inviting me here? Was this the cause of the trouble I was sure he was involved in?

'Tell me, has it made you happy? This pursuit of passion.'

'Happy?' He laughed. 'Happiness is what you feel when you go for a walk on a beautiful day or when you get home from a pleasant evening with friends. No, it has not made me happy. It has brought me to the deepest abyss of despair. It has carried me to the height of rapture.' And then almost in a whisper so that I was hardly certain that I had heard him say it, he muttered: 'And to perdition.'

'If we have the choice,' I said, 'then I would choose happiness rather than passion.'

'You're the undergraduate,' he said, 'if you can brush it aside so easily.' Then in the most contemptuous tone he said: 'You've had enough passion, you say? Your brief marriage all those years ago was enough?'

'Don't say any more about it, Austin.'

'I think you're in a worse case than I am,' he said gravely. 'When you come to die you'll realize that you have not lived.'

'Oh, I've lived, Austin.'

'Once. And that more than twenty years ago.'

I was astonished that he should talk about it so coldly, almost sneeringly. Was he trying to make it look as if he had not understood how much it meant to me? Had he not understood?

'I would prefer that we not talk about it.'

'I suppose you blame yourself?'

'Blame myself? Yes, I suppose I do. I was naive, trusting, unworldly. And since we are speaking frankly, I might as well tell you that for a long time I was angry with you.'

'You were angry with me?'

'But, Austin, whatever I may have felt at the time, you must understand that if I still felt resentment for the part you played, then I would not have accepted your invitation to come here now.'

'What part did you think I played?'

'No, you must make do with what I've just said, I'm afraid. I'm not going to conduct a species of post-mortem examination on what happened all those years ago.'

'Have you really not heard any news . . . ?'

'She is dead. She is dead to me.'

'I heard from an old friend in Naples . . .'

'I don't want to know, Austin. Don't tell me any more. I assume she still lives because someone would have told me if she had died.'

'I heard from an old friend in Naples that they have a child,' he said. 'Did you know that?'

I felt a shaft of pain in my side as if someone had stabbed me. I shook my head. Austin's voice seemed to be coming to me muffled by water.

'A girl. She is now about fifteen. I am told she is very clever and very beautiful. She has the features of her mother with the eyes of her father.' I covered my face with my hands.

'You don't like hearing the truth, do you? A strange quality in a historian. Don't you find it something of a professional handicap?'

I took my hands from my face and turned away: 'I shouldn't have come.'

'It's all part and parcel of your desire for a bland compromise.' He laughed briefly. 'That's your passion: compromise. Don't ridicule anyone's beliefs however wrong you think they are. How middle-class and English and philistine. But there's so much you don't understand. Your life has been so privileged and protected. And you've narrowed it even further and shut out so much. You've lived such a safe, cautious life. I've known such horror and degradation and exaltation that you couldn't begin to imagine.'

He paused. Then he said: 'But I'm so glad you've forgiven me.'

We sat in silence for at least a minute. I became aware of the darkness and the shadows around us in the light of the single candle and the dying embers of the fire. I could even hear the clock ticking on the landing below.

'It's too late to go to a hotel,' I said, standing up. 'But I will leave the house immediately after breakfast.'

Austin looked like a man coming to himself after an anaesthetic or a mesmeric trance: 'Of course you must stay. I'm sorry if I've offended you. I don't know why I said those things. You won't go, will you?'

'I think I should.'

'Look, to be absolutely frank, I'm not myself at the moment. Please sit down.'

Hesitantly, I did as he said and he went on: 'There is something weighing upon my mind. Otherwise I would never have said those things.'

'I guessed as much.'

'I wasn't talking about you just now but arguing with myself. I would have said those things to anybody who was unfortunate enough to be sitting where you are now.' He turned away. 'I tell you in all honesty, in the last few weeks I've come perilously close to the very edge of my being.'

'Won't you tell me about it?'

He turned his anguished face towards me: 'I can't do that. But can you imagine being put in a situation so intolerable that you begin seriously to think of destroying yourself as the only way out?'

'Dear God! You must not let yourself contemplate such a hideous deed. Tell me you are not serious.'

A slow, sardonic smile appeared on his face: 'I have rejected that option. Set your mind at rest on that score, at least.'

'Won't you trust me enough to tell me what this is all about, Austin?'

'You'll stay until Saturday?'

'Very well. Yes, I'll stay.'

'Bless you, old friend.'

I waited for him to speak but it was clear that he had no intention of confiding in me. Even so, I was about to broach the subject he had touched on but at that moment the clock on the landing struck once.

'Is it so late?' I exclaimed.

'It's much later,' Austin replied, taking out his watch. 'Didn't you hear the Cathedral? It's nearly two. That clock keeps time very badly.'

'Then why not have it seen to?' I asked.

He smiled.

Irritating, baffling, unfathomable Austin! I had loved him when we were young and I had been deeply grieved to think that I had lost his friendship. 'I have much to do tomorrow,' I said. 'I should go to bed.'

We shook hands and parted. I went upstairs first, finding the stairs and then the bedroom horribly cold after the warmth of the sitting-room. I pulled a curtain a little to one side and saw that the fog was, if anything, thicker than before. Austin went downstairs and after twenty minutes I heard him come up and go into his room across the landing. I got into bed and read for half an hour—a habit without which I could not sleep—but on this occasion I found it hard to concentrate.

Austin's anger had upset me. I did not recall his having such a short temper when he was an undergraduate. It must be because he had so much on his mind. I wondered once again who it was he was in love with and whether it was that amour that endangered his position at the school. The wife of a colleague? The mother of a pupil?

I could not put from my thoughts the piece of news he had thrust upon me. It was precisely to protect myself from such knowledge that I had at the time severed connections with certain friends and acquaintances. Why had Austin insisted on talking about the past and passing on that cruel piece of information? Did he feel the need to exorcise his guilt? I had seen no sign even of regret for the role—the important role—which he had played at the time.

All I had wanted twenty-five years ago was a life of scholarship and a wife and children, but Austin had clearly not wanted that. I used to think he had wanted less than I, but now I began to wonder if he had wanted more. He had failed to get the degree to which his gifts entitled him because he had got into one of his scrapes—as he called them—just before the examination. There was something naked and dangerous in Austin which I had almost forgotten about until I saw it again just now. He was capable of acting without dignity or self-control. Had a sense of frustration and failure led him to make some serious misjudgement?

I blew out my candle and tried to sleep. Austin was right: the Close was completely silent. It was like college during the vacation. Almost too quiet. I thought of how, a year or two after the great caesura in my life, I had found the house on the outskirts of Cambridge too silent and had moved back into my old bachelor rooms in college. During the term the noise of the undergraduates is comforting, only occasionally disturbing; in the vacations the silence becomes oppressive. The only sound now was the Cathedral clock striking the quarters and when it had uttered its deep chime on the hour, there were answering cheeps from other church-steeples coming muffled through the thick fog that must lie upon the town like an ocean, the spires and towers peeking through. Apart from that, the only noises were from inside the house when the woodwork creaked like an old man's joints as if the ancient building were groaning in pain at its long decline. I thought of all that must have happened in this house: the people who had died, the babies that had been born, the sadness, and the laughter. The creaks were like the groaning boards of an old wooden ship. The house was a ship, but the sea of clouds was over our heads. It was a ship that travelled under the surface of the water, then. My head filled with such nonsense, I drifted into sleep, or a kind of half-sleep.

❖

I woke up suddenly and lay for a moment wondering what had disturbed me. Then I heard again the sound that had broken in upon my sleep. It was a whimpering cry somewhere between a shout and a sob—almost not human. I had some half-dreaming notion that I was hearing the ghost whose story Austin had told me, but this was a real noise and it was coming from somewhere inside the house. I lit my candle and the flickering shadows that this summoned up in the room did nothing to calm my fears. I somehow found the courage to leave my bed, don a dressing-gown and go out onto the landing. The sound was coming, as I had guessed, from Austin's room. I knocked and after a moment pushed the door and went in.

In the dim light I saw a figure on the bed. I held up the candle and saw that Austin was kneeling on the bedcovers in his night-shirt. He had his hands over his ears as if he were trying to protect them from a loud noise. His eyes were open and he seemed to be looking at something at the end of the bed. When I saw his thin legs protruding from the nightshirt I felt pity and faint revulsion at their white boniness.

Looking at his pale, sensitive face in its moment of unguarded pain, I felt a sharp stab of affection despite all that he had done. Was it affection for the man before me or mourning for the youth he had once been?

I approached the bed. He looked at me—at least, his eyes were open and were turned towards me. I had the strangest feeling as I realized that he was looking straight at me and yet was not seeing me. Who or what he was seeing I had no idea.

Addressing me and yet not addressing me, he uttered the words: 'She says he has deserved it for many years. She says it's not vengeance but justice. He has escaped punishment all these years.'

'Austin,' I said. 'It's me. It's Ned.'

Still with his head turned to me and his unseeing eyes fixed on my face, he said: 'His account must be closed. She says so. And she says she'll do it herself if we won't.'

I took him and pressed him to me.

'Austin,' I said. 'My dear fellow.'

He started suddenly and as he stared at me with his eyes wide open I saw recognition and realization dawn. For a moment he stayed in my arms, then he pushed me away quite brusquely.

'My dear old friend,' I said, 'I'm so sorry to find you in such dis-tress. Is there anything I can do to help?'

'It's too late for that.' He breathed heavily twice and then said: 'I'm all right. Go back to bed.'

'Dear Austin, I don't like to leave you in such a state.'

'I'm all right. Go. It was just a nightmare.'

His tone was such that I could resist no longer. With much perplexity I did as I was bid, but it was long before sleep reclaimed me.

My resentment against him was largely dissipated by the vision of vulnerability and torment I had just seen. Had my old friend frightened himself with the ghost-story which he had promised would keep me from sleeping and disturb my dreams? The terror I had read on his face seemed to suggest something much worse than that. I sympathized, for I was often tormented by nightmares, and in particular at the worst period of my life when, for several months, I had almost been frightened to go to sleep. Was Austin's nightmare related to that? Was he haunted by guilt for his part in that painful event? Although I was not clear exactly what role he had played, he had certainly borne some of the responsibility. Had he invited me here to try to make amends? Or was it because he needed help in the mysterious crisis in which he was involved? And was the woman he had spoken of just now in his dream the object of his passion?

Wednesday Morning

✦

I WAS AWAKENED by the Cathedral clock striking the hour, though I came to consciousness too slowly to count the chimes. The room was in darkness, the heavy curtains admitting no light that could give me a clue to the hour. I lit a candle and, with an effort of will, forced myself out of the bed and into the bone-chilling cold of the unheated room. Once I was dressed I looked at my watch. It was eight o'clock! Horrified at such self-indulgence, I pulled back the frayed curtains and found the fog still thick. Even in the muddy light, the time-blackened stonework of the Cathedral was startlingly close to the window.

As I went down the stairs a few minutes later I smelt toast and coffee and in the dining-room I found Austin laying the table for our breakfast. He smiled and the Austin of the nightmare—indeed, the belligerent Austin of our argument late in the evening—had vanished.

'I'm glad to see you've recovered your spirits,' I said.

'I beg your pardon for having disturbed you last night, old fellow,' he said, lowering his eyes. 'As it turned out, I scared myself much more than I frightened you with that story.'

'You certainly seemed to be very frightened. Do you remember that you were muttering about vengeance and punishment and justice?'

He turned away to tend to the coffee. 'I had a nightmare about Gambrill, the Cathedral Mason. You remember that he had a journeyman who was suspected of being involved in his murder? His name was Limbrick and many years before, his father died in an accident on the Cathedral roof in which Gambrill was badly injured and lost an eye. His widow said at the time that the two men had quarrelled and she accused Gambrill of killing him.'

'Gracious heavens,' I said cheerfully as I sat down and began to attack my breakfast. 'What a murderous little town! Then was she the woman you were talking about?'

He looked startled. 'The woman? What did I say?'

'It was hard to make it out. You mentioned a "she" who was insisting on closing someone's account. Was it the young man's mother?'

'The young man's mother?' he repeated staring at me. 'What can you mean?'

I could not hide my surprise: 'Limbrick's widow, of course. The mother of the young workman.'

'I see,' he said. 'Yes, it must have been. She had been brooding for years about her husband's death and goading her son into avenging him.'

As we breakfasted—hastily, because Austin was in danger of being late for school—I said that I was going immediately to the Dean and Chapter's Library in the hope of speaking to Dr Locard, though my letter would only have reached him yesterday. Austin explained that his duties would preoccupy him until the evening but that we would dine together in the town.

We left the house and Austin closed the door behind him. 'You may come and go as you please and have no need of a key.'

'Don't you lock the door?' I asked.

'Never. But I hide the keys.'

I wondered what he meant by that for it seemed strange to hide the door-key when the door itself was not locked. And in fact, since he put it into his pocket as we set off, he must have been referring to another set of keys.

The Close was as cold and foggy as it had been the previous day. Peering up, I noticed some doves cowering under the eaves of the Cathedral and it occurred to me that one sees more clearly in the fog because one has to look harder. The sight of the birds performing their elaborate dance on the narrow ledges brought to mind a Scottish castle I had once stayed in which stood on a perilous cliff beside the ocean. Our room was at the top of a lofty tower and seagulls would perch precariously on the window-sills and utter their melancholy cries like insistent soothsayers.

Austin told me he could not give himself the pleasure, as he put it with a grimace, of introducing me to Dr Locard because he was already late for his first class, but he directed me to the southeastern corner of the Upper Close where the Library was, and then hurried off.

When I had climbed the worn stone stairs and pushed open a heavy oaken door, my nostrils were assailed by the smell of old books, ancient leather, beeswax and candles. A long and handsome gallery was before me for the Library had originally been the Great Hall of the Abbey. This floor was divided at intervals by bays projecting at right-angles from the walls and carrying bookshelves so that there was only a narrow way through its centre. The bays were big old oak constructions rising to a height several feet above a man's head. This part was the old chained library and many of the books were still fastened in that way.

A young man was sitting at a desk near the door. He stood up as I came in. When I told him I had business with Dr Locard and that I had written to him, to my delight he said that the Librarian was expecting me and asked me to follow him.

'This must be a pleasant place to work,' I ventured as we began to walk the full length of the gallery.

My companion was a little plump, in his late twenties, with a face which, though not handsome, conveyed that its owner was clever and amusing. He nodded vigorously: 'It is perfectly delightful in the summer but in the winter, somewhat dark and cold for my taste.'

'It seems cosy and cheerful enough now,' I said. 'And one might almost be back in the seventeenth century, so little appears modern.'

Just before we passed through a door at the end of the gallery into what seemed once to have been a different building, the young man turned and said: 'You're quite right, sir. I often feel as if some of the extraordinary characters who worked here at that time are looking over my shoulder: Burgoyne, Freeth and Hollingrake.'

'That can't be altogether reassuring,' I suggested and he laughed, and then composed his features as he knocked on a door to our left and walked straight in. It was a big ancient room with oaken panelling all round the walls, a number of tall and heavy display-cases, and a large black book-press filled with ancient leather-bound volumes. A man was seated at a desk beneath the window and he stood up as we entered. He was tall and still handsome in his middle fifties, with fastidious grey eyes that conveyed much acuity but little warmth. I knew of Dr Locard's reputation as an excellent scholar—though his field was not my own—and in particular, as a fine Latinist.

He greeted me by name and we shook hands. I seated myself at his invitation and he introduced me to my escort who, he explained, was his first assistant and whose name was Quitregard. The young man made to leave but Dr Locard called out as he reached the door: 'Would you tell Pomerance to bring coffee for my guest and myself.' He turned to me: 'Would you care for a cup?'

I accepted with thanks.

Quitregard, however, replied: 'Pomerance has not arrived yet, sir. Would you like me to bring it?'

'Please don't bother on my account,' I said. 'I've just had my breakfast.'

'Very well. Then we'll defer it until Mr Pomerance condescends to favour us with his presence.'

Quitregard left and Dr Locard nodded at the closing door: 'That young man will make a fine librarian one day. His Latin is very adequate and he is familiar with a variety of early hands.'

I told him his assistant had impressed me very favourably and then we turned to our business.

'Your letter arrived yesterday and I am perfectly intrigued by it,' the Librarian said. 'For although the subject is far removed from my own area of interest, the Library subscribes to the *Proceedings of the English Historical Society* and so I happen to have read both your paper and Scuttard's response to it.'

'I'm very pleased to hear that. But I hope you were not convinced by Scuttard's argument?'

'I wouldn't dream of venturing an opinion in an area of such complexity outside my own province. But he was very persuasive. He is a scholar of remarkable abilities and achievement—though still barely forty—from whom even greater things are expected. His book on the eighth century has blown away much of the mist of unsupported assumptions which has until now obscured the subject.'

I was rather taken aback by this response. 'However that may be—and I think he dismisses too readily some very brilliant insights by earlier scholars—he is wrong in this regard.'

Dr Locard looked at me dispassionately: 'If you find what you hope to, you will completely destroy his argument. What I don't understand from your letter, however, is why you are so optimistic.'

'I don't know if you are familiar with the name of the antiquarian and scholar, Ralph Pepperdine?'

Dr Locard nodded. 'The author of *De Antiquitatibus Britanniae?*'

'Just so. Well, he died in 1689 and left his papers to his old college—my own, as it happens. Shamefully, they have never been properly examined. Just two weeks ago I looked at them because I was coming here and remembered that Pepperdine had once visited this town. I found a letter written by him while he was visiting this Library in 1663.'

'Really? I imagine it might offer an interesting perspective on the Foundation at that difficult time.'

'Indeed so and there is something in it which will, I think, be of particular interest to yourself.' I removed from my portfolio the handwritten copy I had made. 'Pepperdine gives a description by an eyewitness of the death of Dean Freeth.'

'Really? Does it differ significantly from the accepted version?'

'That his death arose from a misunderstanding of the orders given and was completely unintended?'

'Yes, though that version was proffered by the officer in charge who had every reason to account for it in that way.'

'Pepperdine gives a completely different explanation.'

Dr Locard smiled. 'Then it makes all existing discussion of the incident entirely inadequate. When a competent historian of the Foundation appears he will be in your debt.'

'Is there not already such a history?'

'Nothing since a ponderous work published in the middle of the last century. And there is nothing of any quality in prospect, though there are some amateurish efforts being undertaken whose use of the sources is most unscholarly. What does Pepperdine say?'

'The opening of his letter need not detain us. He describes the journey and the state of the roads and says he arrived two weeks earlier and is lodged in the Palace with his old friend, the Bishop. This is the interesting part:

At supper yesternight with Mr Dean I heard an account of the death of the late Dean which gives the lie to the story given out. As you most likely know, when the Parliamentary forces captured the town, they shamefully made the Dean a prisoner in his own dwelling because he was mightily affected to the king's party and it was feared that he might incite the people to resistance. My intelligence is from one Champniss who has been a Canon Residentiary here for upwards of four decades and greatly loved the unfortunate Freeth. On the morning of his death, Champniss saw six troopers enter the Close who appeared to be drunk and who forced their way into the corner where the Library is. Then they started to sack the building—smashing the windows and looting and stealing. The old man told me that the Dean must have seen this from one of the windows of his Deanery and that, mightily perturbed by this act of desecration, he hastened forth from his dwelling in order to restrain them in defiance of the state of arrest under which he had been placed. When Champniss saw him run into the building he feared for his life and himself hurried thither in order to remonstrate with the soldiers. When he rounded the corner of the building a minute or two later he found the Dean kneeling on the ground in front of the soldiers clutching a document and praying. Champniss heard him begging aloud for God's forgiveness for his murderers— one of whom was a mere boy who was in tears. As Champniss came up to him, the Dean saw him and urged him away with his hand. Two of the soldiers seized Champniss and forced him away from that place and just at that moment he saw an officer approaching who he knew bore a grudge against the Dean which was wholly unjustified. As he turned the corner a few seconds later he heard the discharge of two or three pieces. Even as the old man recounted this incident that happened about twenty years ago, he was in tears.

I broke off. 'The implication is clearly that the officer himself ordered the Dean's death, is it not?'

'The image Pepperdine presents is so emblematic that it arouses suspicion.' Dr Locard compressed his lips in an ironic smile. 'Do you know the work of Charles Landseer?' I nodded. 'It would suit his mawkish sentimentality, would it not? Even to the sobbing boy-soldier for there is usually a good-looking lad in his pictures. Can you not imagine a canvas called "The Dean of Thurchester prays for his murderers"?'

I smiled. 'But even allowing that the old man was partial, that does not discredit his account.'

'Of course not. But it is also possible that Pepperdine is misre-porting the old gentleman's words.'

'I can't imagine any reason why he would do that.'

The Librarian regarded me speculatively for a moment. 'Really? My principle as a historian, when I am faced with a conflict of evidence, is to work out what view of events each witness regarded it as being in his own interests to promote. That seems to me to be the best chance one has of arriving at the truth. So in this case, if Pepperdine was writing to a powerful Royalist he might have good reasons for weighting the story in the Dean's favour, might he not?'

'His correspondent, Giles Bullivant, was merely another scholar with no political influence. He and Pepperdine were interested in the transmission of classical texts in the late Middle Ages, and that was why Pepperdine had come to the town. He was to be disap-pointed in his hopes because little had been done to sort out the manuscripts after the sacking of the Library.'

'And I'm afraid that you will find that little has been done in the succeeding two centuries.'

I gazed at him in astonishment.

'That is the literal truth. Nothing has been done to most of the manuscripts since they were roughly sorted out in 1643. What does he say about where he found the manuscript which interests you?'

'He is exasperatingly imprecise: *I searched the upper floor of the Old Library and found nothing of interest. The manuscripts in the un-dercroft of the New Library are grievously disordered and it would be the work of many days, or even weeks, to examine them and not worth the labour since they seem to be for the most part records of the abbey in the old times.'*

I broke off. 'Can you explain what he means?'

He smiled. 'I will show you, for very little has changed since he wrote those words.'

I shrugged my shoulders to express my surprise and continued with my account of the letter. 'Then he writes: *I chanced upon a manuscript of some interest, I suppose, to those who concern themselves with the early history of the uncouth tribes who ruled in this land in the age of darkness before the Conquest. It recounts—in woefully bad Latin—the story of a king whose former tutor is slain before his eyes by the heathen who have captured his capital, of which the old man is bishop. I therefore left it where I had found it.'*

'And what do you believe he had found?'

'Since he knew nothing of the Anglo-Saxon period, Pepperdine did not recognize that the manuscript he was summarizing was a version of a story in Grimbald's *Life*.'

Dr Locard started. As calmly as I was able I said, hoping he would not notice the tremor in my voice: 'I am convinced that it is nothing less than Grimbald's original text.'

'In that case, it would establish beyond all argument how much Leofranc altered his source.'

'And prove that he did not compose the whole thing, as Scuttard absurdly maintains, but merely revised the existing text.'

'That would constitute an earthquake in Alfredian studies, I assume.'

'If Grimbald is largely authentic—as I believe—his *Life* would have to be taken seriously as a major source for the period.'

'You must be eager to begin the search. Let me show you the Library.'

He led me back into the great hall and we ascended an old

wooden staircase to the huge upper floor where daylight came in through the top half of the tall windows allowing me to admire the handsome hammerbeam roof.

'After the looting and the fire,' Dr Locard explained, 'hundreds of books and manuscripts were gathered up where they had been thrown. The printed books were placed on the ground floor and were sorted out over the next months and years, but the manuscripts were an immense problem. Many of them were in obscure languages or in hands that were hard to read so the Librarian made a crude division: they were sorted into those which were to be catalogued as soon as possible and those which could wait.'

'On what basis was this division made?'

'Those that could wait were for the most part the Foundation's own muniments—fabric records, rent-rolls, and so on—and they were taken down to the undercroft of the New Library and have hardly been looked at since then. The important ones were brought up here to be catalogued.'

He showed me the section of the shelves on which the manuscripts were kept.

'And has that been done?'

'That work only started eight years ago when I became Librarian.' He paused and said with quiet impressiveness: 'In another six months I expect to be able to report to the Dean and Chapter that we have finished. Those which remain to be done are for the most part ones which should have been placed in the undercroft in 1643.'

'I congratulate you, Dr Locard.'

He nodded in brief acknowledgement. 'Let us go down to the undercroft now.'

We descended the stairs and as we passed along the length of the lower floor, we encountered the young assistant at his desk in one of the bays. 'Ah, Quitregard,' said Dr Locard. 'Would you bring a lamp and accompany us down to the undercroft?'

A moment later we had passed into the part of the building

known as the New Library and from which the undercroft was entered, and were making our way carefully down a dark staircase with the young man in front of us to light our way. That was essential for it had no gas-lighting and was nothing more than the ancient cellarage of the old hall, and smelt strongly of dust and spiders and old paper.

The undercroft was huge and for several minutes the two men led me around the maze of ancient book-presses, at each turn more shelves laden with bundles of yellowing manuscript and ancient leathern cartularies coming into view in the flickering light in Quitregard's hand. It was immediately clear to me that Pepperdine had been right: it would be the work of years rather than months to sift through these heaps of paper and vellum.

'Thank goodness,' I said, 'that I do not have to search down here.'

Dr Locard stopped and turned to look at me: 'Why do you say that?'

'Simply because Pepperdine did not search through them and therefore did not find the manuscript here.'

Dr Locard seemed to reflect for a moment and then asked: 'Tell me, Dr Courtine, was Pepperdine's correspondent as uninterested in the Anglo-Saxon period as he seems to assume?'

'Oddly enough, Bullivant did some very valuable work on Anglo-Saxon, finding and publishing some important materials.'

'So it is odd, is it not, that Pepperdine should refer to the manuscript as something which would not interest him?'

'You appear to have an idea about that. May I ask what it is?'

'Simply that we should take into account the question of whom Pepperdine is addressing and what his motives might be. Scholarship is competitive at least as much as it is collaborative—rather as a game is. You play to win but you have to obey the rules.'

'Are you suggesting he invented the manuscript?' I asked in dismay. 'That he found nothing?'

'Oh no. That would be to break the rules.'

'Then I'm afraid I don't understand your point.'

'It is possible that the reference to the manuscript was the bait for a trap whose purpose was to lure Bullivant into coming to the town and wasting his time and his money looking for it in the wrong place. Time and money that might otherwise be devoted to his scholarly rivalry with Pepperdine.'

It was odd to hear of such devious tactics from a man of the cloth, but I thought of such practices in my own field and accepted that he was right in principle. 'But Pepperdine said that he had not examined the manuscripts down here. So even if you're right, Bullivant would not have bothered to search them.'

'Let us consider the letter more closely.'

We followed Quitregard up the stairs and then he returned to his duties. Once we were back in the Librarian's Chamber, Dr Locard laid the letter out on his desk and we bent over it together.

'Pepperdine's words—*it would be the work of many days, or even weeks, to examine them and not worth the labour*—clearly imply,' I said, 'that he has not searched downstairs.'

'But his words are not definitive on that point. I suggest that Bullivant was expected to notice the equivocation.'

'You mean that he was intended to assume that Pepperdine had done so and was trying to hide the fact?'

'Precisely.'

With dismay I realized the force of what he was suggesting.

'And since,' he continued, 'the manuscripts on the upper floor have been catalogued—except for a few which have at least been examined—and the one you are seeking has never been found, it must be downstairs if it is anywhere.'

His logic seemed irrefutable. I had only three days for my search and so it would be a matter of luck if I happened upon my quarry. I could not hide my dismay.

'I wish I could offer you some help but my assistants and I are struggling to keep abreast of the work we already have.'

'You've been very generous with your time,' I muttered. 'I doubt if I'll find it, but I can comfort myself with the reflection that if I do, then I'll deserve all the more credit given the conditions down there.'

I was beginning to walk towards the door when he said: 'On further reflection, since we will soon start sorting out the material downstairs, nothing will be lost if I spend part of tomorrow morning looking through it with you.'

I turned back. 'That would be most extraordinarily generous of you,' I replied.

'Very well, then, that's settled. I have a Chapter meeting at eleven—as always on Thursdays, alas—but I am free for a few hours beforehand. Shall we start at half-past seven, which is when the Library is opened on Thursday mornings?'

'By all means.'

'In addition, I will put one of my assistants at your disposal. I can't spare Quitregard—which is regrettable because he's worth an army of Pomerances—but I can lend you that somewhat inadequate young man. He has just arrived, by the way, for I noticed him skulking in one of the bays just now. I will introduce him to you.'

We left the room and passed back into the main gallery where we found a tall thin youth standing in one of the embrasures and staring out of the window. He started as we approached and turned towards us a long bony face which seemed to have been vigorously pinched into shape during its making. I thought of it as a Viking head and face—raw and empty except that in the eyes was visible the pain of being young.

'Allow me to present my second assistant, Pomerance,' Dr Locard said.

We shook hands and he stammered that he was honoured to meet me.

'Please provide Dr Courtine with every assistance,' the Librarian said.

'I will do my best, sir.'

'That's not quite the same,' Dr Locard said with a smile at me.

I took leave of him and thanked him again. Then my helpmate and I descended with a couple of lamps and, in a state of profound discouragement, I gazed around me. It was possible—indeed, likely—that somewhere in here was an ancient folio that could overturn most of what was accepted about the ninth century. If Grimbald were vindicated then his account of Alfred would be beyond impeachment by the sneering iconoclasts who had dismissed as Leofranc's anachronistic and self-interested fabrications the king's passion for the education of all classes, his curiosity about Islam and Moorish culture, his interest in wind-mills for draining marshlands, and so on.

The chances were small but the reward was great, and inspired by this reflection, I started searching through piles of dusty manuscripts. Young Pomerance was not very helpful since he knew no language but his own and lacked the palaeographic expertise required even to spell out the letters of old manuscripts with any facility. But I found his services useful for bringing down great cobwebby bundles of parchment and paper, and cleaning them up a little before I looked at them.

Pomerance left me after a couple of hours, saying it was time for him to go home for his dinner. When I slipped out at one o'clock Dr Locard was not visible but I nodded to Quitregard who smiled back. Just as I was descending the steps outside I encountered a lady coming up them. She was tall and slender and, though only a few years my junior, she was still a beautiful woman with fine features and large grey eyes. She reminded me of someone—though I could not at that moment think who it was. We exchanged the smiles of strangers who suspect that they are linked in some way and are therefore likely to meet.

Wednesday Afternoon

❖

I WENT to the most respectable of the inns I could see among those in the High Street—the Dolphin—and had a quick luncheon. I returned to the Close through the Old Gatehouse on the north side and as I passed it I glanced in through one of its little mullioned windows and saw a big schoolroom in which about twenty boys were seated. It must be a part of Courtenay's Academy. At the sight, it all came vividly back to me—the fizzing of the gas-standards, the smell of chalk and slate. With a sigh for my own long past schooldays I hastened on around the Close, exercising that most important faculty of the historian's resources: the imagination. At the end of the Close I stopped and reflected. It was from the old house before me, which had been Burgoyne's but had become the New Deanery, that the Dean had hurried a few minutes before his death. And then he had gone or been forced into the Cloisters—without doubt through this very door. I was so intent upon imagining the scene and wondering if I dared risk trying to read the inscription, that I failed to realize that someone was standing in front of me and attempting to attract my attention. It was the young Sacrist and he was with another and much older man also clad in clerical garb.

'I do beg your pardon, Dr Sisterson,' I said. 'I was lost in my thoughts. I was trying to see the events of that day in September 1643 when this precinct earned its place in the pages of infamy.'

'A novel mode of procedure,' the other man commented drily. 'It would save a historian a great deal of tiresome research.'

Dr Sisterson laughed and said: 'Dr Courtine, this is Dr Sheldrick, our Chancellor.'

We shook hands. When I mentioned my College, Dr Sheldrick said: 'You must know my young cousin, the Honourable George de Villiers, who is an undergraduate there. He is reading for the Classical Tripos.'

'I know of him, of course, but my own school is the historical.'

'I'm fully aware of your work and reputation, Dr Courtine,' he said rather crushingly as if he was rebuking me for it. 'I am something of a historian myself.'

'Indeed you are, Chancellor,' said Dr Sisterson. He turned to me: 'Dr Sheldrick is writing the history of the Foundation. In fact, the first fascicle has just been published.'

'Ah yes.' It occurred to me that it was odd that Austin did not mention this work as one of the sources for the story of Burgoyne. And even odder that Dr Locard had not done so either, though I recollected that he had referred dismissively to the efforts of amateurs. Then I remembered that Dr Sisterson had mentioned Dr Sheldrick's work when I had met him in the Cathedral. 'So you mentioned last night.' I turned to the older man. 'I believe I noticed the reception to mark its publication that you gave last night?'

There was an odd silence. It seemed that I had raised an awkward topic. 'I should so much like to read your history, Dr Sheldrick,' I said quickly. 'Does it cover the period of Burgoyne and Freeth?'

'It goes down to the end of the thirteenth century only,' Dr Sheldrick replied.

To my surprise he did not offer to give me a copy—the merest courtesy between scholars.

'Dr Sheldrick has, however, written a draft of the next fascicle which covers the Civil War period,' Dr Sisterson said. 'In fact, I have it in my possession since he has kindly asked me to read it and give him my humble advice.'

'I await its publication with the keenest interest.'

Dr Sisterson glanced at his colleague. 'I wonder if I might lend it to Dr Courtine?'

'I see no reason why not,' he answered rather ungraciously.

'I have it in my office,' Dr Sisterson told me. 'Have you time to accompany me there now?'

I expressed my willingness and my gratitude to both gentlemen. We took leave of Dr Sheldrick and walked towards the Sacristy.

'The Chancellor is a little preoccupied today,' Dr Sisterson said as soon as the other man was out of earshot. 'There was a rather unfortunate episode last night during . . .'

'Excuse me,' I said. 'I beg your pardon for interrupting you, but can you tell me the identity of that lady?'

The woman I had seen as I was leaving the Library just before luncheon had been walking along the other side of the Close on a course convergent with that of Dr Sheldrick and at the right-angle where they met, she had stopped to speak to him.

'That is Mrs Locard,' he said with a smile. 'An awfully pleasant woman and a great friend of my wife.'

'And of Dr Sheldrick, as far as I can judge,' I added rather naughtily: 'He is actually smiling.'

Dr Sisterson looked back and laughed and we walked on. 'You are quite right. It is impossible not to like her.'

In the next moment we were in the Sacrist's office where he handed me a thick sheaf of manuscript which I could see was written in a very neat though somewhat inelegant hand.

I could not resist saying, 'I wonder why Dr Locard did not mention Dr Sheldrick's work when I asked him about the history of the Foundation this morning?'

Dr Sisterson smiled and wagged a finger at me playfully. 'Now, now, Dr Courtine. You mustn't try to tempt me into indiscretion.'

I laughed and, thanking him for the fascicle, tucked it under my arm and took my leave. By two o'clock I was back at work in the dusty undercroft. It was not long before Pomerance re-appeared and gave me half an hour of his time but he was so clumsy and forgetful that he was more trouble than he was worth and I was relieved when he went off for his tea.

At about three o'clock Quitregard came down to tell me that Dr Locard wondered if I would care to come up and take a cup of tea with him. I accepted, relieved to get out of the dusty atmosphere.

The Librarian stood up when I entered his room. A pot of tea and two cups and plates were on his desk beside a dish heaped with sandwiches and another filled with cakes.

'Since we were talking of Freeth this morning,' he said, 'you might be interested to see his portrait.' He indicated a canvas hanging near the window and I crossed to look at it.

'It was executed a few months after he became Dean.'

To my surprise the face was not that of an ambitious and unscrupulous man but sensitive and even delicate. I turned to the Librarian: 'If you had told me this was Burgoyne, I would not have been surprised. This is the face of an aristocratic scholar rather than a worldly sensualist.'

'Unfortunately Burgoyne never troubled himself to have his likeness taken, or if he did, it has not survived. But Freeth was a man of considerable merit, despite his weaknesses. He was able and industrious and did much for the Foundation. What has survived of Burgoyne is not his image but his scholarly work.' He indicated a row of volumes in the ancient book-press. 'That is his edition of certain Syriac manuscripts—still the authoritative text. But, on a very different note, let me show you one of the Library's more ambiguous treasures.' He crossed to a glass case against a wall, unlocked it and withdrew a large vellum document. 'What would you say this is?'

I looked at it carefully, anxious not to make a stupid blunder. It looked like a medieval deed engrossed on vellum in a fine Chancery hand. 'It's surely a legal instrument of some kind and dates, I would say, from the early fifteenth century.'

'Indeed. Well, Treasurer Burgoyne wanted to raise money to save the fabric of the Cathedral which was then in a very poor way. He conceived the idea of suppressing one of the institutions of the Foundation in order to pay for it.'

'What was it?'

'It was a college of vicars-choral. A school of church music which trained boys and young men not merely for this cathedral-choir but also for the choirs of other cathedrals. Burgoyne managed to win a majority of the Chapter over to this but Freeth opposed him and characteristically refused to accept defeat. He and my predecessor in this office—a man called Hollingrake—made an extensive search of the Foundation's ancient records and a week or two later produced a document which frustrated Burgoyne's design. (Please help yourself to the sandwiches and cakes, by the way. My wife made them.) This was the document you are holding now—the original deed of endowment dated 1424.'

'So I was right!' I could not help exclaiming.

Dr Locard paused for a moment and then resumed: 'The deed endowed the Foundation with a nearby manor comprising a handsome dwelling and a number of farms for the support of the college. But it stipulated that if the college were suppressed the land should be sold and the proceeds put at the personal disposition of the Dean of the day. Freeth had no difficulty in persuading the old Dean to confirm that in that event he would take the money and put it to his own use. So Burgoyne's proposal was rejected after all.'

'How strange that the terms of the endowment should be so generous to the Dean.'

Dr Locard smiled. 'Strange indeed. You have not perceived that the document is a forgery?'

I felt my face flush. 'Of course, but it's a very convincing one.'

'That's because it was, presumably, copied from an original document. The forger merely added—in very respectable bad Latin—a clause investing title personally in the holder of the office of Dean.'

'Does the original document exist?'

He smiled. 'The best proof of a forgery is the original on which it is based. Since it would have proved this to be a counterfeit, you can be sure that it was destroyed.'

'Do you suspect that Hollingrake was the forger? Incidentally, these cakes are quite delicious.'

'When Freeth became Dean he gave Hollingrake the office of Treasurer—a generous reward since it permitted him to enrich himself. But I'm afraid that Freeth led the way in that regard for, ironically, he made use of the forged deed to close down the institution, sell the land and pocket the proceeds.'

'After his bitter opposition to Burgoyne? What a greedy hypocrite! How could the other canons have agreed to such a thing?'

Dr Locard gazed at me with mild curiosity. 'I assume that Freeth found a way to quiet their consciences.'

It took me a moment to understand what he meant. 'They were bought off?'

'Freeth became a very wealthy man. He was now the owner of a considerable acreage of land and a handsome manor-house a few miles from the town. He was able to be generous.'

'And Hollingrake?'

'Strangely enough, the records of Chapter meetings show that there was open ill-will between the two men so I suspect that they fell out over the division of the spoils.'

'How sad that posterity lost the college of music.'

'It would not have survived the Protectorate anyway in view of the hostility of the Puritans to church music. In fact, it continued to exist in a reduced form for it shrank to become the Choir School, occupying the same building on the north side of the Upper Close—the Old Gatehouse.'

'I saw it this afternoon on my way back from luncheon at the Dolphin.'

'My dear fellow,' Dr Locard exclaimed. 'Did you take your luncheon there? I'm sorry to think of you living like a commercial traveller. My wife and I would be very pleased if you would do us the honour of dining with us while you are here.'

'That would be a very great pleasure.'

'Are you here with your wife, Dr Courtine?'

'No, I'm not. She's . . . That is to say, no I'm not.'

'How long do you plan to stay?'

'Only until Saturday morning. My niece and her family expect me that day.'

'Until Saturday? That is very soon. But I rather think that my wife and I have no engagement tomorrow evening.'

'You're very kind.'

'I will ask her later this afternoon and send you word immediately.'

I thanked him for the tea and said it was time for me to return to my labours.

'After your morning's work, do you feel more or less confident of finding the manuscript?'

'It would be the merest stroke of luck. If it is still in existence, I think you will find it, Dr Locard, during the process of cataloguing the material down there—though that may be some years in the future.'

'That is most unfortunate from your point of view, since I imagine that finding it would increase your chances of the new Chair.'

I laughed uneasily. 'I'm not even a candidate.'

'But you must be a very serious contender, especially now that Scuttard seems likely to withdraw.'

'Scuttard is to withdraw? Why, has something discreditable emerged about him?'

Dr Locard smiled. 'Nothing of that kind. I understand he is likely to be offered the Presidency of his own college.'

'At his age?'

'He is highly regarded by the present administration, as his recent appointment to the Cathedral Commission indicated. He is a very able man of sound views and will go far.'

'He has powerful friends, I agree. And he will certainly repay the government's confidence in him.' I stood up. 'I should keep you no longer, Dr Locard.'

My host likewise rose to his feet. 'Where can I send you word to confirm that my wife and I are not engaged for dinner tomorrow? I take it you are staying at the Dolphin?'

'No, I'm putting up with an old college friend. I believe you know him. Austin Fickling.'

'Of course I know him.' He went across to the glass case and, with his back turned to me, put the document back in its place while he spoke. 'I had no idea you were visiting a friend when I spoke of your dining with us. I imagine Fickling will have other plans for you. I don't want to place you in an awkward situation.'

'You're very considerate,' I muttered. 'Yes, I believe Fickling said something about our dining together tomorrow.'

'I hope that, perhaps, on another occasion you might . . .'

'Certainly, certainly. You're very kind, Dr Locard. I will, however, have the pleasure of seeing you tomorrow morning at half-past seven. I very much look forward to that.' He gazed at me without saying anything but then nodded suddenly.

I thanked him again for the tea and returned to the undercroft. As I resumed my labours I reflected wrily on the complexities of cathedral politics. Clearly my being a friend of Austin's placed me firmly in the camp of the Evangelicals.

About half an hour later, just as I had given up hope that Pomerance would return, he suddenly came down the stairs and approached with a lamp.

'Ah, there you are,' I said. 'I was expecting to see you earlier.'

'The guv'nor decided he needed me upstairs this afternoon.'

'Well, now that you're here, would you be good enough to get those big bundles down from the top shelf?'

'Sorry but I've just come to say that it's nearly twenty past four and the Library is about to close.'

'I had no idea so much time had passed!' During the course of the day I had examined the contents of four shelves out of about seven or eight hundred. The utter pointlessness of my undertaking was borne in upon me as I picked up my lamp and the manuscript Dr Sisterson had lent me and followed the young man up the stairs.

The Library was in almost complete darkness apart from a single light by the door, and it seemed deserted.

'Is Dr Locard in his room? I should like to take my leave.'

'No, he has gone home.'

'And Quitregard?'

'He has gone with him. He often goes to his house to help him with his Chapter business.'

The young man opened the door for me and I bade him goodbye. There was something I intended to do and, anxious that it would soon be too dark, I hurried along the length of the Cathedral to the back of the New Deanery. It was a big rambling old place with gables and mullioned windows and tall chimneys like twisted candy. A high wall separated it from the Close and I went up to the gate and peered through the bars at the rear elevation. I could just make out a large tablet of black marble inserted into the brickwork. There were words incised upon it, but in the thickening dusk they were impossible to decipher at this distance. In order to see it, I had to lean on the top of the gate and crane forward, conscious of the absurd spectacle of myself I must be making—though fortunately there was nobody to see me—and worried that I might lose my footing, for I was encumbered by Dr Sheldrick's manuscript which was pinned under one arm. I could see that the gate was not locked but I was unwilling to slip it open and go in.

Suddenly I saw a moving light a few yards away as a lantern swung and I realized there was somebody in the back-yard. I was surprised as well as dismayed for Austin had promised me that at this hour there was sure to be nobody at home! Before I had time to move, the beam turned in my direction and I heard a high-pitched voice which was so distinctive that I would remember and think about it a great deal: 'I see you. Don't be shy. Pray come in. The gate's not locked.'

I apologized profusely and declined the invitation but the old gentleman—as my interlocutor seemed from the voice to be—came to the gate saying: 'Don't be shy. Come right in.'

He pushed the gate open and smilingly made way for me to enter and so, still flushed with embarrassment, I did so.

He was below middle height and slender though since he was muffled up in a heavy greatcoat with a thick comforter round his neck it was hard to be sure. Beneath an old-fashioned hat I saw a strong face bearing an expression that was both watchful and amused, whose features were delicate, the skin pale and the cheeks smooth. The most striking element was a pair of bright blue eyes that never seemed to leave my face.

'I do most sincerely beg your pardon, sir. I had no idea anybody was here.'

'I'm a foolish old man to be out here in this weather but I couldn't resist putting more straw round the plants. I'm sure the frost is going to bite even harder tonight.'

I noticed that there were flower-boxes on all the sills of the windows.

'I saw that you were trying to read the inscription,' he said, still smiling.

'It was unpardonable of me to intrude on your property like that.'

'Not at all, not at all. I am very proud of that inscription. And of this ancient place altogether. I am fortunate enough to live in a very quaint old house in which many strange and terrible things have happened, and it seems a small price to pay that I should occasionally have strangers exhibit an interest.'

'You are very generous, sir. I do beg your pardon.'

'I don't mean you, sir. They peer through my windows at the front, you know.'

'That must be intolerable. I can sympathize for I live in a Cambridge college and my rooms are subject to the same sort of attention.'

'You are one of the most courteous of all those who have tried to read the inscription. I was afraid you would fall over in your efforts to remain outside.'

'I must have cut a ridiculous figure.'

He advanced a few steps towards the wall and raised the lantern. 'Can you read it now?'

The letters were worn and, where the stone was chipped, altogether lost in places. But the old gentleman knew the words by heart and we spelt them out together:

All things revolve and Man who is born to Labour revolves with them. And therefore in the Ripenesse of Time shall they that are on High be brought Low, and they that are Low be raised on High. Then shall the Guilty be shattered into pieces like unto the Innocent, by their own Engin brought to Destruction even in the Moment of Triumph. For when the Earthe shudders and the Towers tremble, the Grave will yield up her secrettes and all be known.

It was certainly enigmatic, I reflected as I committed it to memory.

'Do you know the story that lies behind it?' the old gentleman asked.

'I've been told that it was found at dawn just after the death of Treasurer Burgoyne and that it denounces the Cathedral Mason, Gambrill, as his murderer.'

The old gentleman nodded: 'In fact, the story passed down in my family has it that Gambrill himself carved it overnight as a confession.'

'It is hard,' I went on, 'to read it that way since its tone seems to be vengeful and triumphant rather than apologetic.'

'That's true,' he agreed. 'But perhaps Gambrill felt that he was entitled to boast of the murder. Certainly the reference to the high and the low seems to refer to the aristocratic Treasurer and the low-born Mason.'

I nodded, reflecting that it also fitted well with an idea that had occurred to me at breakfast that morning prompted by something Austin had said.

'How exactly was Burgoyne killed?'

'That was never established for certain. He was found under a collapsed scaffold which had been erected in order to put the memorial slab in place for his own family's monument. The extra-ordinary thing was that Gambrill had put the heavy slab in place up on the wall.'

'Singlehandedly?'

'So it appeared. And then, according to the story, Gambrill came here and chiselled this shortly before dawn.'

'At night and without being heard?' I asked with a smile.

It was just light enough with the glow of the lantern to see that the old gentleman himself smiled. 'Well, that's the explanation that my ancestors have accepted for more than two hundred years.'

'How did the house come into your family?'

'That's quite a story. The Canon-Treasurer who was Burgoyne's immediate predecessor spent a great deal of money enlarging and improving it with the wealth he had amassed during his period as Treasurer.'

'You mean that he had acquired from the Foundation by embezzlement?'

'Yes, or, rather, by malversation—if you'll pardon a banker's pedantry.' The old gentleman chuckled. 'Shortly after Burgoyne's death there was a new dean and because this was the grandest house in the Upper Close, he persuaded the Chapter to make it the New Deanery. Much to the annoyance of the Treasurer at the time.'

'The Dean was Launcelot Freeth, wasn't he?'

'You *are* well-informed,' the old gentleman exclaimed. 'In that case, you will understand that after his death the Chapter decided that because this house was ill-omened, they should sell it and revert to the Old Deanery. It was bought by my great-grandfather, James Stonex, in 1664 and has retained its name.'

'So it was through this very gate,' I said, turning back to look, 'that the Dean was dragged to his death?'

'It was certainly through this gate that he passed on his way to his death, but he went to his execution of his own free will.'

'Of his own free will? And why do you call it an execution? His death is regarded as one of the most shameful murders in our history.'

'Not according to a tradition that has been handed down in my family with the house.'

'I would be most intrigued to hear it.'

'I haven't time now,' he said apologetically. 'This is the hour when I dine. I keep strange hours because of my business. But come to tea the day after tomorrow and I'll tell you the true story of how the Dean met his end.'

'That is extraordinarily kind of you.'

'Very well, it's settled then. I shall expect you at a little after half-past four. Do please be punctual because my life is ordered by clocks and I will have to leave for my office at six o'clock.'

I assured him that I would be on time. There was an uncomfortable moment when we both stood there and then he said: 'I can't invite you in now, I'm afraid.'

'No, of course, I quite understand,' I said, rather bewildered. Then in a gesture that seemed oddly discourteous, he opened the gate and smiled and bowed as if to encourage me to go through it.

'Until Friday,' he said.

I passed out into the Close again, made my adieus and walked away, leaving him standing at the gate.

Then something strange happened. The corner of the Cathedral was about fifty yards away and I was sure that there was a figure standing there, only very dimly apparent through the twilit gloom. As I approached, it vanished round the corner. I was almost sure it was Austin. How odd that he should have been skulking like that and then have scuttled out of my sight. Yet it was of a piece with some of his other behaviour, I reflected, as I walked round the Close towards his house. It was as if he both wanted me here and did not want me.

I knew I could get into the house since Austin told me he always left the door unlocked. And now that I thought of his odd remark on the subject that morning, I suddenly guessed what he must mean: the reason why he hid the keys—for he had used the plural—even though the front-door was never locked was because one of them was the key to a secure place. So even if someone entered the house, he would not find both the hiding-place and the key to it. What could he have that he needed to hide? I was still thinking about this when I reached the house and was only awakened from my reverie when, as I lifted the latch and opened the door, I felt something obstructing its movement. There was a piece of paper lying on the floor. I picked it up and carried it into the dining-room and turned up the gas. The note said:

Please find your own dinner this evening. I have been un-avoidably held up. I will be back at about ten.

A

I was struck by the curtness, even the rudeness of this. He gave no explanation and made no apology for this failure of hospitality. If it was Austin whom I saw in the Close a few minutes ago, why had he hurried away without speaking if he had something to say to me?

I took off my hat and coat, poured myself a glass of sherry and sat at the table. It was all very strange. I was surer than ever that Austin was involved in some kind of intrigue. I knew so little about his life here, but how could he be happy in this dull little town—he who had been a Senior Wrangler with a brilliant future in pros-pect? I had given him more than one chance to confide in me. Was I wrong to think that he had asked me to visit him because he wished to ask for my advice? In that case, had I misunderstood the sequence of events and had he invited me before this matter—whatever it was—had begun to preoccupy him and did he now find he had little time or thought to spare for me? In that case, why had he not withdrawn the invitation? Or—if he did not want me to be there at that moment—why had he not allowed me to move into an inn when I had given him the opportunity? To have invited me and then to treat me so strangely was inexplicable. The more I thought about the rudeness of his note the more indignant I be-came. This evening we were to have dined at an inn in the town and I had hoped we would have been able at last to arrive at a bet-ter understanding.

A sudden booming sound broke in upon my reverie. The Cathedral clock was striking half-past six. How inescapably the proximity of the Cathedral would remind one of the passing of time, I thought. The quiet life of the college had obscured that from me. The incessant arrival each year of a new cohort of young men somehow dulled my sense of time passing. In one sense, I still thought of myself as relatively youthful and with all my life before me. And yet I knew that that was a delusion. I was nearly fifty and the die had been cast. For better or for worse, my life was set in the mould which it would retain until death.

I realized I was hungry and rose to my feet. My eye fell on Dr Sheldrick's manuscript which I had placed on the table before me and I decided to take it with me and peruse it during my solitary dinner. Tucking it under my arm, I left the house and made my way to the High Street, directing my steps, as a creature of habit, towards the Dolphin.

Wednesday Evening

❖

I SAT in the vast, gloomy dining-room in which there were no other diners, served by a lugubrious waiter with the mournful solemnity of the last priest of a dying church. The ambience seemed all of a piece with this ancient, decaying town with its unlit and dilapidated streets in which nobody seemed ever to be about. I supposed that the town had never recovered from the damage to its commercial life occasioned by the siege during the Civil War. That made me think of my recent encounter with the strange old creature who had shown me the inscription.

I recalled its enigmatic words—*In the Ripenesse of Time shall they that are on High be brought Low*—for when I had read them I had been struck, with Austin's dream fresh in my memory, by the possibility that they were referring to Gambrill's murder of the father of his journeyman, Limbrick. Did the inscription describe the murder? Was Gambrill confessing to having pushed his rival off the roof of the Cathedral in the accident that had cost him an eye? But it was nonsense to suppose that the inscription had really been carved by Gambrill. All the same, I reflected that I would give a great deal to ascend to the roof of the Cathedral and see the place for myself. Austin had said that the inscription hinted at the secret that Burgoyne was obsessed by and I tried to find some clue to its nature in its Biblical phraseology. The words resisted my efforts and I wondered if Dr Sheldrick's fascicle cast any light on this issue.

And so, as I sat over my greasy lamb-chop and thin claret, I found the account of these events in the manuscript. It was not well written—heavy, pedantic and often pompous—but the story it told was fascinating and I read it quickly and then perused it again more carefully. Some of what Dr Sheldrick revealed was very surprising—in particular the nature of the secret which Burgoyne was threatening to reveal. I understood Dr Locard's jibe about its unscholarliness, for it often failed to cite its sources and seemed to rely a great deal on unsubstantiated oral tradition.

When I had eaten I found that I didn't want to go back to the house yet, so I went into the public-bar where I ordered a brandy and seated myself. The only other occupants were two old men who were sitting somewhat conspiratorially in a corner. I wondered whether to have a frank discussion with Austin and ask him if he wanted me to leave. I might even ask him if the reason for his strange demeanour was that he felt guilty about what he had done to me. I kept on going over and over the same ground, telling myself that it had been foolish of me to think that I could restore my friendship with Austin. Too much time had passed and there were still unhealed wounds. I hadn't realized to what extent the past was still painful to me. Moreover, Austin was a different man from the one I had known. I thought of the strangeness of some of the things he had done and said in the brief time I had been with him. There seemed to be a slyness in him that I didn't remember. As a youth, Austin had been so open, so impulsive and so vulnerable. Had he now become devious and secretive? I thought of his heavy drinking, his quickness to anger and his skulking about the Close earlier in the evening. It was as if something had taken him over, some dark power gained mastery over him.

The other drinkers had been joined by a younger man. I was only half-aware of their conversation until I was distracted by the sound of raised voices. One of the elderly men—the one who had a battered hat pulled down over the side of his face—was saying loudly: 'They shouldn't have started meddling with 'em. You don't never know what might not happen in a building as old as that. Leave well alone is what I say.'

'You sound like old Gazzard,' said the young man. 'He's agin anything that's new. He's as pleased as Punch tonight.'

'I'll wager it's them drains,' said the same old man. 'They goes back hundreds and hundreds of years. Lord knows what's down there. Things they've been hiding for years and years.'

'Don't be softer than the good Lord made you,' said the other old man, removing his pipe from his mouth for the first time. 'The Cathedral don't have no drains.'

'Well, mebbe it should,' said the other with a hideous cackle. 'There's been a stink coming out of that place these twenty years.'

'What do you mean?' the youngest man asked indignantly. I now believed I recognized him as one of the vergers whom I had seen in the Cathedral last night.

'I'm talking about what everybody knows about them canons,' said the old man with the hat, and he gave an enormous wink.

'You don't know what you're saying,' said the man who had mentioned Gazzard. 'They watches each other like a dog eyes a bitch. If one of 'em done something he didn't oughter, the others would have him nigh on hung, drawed and quartered for it.'

'They watches each other, all right,' said the first old man. 'But they don't always ketch each other. And if they ketch each other, they don't always turn each other in.'

'You're wrong there. They don't give each other an inch on account of they're split between the Papists with their incense and Romish ways and the other lot that's more like Methodies than proper Churchmen.'

'I'll tell you this, whether Papish, Chapel, or good English Protestants, they all know what's good for 'em and that's to get their snouts stuck as deep in the trough as they can push 'em,' said the one with the hat. And then he added with another cackle: 'And it ain't just their snouts they take such tender care on.'

'You don't know nothing about it,' said the verger. 'If one of 'em so much as took a sixpence that wasn't due to him, the others would have him out of there before you could blink.'

'Don't show how simple you are. I ain't talking about sixpences. What about this to-do at the school?'

'I don't know what you're on about.'

'Oh yes you do.'

'What have you heard?' asked the old man with the pipe.

'Same as you, I reckon. About that canon there's always been talk about.'

Both old men wheezed with hoarse chuckles. Then the pipe-smoker took a long thoughtful pull and breathed out the smoke saying: 'The Headmaster don't know what day of the week it is most of the time.'

' 'Cept Sundays when the Red Lion's closed. That's the only night you won't find Appleton in the back-bar.'

The other old man grinned: 'That's why Sheldrick's done as he pleased for so long.'

'Shame on both of you for passing on such tittle-tattle,' said the youngest man.

'The Dean'd give the gold out of his teeth to get rid of both on 'em and to do that he'd close the school down and sack the lot of 'em,' said the old man with the hat.

'Why that's nonsense!' the verger exclaimed. 'The Cathedral can't do without the school.'

'Oh, it's nonsense, is it? Ain't there a special meeting of all on 'em tomorrow morning?'

'A Chapter meeting, you mean. Yes. What of it?'

'Well, that's what it's all about. Only he can't do as he'd like.'

'And why can't he?'

'Because of that sly devil Slattery. He has all the cards and does as he pleases. And the Dean can't touch him.'

'Whatever do you mean? The Dean can do pretty much anything he pleases.'

'Not to Master Slattery, he can't. Why, he'd make such a stink the whole lot of 'em would choke to death.'

'Aye,' said the other, removing his pipe and laughing silently. 'So they would. They'd all choke to death.'

'You're talking nonsense,' the verger exclaimed.

The old man with the hat ignored him. 'Seemingly he took something last night from Sheldrick's house, and now nobody can lay a finger on him.'

'What was it?' the other old man asked.

His companion shrugged. 'Something that would make a great scandal and bring the whole lot of them down if it were to come out. So the Dean can't do nothing against him though he'd dearly love to give him his marching orders. Him and his wife.' He stared round the table and then gave a wink which almost wrenched his face in two. The other old man laughed at this sally.

'His wife? What are you talking about?' asked the youngest man contemptuously.

'Don't be such a ninny,' the old man with the hat said. 'Haven't you heard what everybody says about him?'

I noticed the other old man touch his companion's arm and glance in my direction and when he, too, looked at me I suddenly felt ashamed of myself. What was I doing, listening to the gossip of malicious and uneducated people? And yet, what they had said had pointed me towards the nature of the weight that lay upon Austin's mind. There was clearly some kind of problem involving the school and that would have very serious consequences for my friend. I remembered that both Gazzard and Dr Locard had mentioned an important Chapter meeting tomorrow morning. But who was Slattery and in what sense did he hold all the cards?

❖

It was late. I got up and made my way to the Close. As I rounded the east end of the Cathedral a few minutes later I was surprised to see lights and shadows moving on the inside of the windows. Last night the head-verger had said the men would be working until eight or nine. I looked at my watch. It was half-past ten. Then I thought of the conversation I had just overheard and mounted the steps. As soon as I entered I gasped for breath and nearly fainted for there was a strong and very distasteful smell. It was the stench of something ancient and rotten—something older and worse, it seemed to me, than bad drains.

Lanterns were moving under the crossing-tower and I advanced towards it. A number of workmen were engaged with their implements and I saw Dr Sisterson standing a little apart and deep in conversation with the foreman. The old verger was watching them as before and greeted me with courteous solemnity.

'What in heaven's name is causing that?' I asked. 'Is it a gas-leak?'

The old man shook his head. 'This is what comes of meddling. They should never have started on it. When they took up the paving just here, that opened up.' He pointed towards a hairline crack about two feet long in the wall of the transept.

'The floor nearby must have dropped slightly,' I said. 'Did a gas-pipe fracture? That would explain the smell.'

He raised his shoulders in a gesture of despair and amazement. 'There aren't any in this part of the building, sir. We don't know where it's coming from.'

'Then I'm as puzzled as you are.'

'The master of works did as you advised, as Dr Sisterson ordered him to.'

He sounded reproachful and I said quickly: 'I'm afraid he has blundered in trying to follow my advice. It's necessary to know a great deal about the construction of these old buildings before attempting work on them.'

'And you do know a lot about them, sir?'

I looked at him sharply. Could he possibly mean to imply that I was in some degree responsible? 'Well, I'm something of an architectural historian—though only in an amateur way, of course. And that reminds me, I would very much like to go up into the tower.'

At that moment Dr Sisterson looked towards me and smiled, indicating with a gesture that he would join me in a moment.

'Why, I'm very sorry, sir,' the old verger replied. 'But that's quite without my power. I don't even have a key to that door. Nobody is allowed up there—by order of the Dean and Chapter. It's too dangerous.'

'I quite understand,' I said. After all, I reflected, the spire had been in a perilous condition two hundred years ago and might well be unsafe now.

Dr Sisterson came over and greeted me. 'This is a worrying business,' he said but even in this moment of crisis a pleasant smile still hovered on his face.

I wrinkled up my nose: 'And the smell!'

'Its source is a complete mystery. I dread to think what Bulmer will say when he returns tomorrow. He has a sharp tongue at the best of times.'

I held the bundle of manuscript towards him. 'I am glad at least of this chance meeting which gives me the opportunity to return this to you.'

'You have read it already?'

'Every word. And I would love to talk about it and hear your opinion.'

'Alas, I have myself not yet had time to read it! But that only makes me the more eager to discuss it with you and find out what

Dr Sheldrick believes is the truth about several mysterious episodes in that period of the Cathedral's history. I know it's late, but would you care to come to my house and talk about it over a glass of wine?'

'I couldn't think of intruding at this hour. Your wife would be most discommoded.'

'On the contrary, I know she would be delighted to meet you. And she is entertaining her friend, Mrs Locard. They were as thick as thieves when I left them an hour ago. I am certain we will find them still conspiring together about baby-clothes and charitable missions to the sick.'

I could no longer resist the invitation and followed him out of the building, relieved to escape the smell. Only a minute or two later we arrived at the house in the Upper Close. It was on the same side of the Close as Austin's but considerably larger—double-fronted with bow-windows on the ground floor. And since it stood on the corner with the opening to the Lower Close, I reflected that in daylight it must have a delightful aspect overlooking the Green. Dr Sisterson ushered me into the drawing-room where I found his wife, a slim young woman, and the lady I knew to be Mrs Locard. Each of them was holding a small child on her lap, Mrs Sisterson a little boy and Mrs Locard a little girl. A somewhat older boy and girl were playing on the carpet.

The introductions were made and Mrs Locard said: 'My husband has spoken of you to me, Dr Courtine.'

'Yes,' Mrs Sisterson said, jogging the child before her and gazing straight into its face. 'I heard Dr Locard say to my husband that you hope to show him how to manage his Library. That must be very generous of you.'

There was a silence. I saw that her husband's face had turned quite scarlet with embarrassment. Mrs Locard saved us all by saying, as if nothing untoward had occurred: 'My husband has mentioned your most interesting theory about a lost manuscript.'

We talked about that for a few minutes and I was offered a cup of tea and, because his wife was encumbered, the young canon poured it for me himself. He explained that he had just met me in the Cathedral and when Mrs Locard asked if the problem there had been resolved, we had to admit that it had not.

'I don't ever recall so much excitement as in the last day or two,' Mrs Sisterson exclaimed. She turned to her husband. 'Is there any news about poor Dr Sheldrick?'

'Not as far as I know,' he answered. 'Did you know, Dr Courtine, that the Chancellor was robbed yesterday evening?'

'Good heavens! I had no idea. Did he not give a reception last night?'

'That is so. In fact, when I met you in the Cathedral I had just come from there. It was shortly after I had returned to his house that the robbery was discovered.'

'It was the Dean who discovered the crime, I believe,' Mrs Locard said.

'Indeed so. Dr Sheldrick took him into his library in order to show him a recent acquisition—he is an avid collector of fine old editions—and the Dean noticed that a secretaire on the other side of the room had been forced open.'

'How unpleasant,' Mrs Sisterson murmured vaguely, her attention taken up by the child on her knee.

'Dr Sheldrick said that all that was missing was a package— about the size and thickness of a large book—containing a set of five miniatures and he did not want to make anything of it, but the Dean absolutely insisted that the police be summoned.'

'Fancy not wishing to call the police!' Mrs Sisterson remarked. 'They must have been worth quite a lot of money.'

Her husband smiled. 'Remember that Dr Sheldrick has substantial private means, my dear. What is a great deal of money to us is a trifle to him.' He turned to me. 'He is related to one of the great ducal houses.'

'As he never stops reminding us,' his wife remarked, entirely without malice.

I caught Mrs Locard's eye and we both repressed a smile at this mixture of vulgarity and innocence.

'Is it known when precisely the robbery was committed?' I asked.

'Dr Sheldrick told the police-officer that he had not noticed the secretaire for several days and that it might have been broken into at any time over that period,' Dr Sisterson said. 'But his house-keeper insisted that she had thoroughly inspected the room earlier that evening and that all was as normal.'

'Is one of the servants suspected or is it thought that someone entered the house during the reception?'

'Dr Sheldrick was adamant that none of the servants was responsible. They have all been with him for many years. And as the police-sergeant said, it was hard to see how anyone could have entered the house undetected while it was filled with guests and busy servants.'

I laughed. 'That leaves only the guests.' Dr Sisterson glanced at Mrs Locard and I said quickly: 'I was joking, of course. I imagine they were friends and colleagues of the Chancellor.'

'Indeed,' said Mrs Locard. 'All the guests were canons and functionaries of the Cathedral and their wives.'

'Then,' I said, 'self-evidently, it's not conceivable that any one of them would have done such a thing.'

'No,' Dr Sisterson said carefully. 'It seems beyond credibility that one of them would have taken such a risk for a set of miniatures.'

'It must have been a stranger,' Mrs Locard said, 'hard though it is to believe that an intruder could have escaped notice.'

'It's very mysterious,' the Sacrist mused. 'The Sergeant gathered all of us in the salon and asked if we had noticed anything or anyone suspicious. Of course, nobody had.'

'Mr Appleton became quite angry, did he not, Frederick?' Mrs Sisterson said, without looking up from the face of her child.

'The Headmaster of the Choir School,' her husband explained to me. 'He became a little overheated and asked if the Sergeant were accusing one of us. He didn't precisely deny it. And then Mr Slattery pointed out that it was self-evident that none of us was carrying anything as bulky as a package of miniatures.'

'What a strange man he is, that Mr Slattery,' Mrs Sisterson murmured comfortably, gazing into the child's face and smiling. 'He even offered to let the Sergeant search him.'

Her husband nodded. 'And he was perfectly correct. It was obvious that nobody had anything on their person that large.'

'What an extraordinary story,' I said.

'Not as extraordinary as the history of Treasurer Burgoyne.' Dr Sisterson laughed. 'I'm very anxious to hear Dr Sheldrick's account.'

'I'm sure it holds little interest for the ladies,' I demurred.

'On the contrary,' Mrs Locard said. 'I am extremely curious. And, after all, Christmas is a time for telling tales round the fire.'

Mrs Sisterson lent her mild support and so when the older children had been collected by a young servant and taken off to bed and with the two youngest sleeping in the arms of their mother and Mrs Locard, I embarked on a summary of the chapter I had read earlier that evening.

Holding Dr Sheldrick's manuscript on my knee so that I could refresh my memory from it, I began: 'This is the story of how the enmity between a canon of aristocratic birth and a man of humble origins led both men to their destruction. Canon-Treasurer Burgoyne was killed, according to Dr Sheldrick, because he was about to make public a hidden offence of great gravity. He met his end during the Great Storm which is still remembered since it was on that night that the Bell Tower above the main gate to the Close fell—though miraculously nobody was killed in that incident.'

'That's true, if I may interrupt for just a moment,' said Dr Sisterson. 'But the storm led to the collapse of part of another building in the Upper Close and that did unfortunately cause a fatality. Does Dr Sheldrick mention that?'

'No, he doesn't.'

'I beg your pardon. Please continue.'

'William Burgoyne is one of the great figures in the history of the Cathedral. He became Canon-Treasurer at the age of thirty-three and while it was probably his scholarship and family connections that had led to his being instituted to a prebend's stall at such an early age, it was certainly his intelligence and strength of will which, during the next ten years, made him the most powerful figure in the Chapter. He was a brilliant man whose abilities showed themselves not merely in his scholarship—he had taught Greek, Hebrew and Syriac at Cambridge—but practically and politically as well. He was also a proud, ambitious and stubborn individual with a strong sense of the dignity owed to his family and to himself. As a result he was soon disliked—even hated—by the many people in the little world of the Cathedral whom he had injured either by his sharp tongue or by the rigour with which he carried out his duties. Yet even his enemies found it difficult to charge him with dishonourable conduct—he was too proud, they said, to stoop to that.

'His appearance was striking and he soon became a well-known figure as he strode round the Close intimidating those answerable to the Church—from the humblest gatekeeper in the Close to the Bishop himself. He was a tall, slender man with a high-bridged nose and piercing grey eyes in a long thin face. He always wore the most severe black garb with a high-crowned hat, and was never seen without his Treasurer's chain of office around his neck. He was unmarried and spent the little time that was not consecrated to his duties in studying and in writing his sermons.'

Mrs Sisterson said, without taking her eyes from her sleeping child: 'That sounds just like Canon Sheldrick!' I glanced up from the manuscript and saw her husband and Mrs Locard exchange a look of amusement.

'He was said to be a man of the utmost probity in personal matters with whose name no scandal attaching to women was ever associated—though a number of young ladies in the town had set their caps at him from the moment he arrived. And he would have been a worthy catch, for in addition to the prebendary income and the dividend he received as a canon, he had considerable expectations from his family. Moreover, given his ambition and his advantages, he was likely to become a bishop at the least. The Treasurer had no close friends in the town, remaining estranged from the conviviality of the community of the Close and openly disapproving—in a manner that must have cast a shadow over the warmth of the Chapter's social intercourse—of the intemperance that was common among the canons of the day. This austere and disciplined way of life lasted until a few months before his untimely death.

'Burgoyne's position as Treasurer, his intellectual gifts and his unwillingness to shirk a battle, quickly made him the Chapter's leading champion in its many disputes with the Corporation of the town. Of course, the Foundation at that period was much wealthier and more powerful than it is now. It possessed many properties in the town and because of that, there was constant conflict with the Mayor and Corporation.

'But although the Chapter could stand with a single purpose against the town, it was itself far from united. Dr Sheldrick suggests that, with its fifteen Canons Residentiary living in the Close, it was like nothing so much as an Oxford or Cambridge college—with all the animosities and rivalries so common there. I know myself how bitter and irrational such conflicts can be.'

'I'm afraid we all do,' Dr Sisterson commented, looking at the Librarian's wife. She smiled sadly and kissed the head of the child sleeping in her arms.

'The Dean was already an old man when Burgoyne came, and during the succeeding years the young canon gained an ascendancy over him as he became more and more infirm and feeble-witted.

The other canons could not or did not wish to stand up against their Treasurer, though many resented his power. When Burgoyne arrived most of the Chapter were Arminians and therefore sympathetic to the old Catholic rites and practices—though hostile to Catholicism itself. Most of the townspeople shared their views—and in fact many had secretly remained Catholics, though that was extremely dangerous. While Laud was Archbishop of Canterbury the Arminians were in the ascendant and clergymen with Calvinist leanings were ruthlessly persecuted. But now all that had changed. The Calvinist faction had gained power in Parliament and at Court, for Laud had over-reached himself by encouraging the king to make war against the Scots over the imposition of his prayer-book. The disaster which followed had brought about his downfall.

'During the ten years before this there had been many arguments in the Chapter between Burgoyne, the most prominent of the Calvinists, and the traditionalists, championed by the Sub-Dean, Launcelot Freeth. The fiercest conflicts were about the fabric of the Cathedral for, as I will explain, it was on this matter that everything came together.

'In all of these disputes Burgoyne and Freeth were well-matched opponents for they were very similar: clever, ambitious and proud. But while Burgoyne had an aristocrat's contempt for dissimulation and intrigue, Freeth was adept at hiding his true feelings and was an unscrupulous opponent. From humble beginnings, he had clawed his way to his present position by cunning and deviousness.'

'Dr Sheldrick puts it like that?' the young canon asked.

'He uses almost those precise words,' I confirmed.

'It seems an ungenerous way of describing a man whose hard work and natural abilities had carried him so far,' he said mildly.

I took his point. I myself had achieved what success I had by virtue of my own efforts, and without the influential connections and other advantages by which Dr Sheldrick had so obviously profited. 'But think of his disgraceful conduct in relation to the college of vicars-choral,' I replied.

'Whatever did he do?' Mrs Locard demanded.

I turned to her and smiled. 'You will hear in a moment. In fact, Dr Sheldrick mentions the college as one of the issues that divided the Chapter most bitterly. From the moment of his arrival Burgoyne made it clear that he was deeply opposed to the important role that music played in the Cathedral services. For according to his strict Calvinist lights, music was a sensual pleasure which, under guise of inducing spirituality, was only too likely to encourage gross and carnal thoughts. He neglected no opportunity to appropriate the college's income for the Foundation, and since the Precentor, the canon responsible for music, was a close friend of Freeth, it may be imagined whether that helped to improve relations between the two men.

'Freeth's hostility towards the interloper increased as it became more and more probable that Burgoyne would defeat him in the succession to the deanship. Not only was the political wind blowing in his direction, but he was a member of the powerful Burgoyne family—a Calvinist-leaning dynasty whose principal estates lay about the town and whose head, the Earl of Thurchester, was his uncle. The Earl had enormous influence both in Parliament and at Court. The Burgoynes' principal seat, Thurchester Castle, was a few miles from here and they possessed huge estates in this county. (Dr Sheldrick gives rather a lengthy account of their history, which doesn't seem quite relevant to me. He mentions that the family has disappeared almost entirely now and the title is extinct.) For centuries, members of the Burgoyne family had been buried in the Cathedral and their monuments are many and handsome. How bitterly Freeth must have resented this man who was destroying everything he believed in and taking from him his one chance of power and riches. Possessing no wealth, but with a wife and many children, he was always in need of money and eagerly looked forward to the handsome emolument he would have received as Dean.

'All these issues surfaced very suddenly when a fierce dispute broke out about the miserable state of the Cathedral. Only the Choir was in use for services because the main body of the building had been sealed off and left unused at the time of the Dissolution. That was done because the spire had begun to show signs of instability and the Foundation could not afford the expense of repairing it. The cutting off of the greater part of the building was easily done because the Choir was separated from the nave by a stone screen.'

'A pulpitum,' Dr Sisterson exclaimed. 'It always makes me think of "pulpit" but it's not that.'

'But the Cathedral doesn't have a pulpitum,' Mrs Locard objected.

'Indeed it does not and the reason for that will emerge very soon. The pulpitum had only a single door at its centre and that had been bricked up. The only way into the body of the Cathedral was through the door at the end of the nave. That was locked all the time and there was only one copy of its key—a huge object nearly a foot in length.'

'I see it every day of my life,' Dr Sisterson put in. 'It is still in use. It is in the custody of the head-verger.'

'As it was in Burgoyne's time,' I said. 'He was at that date a very old man called Claggett. Burgoyne used to take the key from him and let himself into the building at night, for from the moment of his arrival he was deeply troubled by the Cathedral's neglect and dilapidation. He saw it both as a reflection on the status of his family—since the Cathedral was almost their private chapel—and as a threat to his status as the future Dean. He perceived clearly what his fellow-canons either failed or refused to see: that if, as was very probable, the spire were to collapse, it would damage the rest of the building beyond repair. The idea of becoming Dean of half a cathedral was a poor enough prospect, but to become Dean of a ruined cathedral held very little appeal. For several years he failed to find any support within the Chapter for his project of restoring the spire. The canons were reluctant to spend the huge sum of money required since it would have had to come from their own income. Burgoyne argued fiercely with the Sacrist, who was in the pocket of Freeth and refused to concede that the Cathedral was in danger of complete collapse.

'From his frequent visits at night to the great, rotting shell of the nave and transept, Burgoyne knew how close to destruction the building was. The floor beneath the crossing-tower was littered with masonry for timbers and stones from the spire had been steadily falling through the rafters and puncturing holes in the bricked vault for many decades. Burgoyne would frequently be ac-companied by the Cathedral Mason—a man called John Gambrill. The two were in complete agreement on the importance of repair-ing the spire, since Gambrill derived his income from work on the building.'

'I think that's rather unfair of Dr Sheldrick,' Dr Sisterson inter-rupted. 'Gambrill was the best stone-mason in the town—indeed, one of the best in the country, whose work is much admired by ar-chitectural historians to this day. He loved the building—on which he had worked all his life—and must have deeply resented the fact that the Chapter granted him insufficient resources to prevent its deterioration. I know how he feels, for every penny spent on it is grudged by my fellow-canons.'

I had never seen him so close to anger. 'I'm sure that's so,' I said. 'But Dr Sheldrick points out that in the years since his appoint-ment the Chapter had had a number of arguments with him. There had also been a serious incident during his youth in which the darkest accusations had been made against him. That's an interest-ing story in itself. Gambrill had, at the age of fourteen, started as an apprentice under the Cathedral Mason of the time and had risen by hard work and skill. Very soon nobody knew the craft better than he. As well as being a gifted craftsman, he had a shrewd head for business and these gifts aroused the envy of the Deputy Mason who resented him all the more because Gambrill had been promised the hand of their master's daughter, who was his heir, and the Deputy feared that this meant that Gambrill and not he would become the next Cathedral Mason. There was an accident while the two men were working on the roof of the Cathedral and the Deputy, Robert Limbrick, died. Gambrill survived but lost his right eye and afterwards walked with a limp. The widow of Limbrick laid an information against Gambrill in the Chancery Court alleging that he had killed her husband. The quarrel was apparently made up, however, for Gambrill later took on the dead man's son as his apprentice. By the time of the events I am describing all that was long in the past and Gambrill, whose mother had been a washer-woman and whose father was unknown, had, by virtue of hard work, ability and conspicuous honesty, become a prosperous figure in the town. He had inherited his father-in-law's handsome house in the High Street with a fine garden backing onto the Close and had furnished it in an elegant style, and lived in it with his wife and their five children.

'He was a tall, handsome man and was well-liked since he was frank and open-handed, and spoke his thoughts without prevarication. And he was quick to help his neighbours when they were in distress—though he was also swift to anger and he was said to be unforgiving when once he was crossed. There were stories current in the town that he had been unwisely extravagant over his house at the urging of his wife—a greedy and mercenary woman who was anxious to show her superiority to her friends and neighbours—and that he had got into debt. If that was so, it made the prospect of being commissioned to do a great deal of work on the Cathedral all the more important to him. Dr Sheldrick says he embraced enthusiastically Burgoyne's project and the two men, leaving the Sacrist entirely out of the matter, began to draw up plans and estimate costs.

'Despite their differences in social condition and religious affiliation, Burgoyne and Gambrill had a good understanding at first. Apart from the Cathedral, the two men had another passion in common—though at first Gambrill did not know it. He adored music and was a gifted player upon the viols. Despite his conviction that it was a corruption, a source of worldly pleasure, Burgoyne secretly loved music, too. Although in his early years at Cambridge he had indulged freely in this pleasure, he had later schooled himself to resist it by forcing his mind into the paths of prayer whenever he was assailed by this temptation. And when he came to the Cathedral he succeeded for the first few years in remaining undistracted by the choir and the college of young vicars-choral. But now Burgoyne would often find Gambrill standing in a trance of pleasure listening to the choir, or would come upon him singing or whistling and his own love of music began to revive.

'And then one day Gambrill told him that a nephew of his wife's was a gifted singer, and that the family was anxious that he should enter the college and have his education paid for in return for his services in the choir. Burgoyne declined to help on the grounds that the matter lay outside his authority. But it happened that a day or two later he encountered Gambrill with the boy in the Close and the youth was presented to him and for some reason Burgoyne changed his mind and agreed to persuade the Precentor to admit him to the college. The Precentor must have been surprised by Burgoyne's suit to him but he was impressed enough by the boy's singing to grant him a sizarship that would pay for his board and lodging. He was lodged in a part of the college which, conveniently enough, was beside Gambrill's house—the Old Gatehouse on the same side of the Close.

'If the Precentor had been surprised by Burgoyne's change of heart, he was to be yet more astonished for from this moment Burgoyne abandoned himself to his passion for music with all the force of his austere personality. He began to haunt the Cathedral in order to listen for hours to the choir practising—neglecting his duties. His favourite place was in the organ-loft from where he could look down upon the choir without being observed. He set out to win the friendship of the Precentor whom he had previously despised as a man of low birth and to this end sent for instruments and printed music from London and became a kind of patron of the college. They became such good friends that the Precentor would lend him his keys so that he could come and go as he liked.

'All this while Burgoyne, in his position as Treasurer, was making a prodigious effort to find the money required for the work he and Gambrill were planning: increasing rents and pursuing debtors with the full rigour of the law. Then he conceived his masterstroke: closing down the college of vicars-choral.'

'Since he loved music,' Mrs Locard said, 'is it not strange that he should wish to do that?'

'It is, and Dr Sheldrick suggests that his desire to close down the college arose from his fear that it represented a temptation to himself as much as to anyone else. He knew that this suggestion would be strongly resisted and so, before proposing it openly, he attempted to win over a majority within the Chapter. He set about trying to awaken the slumbering consciences of some of his fellow-canons by a quiet reference to various little personal failings and a reminder, in the more recalcitrant cases, of how their little lapses might be perceived if they should fall under the harsh light of public scrutiny.'

I saw Dr Sisterson smile and when he noticed my curiosity he said: 'Dr Sheldrick has a very generous way of interpreting Burgoyne's conduct.'

'Do you think so? He seems a very admirable figure to me.'

'Don't you think,' he suggested, 'that his high-minded fastidiousness for the worldly concerns of his colleagues was a kind of arrogance?'

'No, I don't believe so,' I said, strangely stung. 'He appears to me to have been a principled and ascetic man.'

'I imagine that his wealthy and privileged background,' Mrs Locard put in mildly, 'made it hard for him to sympathize with colleagues who did not have his advantages.'

Dr Sisterson and I nodded. I continued: 'Events played into his hands. In the spring of the year before his death, a crack in the spire that had opened up decades earlier suddenly widened and it became obvious to even the most stubborn of the canons that a severe storm might well bring it crashing down. Now Burgoyne laid before the Chapter his proposal to sacrifice the college in order to save the Cathedral. He demanded a complete restoration of the spire and showed that it could largely be paid for by selling the college's endowments which consisted of a manor-house and three farms in the village of Compton Monachorum. Against him he had all the most powerful canons—Freeth, the Librarian Hollingrake, the old Dean, the Sacrist and the Precentor—who argued that the Cathedral's reputation for music-making was one of its proudest boasts. Burgoyne, however, had won over to his side those whose consciences he had touched, and the proposal was passed by a narrow majority amid great bitterness. Freeth and Hollingrake, however, forged a deed which your husband, Mrs Locard, was kind enough to show me this afternoon. This made it impossible for Burgoyne to suppress the college after all.'

'We're not sure that they forged it,' Dr Sisterson objected. 'It's possible they found an earlier forgery and believed it to be genuine. But even if Freeth did forge it, who can say what his motives really were?'

'Pretty contemptible,' I said, turning to the two ladies. 'You see, when Freeth was himself Dean a few years later he used the forged deed to close down the college and appropriate its endowments for his personal benefit.'

'How shameful,' Mrs Sisterson murmured.

'Isn't it possible,' Mrs Locard suggested, 'that he foresaw the Civil War and wanted to keep the Foundation's property from being sequestrated by Parliament?'

'You're very generous, but everything we know about him shows that he was extremely greedy,' I objected.

Dr Sisterson glanced at the sleeping children and smiled. 'As the father of a large and very young family myself, I find it hard to condemn him even if his motives were entirely worldly.'

I was startled for a moment until I saw that he must be joking. I went on: 'To go back to Burgoyne's story. He had been trumped by Freeth—and he was furious—but he did not abandon the struggle and very soon after he was able to play his own trump card. He managed to obtain promises for half of the necessary money from his uncle and other members of his family. Some of it would be spent on a memorial in the Cathedral dedicated to the previous Earl—his grandfather.'

'The Burgoyne monument!' Mrs Locard exclaimed.

'Indeed so,' I acknowledged. 'When Burgoyne put this new proposal to the Chapter, Freeth saw immediately that the combination of the memorial and a large subvention for the restoration of the Cathedral would constitute an indefeasible claim to the deanship on the part of Burgoyne himself. And yet it was hard to refuse such a gift. But the canons still baulked at the portion of the expense which would have to come from their own pockets. Then it was that Burgoyne made what turned out to be his fatal mistake—as Dr Sheldrick puts it. He asked Gambrill to draw up revised figures for doing the smallest amount of work necessary to save the spire. Gambrill was horrified at this betrayal by his ally. He insisted on taking the Treasurer up the tower to show him how unstable many of the timbers were by rocking them with one hand, and he pointed out how easily one of them might be made to come crashing down. Burgoyne, however, stuck to his decision. The Mason was only mollified by hearing of the Treasurer's plans for the memorial which, it was understood, would be made by him and which he decided would be his masterpiece.

'Now Burgoyne had Gambrill argue before the Chapter that the collapse of the spire would destroy not only the Cathedral—a prospect which they were able to contemplate with some equanimity—but very probably some of the houses in the Close. Faced with this danger to their own lives and those of their households, the canons agreed to surrender from their own income the balance of the money that was required.

'Burgoyne and Gambrill had got their way, and Dr Sheldrick writes that Gambrill triumphed over the Sacrist, losing no opportunity to outwit him, deceive him and humiliate him in front of the workmen, with the consequence that the canon, never a man of robust health, fell ill and had to resign his duties.'

'My heart goes out to that poor man,' Dr Sisterson exclaimed with a smile.

'Poor Dr Sisterson,' said Mrs Locard. 'You cannot be looking forward to tomorrow's Chapter meeting.'

'Indeed not. I will have to break the news that services in the Cathedral will be seriously disrupted for an indefinite period.'

He heaved a comical sigh which ended in a broad smile and a request to me to continue the story.

'Burgoyne and Gambrill now had a free hand to do as they wished. In the months that followed, however, differences between them began to emerge. Burgoyne kept refusing to give Gambrill authority to repair the spire and instead required him to devote his resources to work that the Mason believed to be of much lower priority: for example, preparing for the removal of the communion table to the centre of the building.

'The antagonism between the two men was held in check—or so

at least it appeared—by Thomas Limbrick, Gambrill's foreman. He was the son of the man who died in the accident in which Gambrill was injured and many in the town said that giving him employment showed Gambrill's generosity—though some attributed his action to other motives. Limbrick was a hard-working and able young man who had the trust of both the Treasurer and the Mason and was therefore in a position to smooth the difficulties that lay between them.

'Burgoyne now had what he desired: the Cathedral was being restored and would be reopened in a manner that would hugely strengthen his position. Yet he seemed far from happy and it began to appear that something was troubling him for although he had always been extremely fastidious, he now appeared on occasions unshaven and dishevelled. He was late for meetings of the Chapter, increasingly neglectful of his duties and even abstracted during services. Once or twice while preaching he broke off as if he had lost the thread of his thoughts. He took to pacing restlessly about the town during the hours of darkness and was stopped by the watch several times—to their profound confusion—before they grew accustomed to him and learnt to recognize him, in the utter darkness of the nights in those days, from his great height and his tall hat and clerical garb.'

'Moreover, his habit of sobriety was apparently discarded,' put in Dr Sisterson, 'and he appeared on several occasions the worse for liquor.'

'Indeed? Dr Sheldrick makes no mention of that. Everyone in the town wondered what secret passion might be tormenting the Canon . . .'

'He was in love,' Mrs Sisterson said softly.

We all glanced at her in surprise and she smiled at her husband who blushed and glanced down.

'Well,' I went on, 'although people gossiped about a woman, nobody ever saw him in the company of one. Dr Sheldrick, however, now reveals for the first time the true explanation.'

'He does?' Dr Sisterson said in surprise. He glanced towards his wife who at that moment was giving her full attention to the slumbering child in her lap.

'The truth is that Burgoyne was going through a spiritual crisis occasioned by his discovery of a secret offence, something so dark and shocking that it threw into turmoil all his assumptions.'

'Indeed? Dr Sheldrick says that?' Dr Sisterson looked at Mrs Locard as he asked me: 'And what does he say this secret was?'

'Financial corruption on the part of Freeth. Burgoyne was overwhelmed with dismay when he realized how corrupt Freeth was.'

'I see,' Dr Sisterson said, leaning back with a smile. I wondered if he had expected something else. 'But did he not already believe Freeth to be greedy and corrupt?'

'Yes, but the extent and deliberateness of what he discovered shocked him immeasurably. And he also discovered, Dr Sheldrick suggests, that the trusted Gambrill was deeply implicated in Freeth's misappropriations.' I could see that he was sceptical and I myself found Dr Sheldrick's revelation somewhat unconvincing. 'Then what do you think caused this sudden change in his demeanour?'

'I believe he did indeed discover something that profoundly disturbed him, but I don't believe it was Freeth's financial dishonesty.'

'What do you think it was?'

He glanced at the two ladies whose attention was at that moment taken up by the child in Mrs Sisterson's arms, and spoke quietly. 'I can only conjecture and I have no wish to slander even a man who has been dead more than two centuries.'

I looked at him in surprise but he pursed his lips and shook his head very slightly to indicate that it was not a subject he could pursue in the presence of the ladies, so I went on: 'In the April of that year, Burgoyne made a long visit to London. When he returned he admitted to Gambrill that he had decided to have the memorial executed by Italian workmen in the capital. Gambrill was deeply angered by this insult to his own craftsmanship. A day or two later, he announced that the spire had become so dangerous that he was going to bar access to the tower to everyone except himself and his workmen. Burgoyne, though infuriated by what he saw as an attempt to force him into releasing monies for its repair, could not challenge the Mason's expertise and had to accept that restriction. So Gambrill sealed off the stair at the bottom of the tower by means of a stout door, the key to which only he and one of the canons held.

'If Gambrill had been angered by Burgoyne's decision to commission the memorial in London, his indignation was as nothing compared to his fury when, a few weeks later, he learnt where Burgoyne intended it to be placed: the most prominent position possible, just on the chancel side of the crossing. In order to do this Burgoyne intended to take out the pulpitum. Of course the other canons protested but by this date the political situation in the country had swung decisively in Burgoyne's favour. Archbishop Laud was in the Tower, from which he would shortly be taken to be executed, and the victorious Calvinists were insisting upon the removal of all barriers between the congregation and the celebrants. The Chapter could do nothing. When Gambrill learnt from Limbrick what Burgoyne had ordered him to do he was horrified.'

'So he must have been,' Dr Sisterson said warmly. 'The dismantling of so ancient and beautiful a part of the Cathedral—the building he loved and to whose preservation he had devoted his life and even sacrificed his eye—must have seemed an act of desecration.'

'Dr Sheldrick has a rather different explanation. He claims that Gambrill was a clandestine Catholic—as were many in the sleepy old town. That placed him in grave danger of financial ruin and even imprisonment, but it also meant that in his judgement the Cathedral was still a Catholic place of worship which had illegally fallen into the hands of men dedicated to the destruction of everything that it represented. There was a scandalous scene in the Cathedral when the Mason bearded the Treasurer and loudly reproached him for the damage he was doing. Burgoyne stalked from the building and Gambrill pursued him into the Close and up to the very back-door of his house continuing to shout at him until Limbrick intervened to pull him away. That moment probably sealed the fate of both men.

'Gambrill, of course, had either to resign his post or do as Burgoyne ordered and with a family to support he could not afford the grand gesture. Burgoyne would have dismissed Gambrill from his post, but there was no other mason in the town who could be entrusted with the work, and Burgoyne recognized that Gambrill was a conscientious and skilled craftsman.

'And so Gambrill removed the pulpitum, replacing it with wooden boarding to keep the nave sealed off while the spire was unrepaired.

'Now Limbrick became the intermediary by whose means Burgoyne and Gambrill entirely avoided having to deal directly with each other. At least, so it was supposed. Much later, when events turned out as they did, some people said that Limbrick had in fact made difficulties between the two men for his own purposes while cleverly appearing to be trying to do the opposite.

'From this time onwards Burgoyne never again came to watch Gambrill and his men at work in the Cathedral. Instead he renewed his former visits to the building during the hours of darkness and although it was assumed that he went there in order to examine Gambrill's work without having to meet him, it was noticed that his visits began to last longer and longer and sometimes he returned the great key to Claggett, the head-verger, only at dawn. The old man was often awake all night for he was seriously ill.

'Burgoyne's conduct was causing more and more speculation. His housekeeper described later how he stayed awake all night pacing up and down his room or prowling around the Close as if wrestling with some fearful dilemma. Later, when people learnt what at this time was not known, some of the townsfolk claimed that they had seen him many times at night standing on the north side of the Close and looking over the back wall of the gardens into the windows of the houses that fronted the High Street. Some said afterwards that he was looking into Gambrill's house and debating whether to destroy his happiness and that of his wife and children. Others said that he was a lonely and envious man who resented the domestic content of his enemy. Others suggested yet other motives.

'All of this came to a head two weeks before the Great Storm. That Sunday Burgoyne was the preacher at the main service in the Cathedral. He ascended to the pulpit looking pale and gaunt, and people in the congregation began to mutter among themselves, for his strange conduct over the past weeks was widely known. But when he started to speak his voice was strong and his words flowed without a break. He began by inveighing against sins of corruption and talked passionately of the damnation that awaited a man who yielded to temptation and persisted in his sinful ways without repentance. And then he said he was speaking of a particular man who was among them at that moment and whom he was indicting for his secret offences—offences whose nature he did not reveal. He seemed so intent upon some hidden meaning that some of his hearers thought he was showing signs of mental alienation. Much of what he said was not understood by those listening but his words were remembered: *There is one among us now who has entered this house of God with sinfulness and pride in his heart, though he wears the outward garb of sanctimony. He alone among this assembly knows what darkness he nourishes in the privy mansions of his being. He alone knows how he has wandered out of his way into the foul and strange path that leads to the sty of pestilential filth.*

'When he stepped down from the pulpit he left the townspeople and his fellow-canons stunned. In the days that followed nobody could talk of anything else. A number of people were suspected of various offences and the atmosphere of the town became quite poisonous with rumour. It was noticed that Gambrill remained silent when the topic was brought up, and this laid him under suspicion—though no more than many others. Freeth, in particular, gave clear evidence by his nervous demeanour that he believed he himself was the man referred to by Burgoyne. And if Dr Sheldrick is correct about his financial improprieties, he had good reason for this fear.

'The following Sunday a large proportion of the population of the town—squeezed into the Choir and even overflowing out of the door—was present when Burgoyne rose to preach. His words became more precise, though they were still vague enough to puzzle his listeners. Burgoyne said: *Woe unto the man that in the mountainous pride of his ignorance thinketh to hide his shame. Though he be raised up in the sight of men and ween his sin to be hidden when he wrestles foot to foot with his Enemy in the high places and is cast down, yet shall his wickedness be laid bare before the eyes of men. Yea, even in the dark places shall his sins be blazoned forth. The truth shall find him out.* At that moment Gambrill drew attention to himself by his demeanour. He turned pale and was seen to be trembling as Burgoyne announced that the following Lord's Day he himself would make manifest the sinner in that very place.

'All eyes turned to Gambrill who, looking as if he had seen his own death, suddenly stood up and forced his way through the crowd to the door. Many of Burgoyne's hearers, who had trembled to think that he might mean them, were relieved by this conduct. Yet Burgoyne made no charge against him.

'In the course of the week that followed, a space for the memorial was hollowed out in the wall where the pulpitum had been. The memorial itself arrived from London on the Tuesday, and when Gambrill saw the wagon carrying it come rumbling and clattering into the Close, he told Limbrick that he was horrified as much by its ugliness as by its weight, and said that he feared for the consequences once it was sealed into the wall.

'Saturday dawned as an unseasonably sultry and oppressive day of low clouds and short angry bursts of fierce rain. Old men shook their heads and forecast a violent storm, and some of them muttered and grumbled over the state of the spire. By the close of work that day, Gambrill—ever the conscientious workman however much he resented what he was being required to do—had made all ready. The heavy slab had been raised to the top of the scaffolding under the crossing-tower ready to be lowered on Monday into its final position on the wall about twelve feet up. Gambrill ordered work to end early on account of the imminent storm, for as the sun set, the clouds seemed to be boiling around it like a witches' brew.

'As he often did, Burgoyne came to Claggett's house at about ten o'clock—just as the wind was rising. The old man was gravely ill by now and his wife and daughters were busy with him, but his young maidservant handed the great key to the Canon. An hour or two later the storm burst over the town in its full rage, launching a bombardment of hailstones as big as thrushes' eggs and stripping off roof-tiles and sending them flying through the air like leaves, breaking windows, and even knocking over chimney stacks. Amid all the noise and confusion of doors and shutters banging and glass breaking and thunder rumbling, old Claggett lost consciousness and it became clear that he was dying. A surgeon was sent for and a servant was also dispatched to the house of the Precentor who had been a particular friend of the old man. In the excitement of all this, nobody remembered that Burgoyne had not returned with the key.

'As the tempest reached its height, at about two o'clock in the morning, those who were sleeping—or trying to sleep—in the houses around the Close heard a terrible noise and the whole of the Upper Close shuddered. Several of the canons and under-vergers hurried out to see what was amiss and found that the roof and upper storey of the ancient Bell Tower above the main gate had collapsed. As a frightened little crowd—Freeth, the Precentor and even the old Dean—stood surveying the ruin and offering up thanks that it was unoccupied at night, they heard another crash. This time, to their horror, they realized that it came from the Cathedral. They scanned the building as far as they were able to in the thick darkness and saw that the spire appeared to be intact, but nobody was prepared to venture into the building while the storm still raged. Now it was learnt from Claggett's servant-girl that Burgoyne had not returned the key. Even so, none of those present offered to go in and look for him.'

Dr Sisterson stood up and crossed to the window which he opened. 'I can imagine why not. It's a peaceful night now. But imagine a storm raging.'

I crossed to stand beside him. The lamps were guttering in the Close. Through the fog and in the darkness the bulk of the building was beside us as if we were up against a cliff. 'How frightening it must have been,' I agreed, 'to be in the shadow of that vast building and dread that the tallest part of it might come tumbling down.'

Gratifyingly, the Sacrist shivered.

'Please close that window, Frederick,' Mrs Sisterson protested, misinterpreting his gesture. 'It's freezing and you'll wake the children.'

My host did as he was bidden and we sat down. I went on: 'Some of the other canons came to the Deanery to see what was afoot but nobody would venture into the Cathedral. Indeed, some people were frightened even to stay in their houses nearby. Limbrick arrived and strongly advised against entering the Cathedral during the tempest. And so they waited. By the time the first streaks of daylight appeared in the sky over Woodbury Downs, the storm had largely abated. In a state of considerable trepidation the old Dean, Freeth, the Precentor, Limbrick and one of the under-vergers cautiously crept into the Cathedral.

'Imagine what it must have been like to advance along the vast length of the nave with just the light of two or three lanterns to guide you and with the wind still howling around the spire and the tower to remind you of the possibility that stones and timbers might come crashing down upon you. And beneath the sound of the wind they heard another sound—a noise that made the hair rise on the backs of their necks: a sound like a human voice moaning and muttering in pain and despair.

'As they approached the crossing, a huge shape loomed up suddenly from the darkness. Their terror was only slightly diminished by the realization that they were looking at the scaffolding which had collapsed and lay in a heap of planks and splintered wood. That was the origin of the loud noise heard from within. Then as they drew closer and raised their lanterns they saw a patch of dark and sticky liquid that had seeped out from beneath the broken timber. They listened and now they realized that the human voice they had believed they had heard was merely an effect of the wind. Otherwise, there was silence. Limbrick told the others that he had a premonition that they would find the body of their colleague beneath the debris. It was also he who pointed out the astonishing fact that there was no sign of the marble slab that had been on the scaffold the night before. He raised his lantern towards the place where it was destined to go and to the amazement of all of them, there it was in its intended position high up on the wall. They stood staring at it in disbelief. It had been neatly inserted into the space prepared for it and the brickwork sealed up around it.

'Limbrick sent for his workmen and for the next two hours they laboured to clear away the mass of broken wood. It was now realized that Gambrill had not been seen since the storm started. Limbrick hurried to his house and learnt that his master's wife had not seen him since the previous evening at about nine o'clock. She had assumed that he had stayed out all night dealing with the dangers posed by the storm, and was only now becoming worried by his absence.

'By the time Limbrick had returned to the Cathedral with this news, the last of the fallen scaffolding was being lifted from the body. It was so badly crushed that it could be recognized as that of Burgoyne only by the canonical garments, the Treasurer's chain of office and the great key to the west door which Burgoyne had taken from Claggett. Limbrick confided to Freeth—for a close understanding was growing up between the two men—that he feared that Gambrill's disappearance suggested that he had murdered Burgoyne. Gambrill did not reappear that day and, in fact, was never seen again in the town. By disappearing he convicted himself. The prospect of imminent denunciation had driven him to murder.'

'I don't understand,' Dr Sisterson objected. 'What was it that Gambrill believed he was going to be denounced for?'

'Well, Dr Sheldrick has a theory about that. Limbrick suggested to Freeth that a clue might lie in the Treasurer's Accounts kept by Burgoyne and relating to Gambrill's work on the fabric. The two men broke into Burgoyne's study and found the account-books, examined them, and a few days later disclosed that they had discovered, from comparing the accounts with the work actually carried out, that Gambrill had embezzled some of the funds allocated for work on the Cathedral.'

'That seems straightforward enough,' Dr Sisterson said.

'But you said that Dr Sheldrick has a theory about it,' Mrs Locard put in. 'So does he not accept that explanation?'

'He argues that Freeth persuaded Limbrick to help him falsify Burgoyne's accounts in order to put the blame solely on Gambrill.'

'Whereas Freeth himself had involved Gambrill in his embezzlement of Foundation funds?' Dr Sisterson suggested.

'Precisely. Incidentally, I understand that the correct term is malversation. And that is why he was able to persuade him to kill Burgoyne.'

'Good heavens!' he exclaimed. 'Has he any evidence for that?'

'Only inferential. It fits the facts and Freeth seems capable of it.'

'Capable of inciting a man to murder!' Mrs Locard exclaimed. 'Surely that is too dark a view of human nature, Dr Courtine.'

I was taken aback. 'The record shows him to have been greedy and unscrupulous in his use of forgery to steal the Foundation's property.'

'Even if he did those things, they fall very far short of murder,' she said with a smile. 'And the role which Dr Sheldrick ascribes to the Mason also puzzles me. The proud and conscientious man you described would surely not have stolen from the Cathedral which he loved, however he felt about its canons?'

'Well, someone murdered Burgoyne,' I protested.

'If it was Gambrill,' Dr Sisterson said, 'I believe it was nothing to do with money that motivated him. What we do know about him is that he loved the Cathedral and he believed that Burgoyne was bent on destroying it.'

'Freeth and Limbrick convinced people at the time that the murderer must have been Gambrill,' I went on. 'The only mystery now was how the memorial had been put in position. Limbrick and the other men who had been working there the night before insisted that it weighed far too much for one man to have done so. The townsfolk settled it among themselves that Gambrill had had the aid of the Devil.'

'That certainly seems the only rational explanation,' Mrs Locard remarked with a smile. Then she said: 'One thing that puzzles me is why he chose to flee the town?'

'That struck me, too,' Dr Sisterson agreed. 'Burgoyne's death could have been passed off as an accident and if Gambrill had simply gone quietly home, nobody would have known about the part he had played.'

'To have abandoned his wife and young children!' Mrs Locard exclaimed softly, glancing down at the child sleeping on her lap. 'That seems to me quite extraordinary.'

'I suppose it is odd,' I agreed.

'As a bachelor, Dr Sheldrick might not have given enough weight to that consideration,' Mrs Sisterson said.

Her husband chuckled. 'I'm tempted to say that, on the contrary, we may have discovered Gambrill's motive for fleeing the town.' As we smiled, he went on: 'Incidentally, does Dr Sheldrick reveal what became of Limbrick in later years?'

'He took over Gambrill's business and conducted it on behalf of his widow.'

'Did he indeed! And what happened to the widow—and the children?' he asked.

'A few years later she applied to the justices to have her husband declared dead and after a long delay this was done.'

'And Limbrick married her?' Mrs Locard suggested.

'Very shrewd of you, if I may say so. It appears that in the interval she bore several children by him.'

'It strikes me,' she said, 'that he played a crucial role in the story.'

'Could it be,' Dr Sisterson suggested, 'that he made trouble between Burgoyne and Gambrill while pretending to be a peacemaker?'

'You suspect he was involved in the murder himself? That is possible, but Burgoyne's family made extensive efforts to find out the truth and Dr Sheldrick does not mention such a hypothesis. Burgoyne's nephew, a young man called Willoughby Burgoyne, spent a couple of weeks in the town trying to find out what had happened. He knew, of course, of the hostility towards his uncle within the Chapter but he failed to find any evidence on which to bring charges.'

We discussed it for some minutes more and then the booming of the Cathedral clock reminded us how late it was. Dr Sisterson asked me if I would escort Mrs Locard to the Deanery and although she insisted it was not necessary, I was only too pleased to do so. We left the house a few minutes later and on the short walk through the Close we talked about Dr Sisterson and his wife, and their evident happiness.

As we approached the Deanery, she said: 'I found your exposition of the story of Canon Burgoyne fascinating. You brought it all to life so vividly. I imagine you are a wonderful teacher.'

'I don't know about that but I certainly try to make the past live again,' I said. 'I believe it's so important that the young realize that the men and women of bygone times were once human beings with our own passions and fears.'

'And yet we can never be sure, can we, that Canon Burgoyne was as noble as Dr Sheldrick would have us believe or Sub-Dean Freeth such a monster?'

'Absolutely sure, no. But if all the evidence in a given case points in one direction, we can be as sure as we need to be.'

'Don't you think that we read our own desires into the figures from the past about whom we reflect because, as erring mortals, we cannot be dispassionate?'

'That is a danger, certainly. The only protection against it is to try to understand our own motives and so take our prejudices into account.'

'That is assuredly the path of wisdom,' she said with a smile. 'But it is not an easy one to follow.'

To my regret, we had already arrived at the Deanery. I had realized during the evening who it was she reminded me of and when I took leave of her I said that I hoped we would meet again before my departure. She replied, as she shook my hand, that she very much hoped so, and when the yawning servant opened the door I bowed and turned towards Austin's house.

Wednesday Night

✛

A S I CROSSED THE DARK CLOSE I thought of the noise
and warmth and affection I had just left behind, and my
own life seemed very quiet in contrast. There was no
sound at all now, and although I had always loved silence, it began
to take on a sinister air. Sisterson, ten or fifteen years younger than
I, had gleefully encumbered himself with cares and obligations that
I had, in one way or another, avoided. It occurred to me that of the
three canons I had met, he was the least concerned by the petty rivalries of the Chapter.

Austin's door was before me now but, feeling that I did not want
to enter yet, I decided to take a turn around the outside of the
Cathedral, which squatted like a great beast in the black cage of
the Close. Was I cheered by the ungenerous reflection that Austin
had made a mess of every department of his life? Although I did
not have the domestic contentment of Dr Sisterson, at least I had
an interesting, respected and well-paid position whereas my friend
seemed to be entombed in a world of provincial dreariness and op-
pression. In contrast to him, I was doing what I had always wanted
to do and I enjoyed doing it: teaching undergraduates, carrying out
my researches and writing my books. Of course, Austin was right to
say that happiness is much more than merely the absence of misery.

And now that I thought about it, I supposed it could not be said that I was happy. It seemed to me that some people have a talent for being happy and others appear to find unhappiness almost as if they sought it. Perhaps that was from the fear of being disappointed. I had always thought of happiness as something that would eventually come if I avoided doing the wrong things. I had been careful and made very few mistakes in my life. I had, of course, made one grave error and I was still paying the penalty.

Absurdly, I had continued to think of myself as young. Even surrounded by undergraduates I had persevered in imagining myself as a slightly older contemporary of theirs. Was that because I had gone on thinking of my proper adult life as being about to begin at some point in the future? But now, suddenly, I found I was nearly fifty and it was too late. My life would continue to unfurl in precisely the way it had for the last thirty years.

Yet while I thought of myself as still young, I sometimes wondered if—because I had read too many books too early—I had become so theoretically sophisticated about later life that I almost avoided going through adolescence and youth. So in a way I was much younger than I should have been when I fell in love with my wife.

As I rounded the eastern end of the Cathedral I felt like a ghost in the deserted Close. But unlike Canon Burgoyne, nobody would remember me in two hundred years. Not in fifty. And nobody would bear my name. What would I leave behind? A few dusty books that would lie unread on the shelves of libraries? Fading memories in the minds of my students—if they ever thought of me at all, and why should they?

I saw that my unwillingness to bestow my time and attention on things and people that bored me had led me to exclude a great deal from my life. Ancient texts, conflicts or lacunae in the historical record, forgotten languages—these things were endlessly fascinating and, moreover, had the advantage that they could be immediately put aside if my interest in them should become exhausted. All my passion had gone into that aspect of my life and in the last twenty-two years I had never allowed myself to feel tenderness for another woman. Had I used as an excuse the fact that a wife was an impossibility for me? And yet I knew that I had only ever cared for myself to the degree that I believed that someone else cared for me. We only value ourselves as others value us, for it might be said that we hold ourselves in trust for others. In that case, what reason had I to value myself? Was I really content to believe that any prospect of love—or even of domestic happiness—was out of the question? Had that distant experience frightened me from entrusting my peace of mind to another person for all time? Perhaps, to anticipate for a moment, it was because that hare had been started in the deep coverts of my imagination that I had the most disturbing dream of my life in the early hours of Friday morning.

When I opened the door I found the gas in the hall turned down and so I assumed that Austin was still out. I took off my hat and greatcoat and picked up and lit a candle, but as I reached the first-floor landing, I heard a cry of greeting from the sitting-room. When I went in, I found the chamber in almost complete darkness with only the smouldering coals in the grate casting a flickering reddish light. Austin was sitting at the table with a bottle and two glasses before him.

'Come in and sit yourself down and take a glass with me,' he said effusively.

'May I light a candle?' I asked and, when he nodded, quickly did so.

As the light flared up, I saw Austin's smiling face raised towards me. For a moment in the candle-light he looked like the young man I had known long ago.

He lifted the bottle to pour some wine into the untouched glass.

Then he smiled and said: 'How mysterious. There appears to be none left. Be a good chap and fetch another bottle from the cupboard.'

I moved towards the armoire and tugged at its door. 'It's locked, Austin.'

'Not that one,' he said sharply. 'I meant the one over there, for heaven's sake. But sit down and I'll do it myself.' He jumped up and hastened towards a cupboard near the door while I did as I had been ordered. He brought over another bottle of old port and opened it, his affability now apparently restored.

'My dear old fellow,' he said. 'I was growing quite alarmed about you. I was afraid you might have taken offence and decided to leave and that's the last thing in the world that I want. The very last thing.'

I was touched even though I could see that he had drunk heavily and so his words were not to be taken completely at face-value. As I looked at him—merry and intoxicated—I thought of our many late-night carouses in our lodgings and felt an ache of sadness at what had been and what might have been.

'Why ever should I do such a thing?' I asked, seating myself opposite him.

He poured me a glass of wine to the brim. 'Because I've been abominably rude. Being irritable and argumentative. Leaving you that note. But I . . . If only you knew. I've been so . . .'

He broke off as I placed my hand upon his.

'Dear Austin, I'm not offended, not the least little bit in the world. I know that something is preying on your mind.'

He looked startled: 'You're quite mistaken. I have nothing troubling me.' He took his hand away.

'My dear old friend, you need not put on a brave face to me. I've noticed how nervous you have been. And there was your nightmare. I know you are preoccupied by something and I think I know what it is.'

He stared at me: 'What do you mean?'

I felt embarrassed. I had not meant to say anything. The truth was that I had been thinking of the gossip I had overheard that evening. 'I know that there are grave difficulties at the school.'

'At the school? What are you talking about?'

'I've heard—please don't ask me how or from whom because I can't tell you—that the Headmaster is not generally respected and that . . .'

'The High-master, you mean. He's certainly not respected by me.'

'And that things are coming to a crisis.'

'A crisis! There's always a crisis there. Mediocrities thrive on spurious excitement. It's a substitute for a life of the mind. But there's nothing happening there of any significance. You've invented some sort of story about it, haven't you? You have too much imagination. As a result, you don't see what's in front of your nose. You're so eager to look beyond it that you miss things that are obvious to less perceptive people. Well, I'm sorry to disappoint you.'

I laughed a trifle uneasily. 'Are you sure? I've heard that the school might be forced to dismiss some of its staff.'

'So? Do you think I want to spend the rest of my existence in this damned little town? My whole being frets with impatience to get away.'

'But, Austin, you need your salary to live on.'

'Money is the one thing one should never waste time worrying about.'

I found his attitude astonishing. And yet he had been just as insouciant as an undergraduate, with an attitude that was much more characteristic of those from wealthy families. Austin's father, however, was even less prosperous than my own. And while my comparative lack of resources had given me an urgent desire to find a secure, interesting and reasonably remunerated post, Austin had never bothered about such matters.

'Do you mean you have money now?'

He smiled. 'I haven't a penny to my name.' In a gesture of self-mocking surrender that I remembered so well he threw back his head and extended both arms to indicate the room—the thread-bare carpet, the ancient rickety furniture. 'I barely manage to survive on my wages and I have not succeeded in saving anything. If the venom and hostility that are rampant here meant that I left without a reference, then my situation would be abject. But I rather doubt if it will happen.'

'Does Appleton have anything against you?'

He looked at me in alarm: 'Appleton? What has it to do with him?'

'He is the Headmaster or High-master, isn't he?'

'Of the Choir School!' Austin exclaimed. 'He is the Headmaster of the Cathedral Choir School!'

'Is that not part of Courtenay's?'

'Certainly not. The two institutions are entirely separate. We have a High-master.'

'I thought the Choir School was simply a department of the Grammar School.'

'Far from it. The Choir School is the direct responsibility of the Dean and Chapter.'

'Then Courtenay's is not?'

He shuddered. 'What a thought! Because of the meddling of those petty-minded old women, the canons, the educational attainments of the Choir School are beneath contempt. I'm quite offended that you should think I had anything to do with it.'

'I apologize. I had no idea there was such a difference between the two schools.'

'Courtenay's has ten times as many scholars, for the Choir School educates merely the choristers. Courtenay's is a great deal better than the Gatehouse. That's our old name for the Choir

School and it's rather insulting for there has always been considerable ill-feeling between the two schools.'

'I suppose the boys fight.'

'They certainly do. But, unfortunately, such is the ill-feeling between the schools that friendship between masters is frowned upon. I happen to have a good friend at the Choir School—an excellent fellow and I intend that you shall meet him—and the fact that we are chums has occasioned some ill-will in this poisonous little community.'

'That would be hard to believe if I did not know the world of a Cambridge college so well.'

'Where did you pick up this story?'

I was too embarrassed to admit that I had eavesdropped in a public-bar. Without exactly lying, I said: 'You remember that I spoke to the old verger last night and he mentioned the school? He said it was to be discussed at the Chapter meeting tomorrow.'

'Yes, there is some issue involving the Choir School that is wringing the canonical withers. But it doesn't affect Courtenay's. I misunderstood you. There is nothing going on there but the usual schoolmasterly bickering and pettiness.'

He uttered the words so irritably and then turned away so abruptly that I could see how much I had annoyed him. After a long silence I said: 'Do you want me here? Am I in the way?'

He reached across and patted my hand.

'No, no. Don't go. It's very important that you are here. That's how you can help me.'

I was deeply touched by his words.

He went on: 'Just stay here for the next few days.'

'I can't stay longer than Saturday.'

'Saturday, yes, that's excellent.'

'I have to reach my niece's that afternoon, so I can't stay any longer.'

'Then Saturday it is. That will be quite long enough. I haven't been a very good host, I'm afraid. I shall endeavour to do better.' He rose and re-filled my glass. Then he sprawled sideways across his chair in his old manner, gradually sliding down so that eventually his face was framed for me between his feet.

In the comfortable silence that followed I was reflecting on his rather odd words—'Saturday will be quite long enough'—when he asked: 'How did your visit to the Library go? Did you find what you were looking for?'

I laughed. 'Good heavens, Austin, it's not going to be as easy as that. But Dr Locard was very helpful.'

'Now there's a delightful fellow.'

'I found him pleasant enough,' I said cautiously.

'I'm sure you did. As long as you can be of value to him or advance his career in any way, he'll be perfectly pleasant. Not charming because he has no charm. Charm would be rather suspect and certainly beneath him.'

'Well, he was perfectly all right with me. We talked about the murder of Dean Freeth.'

'That must have been exciting.'

'It was very interesting. Just before I left Cambridge, I found a letter, written in 1663, which casts new light on it and I believe there will be material for a contribution to the *Proceedings of the English Historical Society*. And one that might cause quite a stir.'

'Then you'd better hurry up and write it or Locard will do it before you do and steal all the glory.'

'I hardly think so, Austin. He has published little but that little is of very high quality and, I understand, has made a very significant contribution to scholarly knowledge of Celtic culture of the early period—an area which is only now receiving attention—by demonstrating the erroneousness of amateurs who have done most of the work until recently. I hardly think such a man would stoop to theft and plagiarism.'

'It's precisely his ambition that has led him to stake out a claim to a new empire of scholarship, not his love of learning. He is not a scholar but a politician, and you shouldn't assume he has any desire for your success.'

'On the contrary, he was extremely anxious to help me and he put at my disposal one of his young men—not an awfully impressive individual, I'm sorry to say.'

He looked at me with sudden interest: 'You don't mean that strange creature Quitregard, do you? He's the most old-womanish gossip in Thurchester and you shouldn't believe a word he says.'

'No, the other one, Pomerance. He's not very useful. Or very charming. On the other hand, Quitregard seems to me to be a most pleasant young man. I don't know why you call him strange. However that may be, I spent the rest of the morning and afternoon searching for the manuscript—without success, I fear.'

Despite his promise to make more of an effort, Austin seemed to have relapsed into a gloomy silence. 'Talking of Dr Locard,' I said, 'I met his wife this evening.'

'How did that come about?' he asked perfunctorily.

'It was at Dr Sisterson's house.'

'Sisterson is a fool but there's no harm in him.'

'Mrs Locard was charming. And she is like a second mother to those children.'

'Nobody has any ill to say of her,' Austin said, rather as if regretting it. 'Except that she can't leave people's children alone. She had one that died when it was a baby and afterwards it was found that she could not have any more.'

'How sad!' I exclaimed. 'Such a kind, motherly woman. And so beautiful. Really quite . . .'

'How did you come to be invited there at this late hour?'

'I fell into conversation with Dr Sisterson.'

'In the Close? You must have been very cold. What possible topic could keep you both warm enough out there?'

'It wasn't in the Close. On the way back here from taking dinner at the Dolphin, I saw lights on in the Cathedral and went in and he was there.'

'Surely not. It should have been locked up hours ago.'

'No, the men are working late.'

'Yes, to make ready the organ for Friday. But they always finish by nine at the very latest.'

'Something has happened to cause them to work all night. That was why Dr Sisterson was there.'

'What are you talking about?' Suddenly I had his attention.

'Those blundering fools working on the Cathedral have done some serious damage, precisely as I feared. A crack has opened up in the wall of the transept and there's a terrible stench.'

He pulled himself back into a more usual position in his chair and stared at me in alarm. 'What does that mean?'

'It's just possible that the base of a pier has dropped slightly. If the Cathedral was built on water-logged ground there could be marsh-gas trapped down there which is now being released.'

'Will this delay the inauguration of the organ?'

'I don't know.'

'Didn't you ask?'

'No,' I said in bewilderment. 'Is it important?'

He slowly shook his head.

At that moment the great clock of the Cathedral began to sound the hour.

'One o'clock,' Austin muttered. 'You should be in bed.' Then, as if correcting this remark, he said: 'I'm keeping you from your bed.'

'You're quite right,' I said. 'I have to be at the Library early to-morrow. I will try to leave the house without waking you.'

'No, don't worry about that,' he said somewhat distractedly. 'I have much to do tomorrow. I will be up as early as you. Probably earlier.'

We shook hands and parted. Within fifteen minutes I was in bed with my book propped open in front of me. I could hear Austin moving about in his room across the landing for, prompted by some vague notion that he might have another nightmare, I had left my door ajar.

❖

Although my eyes were passing over the page before me, I was not taking anything in. As I reflected on how irritated Austin had been by my curiosity about his affairs, it occurred to me that he had asked me virtually no questions about myself. I had thought at first that it was from a delicate fear of wounding me, but now I understood that he was simply not interested. I had not realized when we were both young how intensely self-absorbed he was, perhaps because I was as wrapped up in myself as he was. But as I had grown older I had increasingly found others more interesting than myself.

Yet, I suddenly remembered, he had followed me when I had visited the New Deanery to read the inscription. In that case, was he, after all, interested in my doings?

Between Wednesday and Thursday

❖

IT WAS CLOSE TO TWO O'CLOCK when I blew out the candle and made an effort to sleep. I was in a confused land of shadows and half-understood images when a sound from the landing brought me back to full wakefulness. The old house creaked constantly but this noise had been sharper and louder. I listened hard and heard a soft weight on the stair. Then another. And another. Austin was descending the stairs! Immediately I conceived an image of my friend walking out through his front-door with his eyes wide open but his mind still lost in the world of dreams. I rose and, in the darkness, pulled on some of my clothes and felt my way to the door. I crept across the landing and down the first flight as quietly as I could in order not to wake him, remembering that it can be dangerous to rouse a sleepwalker suddenly. Straining my ears I could detect nothing but the old clock ticking loudly on the landing below me. Then I heard the front-door softly open and close just as I reached the top of the stairs. I hurried down as quickly as the utter darkness permitted, holding on to the hand-rail of the banister. Once in the hall, I groped my way to the coat-hooks and found my overcoat. Pulling it on I cautiously opened the door and peered round it. There was a wind for the first time in several days and a few scattered flakes of snow were falling—or, rather, blowing about. The fog had dispersed and a faint moon was peering through the streaky clouds by whose pale light I saw a figure moving quickly round the corner of the transept.

I hurried after him and as I turned the corner myself I was just in time to see him disappear into the mouth of an alleyway between the corner of the Close and the New Deanery. Walking as quickly as the need to keep silent permitted, I entered the lane in pursuit. Unbidden, the memory came to me of following someone in much the same fashion many years ago.

Austin did not seem to be sleepwalking: he was moving too fast and too purposefully. The alleyway twisted and turned several times so that although he was only a few yards ahead of me, already he was not visible. If he was not sleepwalking then he was not in danger and it occurred to me that I had no right to follow him. But had enough strange things not occurred since my arrival to give me good reason to suppose that he was in some kind of trouble and to justify an action which would otherwise have been dishonourable? I was quickly relieved of my ethical dilemma, however, for when I came out of the alleyway Austin was no longer in sight. The alley debouched into a short row of little cottages and it was possible that he had gone into one of these, or taken one of the lanes that led off the street. I stopped. I could hear nothing. It was as if the whole town was breathing as quietly as a sleeping child. I hurried on. If he had gone into one of the houses I might see a light or hear voices. I hastened down the row but saw and heard nothing. At the end there was another street cutting across it at a right-angle and, as far as I could ascertain given that it was unlit, it was deserted in both directions. I had lost him.

I was also lost myself. For some minutes I wandered the silent streets in bewilderment. Was this the way I had come? Was this the little alleyway I had taken? It all looked the same in the dark and I might have been wandering around the same few streets for all I knew. But the sharpness of the night air and its clarity after the stifling fog of the last few days were pleasant, and the regular motion of my legs was an appropriate accompaniment to my anxious thoughts. Where could Austin be going at this hour? What business could he have and with whom? Why had he seemed so concerned with the problem that had been found in the Cathedral?

At last I found the little alley again and returned to the Close. The Cathedral loomed up disconcertingly large ahead of me, gleaming where it caught the moonlight. I thought of how everything around it had crumbled away and been demolished and built over, including even the huge abbey that once surrounded it. The Cathedral's vastness made the town seem like a capital city and then I reflected that it once was—and remained for a long time—one of the great centres of learning in medieval Europe to which scholars and students came from as far away as Córdoba and Constantinople. I grieved for the lost treasures of the vast library dispersed at the Dissolution and for the lost community of ascetic scholars.

The story of the murdered Canon Burgoyne came to me unbidden and then images of the death of Dean Freeth as I moved past the cold stones where so much passion had once been felt. Something prompted me to walk past Austin's house and then make a circuit of the Close. It was in almost complete darkness. There was only a dim oil-lamp at the western end of the nave which should have burnt out by midnight and was just about to be extinguished now.

The ancient fear of the dark possessed me; the terror that there is evil and that it comes into its own at night. The image of a face that was a grinning skull took hold of me. I could not stop thinking about the story of Burgoyne. I knew that as a historian I should be perfectly rational and accept that the past is gone, yet my avocation makes me keenly aware of the pain and horror suffered by the dead even among the peaceful meadows or back-streets of England,

and so allows me to believe that something lingers on rather like a photographic plate on which a second image has been exposed. How do we know what happens to us after death?

I heard a muffled clinking and realized that the workmen might still be engaged in the Cathedral. The windows were indeed faintly illuminated and shadows were moving upon them. I went back to the door at the end of the south transept and pushed it. It opened and I slipped quietly in. The great stone columns were covered in droplets—as if perspiring, in spite of the cold. Indeed, the whole building seemed to be breathing. It was a vast living creature. I felt the skin on the back of my neck prickle as I heard a soft bubbling sound which seemed hideously like a human voice moaning and muttering in pain and despair—even though I knew it was only the wind.

I walked very quietly towards the chancel where the men were working. Three of them were at their labours and the old verger, Gazzard, was standing watching them with his back to me.

None of them noticed me standing under the crossing-tower. And then suddenly I felt I was being observed and that made me glance up at the organ-loft. I did so without thinking. It was one of those moments of inattention when mind and body seem to drift apart as if an effort were required to hold them together, when time appears to lose its motion. Or rather, when it later seems like that, for such moments can only be captured retrospectively. It was like those many times when I would realize I had read several pages with apparent concentration but without being able to remember a word. At such times I wondered, if my mind were not on my book, where was it?

And so it was on this occasion. When I glanced up at the organ-loft I suddenly became aware of where I was and had no idea how much time had passed or how I had got to where I found myself. Over the edge of the rail was a pale spot in the darkness and as I watched, it resolved itself into a face which seemed to be gazing straight at me. A cold, white, empty face with eyes that were two pieces of glass—empty and yet they seemed to peer into me. They looked through my soul—or rather my lack of a soul for they found or created an answering emptiness within me. It was the face of a creature not of our world. How long we stared at each other—or rather I stared at him for I cannot be sure that he was looking at me—I have no means of knowing. The face disappeared and I seemed to awake with a shudder and in a cold sweat, and it was at that moment that I reconstructed the sequence of events. I had an idea about who it was that I had seen, but I could not accept it. Everything I knew and believed would be thrown into confusion.

I stood there waiting to see who would emerge from the doorway which led down from the organ-gallery. Eventually, realizing that nobody was going to come down those steps, I turned and in a trance I made my way along the transept towards the door.

As I stepped through it and pulled it shut behind me my eyes were almost dazzled by unexpected whiteness. The air was filled with movement as myriad drifting snowflakes turned black and white when they caught or lost the moonlight. While I had been inside, the snow had begun to fall in earnest and enough had descended to cover the cobbles and roofs. I had not realized that I had been in the building for long enough for that to have happened. Always, with the first snow of the winter, the world was reborn. Involuntarily I remembered my childhood—hurrying through the snow with my nurse to watch the skaters on the nearby pond, coming back from school at the end of my first half when the coach laboured through deepening snow as it approached London, and waiting for my father to return on Christmas Eve when I knew I would be allowed to stay up late and sip hot punch with my parents. The memories moved me so deeply and seemed so innocent in contrast to what I had just experienced that I felt tears coming to my eyes.

And then it happened. I record only what I saw and believed at the time. The reader must be patient with me.

About sixty yards away in the pale moonlight and clearly distinct against the snow, there was a black figure standing at the entrance to the alleyway into which Austin had vanished. But this was not Austin. It was far too tall. The face was that of the being I had just seen in the organ-loft. *If he were a mortal being, I knew of no way he could have got from there to where he now was without my having seen him for I had watched the stairway from the gallery and then walked straight out of the only unlocked door of the Cathedral.* And once again the figure seemed to be looking at me. A long contemptuous stare. Then it turned away and entered the mouth of the alleyway making ungainly movements as it went. It was limping and that made it seem like some wounded creature dragging itself away, filled with pain and misery and rage.

I had seen William Burgoyne. I was sure of it. In that case, the world was not as I had imagined it. The dead could walk again, for a man who had died two hundred years ago had appeared before me. That meant that all that I believed—all the decent, rational, progressive ideas by which I lived—were childish games that could only be played in the daylight. When it grew dark then the real powers reassumed their place and they were irresistible, irrational and evil.

I don't know how long I stood there—ten minutes, fifteen, half an hour—for never had time seemed to me so illusory. When I came to myself I looked at the snow-covered cobbles. I could see in the faint moonlight that the surface of the snow between where I was and where the figure had stood was untouched. If it was anything but some insubstantial being, it could not have got there without leaving traces in the snow!

I wanted to get away from that place, and yet to return to Austin's house was unthinkable. I could not bear the thought of being confined and least of all in that old house that now seemed to me to be full of mocking shadows, of half-heard voices muttering in the creaking of the ancient timbers. I hastened along the side of the Cathedral in the opposite direction, passed under the entrance and found myself in the silent High Street. I set off fast and at random. How long I strode around the sleeping streets I do not know.

The town's peacefulness reassured me that the world of ordinary life, of the patterns of sleep and work, still existed, for what I had seen was like a cry of agony in the middle of a chamber concert—a glimpse of pain and anger powerful enough to raise a man from his death two hundred years after the event. I let my legs carry me where they would and I hardly knew where they took me. Wherever I passed, my footsteps were the only stains upon the light dusting of snow that now lay upon the town. I remember that at one moment I was climbing a gently sloping hill along a curving road lined with big villas, each with a wrought-iron balcony and verandah and painted wooden shutters, and I remember pausing near the summit to look down at the houses and their long gardens that led down to a little stream sheltered by weeping willows all along its length, and I remember thinking that it must have been charming in the summer although the trees were now silent and gaunt in the winter moonlight. I thought of the parents and children and servants sleeping inside them, and sighed as I imagined what a pleasant place those dwellings would have been to grow up in or to bring up a family.

From up here the little town lay before me like a child's toy, my sight of it slightly misted by the falling snow. In the centre the dark shape of the Cathedral thrust upwards from the low roofs around it, and as I thought of the dark little Close huddled in its shadow I felt an unwillingness to return there out of the clear air of the hilltop.

After a few minutes I set off. I descended the hill again by a different way and saw nobody until at last in some street on the edge of the town—more like a country lane with its thatched cottages and rutted carriageway than a town street—I met a milk-cart driven by a burly young man who called out a cheerful greeting. This communication with a breathing human being brought me back to my senses. Now I hurried back towards the centre of the town, taking as my landmark the spire of the Cathedral that loomed up against the dark sky. After a few minutes I was so close to it in among the houses that I could no longer see it. And then I heard its clock sound the half-hour and knew I was near it. It was half-past three. I was completely lost among narrow back-streets and gardens until I found myself in one of the lanes I had taken after losing sight of Austin. Suddenly I smelt butter and ginger. Something was baking! I followed the smell. As I turned into a long narrow street I saw only one light along its whole length. It was a street of tall old houses of faded red brick, now somewhat dilapidated with the paint on the doors and window-frames peeling and the wood rotted beneath it. All of them had several bell-pulls and name-plates—sure signs that they had been made down into separate dwellings. I went up to the sole window where there was a light and looked in.

There was a gap in the frayed curtains and through it I could just see a part of Austin's face and the lower part of his body. He was sitting in a chair and talking but I could not see whom he was addressing. I saw him raise a glass to his mouth and drink. I strained to hear and could just make out a murmur of voices—one of which was a woman's. I could not tell if she was the only other person in the room with Austin or if there were more than those two. And then as I watched, a hand which seemed too large for a woman's but whose fingers were slender and delicate, reached towards Austin and rested for a moment on his knee in a strangely intimate gesture.

Austin smiled at his invisible companion with such tenderness, his face illuminated with such evident happiness, that I had a sudden memory of him looking at me that way many years before and felt a sharp stab of regret, remorse, even jealousy. I only looked for a few seconds, terrified that he might glance out and see me, though I suppose that the lights inside the room would have turned the window-panes into black mirrors. I backed away from the window and walked down the street in a daze.

So that was his great passion—a squalid liaison with a woman of the town in this shabby district. What a fool I was not to have thought of that as a reason for his going out in the middle of the night! I was horrified at the idea that he might find out that I had followed him. And at the same time, I was astonished. The Austin I had known had never gone in for mercenary amours—as many of our contemporaries at the University had done. Indeed, he had never been involved with women at all, as far as I knew. I had never had a moment's unease on that score during his friendship with my wife.

I thought of him hurrying through the dark and silent streets to his lover. How ridiculous at his age. And yet how enviable. I found I had to pause and take a deep breath as I thought of the sheer naked shamelessness of my friend's indulgence in this adventure.

At the end of the street I seemed to come to my senses and found that I knew where I was. I was at the corner with the street which led to the alleyway in which I had lost Austin. I retraced my steps. Now it occurred to me that the affair might not be what I had assumed. Perhaps Austin was truly in love with some woman who was worthy of his love. Yet their meeting like that in the middle of the night implied that their relationship was in some way illicit. Was she married? Was she even the wife of a colleague or one of the men attached in some capacity to the Cathedral? In that case, who could she be? I thought of the cycle of disappointment, excitement, resentment and desire through which I had not been forced for two decades. Who was this imperious, unreasonable creature who had such power over him—summoning him, perhaps, to come to her in the middle of the night regardless of the risks? Recalling him, it might be, after a period of anguished banishment, during which he might have had to watch her smiling with affection upon a rival. When I remembered what I had suffered, I hardly knew whether to envy or to pity him.

Then a horrible idea came to me about who the woman might be. I could not believe that it could be true. How could such a woman find Austin worthy? And yet it occurred to me that the real Austin, the Austin I had known if he still existed, might be worthy, for the best qualities in him were admirable. And of all women in the world she would be the one to find and encourage them for, as I had seen, it was characteristic of her always to think the best of people and try to understand and forgive their worst actions. What horror it was to reflect that it is often the very generosity of the lover which makes an unworthy beloved seem deserving.

I went back to the house, shaking the snow off my boots before I went inside, and took a lighted candlestick up to the sitting-room. I had determined upon a certain course of action. Austin's behaviour was of a piece with other strange acts since my arrival: his watching me that afternoon in the Close, his abrupt changes of mood and swings from friendliness to resentment. The circumstances now—the fact that it was the middle of the night, the snow, the figure I had just seen—all of these factors seemed to mean that I had stepped out of the ordinary world and was therefore allowed to take measures that I would not normally permit myself. I had begun to think that there might be a connection between the theft of the miniatures—if they were indeed what had been taken—from Dr Sheldrick on Tuesday night and the odd business of the package that had mysteriously arrived inside Austin's front-door.

I crossed to the armoire. The doors were solid and when I tried them, I found they were indeed locked.

I scrutinized the room for any other clues. It struck me that the bookshelves were the tidiest thing in the house. Did that mean that Austin never touched his books or, on the contrary, that he was so devoted to them that he was careful to keep them in order? Because of the orderliness, it was striking that on one of the shelves there was a single volume out of place and lying on its side. Noticing that it had a book-mark inserted in it, I picked it up and found that it was a collection of fairy-tales and bore inside a gummed label indicating that it was from the library of Courtenay's. On an impulse I took it up to my room, made ready for bed and got under the covers.

I opened the volume at the place where the book-mark had been put and, finding that it was the beginning of one of the stories, began to read it. My attention wandered, however. Could it be that I had imagined the figure I had seen in the organ-loft and again in the Close? It was true that I had drunk several glasses more than was customary during the course of the evening. Now that I considered it, I could explain some of what I had seen, but not everything. It might be, for instance, that I had stood on the steps for longer than I had realized and that the falling snow had covered the traces of the figure I had seen before I had thought to look. Yet the fact remained that he could not have got from the organ-loft to where I had seen him without passing a few feet in front of me. Even now that I was tucked up in bed I was unable to feel amusement at my superstitious terror for I still had a strange feeling that I had seen something from another world or another time. Austin's remark about being damned—that his mysterious passion had led him to perdition—came unbidden into my mind. The creature I had seen that night was evil—even damned—if that word meant anything.

Curious to know what Austin had been reading, I forced myself to peruse the tale open before me. To my surprise, although it was a conventional enough story of a brave young prince and a beautiful princess and an enchanted castle, I found it profoundly disturbing.

When I had finished it, I lay for some time thinking again about certain passages in my life. After about an hour I heard Austin creeping into the house and up the stairs. It was another half-hour before I was able to fall into an uneasy slumber.

Thursday Morning

❖

AUSTIN PROBABLY SLEPT worse than I did, for when I came down for breakfast at a quarter to seven he was not there. I prepared coffee and toast for both of us and he descended a few minutes later looking pale and haggard. I waited in the hope that he might say something about what had happened during the night and, as a result, neither of us spoke more than a few sentences while we ate our breakfast. I noticed that his hand was shaking as he lifted the cup to his lips. He seemed to be avoiding my gaze and I was trying to do the same for I felt embarrassed in case he had by some means discovered that I had followed him. He might have seen me or, it now occurred to me, have noticed traces of melted snow in the hall when he returned.

At last he spoke: 'I will wait for you outside the Library when it closes.'

'Whatever for?'

He looked at me in apparent surprise: 'Have you forgotten that old Mr Stonex is expecting us to tea this afternoon?'

For a moment I could not think what he was talking about. Then I realized that the name he had uttered was familiar. Of course! It had been mentioned by the elderly banker yesterday as that of his ancestor who had purchased the house. 'But it was for tomorrow that he invited me. Us.' I couldn't imagine how Austin knew of this.

'Today. He meant today.'

'I'm certain he said tomorrow. Friday.'

'He has altered it.'

'But, Austin, how do you know about it? I forgot to mention to you that I met him yesterday when I went to read the inscription.'

'I am aware of that.'

I was astonished. Was he admitting that he had been spying on me? Feeling suddenly embarrassed on his behalf and not wanting him to say any more about his strange behaviour, I went on: 'I didn't even think you would want to come. How do you know he has changed the date?'

'How do I know? Because he told me. I happened to meet him yesterday evening. I myself forgot to inform you of it last night.'

'But how did he come to learn that you are a friend of mine? I'm sure I didn't tell him.'

'There are no secrets in this town,' he said flatly, and it seemed that I had to be content with this. 'So I will meet you outside the Library when it closes and we will go there together.'

I nodded. It was strange. If Austin had not been watching me yesterday afternoon while I conversed with the old gentleman at the back of the New Deanery, why should he have spoken to Mr Stonex? My suspicion that he had been following me must be correct. And he had presumably wanted to find out what had passed between me and the old man.

A few minutes later Austin, who had made a hasty toilet but still looked ill-shaven and untidy, was ready to leave. I had waited for him so that we would leave the house together. When we opened the door we found that several inches of snow had fallen in the last few hours. We trudged in silence through the almost immaculate whiteness.

As we reached the door of the transept, we passed two boys. One had hold of the other and I smiled at Austin, wondering if he saw them as reminders of our youthful selves, but he appeared not to have noticed them. The bigger boy, who glanced at Austin with contempt, was in what I assumed to be the required dress of the Grammar School—blue gown and knee-breeches with buckled shoes—while the other wore a plain black jacket and breeches and was presumably a Choir School pupil. I remembered that Austin had talked of the rivalry between the two institutions which this vignette seemed to belie. As we passed them, the younger boy was saying something—or trying to say something for he stammered agonizingly—about being late and getting into trouble.

A moment later I looked round and saw that the larger boy had seized the other by the neck and was stuffing a snowball down the back of his collar. The younger one struggled and his antagonist hit him quite hard twice on the chest in rapid succession. I was about to turn back but I saw him release the smaller boy who ran off. Austin—unlike the ever-vigilant schoolmaster of my childhood— gave no sign of having noticed.

We reached the end of the Cathedral in silence and parted with another reminder from Austin of our appointment. At that mo- ment I saw young Quitregard rounding the corner of the ambula- tory and we greeted each other and covered the last few yards together. I mentioned the incident I had just witnessed and he said he had seen the Choir School boy a few minutes earlier, remarking that he himself had a brother at the school. It was a few minutes before half-past seven when we reached the Library, whose great door Quitregard unlocked.

'Were you a pupil there yourself?' I asked.

'I was at Courtenay's—the Grammar School.'

'I'm surprised that brothers should be sent to the two institu- tions,' I said as I stamped my feet on the mat just inside the door to get the snow off my boots.

'I can't sing a note, you see.'

'Even so I am puzzled, for I understood that the two schools de-tested each other.'

He laughed. 'The boys fight each other, of course. But I don't be-lieve there is any official ill-will between the schools.'

'My friend—Fickling—told me that suspicion between the two institutions went so far that his friendship with a master at the Choir School was disapproved of.'

The young man said quickly: 'Oh, I don't think it's the friend-ship itself which is frowned upon.' Then he flushed and said: 'Dr Locard has asked me to convey his apologies, Dr Courtine. He will not be able to help you this morning as he had hoped. He has to prepare for the meeting of the Chapter. Some important business has unexpectedly arisen.'

'That is most regrettable from my point of view.' It was of a piece, I reflected, with the invitation to dinner which the Librarian had offered and then withdrawn, and it reduced even further my chances of finding what I was seeking.

The young man must have seen the disappointment on my face for he offered me a cup of coffee before I resumed my dusty labours in the undercroft and added: 'When Pomerance arrives he'll light the fires so if we wait a while it will be warmer.'

I accepted with gratitude, though reflecting that the heat would not penetrate to where I would be working. As he led the way to the snug bay in which he made coffee, he said: 'I think I can tell you without betraying any confidences that there is something of a crisis today. The Chapter meeting will be long and difficult.'

I remembered Gazzard saying that the school was to be discussed this morning and assumed that the crisis was connected with the gossip I had heard in the tap-room last night. I was unwilling, how-ever, to put Quitregard in an embarrassing situation by asking him any questions. We seated ourselves and waited while the kettle boiled.

'Of course I'm very sorry that Dr Locard is unable to lend me his valuable assistance,' I remarked. 'But I fear that all the help in the world would not advantage me. Even if the manuscript is here I could spend six months searching down there and still miss it.'

The young man looked a little self-conscious as he bent over the stove. I wondered if he was embarrassed because he had overheard me talking to Dr Locard about this. 'I wish I could help you,' he said. 'I would give anything to find it for you, and I'm sure Dr Locard would much prefer it to be found by one of his staff.'

'I wish so too. Dr Locard talked of you in very flattering terms and was kind enough to say that he might be able to release you for a few hours to give me the benefit of your assistance.'

'Did he?' Quitregard turned away to reach down a jar of coffee and said over his shoulder: 'However, I'm dismayed to have to tell you that Dr Locard reminded me only yesterday afternoon how important it is that we continue with our cataloguing of the manuscripts and has given me work that will keep me occupied for the next week or more.'

'That is unfortunate. But I have at least had the advantage of Dr Locard's advice. His interpretation of the single piece of evidence I have was masterly. I should explain that it is a letter written by an antiquarian of the Restoration called Pepperdine who . . .'

'I have to confess that I overheard your conversation,' the young man said apologetically, looking up from his labours over the coffee-pot. 'I had no reason to assume it was confidential.'

'It wasn't in the least confidential. But in that case you will know how brilliantly Dr Locard read beneath the surface appearance of the evidence to find its truer significance. It was an impressive demonstration of historical analysis.' He bent over the kettle so that I could not see his face. I went on: 'And you probably also heard us talking about the new perspective the letter gives on the Freeth affair?'

'Yes, I did. And it's an incident which I've always been fascinated by.'

'In that case you will be interested to learn that I am to hear yet another version of it this afternoon. Yesterday I went to read the inscription on the wall of the New Deanery.'

'The famous Satanic inscription,' Quitregard said turning round with a smile. 'Though I doubt if it has anything to do with the death of Dean Freeth.'

'No, indeed. It was in connection with the story of Treasurer Burgoyne that I went to read it.' The young man raised an eyebrow to express equal scepticism. 'But that's beside the point,' I went on. 'I was going to tell you that I happened to fall into conversation with the old gentleman who now lives in the house, and he invited me to tea tomorrow.' I corrected myself. 'I mean this afternoon.'

Quitregard looked astonished. 'Really? Mr Stonex?'

'Yes. He mentioned that he knows a story about Freeth's death which he inherited with the house. He is to tell it to me this after-noon.'

'I can't tell you how surprised I am. You are honoured indeed. He is very reclusive. Or perhaps you are not so fortunate. I've heard that he is far from gracious.'

'Well, he was perfectly charming to me.'

Quitregard raised his eyebrows. 'You astonish me immensely, Dr Courtine.'

'That anyone should be charming to me?' I asked playfully.

He smiled. 'Such an invitation is quite at odds with all that I have ever heard about him. And I grew up in Thurchester and have heard gossip about him all my life. He is friendly to children only—in fact, only to the boys of the Choir School which he at-tended himself. As it happens, I saw him talking to one as we were arriving.'

'And what is said about him in the town?'

'Although he is a personage who is much talked about, very lit-tle is known for sure about him. He is very prominent in his capac-ity as the sole proprietor of the Thurchester and County Bank.'

'It's possible that he is affable only to people who have no knowledge of his position in this town—like children and strangers. But I may take it, then, that he is wealthy?'

'Did he not give you that impression?' the young man said with a smile.

'Very far from it. His appearance was somewhat threadbare. And the house looks—from the outside at least—to be in a poor way.'

'He is—not to mince words—a famous miser and spends as little as possible on himself and his comforts and nothing on anyone else's. But the truth is that he is one of the town's wealthiest citizens—probably the wealthiest. Yet he lives in the most frugal and reclusive manner. I have never heard of anyone being invited into his house.'

'He has no friends or relatives?'

'No relatives with whom he is on good terms—or any sort of terms—though it is said that he had a sister with whom he quarrelled many years ago. And certainly no friends.'

'Then I have been favoured indeed. I wonder how I shall be received. What shall I find?'

'I shall be intrigued to hear from you,' the young man said with a smile. 'The house will be clean and tidy for a woman comes every day to take care of it. Everything will be in its exact place but you will notice that nothing in the house has been newly purchased. Apart from his collection of old maps, he has an absolute horror of spending money.'

'Is he merely eccentric, or is it something more serious?'

'He is not in the least deranged. Perhaps I should not even say that he is eccentric since a prosperous banker to whom people entrust their money can hardly be said to be eccentric—but, rather, that he is an original. And his originality might be said to lie in the extreme orderliness of his life. He is like Kant, the philosopher, whose daily movements were said to be so regular that the citizens of his town would set their watches by him.'

'Is there any reason for his punctiliousness in regard to time and for his unsociability?'

'Both seem to arise from his terror of being robbed. They say that he keeps a fortune in cash and gold in a hiding-place in his house. I have no idea if that is so. I would imagine that he entrusts his valuables to the strong-room at the bank. But that is the belief in the town and I suppose that it might have been prompted by the elaborate precautions he takes to avoid being robbed. And perhaps he now has to take such precautions only because of the belief that his house is worth breaking into.'

He laughed and I smiled with him.

'What are these precautions?'

'He receives nobody at the house. Hence the unusual honour accorded to yourself.' Here he half-rose and gave me a little mock-bow. I was beginning to like this young man a great deal. 'The house is never left unoccupied and he himself leaves it only to go to the bank. There is only one set of keys which he keeps on a chain on his person and so nobody apart from himself has a key—not even the single servant—an old woman, Mrs Bubbosh, who comes every day to clean and do the laundry and prepare his meals.'

'If she has no key and Mr Stonex spends much of the day at the bank, how does she enter and leave?'

'A very good question. This is one of the most original elements of the old gentleman's way of life. He admits her at seven and she makes his breakfast. He leaves the house at half-past seven, locking her in.'

'She is locked in all day?'

'Until he returns for his luncheon at noon. And all the windows are barred by shutters which are locked so that she cannot let anyone in. The old woman has a few hours' leave in the afternoon for her employer's dinner is brought by a waiter from an inn nearby. It arrives punctually on the stroke of four. So he opens the door only at those times: seven, four, and six when Mrs Bubbosh returns and he goes back to the bank. He comes home at nine for his supper and she goes home.'

'When I met him yesterday he mentioned his dinner. I thought he said he was expecting it, and yet it must have been long after four for I left here at a quarter past when your colleague closed the Library.'

Quitregard smiled. 'I think you must have misunderstood him. I assure you that any alteration in his daily routine would be widely talked about in the town.'

'The rigidity of his daily round intrigues me. I wonder if there is something in his past that he is trying to protect himself from.'

The young man looked at me quizzically.

'People sometimes attempt to shield themselves from painful memories by adopting a fixed pattern in their lives.' At the worst time in my life I had turned myself into a figure on an old clock—popping up from my desk or out from my study merely for meals, lectures and tutorials. The youthful librarian clearly had no idea what I was talking about, so I dropped the subject. 'How long has he led that life?'

'He has been miserly and solitary all his life, but it was about eight or nine years ago that he started to take such elaborate precautions.'

'If he has no relatives, what does he plan to do with all his carefully guarded wealth?'

'The town would love to know the answer to that.'

'Has the town no conception at all?' I asked with a smile.

'The town suspects—and certainly hopes—that he will leave it to the Cathedral Foundation for the benefit of his old school. He holds it high in his somewhat flinty affections for he had a difficult childhood and one or two of the masters at the school were kind to him.'

The Cathedral clock sounded the hour and I stood up. 'Well, this has been very pleasant but I must return to work.'

Quitregard also rose to his feet. 'You are going to continue to search in the undercroft?'

'Indeed,' I said, surprised by his question after what I had told him.

He hesitated for a moment as if he was on the point of saying something he found awkward, but then he laughed and said: 'I'm afraid it will be cold. Pomerance has not arrived to light the fires yet. He knows Dr Locard is as a rule busy with the Chapter meeting on Thursdays and is usually late that day.'

I thanked him for the coffee and went down to the heaps of mouldering manuscripts and resumed my search. Quitregard's question had seemed idle enough but it made me wonder: was this arduous search the right course of action? Something had begun to occur to me even while I was talking to the young man. The Librarian's strange conduct in cancelling his invitation, breaking his appointment and, Quitregard had implied, withdrawing the assistance of his staff, had made me start to wonder if Dr Locard—so obsessed with scholarly rivalry and elaborate bluffs and counter-bluffs—could be envious of my discovery that Grimbald's manuscript might be in this building. Could it be that he had decided that he would find the manuscript himself? As Mrs Sisterson's unguarded words had implied, it might be humiliating to him to have such an important discovery made under his own nose by an outsider, and he and his assistants were about to start cataloguing the remaining material quite soon. Austin had warned me about his ambition and, he had implied, his unscrupulousness, and although I had accepted the former I had declined to see the latter quality in him. Had I been naive? Had Dr Locard deliberately given me advice that would lead me into wasting my time? Had he, in fact, done to me what he had convinced me Pepperdine had done to

Bullivant? Could it be that he had decided to enter the field of Anglo-Saxon scholarship and that was why he had read my article and Scuttard's response—which was otherwise a surprising coincidence?

All morning I sorted through piles of cobwebbed and crumbling manuscripts, my task made harder by the fact that Pomerance failed to appear—although he could have shared only the physical and not the intellectual part of my labours. At noon I left the Library, tramping with difficulty through the snow which had by now been trampled into slush and then frozen into a mass of icy mud and stones. I went to take my luncheon at the inn to which I had gone the evening before, though this time I did not enter the public-bar. When I returned at a little after one I found Quitregard making coffee and accepted his invitation to share it with him.

Just as the kettle boiled Pomerance burst in crying: 'The Guv'-nor's won! Sheldrick's down. They've knifed him properly. He's cat's meat now. He'll have to sack himself. All the fellows were talking about it.' Then he stopped suddenly at the sight of me and his long bony face turned quite crimson.

Quitregard smiled. 'Sit down and have a cup of coffee, Pomerance.' The young man slumped into a chair like a puppet whose strings had been cut. 'He's just come from choir practice,' he explained to me. 'Where I understand singing occurs in the occasional pauses in the flow of gossip.'

'I say, that's not fair. The choirmaster is a real dragon. He makes us work jolly hard.'

'Then perhaps I should emulate his dragon-like qualities.'

'That reminds me,' Pomerance said, 'I won't need to have tomorrow afternoon off.'

'But what about the service for the organ?'

'Oh, that has been cancelled.'

Quitregard looked at him in astonishment.

'There's something rum up with the Cathedral,' Pomerance

explained. 'So the organ will be out of use from after Evensong tonight.'

'Something rum?' Quitregard echoed. 'Can't you deploy the resources of the English language with a little more finesse, Pomerance?'

The young fellow shrugged to indicate that he knew no more.

'The workmen may have done some slight damage to the base of a pier,' I said, delighted to be able to contribute some information about his native town that Quitregard did not have. Gratifyingly, the young man turned to me in surprise. With a flourish I added: 'And there's a mysterious smell.'

Pomerance wrinkled up his nose. 'Yes, it's utterly foul. It was beastly having to sing when you wanted to keep your mouth shut.'

'I can't believe you've ever wanted to keep your mouth shut since you drew your first breath,' Quitregard said. 'But when will the service take place?'

'Probably next week.' The youth glanced quickly at me and then turned back to his colleague: 'And by then it's very likely that there will be a new organist.'

Quitregard smiled. 'Possibly. We will see.'

'Well,' I said, 'it's time for me to return to my labours. My somewhat hopeless labours.'

Quitregard glanced at Pomerance. 'Go and start copying yesterday's work into the register, like a good fellow.'

The young man drained his cup and got up.

'I missed you this morning, Mr Pomerance,' I said with ironic politeness. 'Will you be able to come down and give me a hand later?'

'Oh no,' he said immediately. 'The Guv'nor says I'm not to any more.' Then he caught Quitregard's eye and reddened.

'Hurry along now, old chap,' his older colleague said mildly and the youth walked down to the other end of the long gallery.

I waited for Quitregard to say something but he seemed to be lost in his thoughts. To break the silence I asked: 'Are the reverend canons really so fierce with each other?'

He smiled. 'They are for the most part honest and intelligent men who find it curiously easy to attribute to their colleagues the most heinous motives.'

'I know the truth of that from my own college. It's extraordinary how a group of entirely honourable men can come to see each other as unprincipled demons simply because they take a different position on some issue.'

'And almost invariably their suspicions are unjustified.'

'I believe I can guess what the real issue is in this case.'

He looked at me in astonishment. 'Can you?'

'It's universal, is it not?'

'Is it?' He turned away to sort out the used crockery.

'It is widely known that most of the Thurchester canons are High—the Dean especially—but that others are on the Evangelical wing. Every Chapter in England has such a division.'

He turned back to me and nodded pleasantly. 'I see what you mean.'

'I assume Dr Locard is High?'

'Vertiginously.'

'But Dr Sheldrick is Low,' I suggested.

He nodded. 'Almost perfectly horizontal.'

'Well, there is the whole explanation. I imagine the canons have been bickering—I beg their pardon, disputing—for years about the usual issues of incense and vestments and anthems and so on. But presumably something much more serious has been debated to-day.' When he said nothing I asked: 'As the Chancellor, does Dr Sheldrick have any responsibility for the Choir School?'

'Not directly,' he replied, glancing up curiously. 'But one of his duties is to oversee the Headmaster's conduct of it.'

'And has the Headmaster's conduct been questionable?'

'It has certainly been questioned.'

I was longing to quiz him: What accusations had been made against Dr Sheldrick and why was he apparently being forced to resign if he had merely been negligent in his supervision of the Headmaster? Was there a connection with the mysterious theft from his house on Tuesday evening? But it was clear that I was putting the young man in an increasingly awkward position. I permitted myself one carefully phrased enquiry: 'It is Dr Locard who has been foremost in insisting that the Chapter take action?'

He smiled. 'Dr Locard has shown characteristic resolution in what he sees as his duty.'

'I can believe that he is very resolute,' I said. 'And I believe he has a somewhat sceptical vision of human nature.'

'Perhaps at times too sceptical.' He stopped and looked at me nervously. 'If I may speak for a moment with perfect frankness, relying on your discretion . . .'

He broke off.

'You may rely on it completely,' I responded.

'I believe that Dr Locard has a tendency to over-complicate matters, and especially the motives of others.' He paused for a moment and then said cautiously: 'His scholarship is somewhat combative because of that. For example, with the greatest respect to him, I'm not sure that I agree with his interpretation of Pepperdine's letter.'

'Indeed? You don't accept that Pepperdine tried to mislead Bullivant?'

'I think he unintentionally pointed towards the undercroft simply because of the ambiguity of what he wrote.'

'So where do you believe he found the manuscript?'

'On the upper floor.'

'But almost all the manuscripts up there have been catalogued.'

'Almost all. But if it turns out not to be among those that are still uncatalogued, you will have lost very little since if it is in the undercroft, you won't find it in the next day or two except by the merest accident.'

His logic was impeccable. I wondered if Dr Locard had deliberately pointed me in the wrong direction, and then it occurred to me that the young man certainly suspected that that was the case. 'You have given me excellent advice. I'm very grateful.'

He could not hide his pleasure and insisted upon accompanying me to the upper floor. There he showed me which shelves held the uncatalogued manuscripts and it was immediately obvious that I could search through them in two or three days. It was so much pleasanter up here—dust-free, light, clean and very much warmer. The conditions in which I was working as well as my prospects for success had been transformed.

I began taking down heavy bound volumes of manuscripts and depositing them on the table and searching through them. After a couple of hours I had examined four and was becoming weary of sitting. I stood up and walked round the table to stretch my legs and as I glanced at the books in the section that had been catalogued, my eye fell on three large folios on one of the uppermost shelves. I climbed onto a chair and saw, written on the spines in a hand characteristic of the late seventeenth century, the words: 'Records of the Chancery Court of the Liberty of St John' followed in each case by a set of dates: 1357–1481; 1482–1594; and 1595–1651. They must refer to the long-abolished court—the equivalent of a magistrate's—which had jurisdiction over the Cathedral Close and I wondered if I might find a reference to the incident in which Limbrick's father had died and Gambrill been injured. In the hope of satisfying my curiosity and as a brief respite from my labours, I lifted the third volume down and opened it upon the table.

I leafed quickly through it and saw that for each adjudication someone—presumably the clerk of the court—had written a brief account of the charge, the evidence given by witnesses and the decision of the Chancellor. I found the date 1615, which I reckoned must be the earliest that the incident could have occurred, and began to read more slowly. And then, under the year 1625, I found what I had been looking for: Alice Limbrick, relict of the late Deputy Mason of the Cathedral, had laid an information against John Gambrill that he did 'by negligence or malice' bring about the death of her husband, Robert Limbrick. She alleged that they had quarrelled because Gambrill had *conceived the desire to take for himself the office of Mason, which office had been promised to her husband,* and had therefore accused her husband—without good cause—of cheating the Cathedral authorities and endangering his fellows by supplying wood of poor quality for the timber bracings.

There then followed a brief account of the accident given by two fellow-workmen who had seen it and by Gambrill himself. Presumably because the three gave the same account, the clerk had not differentiated between their testimony. Gambrill and Limbrick had been working on the vaulting of the tower above the central crossing when the accident had occurred: *They were raising dressed Stone by their Engin when by the slipping of the Knot on a Rope, John Gambrill missed his Footing and fell, to the Destruction of Robert Limbrick who was on high and was thereby grievously injured, his Body broken in an Hundred Places.* The account was strangely unclear but Gambrill's fall must have brought down the other man in some way.

The Chancellor found that Gambrill had no case to answer. But the clerk had recorded that Limbrick's widow did not accept that finding and that, with the intervention of the Chancellor himself, Gambrill offered to make up the quarrel by taking on her eldest son, Thomas, who was then aged twelve, as an apprentice without requiring a premium. The resemblance to the words of the inscription struck me. And in particular, the word *Engin* which appeared in both and about which an idea was beginning to form. In the early seventeenth century the word could designate three things: ingenuity, a conspiracy, or a piece of machinery. Here it was clear that some kind of mechanical device was being referred to, while the inscription was much more enigmatic in its allusion to *the Guilty . . . by their own Engin brought to Destruction.*

That was the end of the record. Idly I turned over the leaf in order to ensure that there was nothing more, and found a page which was not bound into the volume but loosely inserted. I stared at it for several seconds before I realized that I was looking at a folio of manuscript from a very much earlier period—about the eleventh century, I judged, from the style of the somewhat inelegant proto-gothic bookhand. I read the first words—*Quia olim rex martyrusque amici dilectissimi fuissent*—and felt my heart beat faster. I quickly read on and recognized, as I had guessed, the story of the siege of Thurchester and the martyrdom of St Wulflac. With an extraordinary calm, I told myself that I had found what I had been seeking: part of an early version of Grimbald's *Life*. My judgement had been vindicated. The work had indeed existed before Leofranc had done anything to it.

Nobody had looked at it for more than two hundred years. It suddenly came to me that the folio was here because Pepperdine had consulted this volume of records after his accidental discovery of what I now thought of as 'the Grimbald manuscript'. He had simply left the folio where I had found it because he had had so little interest in what he dismissed as *the age of darkness before the Conquest.* He had searched for the Chancery Records because, like me, he had become interested in the story of Burgoyne and Freeth. He must have realized that the Treasurer's death was in some way connected with the early life of his assumed murderer, and like a good historian, he had gone to the available sources. Dr Sheldrick, it occurred to me, had failed to do so and had thereby lost an opportunity to pique Dr Locard by finding the manuscript under his rival's nose.

At that moment I heard someone bounding up the stairs, and

without pausing to reflect, I closed the volume with the manuscript still where I had found it and pushed it back onto the shelf.

Young Pomerance burst in to tell me that he was closing the Library. I turned and followed him unthinkingly and made small talk while my thoughts were elsewhere. Why had I hidden the manuscript? Would I have done so if it had been Dr Locard or even Quitregard who had approached? Why had I not shouted out to Pomerance that I had found what I was seeking and told him to fetch Dr Locard? Perhaps it was because the secrecy in which the manuscript had dwelt for so long was too powerful to break without reflection and ceremony. Or did I have another motive of which I was not fully aware?

I left the Library in a trance, fortunately without seeing either Dr Locard or Quitregard.

Thursday Afternoon

❖

AS I WALKED OUT INTO THE DARK Close and began aimlessly to take a course, someone came forward from the shadows beside the entrance. It was Austin. I had completely forgotten that we had an appointment.

Should I tell him of my discovery? Something made me decide not to. He was pale and seemed nervous.

We greeted each other with some meaningless formula and I fell into step beside him as we made our way round the Close. I walked mechanically, not knowing where we were going or remembering why he had come to meet me. We walked in silence for Austin seemed as preoccupied as I was. I tried to think of something to say, but everything seemed trivial in comparison with my discovery. Somehow I had to get through the coming evening and the long night until the Library opened again in the morning. How unfortunate that it opened early only on Thursdays. I would have to wait until half-past eight!

We made a complete circuit of the Cathedral in silence and then suddenly Austin exclaimed: 'We're too early. He is not ready for us.'

I had to force myself by an effort of the will to think what he was talking about. I saw that we were standing at the back-gate of the

New Deanery and then I remembered: we were having tea with Mr Stonex.

I pulled out my watch and read its dial by the light of a gas-lamp a few yards away. 'On the contrary. The old gentleman said half-past four and that is exactly the time now.'

'Nevertheless, he's not ready so we'll go to my house for a few minutes,' Austin said, already striding on ahead.

Puzzled, but not able to deploy enough of my mental resources to think about it, I tagged along beside him as we continued our circuit of the Cathedral. It was getting dark and we saw nobody. I recalled how punctual the old man was, according to Quitregard, and was the more perplexed. As we passed the Chapter House, the dim glow through the windows created dark shadows among the buttresses as if a figure were hidden there. The light, together with the muted sounds of a piano and voices raised in harmony, indicated that the choir was practising. As we rounded the corner of the transept, I remembered that this was where the apparition of the night before had been standing and asked: 'Does he limp?'

Austin started and turned towards me in alarm: 'Why do you ask?'

'Oh, just that I'm intrigued by his story.'

'His story? Who are you talking about?'

'Burgoyne. Does his ghost limp?'

He seemed to scrutinize my face. 'Burgoyne didn't limp,' he said, almost angrily. 'It was Gambrill who was lame. You've confused them.'

I didn't bother to correct him.

'What on earth makes you think of that now?' he demanded.

'I merely wondered if people have reported that the ghost limps.'

'The ghost?' he almost hissed.

'The ghost of Burgoyne.'

He stopped and looked at me. 'What are you talking about?'

I was in a quandary and could say nothing. I could hardly tell him what I believed I had seen, only a few yards from where we now were, in the early hours of the morning. How could I have accounted for my being there at that time?

We walked a few steps in silence and as we reached the door of his house, I said: 'I've been thinking about the idea that a spirit is restless because its body is not buried. And so I've been wondering if it really is Burgoyne who haunts the Close, for since his corpse *was* buried, why is his ghost walking?'

'What in heaven's name are you babbling about?' Austin asked as he removed his greatcoat.

'The corpse. The body of the murdered man.'

'The murdered man?' he stammered, looking at me in dismay.

'I've been saying that it has struck me as puzzling that Burgoyne's ghost walks since he was buried.'

'That's a story, for heaven's sake. You can't believe all that nonsense.'

'But they also say, don't they, that the ghost of a person walks if his murder has not been avenged. I suppose Burgoyne was unavenged since Gambrill fled unpunished.'

'Why on earth are you drivelling on about this?'

'My dear fellow, only for the sake of saying something.'

'Well, if that's all you can think of, perhaps you'd do better to hold your tongue.'

Then he turned away and, quickly tugging at the cord of the gasmantle to bring up the flame, mounted the stairs ahead of me. I picked up a candle, lit it and followed him. When we entered the sitting-room, I placed the candlestick on a low table and seated myself in front of the fireplace, but Austin crossed to the window where he squeezed himself into the corner, pulling the curtains but holding back a corner so that he could peer out. I picked up a book and tried to read since he seemed not to be in the mood for conversation. Austin took out and looked at his watch several times in the three or four minutes that passed.

What would happen to the manuscript now? I wondered. Although I would take the credit for having found it, it would not necessarily be to me that its publication would be entrusted. Dr Locard would presumably be the person who decided its fate. Could I bear to think of it being put into the hands of an ignorant blunderer, or, worse, of someone determined to discredit its importance? Of Scuttard, even! From my rapid perusal of it, I could see that it was highly susceptible to misinterpretation.

And then it was that perhaps the most shameful moment of my life occurred. It came to me that since I had put the manuscript back where it had lain for two centuries, nobody need know that I had found it. Or, rather, that I had found it there. It would be the simplest thing in the world to claim to have found it among Pepperdine's papers in my own college library. There was no reason why he should not have purchased it from the Library of the Dean and Chapter of Thurchester Cathedral. In that case the manuscript's fate would lie entirely and exclusively in my own hands. But what was I thinking? I had a momentary, insane vision of myself smuggling the manuscript out of the Library. Unthinkable. Quite unimaginable. That would be to sink lower even than Scuttard. And besides, since Dr Locard would know that I had hoped to find it there he would realize immediately what I had done.

Suddenly Austin exclaimed: 'We must go!'

To my astonishment he hurried from the room and down the stairs and quickly threw on his coat and stood waiting impatiently for me at the door while I cautiously descended the ill-lit stairs.

So we retraced our steps and a couple of minutes later arrived back at the New Deanery. Since I was later required to describe everything in detail and there were crucial conflicts of evidence, I will now recount precisely what I saw and heard—although it was only by reflecting later on what had occurred that I was able to understand it.

We passed through the back-gate into the back-yard and

knocked on the door. It was opened instantly and standing there was the figure I had seen the previous day.

'I am delighted to see you, Dr Courtine,' the old gentleman said with a smile and nodded familiarly at Austin. He shook our hands and invited us in. I noticed that Austin was trembling. The house was cold but it seemed to me that that could not account for it.

As I entered I said: 'I'm very excited to think that this was William Burgoyne's house.'

'And Freeth's,' our host said. 'Don't forget Freeth, who is a much better known figure in our history.'

'But remembered more for the manner of his death than anything he did during his life,' I riposted and he nodded vigorously. 'For the things he did were shabby and mean-spirited, whereas Burgoyne was a much more admirable figure: a scholar of brilliance cut down in his prime.'

As I was speaking, we passed through a big old kitchen with sculleries and pantries leading off it, and then into a dark passageway. 'Shabby and mean-spirited indeed,' our host agreed, turning towards us as we came to another door. 'Take off your hats and coats,' he said. While we were hanging them up on a row of pegs, he added: 'We will have tea in the houseplace. It's much cosier than the dining-room.' Then he led us through another door and we found ourselves in the big main room which, in the old style, had a door straight onto the street. It was a true 'houseplace'—a cross between a dining-room and a kitchen with a big range along one side on one of whose hobs a kettle was boiling. A vast dresser took up almost the full length of one wall and there was a handsome old clock by the street-door and a huge oaken table in the middle of the room with four or five chairs round it.

'I have a housekeeper but she is not here during the afternoon so we will have to manage for ourselves,' Mr Stonex said as we entered.

In the light of what Quitregard had told me, I was astonished to see that the room was in great disorder. Scattered about on the floor were a coal-scuttle, tongs, a poker, two ewers, a bucket and a number of empty preserve-jars. The drawers of the dresser were pulled open and their contents—cutlery, napkins, place-mats, and so on—were spilling out. On the dresser everything was in disarray—cups, plates, saucers, dishes lying higgledy-piggledy. A cupboard door was half-open and I could see that everything inside it was similarly topsy-turvy. Most striking of all was a big old sideboard against the wall which was heaped up with deed-boxes, bundles of letters tied up with red ribbon, papers, legal deeds, receipts, etc. These were piled up and spilling across its surface in such profusion that some of them had fallen onto the floor. Rather incongruously, in among the confusion was a child's slate with something written on it and some pieces of chalk lying beside it. In the midst of this disorder, the oaken table in the centre of the big room was an island of order with a fine damask tablecloth upon it on which were three places neatly laid for tea with plates containing bread and butter and two large cakes—one of fruit and the other chocolate—as well as some smaller ones.

I wondered where our host's dinner was and then I saw dirty dishes piled up in a crowded corner of the sideboard. According to what Quitregard had told me, the old gentleman's servant-woman, Mrs Bubbosh, must have left at noon and would not return until six. I supposed she had prepared this repast.

Seeing me looking round the room in obvious and highly discourteous surprise, Mr Stonex said: 'I've been looking for something. A document. I wanted to show it to you.' Then he turned to Austin and said: 'I haven't succeeded in finding it.'

'You haven't found it?' Austin repeated.

The old gentleman smiled. 'It's most frustrating. However, pray be seated.'

'But you must find it!' Austin exclaimed.

'I very much hope to do so.'

We established ourselves around the table and I said: 'Might I ask what it is?'

'I intend to tell you,' he said and I saw Austin glance at him in surprise. 'It's an account of Freeth's death which was written about fifty years after the event,' Mr Stonex said. 'There was an old serving-man in the house who had been here at the time as a kitchen-boy. When my grandfather was a young man he was interested in the story and took the account down verbatim from the old fellow's lips shortly before he died.'

'I would be fascinated to see it, but you really shouldn't have gone to so much trouble,' I said, looking round at the confusion he had created.

'I didn't imagine I would need to turn the house upside down for I thought it would be with all my legal documents,' he said, addressing Austin rather than me. 'But it turned out not to be.'

'Then where do you think it might be?' Austin demanded. I was surprised at the intensity of his response for I had not thought he cared so much for the story of Freeth.

The old man half-turned to indicate the boxes and papers piled up on the sideboard. 'Assuredly among those. I've brought all the boxes of documents in the house here and will look through them while we take our tea. Speaking of which, please help yourselves. I dined very recently, so I will take nothing myself.'

I acted on his invitation and began on the bread and butter. Austin seemed not to be hungry for he took nothing.

Our host crossed the room, lifted the kettle and made tea in a large pot beside the range, continuing to talk to us over his shoulder: 'I can remember most of the story even without the written account, for my brother and I made a game of it.' He paused and then said quickly: 'And my sister, too, of course.' He turned and addressed me: 'You know that I grew up in this house?'

'It must have been a wonderful place for a child,' I said.

'There are so many passages and dark corners where we could

hide that we used to play elaborate games of hide and seek that lasted for hours. And how we plagued our elders by secreting ourselves and spying on them or leaping out at them when they least expected it.' He laughed. 'We loved dressing up—swords, cloaks, beards. I was wonderful at it. And then we re-enacted famous moments from history: the execution of Mary Queen of Scots, the burning of Joan of Arc. And one of our favourites—bloodthirsty young savages that we were—was the death of Dean Freeth.'

I smiled. 'How did you do that?'

As he placed the tea-pot on the table he said: 'Our text was the story handed down from the kitchen-boy and we took on the different roles. I always liked to play the officer in command of the garrison. He is the real hero of the affair.'

If I had been surprised by the condition of the room I was even more astonished by the affability of our host. The old gentleman was showing himself to be even more utterly unlike Quitregard's description of him than he had at my first encounter. It must be, I speculated, that he was much more affable with strangers than with his fellow-townsmen. And yet that could not be true since he was so familiar towards Austin who had lived there for so long—though perhaps he regarded him as an incomer to the town after a mere twenty years. And it was hard for me to judge how well the two knew each other for Austin appeared to be awed by and even frightened of the old gentleman.

'Is he the hero?' I asked. 'Surely he played a repugnant part in the Dean's death?'

'He acted boldly and decisively as one needs to in a situation of crisis,' our host replied. Then he cried: 'But we'll play the game again now and see for ourselves!'

'What do you mean?' Austin asked.

'We'll enact it.' He turned to me: 'You're a historian. You can put flesh on the dry bones of the past.'

'Historians are not required to have any imagination,' I objected. 'In fact, it's a positive handicap.'

'I think you have quite enough imagination to handicap a whole college of historians,' Austin said rather bitterly.

'Then you are well qualified to play the game,' our host broke in.

He stopped in the middle of the room: 'Imagine that it is the morning of September the tenth in the Year of Our Lord 1643,' he began theatrically. 'Dean Freeth is in his study next door. The kitchen-boy is cleaning pots in this very room. There are two Parliamentarian soldiers in the kitchen, for the Dean has been put under virtual arrest in his own house. It is half-past ten and the Dean has less than an hour to live. He does not know it, but his death has been decided upon.'

'Good heavens!' I exclaimed. 'Then you believe it was not an accident?' I remembered that at our meeting the day before he had referred to the Dean's 'execution'.

'I am convinced of it,' our host said, pouring out the tea for each of us and handing it round. 'But judge for yourself. I need you to imagine the situation. Just three weeks ago a Parliamentarian army reached the city and began a siege. There was panic and terror. Many of the more well-to-do citizens managed to flee—among them the wife and nine children of Dean Freeth. They were sent by him with some of the servants to a place of safety—a handsome manor-house a few miles from Thurchester.'

'That he had stolen from the college!'

'Ah, you know about that! Then you know what a greedy scoundrel he was.' Still standing at our table, he added: 'Please help yourselves to the cakes.'

I thanked him and began to cut slices of the chocolate cake for Austin and myself. The old gentleman went on: 'The majority of the townsfolk, lacking servants to stay behind and protect their possessions, have had to stay with their property—unless they have already lost it, for in the course of the Siege many of the houses were damaged or destroyed. The Cathedral itself was bombarded and some of the buildings of the Close set on fire. Six days ago, the military Governor capitulated on condition that the defenders be allowed to escape and that the town not be sacked.'

He crossed to the sideboard where the sugar-bowl and cream-jug were standing. I noticed that he put them down and was absent-mindedly rubbing out the writing on the slate with a dish-clout. Then he returned to the table and set down the bowl and jug so that Austin and I could help ourselves. He walked over to the table strewn with documents and began sorting through them, half-turned towards us, all the time talking without a pause: 'The Royalists did escape but the Parliamentarians went back on their word and looted and burned many buildings in the town. On the sixth the besieging army moved on, leaving a young officer in command of a small garrison. I am he.' As he spoke he straightened his back, his face took on an expression of youthful resolution and before my eyes he suddenly became a twenty-five-year-old officer brooding over his next move. 'I am in desperate straits. How can a mere handful of men hold down six thousand angry and reckless people? Only by goodwill or, if that fails, by intimidation. Goodwill has been lost beyond recall. Now the situation is becoming even graver. Three days ago—on the seventh—a rumour reached the town: a Royalist army was approaching. The townspeople were enraptured. Salvation was at hand! A mob congregated in the market-square and I had to disperse it by ordering my soldiers to fire over their heads. The temper of the people has become worse.'

As I listened I took one of the little cakes, noticing that Austin had not touched any of the food.

'The next day the Dean, a notorious supporter of the King's party, delivered a sermon in the Cathedral inciting the townspeople to insurrection and there was a riot in front of the Cathedral so that once again I had to order my troops to fire. This time a woman was injured by a stray shot that went too low. The situation was now extremely dangerous and because I was worried that the Dean might become a figurehead for a rising, I took the decision to put him under arrest in his own house and billet two troopers here to guard him. On the ninth I come here to tell him so.'

'But the man was an ecclesiastic,' I said. 'Some respect was owed to the cloth, even though he was an avaricious and dishonest schemer.'

The old gentleman snapped out of character and said to me sternly: 'You *are* Freeth.'

'I beg your pardon. What do you mean?'

'That's your role. So don't talk about him. And certainly not in those terms. Speak up and defend yourself.' Suddenly he became the young officer again: '*Mr Dean, you do not leave this house without my permission.*'

'*I am a reverend of the Church,*' I said with considerable self-consciousness. '*You owe me some respect.*' With a sense of my own brilliance, I added: '*Young sir.*'

'*You are a fool, sir,*' my host said sternly and I found myself blushing. '*And an unprincipled one for you are dabbling in politics for your own ends and risking the lives of many.*'

'*Nonsense,*' I said rather feebly.

The old gentleman briefly reappeared and frowned as if to hint that I must do better than that. Then he instantly vanished again: '*You are a traitor, sir. You hope that if you can help to recapture the town for the King, you will be rewarded with a bishopric. You do nothing except from self-interested motives.*' As he finished speaking he turned away and began scrutinizing a document from among those on the sideboard.

'*Have you any evidence for that assertion?*' I demanded indignantly, feeling myself strangely moved to defend the man.

'*The record of your previous conduct,*' he answered as he threw the document to one side. '*You are a greedy, ambitious man of modest capacity who has advanced by fawning upon those in power while lording it* over those under you. You plundered the Foundation and misappropriated the college's endowments.'

'I deny it. I took the property into my own possession to save it from being confiscated by your Parliamentarian friends.'

'Pshaw! If you really believe that, it only shows how easy you find it to justify to yourself your worst acts, and that's proof of your profound dishonesty. Are you saying you have never had a shameful, ambitious, self-aggrandizing thought? That you never wanted to steal something that was not your own?' He gazed at me with extreme intensity and I was unsure if he was acting or really accusing me. Could he read my mind? At the memory of the temptation I had grappled with earlier that afternoon I felt my colour rise.

'I . . . No.'

'You claim the privilege of your cloth and yet you conspired to murder William Burgoyne in order to remove a rival for the deanship. For that alone, I could have you tried and hanged and nobody in the town would shed a tear for you.'

'I did not plot his death.'

'Are you saying you did not long for his destruction?'

'Yes, I hated him. I hated him because with all his unfair advantages, he was going to become Dean instead of me. And I hated him because he was cleverer than I!' I started. What had made me say that?

'If you insist on killing all those who are cleverer than you, you will be fully employed.'

Before I could defend myself, my host, still speaking as the young officer, said: 'It turns out, however, that I have miscalculated. The townspeople are incensed by this treatment of the man whom they have adopted as their figurehead, however much they despise him personally. And so later the same day an angry mob comes to the Close to try to rescue him. Again I have to order my men to fire and this time several people are injured. I realize that the townspeople will organize another and larger attack, and that my men will be overwhelmed. Now, sir, I ask you, what can I do?'

'I admit that you are in a difficult dilemma. What did you do?'

'What I need to do is to find a way of removing the Dean, but to do it in a way that discredits him in the eyes of his fellow-citizens. I know that he is scorned by them for his greed and venality, and suspected of something even worse in the Burgoyne affair. I need to remind them of that. In some way I have to separate the public Freeth, who is a symbol of opposition, from the private man who is despised. He has to be publicly exposed to shame for the things he is known to have a weakness for. I know that Hollingrake, the Treasurer, is resentful towards him because of some history of past collaboration which has soured. A former ally—like a former lover—is always the most bitter and therefore the readiest for revenge. I have him brought to me privily. *Mr Treasurer,*' he suddenly said to Austin who started. '*You do perceive how Freeth's actions are endangering the whole Foundation? In his lust for office and wealth he is likely to bring down the wrath of Parliament upon the heads of all of you.*'

Rather to my relief, Austin merely gazed back open-mouthed at the old gentleman. I was acquitting myself better than he. 'Oh surely,' I protested. 'You're not suggesting that Hollingrake was implicated?'

He kept his gaze on Austin: '*The Cathedral and all its charitable works are being recklessly staked by this gamester, this man without scruple who has robbed his own family.*'

Austin stared back at our host with naked terror in his face and I began to wonder if he was, after all, performing better than me. And what was the meaning of the reference to Freeth robbing his own family? I knew nothing of that.

'*I ask you to help me deal with this man.*'

'You're suggesting there was a plot?' I exclaimed.

Our elderly host turned his cold, youthful gaze on me: '*The situation justifies it. This is a town in the middle of a civil war with the danger of the death of many people if I lose command of public order. And the loss of the town for the Parliamentary cause. In such circumstances it is permissible to take a single life.'*

I shuddered at how cold-bloodedly he uttered these chilling words.

'But that principle, once conceded, could be extended indefinitely,' I protested. 'There are always ways of justifying the death of an individual for the sake of the many.'

'And sometimes that is right,' the old man said calmly.

I was astonished by this remark. He seemed to realize what effect his statement had had upon me.

'Leading safe, comfortable lives at the end of the nineteenth century it is probably hard to imagine having to act as decisively as that,' he said. 'If you had been in the situation in which the young officer found himself, Dr Courtine, would you have let events take their course and lost the town for your own side? Or would you have rolled the dice and risked everything?'

'I don't know.'

'To dare all like that, that is the incomparably great adventure of life. That is how one knows one *is* alive. Otherwise one is dead without being buried.'

As he spoke those words he kept his gaze fixed on Austin who now nodded slowly.

'Did Hollingrake realize what he was being invited to participate in?' I asked.

The old gentleman turned and stared at me in delight as if I had invented a new twist to the game. Then he swung round to address my friend: 'What do you say, Fickling? You're playing him so you should understand him better than Courtine and I. Did you know that what you were getting involved in would result in a man being butchered?'

Austin replied in a leaden voice: 'Yes, I did know. Though I somehow made myself not know it.'

'Then play the part you've undertaken, man!' The old man

growled. Then in an instant he became the young officer again and said contemptuously: 'Just do what I tell you and you need have nothing to do with the deed itself.'

Austin stared at him like a rabbit before a snake.

'One way or another,' the young officer continued, 'his account must be closed.'

'His account must be closed,' I repeated, and glanced at Austin who was still gazing at his tormentor. 'That is a curious phrase.'

Slowly Austin nodded his head.

'What is the plot?' I demanded. They both turned to look at me.

'Oh no,' the old gentleman cried. 'You're to be kept in the dark for the moment. But I promise you, you're going to find out very soon!'

At that moment the big grandfather clock in the corner of the room made a noise as if it were clearing its throat and then ponderously struck the first quarter.

Our host looked at Austin.

'Can that be right?' Austin exclaimed and pulled out his watch.

'No, that clock is fast,' Mr Stonex said. 'I don't know why, for all the other clocks in the house keep time well.'

Austin turned to me: 'What time do you believe it is?'

I took out my timepiece: 'A minute or two before five.'

'That's what my watch says.' He turned to the old gentleman. 'I'm anxious not to miss the whole of Evensong. Courtine has not heard the organ and this will be his last chance since it's to be out of commission from tonight.'

'Then you may leave at half-past five and still catch the end of it,' our host said. Then he raised a hand and lowered his voice. 'It's now half-past ten on the fatal morning. I'm the kitchen-boy.' At those words he seemed to shrink, to become even younger than the officer he had just been playing, and into his eyes came a look of frightened simplicity. He suddenly hammered on the table so that the crockery jumped. 'Without warning there is a thundering at the street-door.' As the servant-boy, he started at the noise and then made his way timidly towards the door.

As he reached it he straightened his back and was the officer again. I was becoming more interested in the narrator than in the story he was telling for I could not reconcile this flamboyant, expansive individual with the lonely miser Quitregard had described.

'Boy, where are my soldiers?'

He cringed and stammered: 'In the kitchen, please your Honour.'

'Summon them.'

As the boy he scuttled to the other door. Then he turned and seemed to grow larger and fatter, and shuffled into the room with a slightly hang-dog air, wiping his mouth with one hand and then tugging at his forelock. 'At your pleasure, sir.' In some extraordinary way he conjured up a companion, smaller than himself but just as drunk.

The officer barked: 'Where is the third man?'

The soldier turned to his invisible companion, shrugged, and then said: 'He is posted at the back-gate, your Worship, as your Worship ordered.'

'Very well. Now listen carefully, men. A Royalist army is approaching and is about to attack our positions.'

'That is an invention?' I asked.

'A complete fabrication,' he threw over his shoulder. 'But such an army has been created by rumour and is therefore likely to be believed.' Then he went on: 'We have no hope of holding the town and will withdraw immediately to a village a few miles away which controls the only nearby bridge across the river. If we can hold it, then Parliament has a good chance of taking Thurchester back. The village is called Compton Monachorum.' The old gentleman paused and turned to gaze at me significantly.

'Where the Dean's manor-house was!' I cried.

He did not acknowledge my remark but an expression of slow-witted concentration spread over his features. '*What are we to do about his Worship the Dean, sir?*'

'*We are taking him with us as a bargaining counter.*'

I turned to him: 'Is what you are describing derived from the manuscript you have been looking for?'

'Yes. Except that that gives only an account of what the kitchen-boy saw. A witness does not always understand what he is seeing and in this case he most certainly did not.'

'I beg your pardon,' I interrupted. 'I don't take your point at all. The whole of our system of justice is based on the assumption that witnesses can fairly report what they have seen.'

'I don't dispute that,' the old gentleman replied tartly. 'What I do insist is that they frequently misinterpret it. I have used my intelligence and my knowledge of what came later to work out what really happened. Watch and judge. While the three soldiers stayed in this room, the boy slipped out to find his master.'

With long silent strides he stalked to the door, glancing fearfully over his shoulder at us once or twice. Then he straightened and said to me: 'Outside the study he finds you in a state of blue funk. You have overheard everything—as you were intended to—and you understand that your life and that of your wife and children hang by a thread. But how can you escape and take them to a safe place? To reach the back-door you must pass through this room which is full of soldiers. And even if you could get to the back-door, there is the guard at the gate into the Close.'

He pulled open the door and we went into the hall.

'At that moment there is a tapping at the window. You open it.'

I hesitated and he repeated the cue: 'You open it.'

I mimed opening the casements of the window, noticing that they were actually nailed down. I remembered what Quitregard had said about the elaborate precautions the old gentleman had taken against being burgled.

'There is Hollingrake on the other side of the window,' our host said briskly, nodding at Austin to bring him into the action. 'He is wearing a tall hat and a bright red surcoat with a high collar. You are filled with joy at the sight of him. Instantly, all your distrust of him is laid aside. How quickly we forget the wrongs we have inflicted on others when we need their aid! You beg him for help in escaping and Hollingrake tells you he has come for that very reason.' He paused and waited for Austin to speak. My friend, however, stood glowering back at him. Unabashed, the old gentleman went on: 'Hollingrake climbs in through the window and tells you something you are very pleased to hear.' He paused but Austin failed to respond to his cue.

'He tells you he has a project for your escape. He points out that the guard at the back-gate has just allowed him to pass and will not think to stop him as he leaves. You see immediately what the Treasurer means so Hollingrake gives you his very distinctive hat and coat, and he and the boy help you to clamber out through the window. The last thing that crosses your mind is to wonder what are the heavy objects in the pockets of the coat. The boy watches you hurrying out of the back-gate past the unsuspecting soldier. Less than half a minute later he sees me—the officer—and the soldiers hurry out of the house and run after you. We were waiting for you!'

'And I have fallen into the trap!' I said grimly.

'About two minutes after that the boy hears gun-shots. He runs into the Close and finds you lying on the ground surrounded by soldiers at the door into the Cloisters. A number of townspeople are standing nearby looking on in horror. I am searching the pockets of your greatcoat and—shame and dismay!—I pull out a number of large jewels and small pieces of the Cathedral's gold plate. I can't believe my eyes. I show them to the townspeople and they recognize them and are horrified. You're lying there unable to speak but witnessing your disgrace as you bleed to death.'

'Poor Freeth,' I found myself saying. Whatever he had or had not done in his life, this ignominious and unjust death deserved sympathy. To lie there with his life's blood pouring from him and know that he would be remembered as nothing but a cowardly thief.

The old gentleman smiled. 'Even the kitchen-boy who was the chief witness did not understand what really happened.'

'But there are other accounts which differ from that one,' I protested and told him of the antiquarian's letter. 'Pepperdine's eyewitness claimed that Freeth saw soldiers pillaging the Library and rushed across to stop them. So he died like a valiant scholar defending his books.'

My host uttered a high-pitched laugh of derision. 'Stuff and nonsense! Why, you cannot even see the Library from this house.'

'Are you sure?'

'Come, I will show you. The dining-room has the best view of the Close, so if you cannot see it from there you can be certain you cannot see it from any other room.'

As he set off down the passage, Austin almost shouted: 'What are you doing? You can't go in there! You can't mean the dining-room!'

Mr Stonex looked at him with unruffled calm. 'Indeed I most certainly do mean that room.'

'You must mean the study,' Austin protested.

'I most assuredly do not.' He smiled at me. 'That looks out onto the street.'

'That was the Dean's study?' I asked, indicating a door behind us. He nodded.

'Could I see it? I wish to put to the test your hypothesis that the Dean heard the officer saying he had orders to capture and very probably to kill him.'

'Very willingly,' he said and reached into one of his pockets. 'That room is always kept locked.' An expression of dismay appeared on his features. 'Unfortunately I find I don't have my keys to hand. I could, however, go upstairs and fetch them if it would give you pleasure.'

'I wouldn't dream of permitting you to go to so much trouble,' I said, somewhat surprised, for I recalled young Quitregard saying he carried his keys on a chain at all times.

With a careless shrug as if it were a matter of complete indifference to him, he turned and led us along the passage and down a couple of stairs. Then he opened a door and ushered us into the dining-room. It was large but low and dark with only a dim source of light at the opposite extremity. The walls were lined with oak panelling and a long table occupied the centre for almost its full length. Standing at the end of the table closest to the window was a single candle in a stick, still burning but almost extinguished. I looked out of the window and found that the Cathedral was directly in front of us, vast and blocking out almost everything.

Far along the length of the Cathedral in the thick twilight, I could just make out part of the Library which was visible beyond the point where the Chapter House projected.

'The door into the Library is too far to the left to be seen. The Chapter House hides it,' said the old gentleman at my shoulder.

I had to admit that he was right. I looked round the Close and noticed that I could just see one of Austin's upper windows. It must be the sitting-room, I realized.

At that moment the candle on the table guttered and went out.

Our host lit the gas in a wall-bracket and as the light flared up, a portrait nearby caught my gaze. Seeing me looking at it, he said: 'That is my father as a young man.'

The figure was a youth wearing costume dating from the turn of the century. The face was delicate, even feminine, conveying a sense of the sitter's love of pleasure and at the same time, with the lips drawn back slightly from the teeth like a snarling animal, his defiance of anyone who stood in his way. I believed at that moment that I saw, despite the difference in age, a resemblance to the face of my host.

'He was a handsome man,' I said.

'He certainly broke many a young lady's heart,' the old gentleman said with a laugh. 'He had a very wild youth and got himself into many scrapes. He fought several duels with outraged brothers and sweethearts and he very nearly reduced his inheritance to nothing. But he reformed just in time and made a good marriage and settled down to life in his father's bank. Unfortunately he died young—the penalty he paid for his earlier dissipation.'

'Do you remember him?'

He nodded. 'I was very young when he died but I have many memories of him. He was always full of merriment. While he was alive this house was filled with bustling servants and music, and there were guests in beautiful dresses, lights, parties, cards and dinners. Handsome carriages came and went all day and until late at night.'

He shook his head and I wondered how his life, which had started with so much conviviality and warmth, had shrunk to this—one solitary old man in a big empty house with nothing but memories and stories of the distant past. I suddenly felt very cold.

Our host led us back to the houseplace where he urged us to be seated again. I said good-humouredly: 'My sole objection has been removed and I have to concede that your version of the Dean's murder is very plausible.'

'I don't know why you use that word,' the old gentleman said. 'Freeth was not murdered—he was executed. His death was necessary in order to prevent a greater loss of life.'

'It can never be right to assess a man's life so pragmatically,' I protested, looking at Austin for support. He merely shook his head as if declining to express a view.

'That is a religious position which deals in moral absolutes,' the old man replied with complete dispassion. 'I take the humanistic view that there is always a calculus of human interests in which the benefit of many may be purchased at the expense of the few.'

'I call myself a humanist,' I said indignantly. 'But I reject absolutely that point of view. Human life is sacred.'

'Sacred?' the old gentleman sneered. 'You can use that word and claim to be a humanist?'

Before I could find a way to answer that, Austin spoke: 'Courtine is right. Murder is the ultimate evil and its perpetrator cannot hope to escape eternal damnation.'

Mr Stonex swung round and directed at him a strange look which I could not interpret. At that moment the clock by the door started striking the final quarter.

'It must be half-past five,' Austin said. 'We must not miss the end of Evensong. Look at your watch, Courtine.'

Rather puzzled by his request, I did so. 'Yes, you're right.'

'Why is that the only clock that keeps time badly?' Austin said suddenly to the old gentleman. 'Is something interfering with its action?'

'Interfering?'

'Hampering the weights?'

Our host smiled, crossed the room and quickly opened its case. With his back to us he reached into it and said: 'No, there's nothing here.'

As he turned back I thought he slipped something into his pocket and I assumed it was the key to the case though I had not noticed him unlock it.

'Thank you, Fickling,' he said. 'That was a very good thought.'

At that moment all possibility of further argument about the time was ended by the booming of the Cathedral clock. Whatever the time might be by my metropolitan timepiece, it was half-past five in Thurchester.

'We should go now,' Austin said firmly. 'Or we will miss the service entirely.'

Though it seemed a little discourteous to depart so abruptly, I re-called that our host had to return to his place of work at six and would probably not be sorry to see us leave. We rose and went through the kitchen to the back-door where we made our adieus. Just as I was shaking my host's hand, there was a knocking at the street-door. The old gentleman said: 'He is very punctual.' Seeing my quizzical expression, he explained: 'That is the waiter from the inn across the way. He is bringing me a pint of ale.'

I was surprised for Quitregard had not mentioned that as part of the old banker's routine. We expressed our gratitude for his hospi-tality for the last time and left the house. We had been inside it for just a few minutes more than three-quarters of an hour.

Thursday Evening

✣

W E HURRIED round to the Cathedral and found that Evensong was just ending as we entered, so instead of taking seats we stood at the back and listened to the organ playing the end of a Bach Toccata and Fugue. The smell was much more noticeable even than it had been the day before and although the interior of the Cathedral was very cold, the odour seemed warm in my nostrils. I was very relieved that we were not staying long.

The celebrant, the servers and the choir filed from the chancel and the small congregation left. While we were talking together in low voices a minute or two later a man suddenly appeared beside us. He must have come, silently and unnoticed, from the direction of the east end.

'This is Slattery,' Austin said. 'Martin Slattery.'

He was tall, about fifteen years our junior, with a very striking face—handsome, spoilt and demanding. His straight black hair was sleeked down like the sheen of an animal's pelt and altogether he seemed to me like some sort of wild beast. A very vulgar expression which I had heard applied to a hunting-dog came to me: that he had a face that was always 'on the twitch' for something. His staring blue eyes seemed to be searching my face for anything that might be of use or pose a threat. I could sense how very charming he could be, but there was something about him which made me believe him capable of anything. Of course, I had had good reason to mistrust a friend of Austin's.

Slattery was a big man and yet the hand that he now thrust carelessly towards me was oddly delicate. His grip was firm and I was relieved when he relinquished my hand quickly.

'I'm sorry I only heard a minute or two of your playing,' I said.

'I played abominably,' he replied with a charming smile. 'You missed nothing.'

His face seemed familiar. I had seen it very recently but I could not recall where.

'I'm sure that isn't true,' I muttered without reflection.

'I give you my word I played worse than I've ever played in this Cathedral. I could do nothing with my hands. They seemed to have a will of their own.' He held them out in front of him as if lining them up for indictment, looking at them with a suggestion of ironic respect which I found strangely disturbing. 'A damnable leave-taking to the organ.'

'I'm sure you'll play it many times when it is back in commission,' I said.

'I doubt that.' As he said those words he smiled at Austin who had been staring at him since his arrival but who now lowered his gaze. At that moment, I saw the old verger, Gazzard, standing a few yards away and looking towards us. He glanced at me disapprovingly and when I nodded, he turned away.

'Shall we go to a public-house?' Austin asked.

We agreed and followed him out of the Cathedral. Austin and I walked ahead and it was only as we left the Close that I glanced back at our companion and saw that he walked with a kind of swaggering limp. At that moment I realized that he was the halting figure I had seen in the Close last night. That must be why I felt I had seen him before, though there was still some memory which remained unnudged. If it was he whom I had seen going into the alley it must have been he whom I saw in the organ-loft. But in that case, how had he got down from there and out into the Close without my noticing him? There must be another staircase. I slowed down to let Slattery catch up and then let him and Austin walk on ahead.

Although I felt relieved that there was a rational explanation for what I had almost accepted as a supernatural experience, I was discomfited by my memory of the feeling of evil that had emanated from the figure. And what had he been doing there at that hour? Though it occurred to me that the organ-loft was at least the obvious place for the organist to be. I wondered if he had recognized me from our encounter and thought not for he had given no sign of it.

Austin and his friend were talking softly as they walked a few paces ahead of me, their heads close together. At one moment Slattery gripped Austin's arm and held it for a few moments. In a minute or two we were inside a tavern—the Angel Inn in Chancery Street.

Austin went up to the bar while Slattery and I seated ourselves in a snug giving a view onto the street.

'Do you enjoy teaching, Mr Slattery?' I asked, casting about for a topic of common interest. 'Fickling tells me you teach music at the Choir School and have private pupils in the town.'

'Enjoy it? I regard it as a prison sentence. I only do it because I pursued my passion for music when I was young and since my drunken brute of a father not only failed to provide me with the means of earning a living in any other way but crippled me during one of his drunken rages, I was sentenced to take it up professionally. And that has almost killed my interest in it.'

Without revealing my astonishment at this remark, I persevered: 'But the singing-boys are gifted musicians, are they not? They must be rewarding pupils.'

'If the choirmaster knew his business that might be the case. But since he has no understanding of music he chooses boys for any-thing but their voices and abilities.' He smiled dazzlingly and added: 'And bit by bit I find myself adapting to the mediocrity that is all one can expect in a devilish hole of a town like this.'

At that moment, Austin returned, carrying the drinks. He glanced at his friend—uneasily, I thought—as he caught his last words.

'Have you lived here long?' I asked.

'About eight or nine years. I first came because I have kin . . .' He broke off and glanced at Austin before saying: 'I should say, I had kin living here. Only my damnable sloth has kept me here. I'm like a whelk that crawls into the corner of a rock-pool and stays there not because of any affinity with its surroundings but because it's too bone-idle to move.'

'Are whelks bone-idle?' I wondered, smiling at the image.

'Do they have bones?' he parried, and drank from his glass with a grin.

'There are worse places to live than an English cathedral town,' I ventured.

'And better. Places with laughter, music and sunlight in the streets.'

'You are speaking of Italy?'

He nodded.

'Do you know it well?' I asked.

'Not as well as I hope to. I spent the happiest year of my life there. For one thing, the most interesting English people live there. All those, for example, who don't fit into the neat pigeon-holes that Protestantism imposes upon us—couples which consist of a man who is legally married to a woman. That's where I met Fick-ling.'

'Really? I assumed you met here.'

'No, in fact, we first knew each other in Italy. The connection is the other way round for it was Fickling who helped me to obtain my post at the Cathedral. We were introduced by mutual friends in Florence who knew that we both had a connection with this town. You see, I happened to mention that I had just come from a brief and rather unrewarding visit to my relative here. So, as you may imagine, Italy has many happy memories for me. They have such a love of music, the Italians. And such understanding of it. Whereas here I play worse with every day that passes since I play for nobody who is capable of judging well. And because, badly as I play, I never hear anyone play better. I've come to hate my own playing.'

'Not as much as the congregation,' Austin said.

'Then all sides will be equally delighted that the organ won't be in use for a couple of weeks.' Then he added softly: 'Not that I am likely to play it again, anyway.'

'Will it take as long as that to repair it?' Austin asked.

'Do you know what,' Slattery said, ignoring that question but favouring Austin with a smile that included me in his confidence; 'I've found out from that idiot, Bulmer, the Surveyor, why the workmen caused all that trouble. On Tuesday evening some meddling visitor to the Cathedral suggested to that tiresome old man, Gazzard, that they would do more damage by following their original intentions than if they adopted the course which has turned out to be so disastrous. Gazzard—be damned to him for an interfering old blockhead—passed that piece of advice to Sisterson since it happened that Bulmer was away burying one of his innumerable siblings. So the Sacrist, like the cursed fool he is, ordered the men to change course and so brought all this trouble down upon his foolish head.'

'I suspect the advice was not followed correctly,' I said. 'And to have persevered with the original plan might have had even more unfortunate consequences.'

'It's hard to imagine how even that dunce, Bulmer, could have created a worse situation. Now they're having to prop up parts of the floor and the wall in the transept and the devil alone knows where it will all end. They might bring the whole damned edifice crashing about their silly ears. But what do I care now?'

He laughed and drained a long draught of his ale. I caught Austin's eye and he looked away.

'Do you have one of those charming houses in the Close, Mr Slattery?' I enquired, hoping to pilot the conversation into less controversial waters. 'They are very picturesque.'

'Unfortunately not. Fickling's miserable hovel is a bishop's palace compared with mine. I have rooms in a shabby little street near here.'

Following a train of thought of my own, I said at a venture: 'Your wife must regret that your post does not bring with it one of those pretty old houses beside the Cathedral.'

'My wife?' He smiled in amazement and then raised his head and laughed. 'La dame n'existe pas.'

Austin looked down. Had I misunderstood the conversation I had overheard in the bar? Surely they had spoken of Slattery having a wife?

'I know what it is,' Slattery said, baring his vulpine teeth in a smile. 'You've heard people talking about me. You've picked up some of the venomous gossip that this town lives on. What did they say?'

I rarely make hasty judgements, but I decided that I didn't like Slattery at all. He had an air of having spent much of his time in public-bars that didn't appeal to me. He veered between boastfulness and delusions of persecution and gave the impression that he felt entitled to a comfortable living without the necessity of working for it. I had known not a few undergraduates like him—embittered younger sons or scions of families that had lost their wealth. I was saddened that such a man should be an intimate friend of Austin's.

'Stow it, Martin,' Austin said.

'Who was it? Did that old woman, Locard, say something? Fickling tells me you've become very thick with him.'

The young man was intolerable. 'No, I assure you, Mr Slattery, I haven't discussed you with anyone. Why should I? I hardly knew of your existence until just now.'

'This town is filled with the most poisonous gossips, and you've met at least three of them: Locard, his fawning catamite Quitregard, and that babbling brook, Sisterson.'

'People gossip in every enclosed society, and not all such talk is malign,' I said mildly. 'But one can ignore that. In fact, one can learn to ignore many things. Don't you find that one really needs very little to be content? Books, concerts, a few good friends.'

'No,' he said. 'No, I don't find that at all. Life should be an affair of drama, excitement. Most people spend their lives half asleep leading an existence devoid of passion, never taking risks. They might as well be dead.'

Without quite knowing why, I found myself getting angry. 'I find all the excitement I need in literature, in history, in music.'

He merely looked at me with what I interpreted as a silent sneer.

'Doesn't anyone with imagination find enough interest in the most ordinary things in life?' I went on. 'The safest life—a life of what to others might seem contemptible ordinariness—can be filled with unperceived drama.'

'Is any life safe?' he demanded. 'Surely we are all of us walking along a path in the mist and sometimes a gust of wind sweeps it aside and we see that we are on the knife-edge of a ridge with a fall of hundreds of feet on either side.'

I looked at him in astonishment. Before I could respond Austin said: 'You're saying the same thing, both of you.'

We turned to him in surprise. 'You're saying, Courtine, that there's excitement and drama beneath the surface of everyone's life. That's all that Slattery was pointing out.'

I was about to respond when there was an interruption. A man hurried into the bar and called out to his friends in the opposite corner: 'There's something up across the road at the old feller's place.'

He and two of his companions went and stood at the window beside ours. We looked out and saw that there were about a dozen people gathered around the door of a house on the other side of the street, spilling into the carriageway so that they would have obstructed passing vehicles if there had been any. Among the crowd were two police-officers, one of whom was hammering at the door with his knuckles.

'I wonder what can be happening,' Slattery drawled.

As we watched a man came hurrying up carrying a mallet.

'Stranger and stranger,' Slattery commented. Then he said to Austin: 'Isn't it that queer old bird's place? What's his name?'

Austin shook his head as if he had no idea what his friend was talking about.

'I say,' Slattery said raising his voice and leaning back in his chair towards the men at the other window. 'Whose house is that over the way?'

'That's old Mr Stonex, the banker, sir,' said one of the three men looking out of the other window.

'That's the fellow,' Slattery said to us.

Of course! It was the street-front of the house we had just come from. I had not recognized it since I had seen it only from the rear. I looked at Austin who took a drink from his glass.

'We were there not an hour ago,' I said.

'Were you indeed? Well, I'll be damned. Do you have any idea what it can be about?'

'Not the least in the world.'

There was a sudden loud noise and I saw that one of the officers was attempting to break down the street-door with the mallet under the instructions of the other who, I now noticed, was a sergeant.

'Don't you think we should make ourselves known to the officers?' I asked Austin. 'We might be able to help.'

He shook his head to indicate doubt or the lack of any view. But Slattery said: 'I believe you should. It would look deuced rum to come forward later.'

Leaving our glasses of beer unfinished, we went out into the street and crossed over to where a small crowd was gathered. I pushed my way through the onlookers and approached the Sergeant who was watching the constable's efforts to smash through the door. I explained to the Sergeant that Austin and I had been in the house less than an hour before and he was very interested. I turned to beckon forward my two companions and introduced them. The officer nodded and said: 'I know Mr Fickling, of course. And I had the honour of making your acquaintance last Tuesday night, did I not, Mr Slattery?'

Slattery bowed deeply and gave the officer a charming smile: 'The honour was entirely mine, Sergeant, although the occasion was less happy than could have been desired.'

'It was at Canon Sheldrick's,' the officer explained to me. 'There was an unfortunate incident in which a number of miniatures were stolen.'

'I heard about that,' I remarked to Austin who turned away.

'Have they been recovered, Sergeant,' Slattery asked, 'as a consequence of your impressive professional endeavours?'

The officer looked at him coldly and said: 'As a matter of fact, Mr Slattery, they have not. Though I have a shrewd suspicion as to what happened to them.'

'Shrewdness is what I would expect of you,' Slattery said with his most charming smile.

The conversation was punctuated by the regular crash of the mallet.

'Where is Mr Stonex?' I asked.

'That's the question, sir,' the Sergeant replied.

An old woman who had been standing beside him all the while began to speak: 'I've never knowed nothing like it. The gentleman is so regular in his ways.'

'This is Mrs Bubbosh,' said the Sergeant. 'She comes every day to cook and clean.'

'And I come as usual just now to cook the old gentleman's supper but he didn't answer the door, even though I hammered and hammered until my fist hurt. That ain't never happened before.'

'What time was that?' the Sergeant asked.

'Why, just a few minutes before six, as always. So I wondered if something had come up sudden at the bank and he'd been sent for so I went down there and spoke to Mr Wattam'—nodding at a neatly-dressed man standing beside her—'but he said no.'

'Mr Stonex has never failed to return to the bank at a few minutes after six in my entire experience,' said the man. 'And that goes back nearly thirty years. I'm Mr Wattam, gentlemen, and have the honour to be the managing-clerk at the Thurchester and County Bank.'

The Sergeant and the three of us shook hands all round and Mr Wattam continued: 'I was so alarmed by what this good woman told me that I came back here. We banged on the door for some time and then went round to the back-door but found that it also was locked. Then we sent a boy to the station-house for the officers.'

As we were speaking the crowd was increasing and by now there were about twenty gawping onlookers.

'Now you know as much as I do, sir,' the Sergeant said to me.

At that moment the constable swinging the mallet succeeded in breaking through one of the panels of the door. He kicked it until he had made enough space to permit access. The Sergeant stooped and went in through the gap, giving instructions to his colleague that nobody else should enter until he had returned.

'This is very strange,' I said to my companions. 'He was in perfect health when we took leave of him. Was he not, Austin?'

My friend nodded gravely.

Slattery smiled. 'I dare say he was called away on sudden business. When he gets back and finds his house broken into and a crowd of idle busybodies blocking the road, I venture to suggest that even his legendary good humour will falter.'

'Is he reputed so good-humoured?' I began, when I realized that he was being ironic. And yet the old gentleman had seemed perfectly amiable that afternoon.

At that moment the Sergeant's face—distinctly pale now—emerged rather incongruously at about the height of my waist as he crawled through the broken panel. He got to his feet and dusted his knees. The constable came up to him as if awaiting orders but the Sergeant seemed to be ignoring him as he glanced around at us. Almost by accident, as it seemed, his gaze fell on Mr Wattam. 'Send for a surgeon,' he stammered to him in a low voice. The clerk stood hesitating as if wondering whether to ask a question. 'Quickly, man,' the Sergeant said softly, and Mr Wattam hurried away.

'Is the old gentleman unwell?' I asked.

The Sergeant merely shook his head. He took a deep breath and sat down very abruptly on the doorstep. As if to conceal his superior's incapacity, the constable began to wave the onlookers away from the door. 'Move along, please,' he urged. 'Don't block the carriageway.'

Unwillingly the crowd of mainly men and boys shuffled off and stood on the pavement a few yards away trying to look as if they had quite unrelated reasons for happening to be there. After a moment the Sergeant beckoned the other officer over. They conferred briefly in whispers. I saw the younger man's face slacken and his mouth hang open. Then he knelt down and began to crawl through the smashed panel.

'Dick,' the Sergeant called out softly. 'First thing of all, go and check the back-door is still locked.' The constable nodded and disappeared through the gap.

'Is there just them two doors?' the Sergeant asked Mrs Bubbosh—his grammar deteriorating in his state of shock. She nodded.

Mrs Bubbosh caught my eye and I seemed to see in her face the sudden realization that this was more serious than the rather enjoyable experience which had briefly made her the centre of attention. Austin had put his hands over his face and turned away. I noticed that Slattery had gripped his arm and seemed to be shaking him while he whispered in his ear.

At that moment two young constables came up and one of them shouted out: 'We got your message, Sarge, and come as soon as we could.'

The words faded on his lips as he caught sight of his colleague who rose unsteadily to his feet and beckoned both officers aside.

The crowd—now consisting of about thirty people—was talking loudly, perhaps resenting their exclusion. On the other hand, those of us in the little group nearest the door who felt we had some sort of semi-official status—Mrs Bubbosh, the man who had brought the mallet, Slattery, Austin and myself—stayed silent as we watched the three officers, straining to catch their low-voiced conversation. I was just about to demand that we be told what was happening when the constable who had been addressed as Dick crawled through the door. As he joined his colleagues I heard him say: 'The back-door's locked, Sergeant. And I can't find none of the keys.'

The Sergeant nodded and said to the man who had lent the mallet: 'Smash down the rest of it, for God's sake, will you?'

The man took up the implement and began to swing it against the remaining parts of the door. The frame gave way before the panels eventually splintered.

At that moment a thin young man carrying a black bag hurried up with Mr Wattam and spoke for a moment to the Sergeant. Then the two of them entered the house while the three constables were left to guard the door. The Sergeant reappeared a minute later and sent one of the younger officers to the railway-station to dispatch a telegram.

When he had hurried off the Sergeant took Mrs Bubbosh by the elbow and began to lead her towards the door. As he did so he turned to the rest of us: 'Would you come in too, please, gentlemen.'

'All of us?' I asked.

'If you please. You three gentlemen appear to have been the last visitors to the house.'

'Not this gentleman,' I said, indicating Slattery who had shown no sign of resolving the misunderstanding.

'You weren't in the house with the other gentlemen this afternoon, Mr Slattery?' the Sergeant asked.

'Indeed I was not.'

'Where were you, sir?'

'Let me think. I was playing the piano at choir practice from about half-past four until five o'clock. And then the Cathedral organ for three-quarters of an hour. Rather a large number of people heard me on both occasions.'

'Oh yes, you were playing at the ceremony for the new organ,' the Sergeant said.

'No, that was to have been tomorrow. In fact, it has been postponed. I was playing at Evensong as I do every afternoon at five o'clock.'

'I understand perfectly, sir. Your movements can be fully accounted for, just as was the case last Tuesday evening.'

Slattery bowed with an ironic smile.

'In that case,' the Sergeant went on, 'only Dr Courtine and Mr Fickling will be required to step inside.'

Slattery saluted us with an enigmatic grin as we left him and Mr

Wattam on the pavement with the two constables. Mrs Bubbosh gasped as she entered the disordered houseplace and cried: 'I never seen nothing like it!' To my relief—for I was not sure what I should expect to find—the room looked just as it had when I had last seen it not much more than an hour earlier, but I supposed that she was surprised at the virtual ransacking of the place. I noticed that the Sergeant was watching us closely as we came in and looked round. In a strange recapitulation of the occasion earlier that afternoon, we seated ourselves again around the table, myself taking the place where our host had sat—or rather failed to sit since he had stood through most of the meal—Austin seating himself where he had on that occasion, with his head bowed over his crumb-strewn plate, and Mrs Bubbosh, who had fallen silent, taking what had been my place.

The Sergeant stood in the centre of the room holding his note-book and the stub of pencil. Then he said: 'I am Sergeant Adams. I am afraid I have to ask you some questions.'

'Before you do so, will you please tell us what has occurred, Sergeant?' I asked.

'That's what I have to find out, sir.'

'I mean,' I said, 'is Mr Stonex here?'

'I don't want to say nothing until I've spoken to Dr Carpenter,' he said.

'Then I take it the surgeon is with him now?'

'He is. And while we're waiting, I'd like to put a few queries to you. Now, Mrs Bubbosh, according to what you told me a few minutes ago, the last time you saw Mr Stonex was at twelve noon when he returned from the bank?' She nodded. 'You had been working here all morning and when he got back you left the house?' She nodded. 'And that was according to custom?'

'That's right, sir. Oh, what a dreadful thing this is!'

Sergeant Adams waited a moment or two until she had regained some composure.

'You had been here since he let you in at seven o'clock?'

She nodded.

'And after he left for the bank nobody entered the house?'

'Nobody could have done, sir. Both the doors was locked and I don't have no key. There is only one set and he keeps them with him always. He wears them on a ring on his belt.'

'What about the windows?'

'All on 'em is nailed fast.'

'You're certain there was nobody already concealed in the house?'

'How could there have been? I went over every inch of the blessed place cleaning it.'

'From your questions, Sergeant,' I interrupted, indignant at his refusal to state the situation and increasingly alarmed by my suspicions, 'are we to assume that . . . that something quite dreadful has occurred?'

Before the Sergeant could answer, the young doctor hurried into the room and exchanged a look with him and the Sergeant moved over to join him in the doorway. They whispered together for a few minutes and then the Sergeant came back into the room and said mildly: 'Now, Mrs Bubbosh, would you be good enough to go with the surgeon. I think he'll want to say something to you first.'

With an expression of terror on her face she allowed herself to be escorted to the doorway where the young man took her by the arm. The meaning of what I was seeing could no longer be denied.

'Sergeant,' I cried. 'I demand to be told what has happened. Did the old gentleman have some sort of seizure? Did he fall down the stairs?'

'I understand your feelings, gentlemen,' said the Sergeant. 'But the less I say at this moment the better. Meanwhile, I would like you to tell me exactly what happened this afternoon.'

So Austin and I explained—I doing most of the talking—that

we had arrived by the back-door at twenty to five and left at a minute or two after half-past five.

'That's very useful, very useful indeed,' the Sergeant said, writing in his pocket-book. 'What I need to find out is what happened between then and six o'clock when Mrs Bubbosh arrived at the street-door.'

At that moment, the young constable who had been sent to the station came hurrying in.

'He's on his way, Sarge,' he reported. 'He telegraphed straight back.'

Sergeant Adams frowned and took him aside and they said something in a low voice. Then he indicated that his colleague should seat himself on a chair up against a wall and he continued his questioning of Austin and myself.

'Now, did the old gentleman have any other visitor while you were here, or mention that he was expecting anyone?'

'No, I believe not. In fact, I'm sure that he did not.'

Austin looked up. 'The beer.'

'The beer?' I asked.

'Don't you recall, as we were leaving, that there was a knock at the door?'

'Of course. And the old gentleman told us that would be the waiter with the beer.'

'What waiter might this be?' asked the Sergeant.

'Presumably the one who brings him his dinner,' I said, remembering what Quitregard had told me. Then I added: 'Used to bring him his dinner.'

'What's his name, sir? Did he mention it?'

Austin and I looked at each other. 'I have no idea,' I said, and Austin shook his head to express his own ignorance.

'As to the old gentleman's manner this afternoon, did he seem to you to be nervous or frightened?'

'Not at all,' I said. 'He was very friendly and talkative.'

'Is that so? Friendly and talkative?' He wrote laboriously in his notebook. 'Would you say the same, Mr Fickling?' Austin made no response. 'Are you all right, Mr Fickling?'

'Yes, of course I am,' Austin said quickly.

The Sergeant paused and looked at him: 'I'm afraid I'm going to have to ask you to take a look at the old gentleman.'

'Whatever for?' Austin exclaimed.

'It's quite customary, sir,' the Sergeant said.

'The old woman can identify him better than I can,' Austin said. 'I only met him a few times.'

'Nevertheless, sir, I'd like you to do so. I want everything to be done properly.'

At that moment Mrs Bubbosh was led in by the doctor and gently seated in her chair. She had a handkerchief over her face. The Sergeant said mildly: 'Mrs Bubbosh, can you tell me the name of the waiter who used to bring Mr Stonex his dinner?'

She lowered the handkerchief and looked up in surprise. 'Why ever do you want to know that? It's Perkins. Young Eddy Perkins. Old Tom Perkins's lad.'

Sergeant Adams glanced at his colleague. 'You and Harry go and get him.' The constable quickly rose and left the house.

'Mr Fickling, would you follow Dr Carpenter?'

Austin got up uncertainly. The doctor smiled at him encouragingly and they went out together.

'I must ask you if you wouldn't mind waiting here, sir,' the Sergeant said to me.

'Very well,' I answered.

He got up and went out after the other two, leaving me and Mrs Bubbosh in the houseplace. To my surprise I had to wait more than forty minutes. Mrs Bubbosh and I made desultory conversation at first, but our common topics of interest were soon exhausted. She kept saying over and over again: 'Who would ever have thought it? Who would have thought it?' I was wondering where Austin was and what he and Sergeant Adams could be talking about. The conversation between the officer and Slattery had given me much food for thought and various strange possibilities were passing through my mind.

At last the Sergeant came in and said, 'Would you come with me, sir?'

I followed him into the hall. As he closed the door he took my arm and said gently: 'I should warn you that what you are about to see may upset you.' Then he opened the door of the study and ushered me in.

The doctor was kneeling in the middle of the little room but rose to his feet and stood back as I advanced. The first thing I saw was an axe lying on the floor, of which both the blade and the handle were smeared thickly with blood. The body was lying so that the face was turned away from me. I walked round it, stepping clear of the pools and splashes of blood that covered the floor. I looked at it from the other side and for a moment I believed I was going to faint. I have tried ever since to forget what I saw then, so let me say merely that it was a brutal reminder of the frailty of our mortal envelope.

'Is that the person whom you last saw at half-past five here in this house, sir?' the Sergeant asked.

I nodded, not trusting myself to speak.

'How can you be sure, sir, in view of the fact that . . . ?' He broke off, delicately.

'The clothes,' I managed to say. 'I remember the clothes.'

The Sergeant took me by the arm and led me out into the hall. I thought we were returning to the houseplace but he escorted me down the passage and saying, 'In here, if you please,' ushered me into the dining-room. Then he closed the door and stood beside it.

Finding myself alone with him like this, something suddenly occurred to me which—given the highly wrought state of my nerves—made me laugh. Sergeant Adams looked at me curiously

and invited me to take a seat. I had laughed because it had occurred to me that I might be under suspicion. I had had a vision of
myself being kept in this room for hours while questions were fired
at me by the Sergeant and his constables until I broke down and
confessed.

'Are you all right, sir?'

'Perfectly, Sergeant Adams. Just a little upset.'

'Quite understandable, sir.'

I seated myself at the big old table and, first turning up the gas-
mantle, he placed himself at the opposite end, with his back to the
window.

'Is there anything you would care to tell me now that we are
alone, sir?'

The question seemed to follow from my train of thought so
precisely that I smiled involuntarily. 'Are you inviting me to confess?'

He did not smile. 'I'm inviting you to tell me anything at all that
can cast any light on this sad matter. For example, one thing that
puzzles me, sir, is the time. Are you quite sure of the hour at which
you and Mr Fickling left this house? There hardly seems to have
been long enough for what happened after that? Are you sure you
left as late as half-past five?'

'Yes, absolutely sure. We discussed the time as we were leaving.
Why do you ask?'

'You discussed the time,' he repeated. 'Would you care to explain
that?'

'No, Sergeant, I don't think I would. This is perfectly ridiculous.
I've had a shock and I really don't want to have to answer a lot of
pointless questions.' He gazed at me imperturbably and after a moment I said: 'We simply discussed the accuracy of our watches in relation to the clock in the houseplace which was fast. Mr Fickling
was anxious that we should catch the end of Evensong so that I
should hear Mr Slattery's playing.'

He made a note. 'Now I must ask you if you can tell me anything about the state of the rooms you saw? Is there anything that strikes you now about them?'

'Nothing at all. As far as I can see, they were as they are now.'

'You mean, sir, apart from the fact that the other room has been ransacked?'

'No, Sergeant, I mean exactly what I said—as is always the case. I rather make a point of saying what I mean and meaning what I say. It would greatly expedite proceedings if you would be good enough to bear that in mind.'

To my irritation, he continued to gaze at me with unruffled calm. After a pause he said: 'The rooms were in their present condition when you arrived, sir?'

'Precisely. To be absolutely clear, this room and the house-place—the only rooms I saw—look to me now as they did when I arrived at twenty minutes before five this afternoon.'

'But the disarray in the other room, the drawers pulled open, papers scattered about and so on?'

'I've told you, Sergeant, that was what I found on my arrival.'

'What explanation did Mr Stonex give for this?'

'He accounted for it very reasonably. He told us he had been looking for something.'

'For what?'

'A document.'

'A legal document?' he said quickly.

'No. A manuscript account of the murder of Dean Freeth.'

The Sergeant frowned. 'The murder of who?'

It took some time to explain since the Sergeant had not heard of Freeth's murder and for a moment thought I was referring to a much more recent crime.

'So he said that before you and Mr Fickling arrived, he had opened drawers and spilled their contents onto the floor in the way that you see now?'

'Yes, I think so. Though it looks worse now. No, I can't be sure that it was as much of a mess as it is now.'

He made a long note. Then suddenly he said: 'How long have you been staying with Mr Fickling?'

'Since Tuesday evening.'

'Have you known him long?'

'Mr Fickling has been a friend for more than twenty years.'

'Have you visited him here before?'

'No.' Reluctantly I explained: 'I hadn't seen him for twenty years until last Tuesday.'

'Has he told you anything about any personal difficulties?'

'Mr Fickling has not told me anything about his personal circumstances which could possibly be relevant to this tragic incident.'

The Sergeant continued in the same tone: 'And Slattery?' he asked. 'How long have you known him?'

'I met Mr Slattery for the first time in my life about half an hour before I met you.' It was odd how querulous I was starting to sound. It made me feel as if I were lying. And I was liking the drift of the Sergeant's questions less and less.

'You had never met him or seen him before?'

'Never.' Then I remembered the figure I had seen during the night. 'That is to say . . . No. Never.'

'You seem to be hesitating, sir.'

'No, I've never encountered Mr Slattery before.'

'Has Mr Fickling talked about him?'

'No. That is to say, I don't believe so. He might have mentioned the organist before I realized he was speaking of a friend of his.'

'The organist? Do you mean Mr Slattery?'

'I do.'

'Mr Slattery is the assistant-organist.'

'In that case, I think he has not mentioned him at all. The truth is, I thought Mr Slattery was the organist.'

'An understandable mistake, sir. Mr Slattery has been, in effect, carrying out the organist's duties while the old gentleman who holds that position has been seriously indisposed. But his Cathedral post is not permanent.'

'I see. And now that I consider, I believe Mr Fickling did say something about that. And Mr Slattery himself alluded to it.' I stopped. What an extraordinary situation. I was answering questions from a complete stranger about what had passed between myself and an old friend. And all this was because of what was lying on the floor across the passage. As the memory of what I had just seen returned to me unbidden, I put my head in my hands. 'I can't believe that anybody could have done it. I can't believe there can be such wickedness.'

'It's hard to believe, sir. It's one of the worst cases I've seen.'

'Does he have any relatives? Does anyone care?'

'To be honest, sir, I don't yet know if any of his relatives are still alive.'

'He must have nephews and nieces. He mentioned a brother and a sister.'

'All that will come out in the next few days, I imagine, sir. The estate will be large and that will be certain to bring any relations to light. Now, might I ask how it was that you came to be having tea with Mr Stonex?'

I explained that I had met him at the back-gate of the house when I went to read the inscription supposedly relating to the murder of Canon Burgoyne.

'Another murder,' the Sergeant remarked drily. 'It seems quite to have been the theme of the last few days, sir.'

'Mr Stonex and I talked about that affair and then about the case of Dean Freeth and then he invited me to come to tea in a couple of days.'

Sergeant Adams lowered his notebook and looked at me. 'That

is somewhat surprising, sir, since the old gentleman was very reclu-sive.'

'It was our common interest in the death of Freeth that led him to extend the invitation. He wanted to tell me another version of that incident.'

'So the invitation to tea was made on Wednesday?'

'That is so.'

'Did Mr Slattery know about the invitation for this afternoon?'

'Not as far as I am aware. Why should he? But Mr Fickling might have mentioned to him that we were having tea with Mr Stonex when he arranged to meet him at the end of Evensong.'

The Sergeant wrote at length and at last I asked: 'I hope I may be permitted to leave now?'

'You may, of course, sir. But I would be very grateful if you would attend here for just a few minutes.'

I consented to this with an ill grace. He left the room and I waited. In the event twenty minutes passed before he returned and while I sat in the near-darkness and the silence—for there was no sound from the rest of the house—it came to me with the force of a revelation that *somebody* had done this thing, somebody who was probably still within a few minutes' walk of where I was now. I tried not to think of what I had just seen. The sudden irruption into my life of an act of such brutality made me feel dizzy and as if the room in which I was sitting was not real. Since I was a schoolboy, I had not seen blood shed as a result of violence. The Sergeant's ques-tions about Austin were worrying. He had certainly been behaving strangely during the last few days, but I had no reason to suppose there was any connection between that and this terrible deed. He appeared to be as shocked by it as I was.

The Sergeant returned and sat down again and said: 'Are you ab-solutely certain about the state of the houseplace when you arrived, sir?'

'For the second time, Sergeant, yes I am.'

'Very well, sir. Mr Fickling has confirmed that Mr Stonex was very worried about the time. Did he give any indication of why that was the case?'

'None at all.'

'I hope you won't take it amiss, sir, if I ask you whether anything in Mr Fickling's conduct has been at all strange while you've been his guest?'

'I resent that question, Sergeant. Have you put similar questions to Mr Fickling about myself?'

'I've asked the other gentleman the sort of questions I'm required to, sir.'

'The whole thing is perfectly absurd. I refuse to answer any questions relating to private matters. They cannot possibly have any bearing on this matter.'

'I understand that, sir,' he said with galling equanimity. 'There's just one last point. You mentioned that you met the deceased at the back-gate of this house. That was yesterday afternoon, was it not?'

I nodded.

'The invitation was for which day?'

'Which day?'

'When I asked you about that half an hour ago, sir, you said that the old gentleman invited you to come to tea in "a couple of days". Now if that took place yesterday, was the invitation originally for tomorrow or for today?'

'I see what you mean. You're quite right, Sergeant. It was for tomorrow, Friday. Then he changed it.'

'Do you know why?'

'Ask Mr Fickling. It was he who told me.'

'As a matter of fact, I have asked Mr Fickling. I just wondered if you knew anything about it.'

'If you've asked Mr Fickling, I can't imagine why you're bothering to ask me, Sergeant.'

'Simply in the hope that between you, you will remember more.'

'I resent your manner of going backwards and forwards between us as if you are trying to find discrepancies in what we say.'

'Not at all, sir. I've found that if I examine witnesses together they have a tendency to overlook details. If one remembers something slightly differently from another he might be embarrassed to mention it and yet what he remembers might be correct.'

I got to my feet. 'If I am asked to give evidence at the inquest, I shall respond to any appropriate enquiries put to me by the coroner, but until then I will say no more. I hope I may be permitted to go now?'

He smiled and also stood. 'You can go any time you wish, sir. Not only do I have no power to detain you against your will, but I have not the slightest wish to do so. I'm very grateful to you for giving me your time and assistance. However, the Major is on his way here and I'm sure he would like a word with you, so I would be more than grateful if you would stay until then.'

'Where is Mr Fickling?'

'He is very kindly waiting for the Major in the other room, sir.'

I found Austin sitting white-faced at the table.

'This is a terrible business,' I commented.

He said nothing but sat back in the chair with his eyes on the ceiling.

Thursday Night

SOME TIME LATER I heard a carriage draw up in the street. The door opened and two men burst in. One was a uniformed police-officer and the other was about sixty, burly and military in his bearing with a purplish complexion, slightly protruding eyes and a large white moustache. Hearing the carriage, the Sergeant had entered the room from the hall. 'Oh, Adams, there you are,' the newcomer boomed. They shook hands and the Sergeant said something in an undertone and the large man glanced at us. Then he turned and said: 'I'm Major Antrobus, the Superintendent. I'm very sorry you have been so severely inconvenienced, gentlemen. But might I ask you to wait a little longer?'

Austin and I expressed our preparedness to do so and the Major hurried out with the Sergeant. I took out my watch. It was half-past eight. I was astonished that so much time had passed and it occurred to me that I should be hungry, but I found I was not.

I blush to write this now, but I can be completely honest since I will be dead by the time anyone reads this account. The dismaying truth is that as I sat there I found myself thinking about the manuscript and how much I was longing to get back to the Library and read it. I had been mad to contemplate the possibility of removing it surreptitiously and could hardly believe that I had entertained such a thought even for a minute. The problem I had to face was what I should say when Dr Locard asked where and how I had located it—as he surely would. It would be embarrassing to have to admit that I had ignored his advice and I could not mention that Quitregard had pointed me in the right direction, of course, because that would get him into trouble.

Austin was staring at the floor. What was he thinking about? The fact that we had not yet spoken was becoming embarrassing. At last I broke the silence. 'It's hard to believe he was alive just now. It's a terrible warning to us all. In the midst of life . . .'

'Hold your tongue, will you?' he snapped.

It was clear that the events of the afternoon had been at least as much of a shock for him as for me. After twenty minutes the door opened and the Major came in with the Sergeant and Dr Carpenter.

'That can't be right,' the Major was saying. 'You say yourself you can't judge exactly.'

'No, but it looks probable,' the young doctor answered.

'Probable! It looks highly improbable. In fact, perfectly impossible. Four hours ago he was dispensing tea right here in this room.' Turning from the doctor as if dismissing him from his consciousness, he addressed Austin and myself: 'I deeply regret that you've been delayed, gentlemen, and I will detain you as briefly as possible. I understand you have been here since about half-past six and that in that time you have been required to look at the body—one of the most unpleasant sights I've seen in my long experience. And that you have both been questioned at length?'

'That is so,' I said. 'But I am perfectly willing to assist in what I see as my public duty. I'm sure your subordinate was doing what he thought was right.'

'We're very grateful to you, sir,' the Major said. Then he turned to the elderly servant.

'Now, Mrs Bubbosh, my sergeant tells me that you claim that

you came to the front-door just before six and could not get in. Did anyone see you arrive and find the door locked?'

The old woman looked terrified. 'I don't know, sir.'

'Nobody can say that Mr Stonex did not let you in when you knocked as he has on every other day at six o'clock for the past twenty-five years?'

'How could he, sir? The poor gentleman was laying dead in that room.'

'That is what is precisely at issue, my good woman.' The Major smiled round at Austin and me. 'Was he lying dead at the moment when you arrived at the door? Or did he open the door to you and an accomplice?'

She looked from one to the other of us in dismay.

'Come, my good woman. Don't waste my time. I've been summoned here from a pleasant occasion with my family. Dammit, it's Christmas Eve the day after tomorrow. I intend to clear this business up before the festival. Be frank now. What do you know about this? Do you have any sons, any grandsons, any nephews? Are there any young men in your family who need money?'

He turned and gave Austin and me a significant look as if to indicate, 'I'm getting close to the truth now.'

'We don't none of us have no money, sir. But there isn't a single man or boy among us would even dream of such a wicked deed.'

'Oh, is that so? I can promise you that very searching enquiries will be made about the male members of your family. Very searching indeed.'

'And you won't find nothing untoward. Save my brother, Jim, that was done for poaching. But that was just the one time. He was in quod for two years on account of it.'

'Ah-ha,' the Major exclaimed. 'Now we're coming to it. Did this brother of yours employ violence in order to escape? Is that why his sentence was so long?'

'No, sir, he did not. The magistrate was a friend of the gentleman that owned the land he was caught on. That's why he got dealt with so harsh.'

'An embittered and hardened jailbird! And where might this brother of yours be found, my good woman?'

'In the burying-ground, sir. He has been dead these ten years.'

The Major's smile faded: 'All that will be investigated, I promise you. But it remains the case that you have no way of proving that you were not admitted at six o'clock.'

I was wondering what devious strategy the Major could be pursuing, since the hypothesis that Mrs Bubbosh had entered the house at six with an accomplice was open to a number of objections—above all, that it left very little time for the deed to be done. It seemed that the same thought had occurred to the Sergeant for he drew his superior aside and they held a brief whispered conference.

Then the Major turned to Austin and me. 'Gentlemen, I understand that as you were leaving the house at half-past five there was a knock at the front-door and the deceased told you that it was the waiter, Perkins, who was bringing beer?'

'That is correct,' I said.

The Major spun round and jabbed a finger at Mrs Bubbosh: 'You know this Perkins, don't you?'

She looked amazed. 'I've knowed Eddy since he was a boy. And his father before him. But I don't know why you say it like that, sir, as if there was anything wrong in it.'

'Keep a civil tongue in your head, my good woman. When I ask you a question I expect you to answer it without embroidering your reply. Now give me a straight answer to a straight question.'

'What was the question, sir?'

'Did you and Perkins come here at half-past five?'

'No, I never did! And I don't believe young Perkins did neither.'

'Are you accusing these gentlemen of lying?' the Major interrupted.

She turned and looked at us in bewilderment. 'Why, no, sir. If they say he came then, all I can say is, he never done so before. And I still beg leave to doubt it for I believe that if he had of come at that time, old Mr Stonex would not have opened the door to him. He only opened it to Eddy at four o'clock when he brung him his dinner. Apart from that, he only opened the door to me.'

'He only opened the door to you,' the Major repeated. 'Aren't you virtually admitting that you came here at half-past five with Perkins? Nobody else but you could have gained admittance.'

'No, I am not! And it don't make no sense to say I did. Mr Stonex only opened the door to me at seven in the morning and again at six in the evening. Other times I might knock until my knuckles run blood and he wouldn't open. He was that afeared of being robbed.'

'Go now,' the Major said to her. 'I don't need you any longer just at present. But go home and stay there.'

She turned away, looking angry and frightened.

'Before you go, Mrs Bubbosh,' the Sergeant said, 'I'd like you to tell the Major what you told me about how surprised you were to see the state of this room just now.'

'It's all this mess,' she said, looking round. 'Why, it was as neat as a new pin when I left here at noon.'

'And the tea?' the Sergeant prompted.

'I never seen them cakes before. And he never had no tea-party in all my time with him.'

The Major looked from her to the Sergeant in surprise.

'So you're saying,' the Sergeant prompted gently, 'that Mr Stonex did not tell you he had invited these gentlemen to tea? And you did not furnish the food?'

'That's right, sir. I never knowed nothing about it.'

The Sergeant glanced at his superior. 'All right, go now,' the Major said and watched her leave. As the door closed behind her he turned to Austin and me and said: 'That woman is lying. This case is contemptibly simple. The criminal mind is by definition limited. The murderer was probably this Perkins or a relative of Mrs Bubbosh and she let him in when old Stonex opened the door to her at six as usual.'

'With all due respect, Major,' Sergeant Adams put in, 'if the killer entered the house as late as six o'clock then I don't believe he had enough time to do the murder. I myself received the message to come at a few minutes before half-past six and so Mrs Bubbosh must have had time to go and fetch Mr Wattam and for both of them to come back here and then for him to send someone to summon me from the station-house.'

'There is no difficulty with that,' said the Major. 'The accomplice was in the house all that time. In their cleverness he and the Bubbosh woman agreed that she would raise the alarm while he was still here. That gave him at least thirty minutes. And it might have been longer. You entered the house at about ten minutes to seven, did you not? The accomplice might only have left then because, as you have admitted to me, you failed to secure the rear entrance.'

'That's true, sir. I didn't guess that anything worse had happened to the old gentleman than that he had been taken ill. But the fact that I didn't send my constable round to the back made no difference because when, a few minutes later, I checked the back-door it was locked—so nobody could have escaped that way.'

The Major grunted. 'Well, the front-door was also locked and he must have escaped one way or another! Have you looked for the keys?'

'We've searched the body and looked round the house, sir.'

'Well, have another look, Sergeant.'

The Sergeant went out of the room. The Major shook his head. 'It was grossly negligent not to have posted a man at the back-door immediately. His conduct of a very simple case has been far from exemplary.'

'Is the case so simple?' I asked.

'Open and shut. The robber or robbers managed to get into the well-protected house of a wealthy man who was popularly believed to have cash and valuables on the premises, killed the owner and ransacked the house looking for money. Adams has done his best to muddy the waters, but you can always find a way to make a thing complicated. The art of detection, as I've often said, is to reduce apparent complexity to the simplicity of truth.' He turned to me with a smile: 'For example, the Sergeant tells me that you said that the house appeared to have been ransacked when you arrived for tea this afternoon?'

'Yes, I did say that.'

'Do you really mean ransacked or simply that the old gentleman had opened a few drawers while searching for that story he wished to show you?' Without waiting for an answer he turned to Austin: 'Mr Fickling, I understand that you described it merely as showing signs of a careless search?'

Austin nodded. I looked at him in surprise.

'Are you gentlemen really so far apart?' He turned to me: 'You're not saying that the disorder you see now is exactly as it was when you arrived?'

'I suppose I couldn't swear to every single item.'

'Good. Then obviously the robbers ransacked the house, adding to the untidiness already created. Now we're making progress.' At that moment the Sergeant came into the room. The Major wheeled round: 'Well, Adams?'

'I haven't found them, sir.'

'Have a couple of your best officers search the whole house as soon as it's light tomorrow. Those keys must be somewhere in the house.'

'With all due respect, sir,' Sergeant Adams said. 'The person who did this must have used them to lock the door behind him.'

The Major nodded and the Sergeant went on: 'In that case they might be anywhere. He would have got rid of them as soon as possible since they would hang him for sure.'

'As soon as it's light enough, have the back-yard searched. If they're not found, have your men go over every inch of this corner of the Close.'

As he finished speaking there was a knock at the street-door and Adams opened it to the two constables who came in with a young man handcuffed between them. He looked terrified, his clothes were torn and his face was bruised.

'Ah-ha!' cried the Major. 'The famous Perkins, the waiter. Where did you get those scratches and bruises?'

'He tried to run away, sir,' said one of the constables.

'Indeed? And did you find anything on him?'

'Nothing, sir.'

'No money? No keys?'

'No, sir.'

'Sergeant, go to his house and find the things he stole from here. And look for those keys.'

Adams nodded a farewell to us and hurried away.

The Major turned back to the prisoner: 'Now I understand you are an intimate of Mrs Bubbosh?'

The man gaped and the Major snapped: 'You know her, for God's sake, man.'

'Everybody knows Auntie Meg, sir.'

'What happened when you came to this house at half-past five this afternoon?'

He blushed and looked down. 'I never did. I only ever come at four o'clock. Four sharp by the Cathedral clock. The old gentleman was very strict about that.'

'Mr Stonex told you to come at half-past five and bring a mug of ale.'

'No, sir. He never done!' He was red-faced and kept his gaze on his feet. He was clearly not telling the truth and his very incompetence as a liar aroused my suspicions that he might be innocent.

'You're lying,' shouted the Major. He half-turned towards us: 'Both of these gentlemen heard Mr Stonex say that he had done so. And they heard you arrive at the door at that hour.'

He turned his frightened face towards us. 'I don't understand. That ain't right. It ain't the truth.'

'I shall want to hear more about that from you. Take him into the dining-room.'

'I won't say nothing,' the young man said as he was led away.

The Major turned back to us and smiled. 'Thank you, gentlemen. I don't need to detain you any longer. You may go now and I am very grateful for your help.'

'Please don't hesitate to find me if I may be of any further assistance,' I said. 'I am at Fickling's house.'

'How long are you intending to stay in the town?'

'Only another two days. I leave on Saturday morning.'

'I fear you will have to give evidence at the inquest. Both of you gentlemen,' he said turning to include Austin.

'Of course,' I said. 'Do you know when that will be?'

'Tomorrow, I hope.'

'Then that will pose no difficulty,' I said.

After a further exchange of courtesies and with the Major's renewed apologies for the inconvenience we had suffered ringing in our ears, Austin and I left the house. When we found ourselves in the street outside I noticed that Austin was trembling and gripped him by the arm.

'We should eat,' I said. 'It's late and we've had nothing.' We were facing the inn in which we had been drinking a few hours before, but I didn't want to go back there. For one thing, I had a fear that Slattery might be lurking in the bar. 'The Dolphin?' I suggested. Austin nodded dumbly.

A few minutes later we were sitting in the empty dining-room. With an ill grace the waiter—who had been about to finish work for the evening—had agreed to bring some cold roast meat and boiled potatoes from the kitchen.

'What a business,' I said rather tritely when the silence became awkward.

He made no response and I was not surprised since he had been in a kind of trance ever since the discovery of the crime.

'I found the Sergeant's manner most offensive,' I said. 'He seemed to assume that one or both of us were lying. And he asked me some very impertinent questions.'

Austin looked up. 'Did he? What did he want to know?'

'I refused to tell him anything that was not relevant to what happened this afternoon. He seemed to think it significant that poor old Mr Stonex changed the date of the invitation. He came and asked you about that, didn't he?'

Austin nodded. Another silence fell, interrupted by the waiter slapping down in front of us two plates containing dry slices of meat covered with congealed gravy, and a dish of blotchy, tepid potatoes.

'Adams seems to have some sort of theory,' I went on, 'that the old gentleman was expecting a visitor.'

'It's not worth speculating about,' Austin said. 'The Major is right. It's really very simple.'

'I think he's wrong if he believes that Mrs Bubbosh is implicated.'

'Perkins did it,' Austin said. 'With or without help from the old woman.'

'Without. And yet she must be lying about the cakes, must she not?'

'Certainly.'

'But why? What possible motive could she have for such an unnecessary and trivial lie?'

'Who knows? With a person like that, it's often hard to say. It doesn't alter the fact that Perkins did it.'

'You're sure?'

Austin put down his knife and fork. 'It's very simple. When Stonex asked him to bring beer at half-past five—a thing that he had never done before—Perkins realized that this was his chance to rob him. He would be let into the house without anybody being aware of it. But what he could not have known was that Stonex would have guests that afternoon and mention to them that he had ordered beer.'

I nodded. 'So it was done on an impulse?'

'Yes, but he might have been thinking about it for months. Of course, he knew he would have to kill him.'

I shuddered.

'But, Austin, why did he . . . Why did he do it like that?'

'Like what?' he asked almost irritably.

'You saw it. He surely didn't need to do that.'

He shrugged. 'Who knows? Does it matter?'

We finished our meal and walked home—almost entirely in silence. By the time we got back it was long after midnight and we went straight to bed. For a long time I found I couldn't sleep. If only Perkins had looked more villainous I might have found the whole affair less disturbing, but to accept that that boyish youth—as fresh-faced as one of my undergraduates—could have done that to a defenceless old man whom he had known for years . . . ! To think how much blood must have spurted and yet he had struck again and again and again. To think of the splintering of bone, the vulnerability of the eyes. To think of what he must have done to have inflicted so much damage to the head, to the face. It was hard to believe. It was hard to believe anything good about our species. Was this what we were—cruel apes who wore clothes and washed and perfumed our bodies?

I thought of Gambrill murdering his rival by throwing him from the roof of the Cathedral, and then of young Limbrick brooding in secret for years about the need to avenge his father, urged on by his embittered mother, yet having to conceal his hatred and accept favours from the man he hoped one day to kill. And had Gambrill guessed at his hidden hatred and tried to appease him by promoting him?

And most of all I thought about the manuscript and regretted that all of this was a distraction from it and from the problem of how to ensure that it was not misused in order to promote someone's interests, for it belonged to history rather than to an individual or even an institution. And then at last I fell into an uneasy slumber, the kind which is more exhausting even than sleeplessness. Towards dawn I had the most terrifying dream of my life from which I awoke with my heart thumping and my forehead wet with perspiration. It was one of those dreams—nightmares—which cast a long shadow over the rest of the day as if some part of the mind were trying to pull one back into it.

Friday Morning

❖

THE STATE of brooding depression in which I awoke meant that Austin and I spoke very little at breakfast. Moreover, I wanted to avoid speech since, in order to postpone the problems that I foresaw, I did not want to reveal that I had found the manuscript. I was therefore hoping that he would be as incurious about my researches as he had hitherto been and would not ask what my intentions were for the morning. As we were about to leave the house, however, he enquired: 'Where are you going?'

'To the Library again.'

'You won't forget about the inquest, will you?'

'Will it be today?'

'I assume so. But whenever it is, you have to be there. You have important evidence to give.'

'Is it so important?'

'All you have to do is describe what you saw and heard. A witness of your standing will put paid to any of the absurd theories that Adams might parade in order to make himself seem clever.'

I nodded, pulling on my coat.

After a moment, he said: 'I suppose you'll see Locard?'

'I doubt it.' I was thinking of how he had broken his appointment and withdrawn his promised assistance.

'Well, if you do, be sure not to say anything to him about this business.'

'Why not?'

'He is a trouble-maker. He will twist anything you tell him to his own interests.'

'What interests could he have in this business?'

'Very powerful ones. There has always been a rumour that Stonex was leaving his fortune to the Foundation. Locard would love to get his hands on it.'

'If a testament is found to that effect, then he will. Otherwise not.' I spoke off-handedly, convinced that Austin was voicing an obsession with Dr Locard that arose from the politics of the Chapter. I assumed he was upset because Canon Sheldrick had been defeated by Dr Locard at the Chapter meeting the previous morning. That was not merely a defeat for the Low Church faction, but, I suspected, it probably made certain the dismissal of his friend Slattery.

I was so impatient to be at the Library early that I hurried out of the house before Austin had left, taking a hastier leave of my friend than with hindsight I would have chosen.

I arrived just as young Quitregard was unlocking the door. He greeted me with a smile and as he ushered me in, he said: 'I'm putting on coffee and I should be honoured . . .'

'Thank you, but not this morning,' I said, hurrying past him.

'But have you heard the news about Mr Stonex?' he called out.

'Indeed I have,' I cried. 'I was assisting the police for most of yesterday evening.'

'I know that, sir, and I'm sorry you and Mr Fickling were involved.'

I stopped and turned. 'How do you know that?'

'Oh, there are no secrets in this town. But I meant, have you heard the news that is fresh this morning?' I shook my head and he savoured the moment before saying: 'The waiter, Eddy Perkins, has been charged.'

'That surprises me not in the least. Has he confessed?'

'Not in so many words, but something very incriminating was found in his house late last night when the officers searched it.'

'What was it?'

He pulled a face. 'I don't know. But he admitted that he had taken it from Mr Stonex's house. Apparently it was impossible for him to deny it.'

'So he *has* confessed?'

'No, for he maintains that he knew nothing of the murder.'

'Is he still saying that he did not go back to the house at half-past five?'

'He has now admitted that he did. But only because a witness has come forward who saw him there at the time.'

'A witness? Do you know who it is?'

'No, sir. But isn't it all frightfully exciting?'

I smiled. 'And yet in spite of all this evidence against him, he is insisting that he did not kill the old gentleman?'

'That is so.'

'That hardly seems a logical position. I suppose the man is stupid.'

'Stupid and brutal, on the evidence. What a terrible thing. And what a shock it must have been for you. To learn of the dreadful murder of someone you were with only an hour or two earlier.'

His kind face was so sympathetic that I was tempted to accept his offer and indulge as well the curiosity that he was finding it so difficult to conceal, but the lure of my discovery was too powerful. With an expression of gratitude for his commiseration, I ascended the stairs to the upper floor.

I listened for a moment to make sure that he was not following me and then I removed the manuscript from where I had placed it the previous afternoon, and laid it on the desk before me. Just looking at it was a balm to my spirit. This was real, this was what was important. Here—in the practice of scholarly skills—were order and rationality and truth. As I began to translate the faded script it became clear to me that I had been correct in my first assumption yesterday: I was indeed looking at a manuscript written in about A.D. 1000, considerably earlier than the 1120 recension of Grim-bald's *Life*. And yet as I read on, my conviction that it proved that the work had existed before Leofranc started to revise it began to waver in the face of anomalies. What I had before me was certainly a version of the story of the Siege of Thurchester and the martyr-dom of St Wulflac—although the king and the bishop concerned were not named—but it was very different from the one which ap-pears in the 1120 recension. The events were broadly the same but the interpretation of the motives of those involved was completely different.

I had been working for a little less than an hour when I heard running feet on the stairs and, barely giving me time to slip the manuscript under one of the volumes lying on the table, Pome-rance came bursting in. 'They've found a body!' he cried. 'They've found a body.'

'Dear God!' I exclaimed, rising to my feet. 'Who is it now?'

In an instant, a host of possibilities presented themselves: I had a bizarre vision of Mrs Bubbosh lying suffocated with one of her tea-towels over her face, quickly succeeded by an image of Austin sprawling on his back with his throat cut and a razor beside him.

'It's in the Cathedral,' he gasped. 'I'm going to look.'

In the Cathedral! What could this mean?

Pomerance turned on his heel and headed back towards the stairs. 'Wait a moment!' I exclaimed.

'I can't!' he threw over his shoulder. 'I only came up because Quitregard told me to.'

He ran down the stairs again. In bewilderment I followed him, pausing only to put on my greatcoat and hat. I saw the young man hurry out of the door and when I got outside I found Quitregard standing on the steps, coatless, and peering towards the Cathedral.

'I'd give anything to be able to go,' he said. 'But I can't leave the Library unattended.'

'What is this new horror?' I asked.

'I don't know,' he almost wailed. 'Do please come back and tell me.'

'I will,' I said, and hurried across the Close towards the south transept where I saw a number of people outside the door—the only one open at that time of day. A police-officer and one of the vergers were barring their entry to the building. I saw Pomerance among the onlookers and he looked eagerly towards me as I approached, as if I could help him to get in. I recognized the constable as one of the two who had brought Perkins to the house last night and when he saw me he saluted and stood aside to let me enter as if I had some special right of access to dead bodies.

I could see that there was a group of men standing under the crossing-tower and as I drew nearer I realized that they were beside the Burgoyne memorial which was now a gaping hole of outraged brickwork partly obscured by scaffolding. Before it lay a block and tackle, and the huge slab which had formed the visible part of the monument was propped up on the ground nearby. I noticed my old friend the head-verger, Gazzard, standing at a little distance apart and went up to him. He greeted me with lugubrious courtesy, and I asked him what was happening.

'Why, they realized the smell was coming from there and so they started to open it up early this morning.'

'I suppose that when the paving subsided, the movement must have disturbed the masonry and punctured the seal.'

He shrugged. 'As soon as they removed some of the bricks, the stench became dreadful.'

'I don't understand. It's only a memorial, not a tomb.'

'Well, they found what was making the smell. They've got it over there. This is as near as I'll go for all the tea in China, sir.'

I thanked him and went a little closer, though the smell was appalling. Two of the men, I now saw, were Dr Carpenter and Dr Sisterson, though the third was unknown to me. For the second time in as many days I saw the young doctor bent over a corpse. It looked like a very old man—its face withered, with the lips shrunk away from the teeth in a grimace, and the body shrivelled up so that it seemed not to be big enough for a grown man. I saw that it was wearing linen undergarments of antique style. The words from the inscription suddenly came to me: *For when the Earthe shudders and the Towers tremble, the Grave will yield up her secrettes and all be known.*

'Move back, will you,' the stranger said to me.

Dr Sisterson, however, looked up and said cheerfully: 'But I know this gentleman.' He stepped over to me and shook hands and said: 'How very good it is to see you.' He turned to the other man: 'This is Mr Bulmer, the Surveyor of the Fabric. And this gentleman, Bulmer, is the distinguished historian, Dr Courtine.'

'Yes, I know who you are,' Bulmer said without smiling as he shook my hand. He was a short, burly man of about fifty with heavy jowls and a head that was almost completely bald.

'I know Dr Carpenter,' I said as Dr Sisterson was about to introduce us.

The doctor nodded in a casual way.

Dr Sisterson smiled: 'We now have all the professions we need: a medical gentleman to tell us how this poor man died, an architect to tell us how he got into the wall and a historian to explain what really happened.'

'And a theologian,' said the young doctor rather sarcastically, 'to tell us the ultimate significance of it all.'

The Sacrist said with a smile: 'This will fascinate you as a historian, Dr Courtine. It seems that the body must have been sealed up immediately after death. So it was perfectly preserved in the airless space until the seal was ruptured a few days ago.'

'Ruptured, I will point out once again,' Bulmer broke in angrily, 'because my instructions were irresponsibly countermanded.' As he spoke he thrust his chin upwards in my direction and glared at me for the space of several seconds in a manner that I found quite alarming.

'Yes, Mr Bulmer,' said Dr Sisterson. 'I have apologized for that and I take full responsibility for it upon myself. The foreman was acting on my orders alone.'

'Except that it was not sealed up after death, Dr Sisterson,' said Dr Carpenter, who had been looking silently down at the cadaver. 'The wretched man was placed in the memorial while still alive.'

'How can you know that?' I asked.

Protecting his own hands with a piece of cloth, he knelt and held up one of the corpse's. 'Look. The nails are worn down and the bones of the hand swollen which means that he tried to claw and beat his way out of the tomb. He must have suffocated over a period of a few hours or even days.'

The thought made me gasp for breath, especially as the stench was already stifling. I was possessed by a sense of horror as I imagined the man trying to scratch his way out of his stone coffin, screaming for as long as his lungs could find air, beating his fists against the cold marble.

'So the mystery is resolved at last—two hundred and fifty years late,' Dr Sisterson commented.

'Yes,' I said. 'We now know why Gambrill disappeared. The poor man did not run away. He was himself murdered. And the reason why the slab was inserted to stand proud of the wall is now clear.'

'But now we have another puzzle instead,' the Sacrist said. 'Who killed *him*?'

Bulmer exchanged a look with the young doctor. 'Do you mind letting us in on this?' he said. 'Who are you talking about?'

Between us, the Sacrist and I told the story of Burgoyne. When we had concluded, the Surveyor smiled and said rather grimly: 'As

Gambrill's successor, I can sympathize with his desire to murder one of the canons.'

Dr Sisterson smiled without quite hiding his embarrassment, but the doctor laughed and asked: 'But did he have any specific reason?'

'That's rather enigmatic,' I said. 'They were quarrelling about the Canon's lack of interest in preserving the spire. As you probably know,' I said, turning to Bulmer to try to make my peace, 'the nave was abandoned for more than a hundred years after the Dissolution because of the danger of the spire collapsing and as a result . . .'

'I know nothing about that. To be perfectly blunt, Dr Courtine, I don't care how or why the builders did something in the past. As a practical man, all that interests me is whether it's going to stand in the future.'

There was an awkward silence.

'And in addition to that, Gambrill believed that Burgoyne was about to expose him for embezzlement,' Dr Sisterson murmured, trying to redeem the situation.

'I understand that the precise term is malversation,' I said, remembering my first conversation with the old banker. The Sacrist looked at me in surprise. I was beginning to explain the distinction when I was interrupted by the young surgeon: 'I am rather intrigued, gentlemen. You said it was assumed at the time that Gambrill killed Burgoyne, in some mysterious way raised this slab to its position, sealed it in place, and then disappeared. Where does this discovery leave that theory?'

'It makes it much clearer,' I said. 'There was a third person involved. And that must have been someone who had the skill to seal Gambrill up in the tomb. In other words, it must have been a mason.'

I waited to see if the Sacrist knew what I was implying.

'Thomas Limbrick!' he exclaimed.

'Who was he?' Dr Carpenter asked.

'A young Mason who worked for Gambrill,' the Sacrist explained.

'He was the son of a former Deputy Mason who had been a workmate of Gambrill's,' I added. 'A man who had been killed in an accident on the tower which cost Gambrill one of his eyes. His widow accused him of murder.' As I said that, I remembered that I wanted to ask the Surveyor about the condition of the spire and whether I could go up the tower stairs which Gazzard had told me were closed.

'And after Gambrill's disappearance,' the Sacrist added, 'young Limbrick inherited his enterprise.'

'And his widow,' I said.

'So he had all those motives for killing Gambrill,' said the Sacrist. 'But why did he wish to kill the Canon?'

The doctor had turned back to the body and was kneeling beside it while listening to us. 'If he did,' I said.

'Excuse me, gentlemen,' said the Surveyor. 'This is all very fascinating but unfortunately the Foundation doesn't pay me to stand here and discuss ancient history. I have work to do.'

'Before you go, Mr Bulmer,' I said, 'I'd like to ask you about the spire. I have a particular reason to ascend the tower and look at it. Is it really too dangerous?'

'I beg your pardon?' he said, turning quickly to look at me. 'I don't understand your meaning.'

'I am informed that the tower is closed to visitors because of its structural weakness. I wondered if an exception could be made in my case.'

He stared at me with his eyes bulging: 'I can assure you that the tower is perfectly safe. Frankly, to suggest otherwise is such a serious criticism of my professional competence that I am quite at a loss for words.'

'I must have misunderstood,' I said.

I saw that a vein in his great naked forehead was throbbing.

'That is entirely possible, Dr Courtine.' He repeated slowly and with particular significance: 'Entirely possible. Let me, however, make one thing clear. You are not, despite the excellent condition of the tower, permitted to ascend it under any circumstances.' He glanced significantly towards the gaping hole in the wall and added, addressing himself to Dr Sisterson rather than myself: 'The Cathedral can't afford any more damage.'

He nodded at the three of us and, with a brief 'Good day, gentlemen', hurried towards the nave and the west door.

'I'm afraid I offended him,' I said to the Sacrist. 'I think he blames me for bringing this disaster upon the Cathedral. But the spire and the tower were certainly in danger of collapse in Burgoyne's time.'

'It's a strange business. They are perfectly sound now and yet nobody quite understands why.'

'Nobody understands why?' I laughed. 'Can you explain what you mean?'

'At the Restoration of the Monarchy, the Foundation set about repairing the damage that had been inflicted on the fabric during the civil turmoil. Contrary to all expectations, it was found that the tower and the spire were in no need of repair. And about forty years ago a survey established that they had been very cleverly and effectively strengthened at some point between about 1600 and 1660. Yet no record of such work exists.'

'Why, in that case, is the tower barred?'

'There's some kind of ancient machinery up there which could be extremely dangerous to anyone who got close to it.'

I was intrigued. The record of Limbrick Senior's death had referred to an *Engin* and a possibility came to me as I remembered the words from the inscription: *All things revolve and Man who is born to Labour revolves with them.*

'What is it?'

'Nobody really knows.'

'Indeed? Even Bulmer?' I asked with a smile.

'He has confessed himself completely baffled.'

'Does he know much about the construction of cathedrals?'

'To be frank, not a great deal. He is a fine engineer, I'm sure. He built bridges before he was employed by the Chapter.'

'Does it have a big wheel?' He stared at me as if I had taken leave of my senses. 'The machinery in the tower. Is there a huge wheel attached to it?'

'Like a prison treadwheel?' he said.

I smiled. 'Precisely. Though not quite as large as that. About one and a half times the height of a man.'

'I have to admit that I have never been up there. I have no head for heights. But I believe it has.'

I believed I knew what it was and, if I was right, a number of missing pieces of the puzzle would fall into place. However, it was clear that I had annoyed the Surveyor to the point where there would be no possibility of his allowing me up there.

At that moment Dr Carpenter came over. 'The undertaker's men will be here soon and I'll have them take the body to the mortuary.'

'I've notified the authorities,' said the Sacrist. 'And I assume there will be an inquest.'

'Speaking of which,' the doctor said to me, 'did you know the one on Mr Stonex is to take place this afternoon?'

'A terrible business,' said Dr Sisterson, shaking his head. 'I'm so sorry you were innocently caught up in it, Dr Courtine.'

I thanked him and turned to the doctor: 'I did not. Though the Major warned me it might be today.'

'The Guildhall at two,' he said. 'Probably you know that the police found banknotes hidden in Perkins's house?'

'Then I assume that his guilt is beyond dispute.'

'Presumably,' he said and turned to the Sacrist, holding up a bunch of keys: 'What shall I do with these?'

'Were they found on the body?' I asked.

'Beside it,' Dr Carpenter said.

'I'll give them to Dr Locard,' said the Sacrist as the doctor handed them to him. I noticed that they consisted of two sets, each on a metal ring. 'As Librarian he takes custody of anything like that.'

'I'm surprised he is not here,' I said.

'He was sent for, of course,' said the Sacrist, 'as soon as this unfortunate discovery was made, but he had other calls upon his time.'

'I know he takes a keen interest in this story,' I said. 'He will be delighted to learn that the mystery has been resolved.'

'I'm not sure that it has,' Dr Carpenter said, turning to me. 'Tell me, Dr Courtine, what exactly do you believe happened that night?'

'Burgoyne was murdered by the collapse of the scaffolding precipitated by Gambrill—possibly with the help of Limbrick. But then he himself was overpowered by his deputy and his body sealed up here to die.'

'He lifted the slab into place singlehandedly?' said Dr Sisterson, shaking his head.

'Yes, that could have been done.' I didn't explain my theory because I wanted to wait until I had proof.

'All of that is very persuasive,' said Dr Carpenter. 'But unfortunately, it rests on a false premise.'

'What do you mean?' I asked indignantly.

'Did I understand you to say that Gambrill had lost an eye?'

'That is so.'

'Then this body cannot be his for both eyes are present.'

I stared at him in astonishment. 'That can't be right.'

'If you doubt my clinical judgement, would you like to offer a second opinion?' the doctor asked with a smile.

I shuddered at the thought of going any nearer the body. And I felt resentment at the way this clever young man had led me on to make a fool of myself.

I was about to say something I might have regretted but at that moment three figures entered through the south door—the undertaker's men. Taking a hasty leave of my companions, I hurried out of the building.

Young Pomerance was still among the little crowd on the steps as I passed out and he plucked me by the sleeve and begged me to tell him what was happening. I informed him briefly what had been discovered and then hastened back to the Library. Quitregard had just made coffee and offered me a cup. I accepted, knowing that he was longing to hear my news and disposed, after my grim experience, to talk it over with someone. And so, anxious as I was to get back to the manuscript, I sat down and told him what I had learned. It was clear how much he relished the mystery.

'It's possible,' I concluded, 'that something more will emerge when the inquest is taken, but it's very puzzling.'

Quitregard struck his forehead. 'Talking of inquests, while you were out, the Coroner's office sent a constable here to tell you that the inquest on poor Mr Stonex is this afternoon.'

'So Dr Carpenter told me. It's at the Guildhall. Where is that?'

He gave me directions. 'Do you know, they say his estate will be valued in the hundreds of thousands?'

'And is it left to the Choir School?'

'Well no, sir. I mean, apparently that was his intention but his will has not been found. His lawyer did not have it, I've been told. And so far, a search of his house and of the bank has not discovered it.'

'If he died intestate, his next of kin will inherit—assuming he has any still alive. Is anything known of them?'

'He had a sister but they have been estranged almost since her childhood. Forty or fifty years.'

'And a brother,' I put in.

The young man stared at me. 'No, he did not. That is to say, begging your pardon, you are mistaken.'

'But I distinctly recall that he mentioned him yesterday afternoon. He was talking of his childhood in the New Deanery and the games he used to play with his sister and—he said—with his brother.'

He looked at me in amazement. 'I have never heard of a brother. I know that he quarrelled with his sister, who was much younger, and that she left the town before she was out of her teens. I remember hearing my grandparents talk about her, for they recalled the scandal. It seems she fell in love with an Irish actor from a touring company that was playing at the theatre. She wanted to marry him and when her brother refused to let her, she ran away with him. That is the last the town ever knew of her. I have heard that she herself became . . .'

'Is it not possible that there was another brother who perhaps died or himself left the town at an early age?'

'It's possible, but I believe I would have heard of it. Mr Stonex and his affairs are much discussed in the town, as you may imagine. Could it have been a mere slip of the tongue?'

I smiled. 'You mean he said "brother" when he meant to say "sister"? That hardly seems possible. It's very mysterious. Could I trouble you to ask your grandparents if they ever heard of a brother?'

He smiled sadly. 'Unfortunately they are no longer alive.'

'I beg your pardon. Of course, it was a long time ago. I wonder if anyone now alive remembers old Mr Stonex. I mean, the father of the deceased. His portrait is very striking.'

'Would you call him old, sir?' the young man asked playfully. 'He died in his forties.'

I laughed. 'You might, but I would call that tragically young. And now that I think of it, the old gentleman mentioned his father's death yesterday and talked of his grief.'

'That surprises me. My grandfather told me that father and son detested each other. The father regarded his heir as cold and calculating.'

'Distance softens memories,' I said. 'You'll have learnt that by the time you're my age. And it's possible to hate someone and yet be deeply upset by his or her death.'

'I'm sure that's true, sir. But my grandfather used to say that Mr Stonex had a most unhappy childhood because his father resented him as a dull dog with little capacity to enjoy life. And that's why the boy grew up hating him. The sister, on the other hand, was the favourite and adored her father.'

'I suppose that's one reason why they quarrelled after his death. A man like that arouses strong emotions. From what the old gentleman said about him yesterday, he was a charming, selfish, devil-may-care character.'

'He certainly had a wild and hot-blooded youth,' the young man said with a rather embarrassed air.

'But then he reformed, the old man told me, when his own father died. He returned to the town and worked hard to make a go of the bank.'

'That is what is always said, sir. But my grandfather had a different slant on it and used to say that he only came back here in order to plunder the bank and that it was on the brink of collapse when he died, and his son, the old man, had to spend thirty years repairing the damage his father had inflicted in five.'

'That's rather curious. I wonder what the truth of it is. I suppose we will never know.' I sighed. 'So many mysteries.'

'I've never known so much excitement,' the young man said. 'Poor Mr Stonex, the body in the Burgoyne memorial, the row over Dr Sheldrick yesterday, and even the theft from his house on Tuesday.'

'Could any of them be connected?' I asked.

Quitregard looked at the floor. 'I don't see how, sir. But people are saying the strangest things about the robbery at Dr Sheldrick's.'

'Is someone suspected?'

'People are saying that what was stolen could, in the wrong hands, be very dangerous.'

'Dangerous to Dr Sheldrick?'

'And to the good name of the Foundation. That's what they're saying, anyway.'

'How could a set of miniatures be dangerous?'

He looked up and blushed. It occurred to me that I was being rather stupid. I had finished my coffee and now stood up. 'If Dr Locard arrives, would you be good enough to ask him if I could have a few minutes of his time?'

I had decided to postpone no longer telling Dr Locard of my discovery. He had to be informed and I might as well do it now.

'Dr Locard is here,' the young man answered in surprise. 'He came in shortly before you and has gone to the upper gallery.'

I was horrified, for I suddenly realized that I had left the manuscript lying upon the desk, barely hidden by a single book. If Dr Locard had found it, he would wonder why I had not reported my discovery to him, and I dreaded that he should suspect that I had contemplated concealing it from him.

I hurried up the stairs and, to my dismay, found Dr Locard bent over the table exactly where I had been sitting. As I approached, he looked up and smiled thinly. 'I must congratulate you, Courtine. You have made a very remarkable discovery.'

The manuscript was before him.

'I found it just before Pomerance came to tell me the news about the body in the Cathedral,' I said in embarrassment. 'I was about to come and tell you when that drove every other consideration from my mind.'

'It has been a day of astonishing excitement,' he commented drily. 'Almost as dramatic as yesterday.'

He gestured to indicate the shelves around us. 'It was up here that you found it?'

'Quite by chance. I happened to come across the records of Chancery Sessions and I was looking through them and I found it between the pages.' I gestured at the book which was still open where the manuscript had been.

'What a curious coincidence,' he remarked.

I didn't believe it was anything of the kind, but I decided to say nothing of how I had been looking into the death of Limbrick's father, just as I imagined Pepperdine had more than two centuries earlier. 'I've only had time to glance through it,' I said. 'It seems to be exactly what I hoped to find: part of the original version of Grimbald's *Life*.'

'I've scarcely had twenty minutes to look at it myself,' Dr Locard said. 'But I've noticed that no names are given. Even the invaders are merely called "pagani" while the town is referred to as "civitas". Moreover, there appear to be some distinctly anomalous features and an idea has occurred to me. But shall we see what we can make of it together?'

I felt like a child whose Christmas gift has been seized and opened by a bigger sibling. But I had little choice and so I seated myself beside him and, like two schoolboys sharing a primer side by side on a form, we translated the text between us:

The king and the martyr were once close friends but were no longer so because the latter criticized his former pupil for his failings. In particular, he reproached him for not surrendering the throne to his nephew now that the young man was old enough. The martyr pointed out to the king in the presence of his advisers that as the son of the elder brother of the last king, the young man was the rightful ruler. It was widely known, moreover, that the king had murdered his father and his elder brother. There were many among those present who supported the king's nephew because they believed he would be a stronger and more trustworthy king than his uncle.

'That's interesting,' said Dr Locard. 'Alfred *was* an unlikely successor to the throne, wasn't he?'

'But there's no evidence to suggest that he murdered any of his family,' I replied indignantly. Dr Locard had disclaimed any expertise in the period and yet not only had he read my and Scuttard's articles, but he clearly knew some of the sources. Was that due merely to his brilliance as a scholar or was Austin right to suspect that he was beginning to take a professional interest in the history of England before the Conquest?

'No, but I suppose there wouldn't be, would there, since the king largely determined what was written about him and therefore what has come down to us? But let us continue.'

The king was saved when a sudden danger from outside threatened the kingdom: a huge army of the heathen invaded the country, laying waste, pillaging and stealing as they swept across the land. The king left the martyr in command of the city which was in the path of the advancing heathen, saying he was going forth to fight them. In fact, because he was afraid for his own safety, he led his army in the opposite direction. As a result of the king's cowardice, the enemy captured the city and took the martyr hostage.

'I congratulate you on proving your point,' Dr Locard said with a smile. 'This is clearly a more authentic version of the story and is presumably what Grimbald wrote before Leofranc tampered with his text.'

'On what grounds do you say that?' I asked in dismay.

'It rings truer than the absurdly heroic image of the king in the later version.'

'I don't agree,' I said somewhat stiffly. 'That seems to me to be an arbitrary and dangerous principle of historical investigation.'

'Certainly its failure to idealize the king is not in itself proof of its authenticity, but as I think we shall find in a moment, there is corroborating evidence. But let us continue,' he said, bending his head over the manuscript again.

When news of this reached the king he was forced by his advisers to return and besiege the city. Because the king was too frightened to do so, his nephew acted as intermediary with the enemy. The leader of the heathens said that he would kill the martyr unless the king handed over his gold. When the nephew informed him that the treasury had been sent to a safe place, he said that the king must surrender himself as a hostage while it was being brought. When he learned this, the king refused either to send for the gold or to give himself up. The leader of the enemy said he would kill the martyr the next day if his demands were not satisfied. The king's nephew argued before the advisers that the king should do what the heathen demanded. Once the gold had been handed over and the king released, they could attack the enemy and regain the treasure. The king did not trust his nephew and refused. Then the king's nephew said he would offer himself in exchange for the martyr and the advisers applauded his courage. So he returned to the enemy and was brought into the presence of the leader, and the martyr was brought forth from his place of detention. When the nephew made his offer the leader laughed and rejected it, saying that he was a brave man but it was his uncle whom he wanted. He intended to force the king to accept his terms by suspending the martyr over the main gate of the city. Now the martyr was a wise and learned man and therefore knew that there was going to be an eclipse. He also knew that the king understood such heavenly phenomena for he had, many years before, read and translated Pliny with him when he was his tutor. And so he attempted to convey this to the king by giving the nephew a message which meant nothing to any of his hearers—or, indeed, to the nephew himself who was a warlike rather than a learned man—but which he knew the king would understand. As the nephew returned to the besieging army the martyr was suspended by ropes under his arms from the city-walls in the sight of all.

The king's nephew went back to his uncle and told him and his advisers that his mission had failed. He also conveyed the message from the martyr and the king understood its meaning but pretended that he had not done so. He wanted the martyr to be killed quickly so that the situation should be resolved, for he feared that his advisers were plotting to hand him over to the enemy. He believed that once the martyr had been released they would refuse to surrender the gold so that he, the king, would be killed and they would replace him with his nephew. His suspicions were confirmed when he found that his bodyguard had become his warders. He therefore decided to flee. Because he was watched so closely the king knew that it would be almost impossible to escape. And then he had an idea of how he might succeed—though it was shameful and degrading. Late that night he secretly shaved off his beard and disguised himself by dressing in the garments of one of the women of the household. In this manner he passed through the guards unrecognized and made his way to the stables. There he mounted his own horse but the animal did not know him in the guise of a woman and, because he was an unskilled horseman, when it bucked he was thrown to the floor. In this ignominious situation he was found by a stable-boy who recognized him despite his womanly attire and set up a shout. The king tried to mount again but the boy held on to the horse's bridle and cried out until the bodyguard came and secured his master.

'This makes better sense,' Dr Locard muttered. 'The king's flight is from danger not into it.' He turned to me. 'Do you not find this version of the story of the horse and the stable-boy much more convincing than the sentimentalized account in Leofranc?'

'No,' I said miserably. 'I find Leofranc's just as plausible.'

'How intriguing,' he commented with a hateful compression of his lips. 'Then you have changed your opinion, Dr Courtine, and you are now arguing that this manuscript is not authentic, is not from Grimbald's original *Life*, is not older than Leofranc and was not his source?'

'I haven't made up my mind,' I replied with as much dignity as I could muster.

I was in despair. The manuscript clearly pre-dated Leofranc's period and the parallels were so close that, particularly in view of its Thurchester provenance, it seemed impossible to deny that he had based his own text upon it.

'Let us see how it goes on,' Dr Locard said.

Now the king's authority was destroyed by this act of cowardice. The nephew and the other great lords decided to hand him over to the enemy in exchange for the martyr and to send for the treasure. It was now daylight. The besieging army was drawn up to watch the king being surrendered and as the sun rose over the horizon the martyr could be seen still suspended above the gate, obviously very close to death. Now the king remembered the message from the martyr and he said to his nephew and the other great lords that if they handed him over to the enemy, as a punishment for this terrible act of disloyalty, God would take away the sun. They laughed and prepared to escort him forward. At that moment the sun began to disappear and the land grew darker and darker until complete darkness fell. The king's nephew and the great lords stopped in terror and when the king said to them that if they released him and restored him to full authority, the sun would return, they immediately accepted these conditions. Meanwhile the enemy leader, who was standing atop the main gate, believed that the martyr had made the sun disappear by his magical powers. He therefore ordered that the ropes which were holding him be cut. The old man plummeted to his death just as the darkness began to lift. The king was delighted and knew that he was saved and no longer had to give up his treasure. The king's advisers and great lords believed that the king had first commanded the sun to vanish and had then brought it back again. When he ordered them to kill his nephew most of them therefore supported him. Fighting broke out and the nephew was slaughtered. The heathens, seeing that their enemies were in conflict among themselves, made a sudden and fierce attack upon the king's troops and defeated them utterly. The king was forced to hand over his treasure as the price of the invaders' leaving his kingdom but he was now prepared to do this because his rival was dead and since he had murdered all his other nephews, there was nobody else who had a claim upon the throne. Moreover, he had so little respect for the slain bishop that he . . .

'And there it breaks off abruptly. Well, you have made an extraordinary discovery, Dr Courtine. If it is what you hoped to find, then it will indeed require the rewriting of the history of the ninth century. I don't know if you noticed that it substantiates Scuttard's thesis that Alfred was defeated by the Danes, surrendered to them and paid Danegeld?'

I nodded, not trusting myself to speak.

'It seems to me very likely that somebody in the Alfredian period—let us say, for the sake of the argument, that it was Grimbald—wrote an account of the king's reign which contained much that discredited Alfred. Two hundred years later Leofranc revised it to make it glorify him because it served his own interests, which were to make Wulflac's shrine an object of veneration for all Europe. Does that not seem a reasonable hypothesis?'

'Possibly,' I said in despair. I didn't want him to see how disappointed I was. Was this the truth about Alfred—that he was murderous, cowardly and deceitful? Was my great discovery going to turn out to require a fundamental reassessment of the Alfredian period—as I had hoped—but in a manner which would cause me exquisite pain?

'The Latin is wretched, of course,' Dr Locard said. 'There is a very tiresome stylistic device which reminds me of something, though I cannot place it. Perhaps it will come to me.' He stood up. 'I should find the Sacrist and learn what has been done with Gambrill's body.'

'Not Gambrill's,' I said, with some pleasure at being able to put him right. 'It has both its eyes.'

'Really?' he stared at me. 'How intriguing.'

'Whose body do you think it can be?'

He reflected for a moment and took his seat again. 'There can be only one possibility. Two men died that night.'

'Burgoyne? But his body was found.'

'Was it? The body found under the scaffolding was identified as his by the clothes.'

'But if it was Gambrill's it would have been recognized by the missing eye.'

'I think not, for the face was injured beyond recognition. The two men were tall and of about the same age. It was the obvious assumption to make. Obvious but wrong, as the obvious assumption so often is. My experience as a historian has taught me that.'

His words had reminded me of Mr Stonex and started a train of thought which I had no leisure to follow now. Forcing my attention back to the issue at hand, I said: 'In that case, who killed Burgoyne and Gambrill? And what were his motives?'

'They were not killed by the same man. Gambrill killed Burgoyne and he must have thought it a darkly apt joke that his body should be put into his family's memorial—the hideous object which had been such a cause of contention between the two of them.'

'Dr Carpenter assured us just now he was put into it alive and died of suffocation.'

Dr Locard raised one eyebrow. 'A very grim jest, indeed. But there was another twist to the joke for Gambrill himself was murdered immediately afterwards when the scaffolding was made to collapse on him.'

'Presumably by Limbrick?' I suggested.

'Certainly by Limbrick. And the two murders are linked. For remember that Gambrill was tormented by guilt for a hideous crime he had committed, as is clear from his conduct when he believed Burgoyne was threatening to denounce him.'

'And Gambrill's guilty secret was that he had killed Limbrick's father?'

He looked at me in surprise. 'You know that?'

'How do you think Burgoyne found it out?'

'I believe Gambrill had confessed to him while they were on friendly terms. Now that they had become enemies he feared Burgoyne was about to reveal it.'

'So he killed him,' I agreed. 'But what he did not know was that Limbrick was even more dangerous. How was that?'

Dr Locard smiled. 'Limbrick was a child when his father died but when there is murderous conflict between two men I follow the old

French adage, *cherchez la femme*. I suppose Limbrick's mother poisoned her son against Gambrill by telling him the story over and over again.'

'So for all those years Limbrick was nursing this grievance and waiting for his chance to kill his patron,' I agreed.

'And his opportunity came that night when Gambrill killed Burgoyne.'

'How ironic that Burgoyne started this whole series of events by threatening to expose Gambrill.'

Dr Locard smiled. 'That's certainly what Gambrill believed he was doing.'

I hesitated. 'You believe he was wrong?'

'The participants did not know the whole of the story. Several other incidents occurred at that time. You know that this was the night of the Great Storm?'

I nodded.

'And do you know that the storm apparently killed somebody sleeping in the Old Gatehouse?'

'I remember that Dr Sisterson mentioned it when we were discussing Dr Sheldrick's chapter.'

Dr Locard smiled grimly. 'Ah yes, the famous history of the Foundation. I imagine Dr Sheldrick does not mention that incident?'

'No, strangely, he does not.'

'Did Dr Sisterson tell you who it was who died?'

'No.'

'It was one of the singing-boys—a member of the college of vicars-choral. He was killed by part of the roof falling on him. What was strange was that little damage was done to the building. In fact, some said that he looked as if he had been beaten to death rather than killed by falling debris. His bed was covered in fallen timbers but none of them seemed heavy enough to have killed him.'

'Did nobody see the roof collapse?'

'No. And none of the other boys heard any of this. He slept alone in a little chamber right under the roof.'

'Do you see some connection between that and the other events of that night?'

'Don't you think it would be rather a coincidence if there were none?' He looked at me thoughtfully for a moment.

'If there is,' I said, 'I confess I can't see it.'

'When a crime is investigated, the explanation that is adopted is not the one that best accounts for all the circumstances, but the one that best serves the purposes of those carrying out the investigation.'

I thought about this for a moment. 'You're suggesting that the assumption that Gambrill killed Burgoyne suited everybody at the time, but it wasn't the truth?'

'And although some people knew there was more to the story than that, they had good reason to keep silent.' He paused. 'Yesterday's tragedy is another example. It suits the police to assume that it was a simple case of robbery and murder.'

'You don't believe the waiter killed the old gentleman?'

'On the contrary, I'm quite sure he did. But I think the police have not understood his motive. It's clear that he knew that if he robbed Mr Stonex he would have to kill him to avoid being incriminated by him. Is it conceivable that he would have decided to commit such a grave crime without being certain of being amply rewarded?'

'He presumably believed there was money in the house. And I believe he found it.'

'Twenty pounds, that's all.'

'You are very well-informed, Dr Locard. But that is an enormous fortune to a man in his circumstances. Several months' earnings.'

'Not enough to justify such a risk.'

'Reserving judgement on that point, what is your explanation?'

'I believe he was paid to commit the murder.'

'Paid? By whom?'

'By the party who stood to benefit by the old gentleman's death.'

'And who is that?'

'If he died intestate, then it is his next of kin.'

'Did he die intestate? I had heard . . .' I broke off. It occurred to me that I would do better not to mention that Quitregard had told me the deceased had made a will in favour of the Foundation.

'I don't believe he did,' Dr Locard said. 'Yet no will has been found.'

'I don't understand.'

'I believe that Perkins was paid not simply to kill Mr Stonex but to find his will as well.'

'Then it has presumably been destroyed.'

'Most probably. Proving that, however, might be difficult.' I was wondering what he meant when he said: 'My hope is that Perkins will confess and admit to everything once he is sent for trial at the inquest.'

'You are sure that will be the result?'

'As long as the jury is not led into a state of confusion.'

'There are certainly some confusing features.'

'But it must be made quite clear to the jury that Perkins ransacked the house after committing the murder.'

I looked at him in surprise.

'I have been informed that you mentioned to the officers that the house was already in a state of disorder when you and Fickling first arrived.'

'That's true.'

'That is exactly the sort of thing that will confuse the jury and throw them off the right track.'

'It's very simple. Mr Stonex had sorted through his papers before Fickling and I arrived because he was looking for a document he wished to show me.'

'A document?' he said quickly.

'And one that will interest you: it was yet another eyewitness account of the death of Freeth . . .'

'It wasn't a legal document of any kind?'

'No, no. It was evidence that the killing of Freeth was the result of a conspiracy by the officer holding the town for Parliament.'

'Really? That sounds most unlikely.'

I recounted briefly the story that the old gentleman had narrated to Austin and myself.

'That is complete nonsense,' Dr Locard said briskly. 'It flatly contradicts the most reliable version, which is the one handed down through the Chapter. This has never been divulged to anyone outside because it casts the canons in such a bad light.' He smiled. 'I will reveal it to you now, however. It derives from one of the canons, Cinnamon. He saw the soldiers start looting the Treasury and then Freeth running over from the New Deanery and going into the building. Cinnamon hurried there himself and when he arrived a few minutes later he found the Dean engaged in a physical struggle with another of the canons.'

'Good heavens! Which one?'

'Hollingrake, the Librarian.'

'That is astonishing,' I exclaimed, remembering Dr Locard's own allegation that the two men had collaborated over the forged deed. 'Was he not the Treasurer by that date?'

'You're right, he was! You know the history of the Chapter better than I do. Freeth was trying to knock over a lamp in order to set fire to the Treasury.'

'Freeth was trying to burn it down? That's extraordinary!'

'You can imagine why the story was kept secret. He succeeded in starting a fire and Cinnamon tried to put it out. Hollingrake broke away from Freeth and, while Cinnamon restrained the Dean, went to a chest and unlocked it and took out what looked like a document. When he saw that, Freeth threw himself at Hollingrake and the two men started fighting for possession of it. Freeth was punching Hollingrake and screaming abuse at him. The canons had to flee from the building because it was now in flames. Once they were outside, the soldiers intervened and dragged Freeth off Hollingrake but he rushed at him again and kicked him while he was lying on the ground and it was then that one of the soldiers unfortunately fired at him.'

I could not prevent myself bursting out: 'I'm astonished that you can dismiss Mr Stonex's story and yet believe this!'

'I believe it, Dr Courtine, precisely *because* it is so improbable and so shaming to the Chapter. The fact that it was remembered and passed down therefore lends it weight.'

'The logic of that is always to accept that the most discreditable account is the truest.'

'Why should Cinnamon lie? What did he have to gain?'

'Who knows? But he said that Freeth ran to the Treasury and not the Library?' I remembered how Mr Stonex had dismissed the evidence of Pepperdine's eyewitness because the Library could not be seen from the dining-room window.

'What was at that time the Treasury is now part of the Library. The Treasury was so seriously damaged that it was moved to another building.'

So Pepperdine's eyewitness might have been right! Following a train of thought provoked by this, I asked: 'Was Cinnamon the Precentor by any chance?'

'Yes, he was. Do you think that has any significance?'

'Possibly.' In fact, I had a theory about what might have been going on, for I had been trying to imagine the politics of the Chapter at that time by reflecting on how, in my own College, resentments and misunderstandings had festered over many years within an enclosed group of men with somewhat abstracted interests.

At that moment the Cathedral clock struck the hour and Dr Locard rose to his feet. 'Unfortunately, I must attend to my duties.'

At the top of the stairs he turned: 'I do hope that your testimony will do nothing to discourage the jury from finding the truth: that Perkins ransacked the house in search of the will.'

'I have to describe what I saw, Dr Locard. That is the obligation of a witness.'

He hesitated and then said: 'I understand that Fickling does not corroborate your evidence?'

'He noticed the disorder rather less than I did. That is all.'

'Nevertheless, don't you think it would be a little embarrassing if you were to contradict each other in court?'

He took leave of me with a final 'Good morning' and descended the stairs. As his footsteps faded into the echoes of the ancient building, I sat and stared at the manuscript. He had drained my enjoyment of it and I felt resentment towards him for that. I was also annoyed that he had teased me with his superior knowledge and insight into the story of Burgoyne. I had the feeling that he had been playing with me like an angler with a fish. What was the significance of the boy dying the same night as Burgoyne? Were the two deaths connected, and if so, how? I could not perceive what the Librarian was implying. And I was haunted by the image of the Dean setting fire to buildings in his own Close and struggling violently with another canon just moments before his death. If it had really happened, what could possibly be the truth behind that?

If I was to arrive at the inquest in time I had to have luncheon now. As I left the Library I looked across the Close and could just see the New Deanery. So Pepperdine's witness had not been mistaken and his version of events could not be discounted. I went to the usual inn, reflecting that it was strange that I found the food and the service barely adequate and yet I went back each time. I supposed it was the reassurance of a known evil that influenced me and the fear that I might find something even worse. I wondered where Austin was and how the outcome of the struggle within the Chapter affected him.

As I ate I thought about how, as the canon responsible for music, Cinnamon must have hated Freeth for what he had done. Assuming he was telling the truth, what had the canons been fighting over? Suddenly something Dr Locard had said the day before yesterday came back to me: *The best proof of a forgery is the original on which it is based.* If Hollingrake possessed the original of the deed which he and Freeth had forged in order to prevent Burgoyne from suppressing the college, then he had immense power over the Dean. He would have kept it locked in his Treasury. Could it be that when Freeth had seen the soldiers entering the Treasury he had seized his opportunity to free himself from blackmail by destroying the original deed under cover of the soldiers' looting?

I paid my account and made my way to the Guildhall.

Friday Afternoon

❖

I WAS DIRECTED into a big draughty chamber lined with black oak panelling and only poorly lit by a few gas-lamps in the dark afternoon. Around the walls were huge canvases of past mayors—ludicrously dressed in military uniform as members of the local yeomanry or even more grotesquely seated on horseback. The largest was a painting of a visit by the last king which portrayed the Mayor and the entire Corporation kneeling in a line before His Majesty.

I had left my arrival rather late and a number of people were already occupying the benches at the front, among whom I recognized Sergeant Adams and Major Antrobus. I found a space a little to their rear, rather hoping they wouldn't notice me. A few minutes before the proceedings were due to start, Austin arrived with Slattery. They seemed not to see me and seated themselves on the other side of the aisle. Moments later, the jury of fifteen soberly dressed men was ushered in by an attendant and led to its box. And then the Coroner arrived—a small man a few years my senior with fine features and a reddish complexion—and sat down facing the audience. At that instant, Dr Locard hurried in, accompanied by a bald man of about fifty. He noticed me, smiled and, rather to my surprise, took a seat beside me with his companion on his other side.

'This is Mr Thorrold,' he whispered. 'The late Mr Stonex's solicitor.'

We shook hands across Dr Locard, but had no time to speak before the proceedings began. I wondered why Dr Locard should be with the lawyer for the estate until I remembered what Quitregard had told me about the old gentleman's interest in the Choir School.

The Coroner began by saying that he and the jury had been that morning to the mortuary to view the body and to visit the New Deanery to have sight of the place of death. Evidence of identification had been taken in the presence of the body from the chief clerk to the deceased—Mr Alfred Wattam. Testimony as to the cause of death would be taken this afternoon from Dr Carpenter who had, unfortunately, been summoned to an urgent consultation and would therefore give his evidence later than was customary.

Major Antrobus was the first to testify. He stood confidently in the witness-box, his big hands resting on the ledge.

'Superintendent, what did you find on arriving at the house?' the Coroner asked.

'It had been ransacked and it was immediately clear to me that a murder had been committed whose motive was robbery. The evidence of the two gentlemen who had been having tea with Mr Stonex earlier that afternoon proved that the deed occurred in the half-hour before six o'clock. The two witnesses conveyed to me that they heard the waiter, Perkins, arrive at the front-door as they were leaving by the back at exactly half-past five—the hour at which he had been asked by the deceased to bring beer. I therefore sent two officers to find Perkins and when I questioned him later the same day he denied all knowledge of the crime. He said that he had gone to the house at four o'clock as usual but had found a note on the front-door instructing him to enter and had found the door to be unlocked—all of which was unprecedented. But he said that he performed his duties in the customary manner: he set out the dinner and took the dirty dishes from the previous day and left. And he flatly denied that he had returned at half-past five.'

'Did he mention receiving instructions from the deceased about coming back?'

'He denied that. However, a witness came forward later that evening to say that he had seen him at the front-door of the house at exactly half-past five.'

'That witness is here today?'

'He is. And he is Mr Appleton, the Headmaster of the Cathedral Choir School.'

'Did you confront Perkins with your proof that he was lying?'

'I did and he changed his story completely and admitted that he did go back at half-past five.'

'To deliver beer?'

'No. He claimed that the old gentleman had left him a message simply telling him to return for further instructions. I now went to Perkins's house—this was at nearly midnight—and found a parcel hidden in a cupboard.'

'That is what you found?' The Coroner pointed to a package in brown paper which was lying on the desk in front of him.

'Yes. It was opened and was found to contain banknotes amounting to the sum of twenty pounds. The notes were smeared with blood.'

There were gasps from the jury and the audience, and heads craned to see this horrible object.

'How did Perkins account for this?'

'He changed his story yet again and said that when he had delivered the old gentleman's dinner that afternoon he had found the package on the table in the houseplace with a message beside it.'

'What did it say?' the Coroner asked with a sarcastic smile.

The Major looked at his notebook: 'I copied his words exactly.

He claimed that it said: *I am busy. Do not disturb me. Lay my dinner as usual. Here is a package for you. Keep it by you and don't tell no-body. If a man comes to you this afternoon to ask for it, give it to him. If he don't, bring it back to me at exactly half-past five this evening and I will reward you.*'

'What action did you take?'

'I arrested him and charged him with the murder.'

'Is it possible that he left without committing the murder and that in the remaining half an hour, someone else did so?'

'Quite impossible, given that the deceased was so obsessed by the danger of being robbed that he only opened the door at fixed times to persons he was expecting. That is why I can state with confidence that he must have let his murderer into the house himself.'

'Could someone have obtained a key?'

'No, Mr Attard. He had only a single copy of each of the keys to the two doors of the house. He carried them with him on a ring at all times.'

'Has that key-ring been found?'

'It has not, although my Sergeant is at this moment making a thorough search of Perkins's house because it's certain that the murderer took the keys.'

'How can you be sure?'

'Because both the street-door and the back-door of the house were secured. Whichever door he left by, he locked it behind himself.'

'What a cool customer! Presumably his intention was to delay the discovery of the crime. Thank you for your testimony, Major Antrobus.'

Just before the Major had finished, Dr Carpenter had hurried in and seated himself. He now took the stand and testified that he was Mr Stonex's personal physician and that he had examined the body on arriving at the house at about seven o'clock. He had performed a full post-mortem examination later that evening.

'And what, Dr Carpenter, did you establish to be the cause of death?' the Coroner asked.

'I found that the hyoid bone was fractured and in view of that my conclusion is that the deceased died by strangulation.'

There were gasps from the audience. The Coroner said: 'Not by the blows to the head and face?'

'No, sir. Those blows were inflicted after death.'

'Are you sure of that?'

'There can be no doubt on that point.'

'How was the damage to the face effected?'

'I believe a garment was placed over the head—in fact, a blood-stained topcoat was found nearby—and the face was then hit repeatedly with the axe which was also found beside the body.'

'How many blows were delivered?'

'I estimate between seven and eight. These were very heavy blows which completely smashed the nose-ridge and upper jaw and the teeth and dislodged both eyes.'

'Would the murderer have been splashed with blood?'

'The person who smashed the face,' the doctor said carefully, 'would not have been splashed with blood because the victim was already dead. Consequently the violent flow of blood that would have resulted had the deceased been alive did not take place. That fact—together with the absence of bruising—is my evidence for saying that death had already occurred.'

'If the blows were not inflicted in order to kill, what was their purpose?'

'I can only speculate. Violence in excess of what is needed to kill usually suggests that the murder has been carried out by a relative, lover, or close friend.'

That was very interesting. He had no close friends, a lover was hard to believe and so I began to speculate about his brother. I was convinced that the motive was the key to this murder and that so far Perkins did not seem to have an adequate one—unless he had acted very stupidly on an impulse. What the doctor had just said, taken with the fact that if no will was found the estate would pass to the next of kin, suggested that that was the direction in which to seek the murderer.

'At what hour did death take place?' the Coroner asked.

'By the time I examined the body at seven o'clock, Mr Stonex had been dead for at least two hours, probably three.'

I leant forward in my seat. I had been impressed by the young surgeon's professionalism—if not by his manners—but this was clearly nonsense. The Coroner obviously shared my view: 'Dead for two hours or even three? That is quite impossible.'

Dr Carpenter said quietly: 'Nevertheless, my estimation by simple palpation was that the deceased died at about four o'clock. In arriving at this judgement, I drew on experiments conducted a few years ago at Guy's Hospital by two highly respected surgeons.'

'That is wholly absurd,' the Coroner exclaimed. 'The deceased was seen and spoken to as late as half-past five.'

'I can only report on what I have observed,' the doctor said calmly. 'This estimation was confirmed during the post-mortem autopsy which I conducted late last night. Rigor mortis had started by ten o'clock, which implies that death was at or before four o'clock.'

'You're not suggesting that the old gentleman with whom Dr Courtine and Mr Fickling had tea was a ghost?' The young doctor stared back in sullen and, I thought, arrogant silence while the audience tittered. When they had stopped laughing, the Coroner asked: 'When and where did you qualify, Dr Carpenter?'

'Two years ago at St Thomas's.'

'And how many murdered bodies have you seen in that time?'

'Two.'

'Were either of them cases of strangulation?'

'No. One of them was stabbed and the other killed by a shotgun. However, while I was a medical student I had the good fortune to walk the wards for six months as a dresser to Dr Tallentire who is frequently consulted by Scotland Yard. During that period I learnt a very considerable amount about forensic pathology.'

'While you were a medical student?' he enquired sarcastically. Without waiting for a reply he said: 'Thank you for your evidence, Dr Carpenter.'

The young man flushed at the Coroner's tone and stood down. Mr Attard then asked for Mr Thorrold and he rose and took his place in the witness-box and was sworn in. He explained that he was the lawyer who acted for the deceased and that he had drawn up his will about twenty years before. Under its terms his entire estate was left to the Foundation of Thurchester Cathedral to be used for the benefit of the Cathedral Choir School, which he had attended as a boy.

'Has the will been found?'

'It has not.'

'Who had custody of it?'

'The deceased himself. He usually kept it in a private strong-box at the bank, but he recently mentioned adding a codicil and presumably had taken it home to consider it at his leisure. Both the bank and his house have been searched. I should say that my late client was in the habit of hiding things in strange places, and so the attempt to find it is continuing.'

'What will be the destiny of the estate if the will is not found?'

'If Mr Stonex is declared to have died intestate then his heirs will be his next of kin.'

'And what is known of them?'

'The only relative he is known to have had is a sister. She would inherit, or if she is herself deceased, any heir she might have.'

I was struck by Mr Thorrold's failure to mention that the old gentleman had a brother. Could it be that his existence had been forgotten? Quitregard had never heard of him.

'Is anything known of her?'

'She left the town at a very early age and nothing has, so far as I know, been heard of her for over thirty years. Mr Stonex referred to her once only in my presence when, about eight years ago he mentioned that she had sent her son to him to—as he expressed it—pester him for money. I received the impression that he had refused the request and he never spoke of the matter to me again.'

Mr Thorrold took his place beside Dr Locard and myself, and the Sergeant was called. As he was walking forward I reflected on what I had just heard. It was becoming harder and harder to resist the hypothesis that if the murderer was not Perkins, it was someone closely related to the victim who therefore stood to inherit his estate provided he died intestate.

'Have you found the keys in Perkins's house, Sergeant?'

'No, sir.'

'He presumably dropped them after leaving the house since they were damning evidence of his guilt.'

'If he was guilty,' the Sergeant said quietly.

There was an outbreak of murmurs in reaction to this among the spectators and jurymen.

'Have you any reason to suppose that he was not, Sergeant?'

'There are a number of things that don't quite fit, sir. The deceased had never invited guests to his house before that day. Moreover, Dr Courtine mentioned to me that the house appeared to have been very thoroughly searched by the time he and Mr Fickling arrived. And he also told me that Mr Stonex was very preoccupied with the time. All of that suggests that there is more to this affair than meets the eye, and I believe it might have been the case that the old gentleman was expecting a visitor and that he was looking for something needed by that person.'

What the Sergeant was implying chimed precisely with the direction in which my own thoughts were moving. The old man had seemed unnaturally bright and animated during the tea-party and that might well have been because he was expecting an important visitor. And it suddenly struck me that he might have been searching for his will and only pretended that he was seeking the eyewitness account of Freeth's murder. But why should he have needed to find it? And how odd that he could not remember where he had put it.

The Coroner was unimpressed: 'That seems very tenuous, Sergeant.'

'There's more, sir. Mr Stonex changed the date of the tea-party at short notice. It was originally to have taken place today. It's possible that he did so because of his visitor.'

'How did he account for this alteration?'

'Mr Fickling and he met by chance on Wednesday evening and Mr Stonex told him the alteration was because the ceremony for the inauguration of the organ had been cancelled.'

'That's very strange,' I muttered before I could prevent myself.

'I beg your pardon,' Dr Locard said in an undertone.

'I'm sorry,' I whispered back. 'I didn't mean to say that aloud.' Austin must be confused. It was of a piece with his behaviour over the last few days and might be explained as the distractedness of a man violently in love. But I could not conceal from myself the recognition that some of his behaviour was disquieting in the light of what had happened. There was the odd business of his sudden insistence, as we approached the New Deanery at half-past four, that the old gentleman was not ready for us although that was the time we had agreed. And the fact that he claimed not to have noticed that the house had been turned upside down before we arrived. That went beyond absent-mindedness.

'There is also the strange fact,' the Sergeant went on, 'that the servant, Mrs Bubbosh, insists that she did not prepare the tea or know anything about it. That led me to try to find out where Mr Stonex purchased the comestibles. I have made enquiries of every baker in the town and none of them was the source for the cakes Mr Stonex offered to his guests.'

'I fail to see the importance of that.'

'It confirms my view that there was something strange, that Mr Stonex was taking precautions to hide his actions.'

'Are you suggesting that he baked them himself?' There was discreet laughter from the audience at this sally. 'This is all supposition, Sergeant, without a shred of concrete evidence.'

'But so, with respect, sir, is the idea that Perkins killed the old gentleman.'

'If it wasn't Perkins, can you suggest who it was?'

The audience seemed to hold its collective breath. The Sergeant's face was working and he turned his gaze slowly over the faces of the spectators. 'No. I can't say, sir,' he said at last.

'Then I don't think we need spend any more time avoiding the obvious,' the Coroner said, abruptly dismissing the officer.

I wondered if the Sergeant knew of the existence of a brother and if he had followed the same chain of reasoning as myself: the visitor who was the mysterious brother was the reason both for the victim's search for the will and for its disappearance; and the battering of the victim's face confirmed that he was killed by someone with whom he was closely involved. And yet there were some anomalies. Why had the old gentleman looked for his will? Could it be that he had done so in order to show his brother that he was leaving his entire fortune to the Foundation? In that case, had his brother flown into a rage, strangled him and then gratuitously destroyed his face? And then taken the will? And had there been enough time for all that to have taken place between half-past five and six o'clock?

Or perhaps Mr Stonex had wanted to find his will precisely because he was frightened of his brother since he knew that he would inherit his estate if he died intestate, and wanted to put the will in a safe place. In that case, had he hidden it somewhere else before his murderer arrived?

The next person called to the stand was Mr Appleton, a tall, thin, stooping man with a long and intense face, who confirmed that he had seen Perkins at the door of the victim's house at a few minutes after half-past five.

'How can you be so sure of the time?' the Coroner asked him.

'Very easily. I had come from the Cathedral where Evensong had begun at five o'clock. I had been told by the choirmaster just before the service started that a particular choirboy had failed to attend. This was a boy who had played truant several times before. Failing to find him anywhere else, I went to the New Deanery.'

'For what reason?'

'I had learned that Mr Stonex had struck up a kind of friendship with him and, naturally, I wondered what kind of interest an elderly gentleman might have in a young boy.' There were murmurs from the audience at this and he said: 'I felt it was my duty to look into the matter. I approached from the Close and as I was passing the back of the house I met an old woman and asked her if she had seen a boy in the uniform of the Choir School. She said she had noticed one round at the front as she was passing a minute or two earlier. So I went round there and although I did not find the boy, I saw the waiter from the Angel Inn—the man whom I now know to be the prisoner, Perkins—standing and knocking at the street-door. At that moment I looked again at my watch because I wanted to be back at the Cathedral as Evensong ended at about twenty to six in order to talk to the choirmaster before he left. I saw that I only had four minutes before it ended.'

'So that occurred at precisely twenty-four minutes before six?'

'Exactly.'

'Who was the woman? Has she been summoned as a witness?'

'I have never seen her before or since and was therefore unable to identify her to the authorities.'

'Thank you, Mr Appleton.'

The prisoner, Perkins, was then led into the witness-box by two police-constables who stood on either side of him throughout his testimony.

'I've allowed you to give evidence late,' said the Coroner, 'so that you can hear the case against you and answer it, if you are able to. I must warn you that things are looking bad for you. You are not on trial and my main interest is in finding out how Mr Stonex died. But if the jury returns a verdict that the evidence shows you to have been responsible, you will be charged upon that inquisition and sent for trial. Do you understand?'

'Yes, sir.'

'If you can clear everything up now by telling the truth, so much the better for you, because I have to say that what has a particularly suspicious appearance is the way you have changed your story so many times. Now, I want to begin by going back to when you delivered the old gentleman's dinner. You told the Major that you found a message from Mr Stonex about the package which was later found hidden in your house. Are you still maintaining that that is true?'

'Yes, it is. But it wasn't hidden and I only put it in a cupboard for safe keeping and I never opened it and I don't know nothing about the blood.'

'Tell the jury what happened when you went to the New Deanery at four o'clock.'

'First thing that was strange was, he didn't answer the front-door when I knocked. There was a note stuck up saying "Come in". I tried the door and, sure enough, it was unlocked. I was very surprised since that had never happened before. He was very particular about locking the doors was Mr Stonex.'

'So you went in. What happened then?'

'I put his dinner on the table just like usual. And then I seen the message.'

'Ah, the famous message. Now let's be quite clear about this. When you were first questioned, you said nothing about it and denied that you had gone back to the house at half-past five. Then when Mr Appleton informed the police that he had seen you at the street-door at that time, you admitted that you did go back but said it was because of a message you had found at four o'clock. You still said nothing about the package. When your house was searched and the package found, you now confessed that you had taken it but said it was because the message instructed you to do so. Have I stated the facts correctly?'

'Yes, sir. I was foolish and wrong not to tell the whole truth at once, but I thought nobody would believe me. It looked so bad.'

'Everything hangs on this message. Do you now have it?'

He gawped. 'Have it?'

'Yes, man. Do you have this famous message? Did you take it with you when you left the house?'

'No, sir. How could I, sir?'

'Did you not think to take the message with you as proof that you were to remove the old gentleman's property?'

'I couldn't, sir. It was wrote in chalk on a scholar's slate.'

'Oh, really? Written in chalk on a scholar's slate? Was Mr Stonex learning to read and write?'

The jury and the spectators laughed but I was not laughing. I had suddenly remembered an incident that until that instant I had completely forgotten. While we were starting our tea, our host had absent-mindedly rubbed out a message on a slate that was on the sideboard. In that case, was the rest of Perkins's story true?

I had all the pieces of the puzzle before me but I could not fit them together. Until this moment I thought I had worked out the role of the unknown brother but that hypothesis failed to explain the business of the message and the package. The chalked message and the package looked almost as if Mr Stonex himself had been setting a trap for Perkins. And he seemed capable of it for I remembered the cold-blooded justification for murder which the old gentleman had enunciated just before we left the house. But it was he who had been murdered and whoever had murdered him had had feelings powerful enough to make him batter the corpse's face beyond recognition.

Beyond recognition! An astonishing hypothesis occurred to me. It accounted for the battering of the victim's face as the consequence of fraternal hatred. And it also elucidated the nature and purpose of the trap into which Perkins had been lured. Moreover, I realized, it explained why it had been so important that the will be found—for I was now sure that that was what Mr Stonex had been searching for.

The Coroner continued with undisguised contempt: 'So the truth is that you did go back to the house at half-past five?'

'Yes, sir. But though I knocked and knocked, nobody opened the door and this time it was locked. So I took the package home. When I heard that the old gentleman had been found murdered, I didn't want to say nothing about it. I was afeared. But I didn't hide the package. I just put it in a safe place in the kitchen.'

'Where were you between the time you left the house and ten past six?'

'I went straight home, sir. I was with my wife, as she will say if you ask her.'

'I'm quite sure of it. And while we are speaking of your wife, how long have you been married?'

'Nearly four years, sir.'

'How many children do you have?'

'Four.'

'You must be in need of money.'

'Times are hard, sir.'

'How long have you been delivering Mr Stonex's dinner?'

'A year, sir.'

'Have you heard people say that he is rich?'

'Yes, sir.'

'And you know he takes careful measures to prevent his house being robbed?'

'Yes, sir.'

'Do you know the woman, Bubbosh?'

'Everybody knows Auntie Meg, sir.'

'Did you discuss Mr Stonex with her?'

'We talked of him and his queer ways a few times, sir.'

'And did you talk about how she could get you into the house so that you could rob the old gentleman?'

'No, sir.'

'Take him down, officers,' the Coroner said as if suddenly weary of the man.

I was the next to be called and as I walked to the witness-box Slattery gave me a most charming smile while Austin stared at me, white-faced and miserable.

When I had answered a few questions and the Coroner had thanked me, I said: 'With your permission, Mr Attard, I believe I can propose a hypothesis that accounts for all of the most puzzling facts in this case.'

The Coroner looked surprised but said very graciously: 'I'm sure the jury and I would be most grateful for the assistance of a scholar of your distinction, Dr Courtine.'

'Thank you, Mr Attard. I believe the Sergeant is correct in suggesting that Mr Stonex was expecting a visitor yesterday afternoon. I begin from the fact that he mentioned to me that when he was a child he had played in that house with his brother.'

There was a murmur from the audience and the Coroner said: 'I have lived in this town all my life and I have never heard that the deceased had a brother.'

'Precisely. That is why that remark was so significant and I'm sure Mr Stonex did not intend to make it. It slipped out because the subject was on his mind.'

'Do you mean', the Coroner said with an embarrassed air, 'that he had a natural brother?'

'No, Mr Coroner. I believe he was legitimate—though possibly he was a half-brother by an earlier and secret marriage. I assume he was older than the deceased and their sister.'

'The irregularity of the father's personal life was well-known,' the Coroner said gravely.

I nodded as I thought of the portrait of Mr Stonex's father and of what the old man had said about his rakish existence. 'I suspect that this brother had some sort of power over him and was exercising a form of blackmail.'

'Do you mean that the deceased had cheated him out of his inheritance?'

'Possibly. But if the elder brother knew that his mother was still alive when his father went through a form of marriage with the mother of the two younger children then he could show that they were the product of a bigamous marriage, in which case he might have a better claim on the father's estate than theirs. He might have been blackmailing the deceased for many years. Whatever the truth of that, I suggest that he had unexpectedly announced his imminent arrival and thereby precipitated a crisis.'

'So that is why Mr Stonex changed the date of the tea-party so suddenly?' the Coroner ventured.

'Precisely. Moreover, I believe that the old gentleman needed to find something which he had mislaid before his brother arrived, and that he invented the account of the murder of Dean Freeth—which he claimed to have been searching for—in order to explain the fact that he had virtually ransacked the house.'

'That is most ingenious and very persuasive,' the Coroner said and I was gratified to hear murmurs in support of his opinion from the audience and the jurors. I saw Slattery smiling at me and Dr Locard leaning forward in his seat intently.

'Something else I remember supports this. Just before we left, Mr Stonex searched inside the case of a grandfather clock. He pulled something out without letting me catch sight of it and with hindsight I now believe that he found what he was looking for.'

'And what do you think it was?'

'I assume it was his will.'

As I said those words I noticed out of the corner of my eye that Dr Locard started whispering animatedly to the lawyer sitting beside him.

'It seems strange that he should need to ransack the house to search for his own will.'

'He was an old man and perhaps had become forgetful.'

'But why should he wish to find the will so urgently?'

'May I continue with my hypothesis and explain that fact in its proper place?'

'Indeed you may, Dr Courtine,' the Coroner said with a courteous nod of his head. 'As you see, you have the full attention of the court for what, if I might be so bold, is an impressive demonstration of your forensic expertise.'

'Thank you, Mr Attard. In order to explain what I believe was happening I have to return to the chalked message on the child's slate that Perkins told the Major he read. I can confirm the truth of this for I saw it myself.'

There were exclamations of surprise from the spectators.

'Did you read the message, Dr Courtine?'

'Unfortunately, I did not read it. I merely saw Mr Stonex absent-mindedly rub out some words. The reason why I have not mentioned it before is that I completely forgot about it and only remembered it when the prisoner mentioned it half an hour ago.'

'Then are you suggesting that Perkins is telling the truth?'

'I am. I believe that Mr Stonex did prepare the package and entrust it to him by means of the chalked message.'

'Ah-ha!' the Coroner exclaimed. 'I begin to follow your drift. He did this so that the brother—who was the mysterious man referred to in the message—should collect it from Perkins!'

'No, Mr Coroner. Why should he do that? If he was expecting his brother to arrive late in the afternoon, why did he not simply give him the package himself?'

'I'm at a loss to account for his actions. But what is becoming clear to me is that you are suggesting that Mr Stonex was murdered by this mysterious brother.'

'Indeed, I most certainly am not, Mr Coroner. I have an even stranger explanation than that.'

I was gratified to hear gasps of astonishment from the spectators.

'You amaze me, Dr Courtine. I thought you had an explanation which accounted for everything. If the old gentleman was killed by a legitimate brother, then the motive was obviously to inherit his estate.'

'As a historian I have learnt to distrust the obvious, Mr Coroner. That explanation, of course, occurred to me but it does not explain the crucial mysteries: the fact that Mr Stonex gave the package containing blood-stained banknotes to Perkins, that the face of the corpse was unnecessarily battered, that the old gentleman was searching for something earlier that afternoon, that he had an obsession with the time, and that he changed the date of the tea-party at short notice. Of all of these, the strangest mystery is why the face was beaten in and I believe that I can explain that in such a way that the other puzzles will then resolve themselves.' I paused until there was complete silence—a rhetorical device perfected during my years as a lecturer. 'There could have been only one motive: to disguise the identity of the corpse.'

I saw members of the audience and of the jury turn to each other in astonishment.

'But the corpse has been identified as that of Mr Stonex,' said the Coroner.

'The corpse is certainly wearing his clothes and is that of a man of his age, height and approximate appearance. And yet if the face was destroyed in order to disguise his identity, then it follows that the corpse cannot be that of Mr Stonex.'

The Coroner stared at me in amazement. As the murmurs of the audience rose to a pitch, he had to bang his gavel. I noticed Slattery grip Austin's arm and whisper something.

'In that case, who in heaven's name is it?'

'Who but someone of the same age and general appearance: his brother.'

Many of the spectators gasped.

'Pray go on, Dr Courtine,' the Coroner said, shaking his head. 'I confess I am completely at sea now.'

'The brother arrived after Mr Fickling and I had left. He possibly entered by the back-door while the unfortunate Perkins was knocking at the street-door. I suggest that Mr Stonex killed him by strangulation.'

There was a moment's stunned silence and then a surge of noise from the spectators. The Coroner banged for silence and after a few moments I was able to go on: 'Mr Stonex then put his own clothes on the dead body and destroyed its face.'

'But, Dr Courtine, I simply don't understand what motive he had for this.'

'That brings me back to the will. The reason why he needed to find and destroy it was in order to prevent the estate from passing to the Cathedral Foundation. If no will were found, it would pass to his next of kin.' I paused triumphantly.

'I must be rather obtuse for I don't follow your meaning.'

'Who was his next of kin but his brother? And so he intended to assume his brother's identity and claim the estate.'

There was silence. Someone in the audience tittered but the

sound was quickly stifled. Mr Attard stared at me. 'He intended to return disguised as his brother?'

'Exactly,' I said. Even as I spoke I could see how preposterous the idea was. And yet it explained so much. I was sure that impersonation played a part in this story.

I heard one of the audience stifling giggles.

'What about his sister? Surely she has a better claim as his acknowledged sibling?'

'I assume she is dead. Or if the elder brother had proof that his younger half-brother and sister are illegitimate, then Mr Stonex will be able to use that to exclude her from the inheritance.'

The Coroner stared at me in amazement.

At that moment Mr Thorrold stood up: 'As the lawyer acting for the estate of the deceased . . .' He broke off and smiled at me: 'The presumed deceased, I should say, since doubts have been raised on that score, I am bound to say that although I have heard nothing yet to shake my belief that the body found yesterday is that of my late client, Mr Stonex, I believe that this point should be resolved beyond the possibility of dispute, and I therefore suggest that his physician be asked to give evidence on this issue.' He sat down again.

'I was about to do precisely that, Mr Thorrold,' the Coroner said rather testily. 'It is the first requirement of an inquest that it establish the identity of the deceased.'

The solicitor rose and bowed. 'I had no wish to anticipate you, Mr Coroner. I made the point simply because a very considerable estate is at issue.'

The Coroner nodded at him and then said: 'Is Dr Carpenter still present?'

The young doctor rose to his feet.

'Do you have any doubt, Dr Carpenter, that the body you examined and on which you later carried out an autopsy was that of Mr Stonex?'

'None whatsoever. He was a patient of mine for two years and I treated him for a variety of ailments. During the autopsy I recognized a number of unmistakable features including scars and discolorations of the skin. The idea that the body was that of Mr Stonex's brother—or even an identical twin!—is, frankly, quite absurd.' As he spoke those words he glanced at me and, as the audience laughed at his remark, I felt myself blushing.

'Thank you, Dr Carpenter,' said the Coroner. He looked at the lawyer: 'Does that satisfy you, Mr Thorrold?'

He stood again. 'On that point, very fully, Mr Coroner. But there is another issue. The present witness has referred to what he takes to be the discovery of the will of the deceased and I would like your permission to ask him about that incident.'

'Indeed. But before you do so, I wish to put a question to you. You have said that the only relative the deceased is known to have had was a sister who may or may not be living and might have a son. What of the suggestion that the deceased had an elder brother or half-brother?'

Mr Thorrold smiled. 'I have never heard of it. My father and grandfather acted for the father of the late Mr Stonex and I am certain they had no knowledge of a legitimate brother.'

'Could there have been a natural son?' Mr Attard asked.

The lawyer smiled again. 'There might very well have been one but he would have no claim. However, the point I wished to make is that since the testament which I myself drew up has not been found, it is of the utmost importance to establish what might have become of it.'

'To what purpose, Mr Thorrold?' the Coroner asked.

'It is premature to speak of this now, but if the deceased had it in his possession just before his death but it was missing when he was found robbed and murdered, then it is a reasonable assumption that it was destroyed by whoever murdered him.'

'And what consequences might follow from that?'

'Very significant ones. In English law a will is literally that—the will of the testator. It need not even be written so long as it satisfies certain conditions. It is important to establish what the testator's final intentions were, and if it can be proved that he had no thought of revoking his will and that it was stolen and illegally destroyed, then it could be executed.'

'Executed? How?'

'I believe I am able to recall its terms very precisely both from memory and from notes made at the time.'

'I understand. In that case, what question would you like to put to the witness?'

The lawyer turned to me. 'It would be very useful, Dr Courtine, if you could remember anything that proved that the document you saw was indeed the will of Mr Stonex.'

'I'm afraid I can tell you no more than I have said: he put something in his pocket which I believed he had found in the clock-case.'

Mr Thorrold put his head on one side and, accompanying his words with a charming smile, said: 'He put it carefully away in his pocket as if he was going to cherish it rather than thrust it in as if it were of little importance?'

'I can't go beyond what I've said,' I answered.

The lawyer thanked me very affably and then sat down and conferred quietly with Dr Locard.

At that moment Sergeant Adams stood up and the Coroner asked him: 'Do you wish to put a question to the witness?'

'Yes, sir. I've been listening with great interest, Dr Courtine, and I believe you may have hit upon part of the truth. But there are some important matters that are still unaccounted for. Why do you think Mr Stonex left the chalked message for Perkins with those instructions?'

'He needed someone to be blamed for the murder. And so he intended to collect the package himself disguised as a mysterious stranger. But for some reason he had to abandon that part of the plan.'

'I see. And why did he put blood-stained money into the package?'

'So that if he did not collect it, then Perkins himself would be suspected of the murder.'

'I thought you would say that, sir, and my own suspicions were taking me in that direction.' He paused as if embarrassed by what he was about to say. 'Finally, Dr Courtine, can you throw any light on Dr Carpenter's belief that the deceased died at about four o'clock?'

I was disconcerted myself by this question for it had crossed my mind that the doctor must have been bribed into giving that extraordinary evidence, although remembering the young man's arrogance in the Cathedral that morning, I would have thought he was too proud to compromise his integrity for money. 'I can only suppose', I ventured, 'that Dr Carpenter's confidence in his expertise has on this occasion—if on no other—proved somewhat premature.'

I was gratified by a few titters from the spectators and a thin smile from the Coroner. Adams, looking disappointed, resumed his seat.

'Thank you, Sergeant,' Mr Attard said and turned to me: 'And thank you, as well, Dr Courtine. I don't think we need detain you any longer. Your evidence has given the court much to think about.'

As I stepped down I reflected on the Sergeant's last question and rather wished I had not exercised my wit at the expense of the young surgeon. Yet he must be mistaken. And it was precisely at that moment that a strange idea—even stranger than the one that I had explained to the Coroner—began to take shape in my mind and I felt my face burn with excitement as I pondered its implications. If I was right, then I knew why Mr Stonex had changed the date of the tea-party: it was because he wanted Austin and myself to be there as witnesses.

My mind was on that as Austin was now called and he shuffled into the witness-box unsteady and shaking, like an old man.

'Was anything that you saw at the New Deanery on Thursday afternoon untoward or suspicious?' Mr Attard asked him.

'Nothing.'

'Then do you have anything to add to what Dr Courtine has said?'

'Only that I saw no indication that the house had been ransacked when we arrived. It's true that the old gentleman told us he had been looking for the manuscript describing Freeth's death, but he was certainly not responsible for the disorder I saw when I went back later that day.'

His answer surprised me. The houseplace was in turmoil when we entered it. He was clearly not himself, for he was speaking slowly and very carefully.

'Did you notice the deceased take something out of the case of a grandfather clock?'

Austin smiled: a horrible grimace intended to suggest amusement. 'I would most assuredly have remembered such an odd proceeding. No, I did not.'

That was extraordinary! After all, it was he who had suggested looking there!

'What about the message chalked on the slate which the deceased rubbed out?'

'I did not see that either. That is to say, I noticed the slate but to my certain recollection there was nothing written on it. Mr Stonex merely picked it up and absent-mindedly stroked it.'

'And what of Dr Courtine's testimony that the deceased mentioned a brother?'

'I did not hear such a reference. I believe Dr Courtine must have misheard the old gentleman. He certainly referred to his sister.'

'Thank you, Mr Fickling. You may resume your seat.'

For the sake of the hypothesis that was taking shape in my mind, it was important to clear up a point on which the Sergeant must have misunderstood Austin. I stood up.

Austin halted in his progress from the witness-box and gazed at me in amazement.

'Do you wish to put a question to Mr Fickling?' the Coroner asked me in surprise.

'I do, Mr Attard. I'd like to ask about something that the Sergeant said.' I turned to Austin: 'You told him that Mr Stonex met you by chance on Wednesday evening and informed you that he wished to bring forward our appointment for tea to yesterday?' Austin nodded cautiously. 'You said the reason he gave was the postponement of the ceremony for the organ?' He nodded again. 'Can you explain that?'

'He said that his bank had been going to close on Friday afternoon but now that it had been cancelled, he would be at work.'

That could not be right. 'At what time did you meet him on Wednesday?' I asked.

Austin hesitated. 'It must have been early that evening.'

I was astonished. Austin was clearly very confused. 'Your recollection must be at fault. It was I who told you about the organ and that was very late that evening.' He opened his mouth as if to speak but said nothing. 'Do you not remember,' I went on, 'the conversation that you and I had that evening?'

'The conversation?'

'The discussion we had of events twenty years ago.'

He nodded.

'Then do you not recall that it was after that that I mentioned going into the Cathedral on my way back from dinner and learning of the delay to the organ?'

Austin stared at me for several seconds. 'Yes, that must be so. I was mistaken about the time but I remember the whole thing very distinctly. It was after our conversation. I found I could not sleep that night and so I went out for a constitutional after you had gone to bed and met Mr Stonex then.'

'Where did you meet him?' I asked.

'As I came out of my house and was passing the back of the New Deanery, he was about to enter.'

He was lying. He could not be confused about that. However much he had had to drink that night. Or earlier today. And if he was lying he had a reason and that raised some disquieting possibilities. It was not forgetfulness or intoxication that had made him deny the incidents I had described. I suddenly felt a desire to expose the truth whatever it cost.

'And where did you go after that?' I asked. I knew he would be gravely embarrassed by this public allusion to the visit he had made in the middle of the night.

'Dr Courtine,' the Coroner interrupted, 'I hardly think that can be relevant.'

'I have a reason for putting the question, Mr Coroner, if you will bear with me for a moment I think it will become evident.'

Mr Attard nodded. Austin stared back, his hands gripping the edge of the box. 'Where did I go? I went nowhere. I merely walked around the town for twenty minutes and came home.'

'You did not go into a house?'

He looked at me in dismay. 'No. No, I did not.'

'That's very strange. You see, I, too, found myself unable to sleep that night and when I heard you go down the stairs I left the house myself.' I could see from his face that he had had no idea and that this revelation horrified him. 'I meant to catch you up, but you were too quick for me and disappeared into that alleyway that runs from the Close into Orchard Street.'

The room was absolutely silent.

Austin was frightened. Clearly there was something in what I saw on Wednesday night that alarmed him. I wished I could work out what it was but I could not see how everything connected: the mysterious woman seen by Appleton, the brother of the victim, the ransacking of the house. It occurred to me that there was another mysterious woman in the case—the one who had been in the house in Orchard Street in the early hours of Thursday morning— but I could not imagine how she might be related to Austin's evident anxiety.

I turned to Mr Attard: 'Mr Coroner, I think I know how the murder was committed in such a way as to confuse all of us about the time of its occurrence. I believe the victim was killed much earlier than has been assumed.'

Austin stared at me white-faced. I noticed that Sergeant Adams had leant forward to gaze at me intently while the Coroner looked at me, his pen poised motionless in his hand.

I turned back to Austin: 'I believe the victim was lying dead in another room of that house before you and I even arrived for tea.'

There was a buzz among the spectators. The noise was so loud that I believed I was the only person who heard Austin exclaim: 'In that case, who was it who gave us tea?'

I was astonished by the remark. It made no sense. My eye happened to fall on Slattery who was staring at Austin with an expression of terrifying intensity and mouthing something I could not make out.

'I see what you are trying to do!' Austin shouted. 'But I had nothing to do with it. I was teaching all afternoon—as dozens of witnesses can prove. I was in front of my class until after four o'clock and then I was with you from the moment the Library closed until the body was found by the police.'

'Gentlemen, please,' said the Coroner. 'Mr Fickling, please calm youself.'

Austin turned to him: 'This man has a grudge against me for an imagined wrong that goes back more than twenty years.'

'That is not true,' I exclaimed. 'If I had not forgiven you many years ago I would not have come to visit you.'

'You forgave me,' Austin repeated mockingly. 'How generous of you.'

I looked at his jeering, drunken face filled with venom and wondered how I had ever convinced myself that I had forgiven him. Or that he had ever intended anything but harm to me.

'You may take your seat, Mr Fickling,' the Coroner said.

Fickling shuffled back to his seat while Mr Attard turned to me and said: 'Dr Courtine, I don't understand what you meant just now when you said that the victim was dead before you arrived at the house.'

'I was suggesting,' I said, 'that Mr Stonex had killed his brother before Fickling and I arrived. His body was lying in the study.'

'Dr Carpenter has already testified to the impossibility of that,' the Coroner said. 'The corpse is certainly that of Mr Stonex the banker and not some hypothetical brother of his.'

I opened my mouth to say that the doctor had obviously been bribed, but thought better of it.

'And so,' the Coroner went on, 'I'm going to advise the jury to dismiss this red herring from their consideration. Thank you, anyway, Dr Courtine.'

I sat down and as I did so I glanced towards where Fickling and Slattery were sitting. The latter was smiling at his friend who was still shaken and wan but was nodding. It was clear to me that, far from alarming them, what I had just said had reassured them. I must have approached very near to the truth but without quite attaining it. I had another surprise, for at that moment Dr Locard turned and smiled encouragingly at me.

The Coroner announced that there were no further witnesses and that he would proceed instantly to his address to the jury.

'Some of the witnesses you have heard,' he began, 'have tried to complicate a very straightforward matter. But from my long experience on the Coroner's bench I know that there are in every case issues which are never fully understood. That is particularly inevitable here for we are dealing with the perverse mind of a human being capable of cold-blooded murder, and therefore it is wrong to seek the enlightened rationality which guides the more elevated representatives of our race. I advise you, therefore, to see the case in all its evident—though brutal—simplicity. You should treat with considerable scepticism the evidence of Dr Carpenter relating to the time of death. You should also set aside the ingenious theory of Dr Courtine, which is a plot for a sensational novel rather than evidence for a court of law. Every fact upon which reliance can be placed points towards Perkins as the murderer: the testimony that Mr Stonex admitted him to the house at half-past five, the blood-stained banknotes hidden in his house, and the fact that he kept changing his account of events as each new piece of evidence against him emerged. Foreman of the jury, will you now decide among yourselves whether you are able to reach a determination here and now, or whether you need to adjourn to the room that is available for you?'

The jurors conferred briefly and then the foreman, a burly, red-faced man who looked like a prosperous grocer, said: 'We don't need to withdraw, your honour. We've decided already.'

'Very well. What is your finding?'

'We have determined that the deceased was unlawfully killed and slain by the prisoner, Edward Perkins.'

There was an anguished cry as if someone had been dealt a physical blow. We all looked at the prisoner whose face was twisted in horror and fear. The Coroner gave instructions that he be held in custody until his trial and we watched silently as he rose to depart and the prisoner was led away.

I got up and went to the end of the row of seats but found I could not move because the ample figure of the Major was obstructing the aisle, and so I turned back to go the other way but found Dr Locard talking to the lawyer. Beyond them I noticed Sergeant Adams looking at me as if he wished to speak, but, like myself, he was trapped where he was. As I stood there, unnoticed and feeling rather uncomfortable, I heard the Major's voice booming behind me, in answer to a question which I had not heard: 'A formality, I promise you. On that evidence, no jury could acquit. He will hang before Easter.'

I advanced towards Dr Locard and heard him arranging to come to Mr Thorrold's office later that afternoon and saw the lawyer hurry away. I was relieved to see out of the corner of my eye that Fickling was also leaving—accompanied by Slattery.

To my surprise Dr Locard turned towards me and smiled and said: 'Dr Courtine, my wife and I find that we are unexpectedly free this evening. You would be doing us a great honour if you would dine with us. There are several matters I wish to discuss with you.'

I could not think quickly enough of a convincing reason not to do so and therefore I accepted and we agreed the hour.

We shook hands and he walked over to talk to the Major and Mr Wattam. Before I could get away, Adams was beside me blocking my escape: 'I found what you said very interesting, Dr Courtine. Very interesting indeed. Although I have to confess that I don't believe your idea about Mr Stonex murdering a brother is correct, I think you might have hit upon something not that far removed from the truth.'

'I don't know, Sergeant Adams,' I said. 'I really don't know.'

Lowering his voice and glancing round he said: 'Did you notice something Mr Fickling said just at the end?'

'Forgive me. I don't have time to discuss it now.'

'You could find that house in Orchard Street again, couldn't you, sir?'

'I must ask you to let me pass, Sergeant.'

'Will you come to the station-house tomorrow? Any time at all. I'll be there all day.'

'I doubt if I'll have a moment before I leave.'

'I have your address in Cambridge, Dr Courtine. I could visit you at your convenience.'

'If you'll forgive me,' I said, pushing past him. I left the building and walked quickly towards the Close.

I had not a minute to spare. The Sergeant was right: I had come near the truth. Yet I had still failed to perceive it. Why had Fickling been so ready to defend himself with an alibi when I had not accused him of anything? What was it that he was afraid I was going to say? Above all, as I walked I could not get out of my mind those extraordinary words which had also intrigued the Sergeant: *In that case, who was it who gave us tea?*

I was anxious to get back to Fickling's house, pack up my things, and escape before he returned. As I hurried through the silent streets, I hoped that he and Slattery had not gone back there. It was already getting dark and the gas-lights were being lit, although the Close, which I turned into through the North Gate, was still unilluminated. Why was Dr Locard suddenly so friendly? Why was he not disgusted by my public confrontation with Fickling? Surely what he feared above everything else was scandal.

When I entered the house there seemed to be nobody there. I did not want to draw attention to my presence and so, instead of turning up the gas in the hall, I merely lit a candle from the pilot-light. I went straight up to my room and quickly packed my bag.

Fickling had been involved in the murder. I was sure of it. And an idea about what had really happened was forming in my mind. My theory about the brother was wrong, though it had been close enough to the truth to have frightened him. I was sure that Perkins was innocent, and in that case, I must try to find evidence to support my new hypothesis. The keys from the victim's house would be the best proof for they could not be destroyed and must have been abandoned or hidden somewhere.

As I came down the stairs my eye fell on the grandfather clock which was shamelessly wrong about the hour. I remembered that it kept time badly. *Just like old Mr Stonex's!* I put down the bag and the candlestick, opened the clockcase and reached down to the weights. There was something attached to one of them. I lifted it and found it was a set of keys. At that moment I believed I had solved the murder. Here were the keys by means of which the killer had left the house of the victim and locked it behind him yesterday afternoon. I was also frightened and horrified at the thought of what I might be about to unleash. This would destroy Fickling and several other people, but it would save an innocent man from the gallows. I found that I could face the prospect of Fickling's disgrace and punishment with equanimity. He had betrayed and made use of me, exploiting our former friendship—our boyish love—without shame. He had treated me like a fool. I doubted if he would hang for what he had done and I did not go so far as to hope that he would. But he had committed—or at least aided in the committing of—a terrible act, and justice must take its course. I removed the keys and looked at them in the dim light of the candle. There were two keys on the single ring, the larger of which was evidently a house-key. Picking up the candlestick I hurried down the stairs and tried the key in the lock of the door. It turned. So it was not the key to the New Deanery. I felt a surge of disappointment. Of course, it made no sense that the murderer should retain the keys. He would have discarded them as soon after leaving the New Deanery as possible.

The other key was too small to fit a door and was probably for a cupboard. A cupboard! I had a sudden vision of the moment on Tuesday night when I had seen Fickling ascending the stairs as I was coming down from my room. Could he have been putting the key back in its hiding-place after concealing that mysterious package? I hurried up to the sitting-room with the candlestick to light my way. The key fitted the armoire and the door swung open to my touch immediately. There were several objects inside, one of which looked like the package. I opened it and removed several layers of wrapping paper until I was able to examine the contents by the light of my candle. Their nature first surprised and then appalled me. What I saw was from a certain point of view charming and could be entirely innocent, and yet I knew from hints and overheard fragments of conversation that they were far from it. What they were I do not propose to reveal beyond saying that they were photographic plates. Many things that I had heard, overheard, witnessed and even guessed, were now explained and confirmed. I had very little time to decide what to do with them. In one sense I had no right to take them but at the same time, they were quite improperly in Fickling's possession. Neither did their owner have the right to have them back since such photographs should not have been taken. If Fickling found them gone he would know that I had removed them, but that was not a consideration that detained me. But what in heaven's name should I do with them?

I sealed the package up again, took a pencil from the table nearby and wrote on the outside 'For the personal attention of the Dean'. Although I had only a vague understanding of the complications involved, I assumed that possession of them would untie the Dean's hands and make it easier for him to see that justice was done. Then I locked the armoire and went back down to the half-landing. I had just replaced the keys inside the clock when I heard the street-door open and the sound of voices.

Because I had not turned up the gas, they did not realize I was in the house! Without thinking, I blew out the candle. To my relief I heard them go into the front-parlour. I placed the package in my bag, picked it up and crept down the stairs in the darkness.

As I passed the door I looked into the room and saw them. They did not see me because they were otherwise occupied. I was so stunned by what I saw that I could not move. Of course, as a man of the world and one who has spent his entire adult life in the University, I have heard of such things. But to be presented with the reality of it so suddenly was disconcerting, to say the least. And yet, what after all was love? If it was a good in itself, did it matter what form it took? Could it ever be called perverse and unnatural? The ancients had accepted many forms of love and it was only the narrow, bigoted, mean-minded spirit of Judaeo-Christianity which was so censorious about it.

So much was now clear to me. There was no unknown mistress to whom Fickling had gone late on Wednesday night and it was Slattery's hands that I had seen through the window. But in that case, who was the woman whose voice I had heard?

I must have stood transfixed for ten seconds, and then Slattery, who was facing the door, looked over Fickling's shoulder and saw me.

Slattery smiled and said: 'I suppose you're profoundly shocked, Dr Courtine.'

Fickling whirled round to face me and I saw naked hatred and fear on his countenance. "What the hell are you doing here?'

I glanced down at my bag. 'I had hoped we might avoid meeting again.'

'I can't feel that more than you do.'

'You say I'm shocked,' I said to Slattery. 'What I'm shocked by is what you two have collaborated in during the last few days. I now know why you lied about meeting poor old Mr Stonex on Wednesday night,' I said to Fickling. 'I understand everything now.'

'In that case . . .' Fickling began, but Slattery held his arm in a disturbingly intimate manner and said softly: 'What do you understand, Dr Courtine?'

'You're going to watch an innocent young man hang for a murder you helped to bring about. Both of you.'

Fickling looked down at the floor but an expression of entirely meretricious amazement appeared on Slattery's face: 'I was at choir-practice and playing the organ all afternoon and Fickling was with you. How on earth can either of us have been involved?'

'I've told you, Mr Slattery,' I said flatly, 'I understand how the trick was worked. It wasn't the victim who gave us tea.'

'Are you going to try to persuade the authorities of yet another remarkable theory?' he said, still smiling.

I said nothing.

'Is this your revenge?' Fickling said.

'What should I avenge?' I asked. He said nothing. 'What did you do to me that I should want to avenge?'

He smiled spitefully. 'You said you'd forgiven me.'

As he said those words I felt such a violent desire to seize him and bang his head back against the wall and throttle him that I staggered sightly and had to put my hand on the back of a chair.

When I could trust myself to speak I said, as calmly as I was able: 'You helped him to win her from me, didn't you?'

'Win her from you!' he repeated mockingly. 'He didn't win her. What an absurd idea. She won him. But it's true that I introduced him to her because I believed he might be the person to rescue her.'

'Rescue her?'

'She told me she only married you to get away from her mother. She found you unendurably dull. And physically repulsive.'

'You're lying. She loved me. When we married we were both in love.'

'You really don't understand, do you? You're the worst kind of fraud—the kind who deceives himself. You're a sentimentalist. You tell yourself comforting lies.'

'You're the liar. A liar and a traitor. You conspired to betray your closest friend, to destroy his happiness. And now you boast of it.'

'Betray,' he sneered. 'You want people to betray you because it confirms your sense of moral superiority.'

'Then I should be happy now because that's why you invited me, isn't it? To betray me again. You wanted to make use of me. To use my good name to provide you and your accomplices with an alibi. You only told me about Burgoyne so that I would go and read the inscription—which has nothing to do with him!—and meet that man at the back of the New Deanery.'

'You mean Mr Stonex?' Slattery said, looking puzzled.

'I'm not a complete fool, Mr Slattery,' I said. 'I admit that I've been obtuse much of the time, but I've also been fairly acute.'

'Well, I half agree with you about that,' he said, with an odious smile.

His words stung me into saying: 'The individual whom I met on Wednesday afternoon was not Mr Stonex who at that moment was eating his dinner a few yards away.'

Slattery struck his forehead. 'Of course! It was his brother.'

I turned from him with contempt. I had built a mistaken hypothesis on that slip of the tongue and I was embarrassed to think of it now. Yet I had at least noticed anomalies that others had overlooked even if my attempt to fit them together had been misguided.

Fickling drew his lips into a weak, venomous, drunken smile and said: 'His twin brother. Don't forget that, Martin.'

'Not his brother. I was wrong about that. His brother-in-law. That was the slip of the tongue that I spotted, even though I misunderstood it.'

I had thought my revealing this would stun them, but although they glanced at each other nervously they were not devastated by my remark. Did that mean I had still not hit upon the entire truth?

'So what are you going to do?' Slattery asked with no more than mild curiosity.

'I don't know. You seem to have taken everyone in. Though I believe the Sergeant has perceived most of the truth. I suspect that some of the others have, too, but they have reasons for not wanting your role to be exposed. You see, I understand now how and why you have been protected by the canons. I warn you, however, that you may not be safe any longer.'

To my delight I saw that at last I had upset them. Fickling started and even Slattery was clearly shaken by what I had said.

Having done what I wanted, I quickly opened the door and left the house. They deserved it. I had no compunction about what I was about to do. Fickling's words had struck home. In that moment I believed that what he had said was true. She had not loved me. She had found me unlovable.

I made my way across the silent and deserted Close to the Deanery where I carefully pushed the package through the letter-box. Then I passed into the High Street and engaged a room at the Dolphin. I was so upset and depressed that I almost decided to send my apologies to Dr Locard and excuse myself from the invitation to dinner. I couldn't face any more questioning about the Stonex murder or any more politicking over the fate of the manuscript. But then I thought how much I would regret losing another opportunity to talk to Mrs Locard and I made up my mind to go.

Friday Evening

❖

DR LOCARD'S DWELLING—the Librarian's House—was a large, comfortable old place in the Lower Close. The maidservant who answered the door took my hat and coat and told me she had been instructed to show me into her master's study and so it was there, a moment later, that I found my host seated at a desk in the window with a blazing fire in the grate. He rose and greeted me warmly.

'I was looking again at the manuscript,' he said, indicating the desk.

'You have it there?'

'One of the few privileges of my post,' he said with a smile, 'is that I may remove items for private study. But would you care to seat yourself and we'll look at it again together?'

'Indeed I would!'

We established ourselves at the desk.

'I think you'll be interested to know,' he said, 'that I've found its source.'

'Its source?' I stared at him in amazement.

'When we looked at the manuscript this morning, I thought something about it was familiar.'

'You mentioned a tiresome device for which the writer had a weakness but you did not specify it.'

'Using the superlative excessively. I was sure I had encountered it before and then I remembered this.' He picked up and opened a book that was lying on the desk. 'It's the *Vita Constantini*, which, as you probably know, is the life of a Frankish saint of the tenth century that was written in the eleventh.'

'But how can it be the source if it's a century or two later than Grimbald?'

'Bear with me for a moment, Dr Courtine, if you will. I'll start reading a few sentences before the crucial point in the text, and I should explain that the author is talking about how bravely Saint Constantine stood up to the rulers of his age.' He read the text in Latin, translating every few phrases: '*King Hagebart showed little respect for men of the Church, as his conduct in regard to the learned Bishop Gregorius, the martyr, illustrated very clearly.*'

'*Doctissimus* and *apertissime*!' I exclaimed. 'There are two of your detestable superlatives.'

'And in the same sentence!' he added with a shudder. 'And now here is the interesting sentence: *Because as a boy the king had been a pupil of Bishop Gregorius when the learned old man taught the sons and nephews of the old king, Hagebart's father, he did not bury him with honour or even decency as he should have done in the case of such a learned and holy man.*'

He looked at me in triumph.

I gazed back. 'What is so significant, Dr Locard?'

'The ellipsis.'

'I'm afraid I don't understand.'

'It does not make sense that the king did not bury his old tutor with dignity *because* he had been his pupil.'

'You're right. Unless, of course, one takes a peculiarly dark view of the relationship between teacher and student.'

He went on without noticing my joke: 'But if we insert the folio you discovered into the text in the middle of this puzzling sentence, we find that at both points the newly discovered sentences make perfect sense. And now the account of the bishop's death illustrates the point the author is making. So the first sentence of the manuscript you found this morning should read: *Because as a boy the king had been a pupil of Bishop Gregorius when the learned old man taught the sons and nephews of the old king, Hagebart's father, the king and the martyr were once close friends.* And the final sentence should be: *Moreover, he had so little respect for the slain bishop that he did not bury him with honour or even decency as he should have done in the case of such a learned and holy man.*'

When I had read it again a few times and thought about it, I had to concede that he was right.

'Somebody removed the page you found from the manuscript containing the *Vita Constantini*,' Dr Locard said. 'And by chance or design, it happened to be the sole copy of the *Vita* that survived, which is why the story has dropped out of that text leaving only a nonsensical sentence to show that something is missing.'

I tried to hide my disappointment. 'I congratulate you upon a magnificent piece of scholarship, Dr Locard.'

'Moreover,' he went on as if he had not heard or as if my compliment was not worth noticing, 'I have found an additional piece of evidence in support of that interpretation. The events described at that point in the *Vita Constantini* took place in 968. Now I've looked through various annals relating to that period and in the *Chronicon de Ostberg* have found this entry for that date: 'To the great dismay of all men, the sun fled from the sky for several minutes a little after noon on the twenty-second day of December of this year."

He looked up in delight.

'Yes, that's conclusive,' I said. 'Then I suppose it's certain that

Leofranc tore this page out of the Frankish manuscript and used it as the source of his *Life*.'

'Rewriting it in order to glorify Alfred and Wulflac,' he added.

Far from confirming the authenticity of Grimbald's *Life*, my discovery had virtually proved that Leofranc had invented it. And had cast grave doubt on the existence of Wulflac. Dr Locard had destroyed my hopes of bringing about a fundamental re-assessment of Alfred, and had done it as a mere amateur. I felt humiliated. I told myself I was as good a historian as he, even though he had apparently read everything in my subject and had an astonishing memory and linguistic gifts. He seemed to me to be a mere logic-chopper, a destroyer rather than a creator, who was so cold and logical and lacking in imagination that he missed the spirit of the past. And he was repulsively calm in his moment of triumph. As I looked at him I believe I almost hated him at that instant for not savouring his victory over me. It was as if he was so far above me that it gave him no pleasure to have crushed me so comprehensively. My one consolation was that what had looked like an account of Alfred's deceitful and cowardly conduct was now proved to have nothing to do with him. There was one important question that remained to be resolved.

'What are your intentions with regard to publication, Dr Locard?'

'This is so important that the world of scholarship should know of it as soon as possible. It virtually proves that the whole of Grimbald is to be rejected as a source. Ideally what is needed is a scholarly edition of the manuscript together with the related sources. A series of volumes, in fact.'

'Absolutely,' I agreed excitedly. 'But such an undertaking would be prohibitively expensive even for one of the university presses.'

'The manuscript was found in this Library where it had lain for nearly eight hundred years,' he said with the calm passion of an archivist. 'Leofranc was the bishop here. I would like to see the Dean and Chapter support such a project. The *Annales Thurcastrienses*.'

I stared at him in amazement. 'Is that possible?'

He gazed at me speculatively. 'It might be. At present the Foundation has a number of demands upon its resources, but if that should change then certain funds would become available.'

There was a brief silence.

'Such an edition would require,' I said cautiously, 'a scholar with a profound knowledge of the period and the sources.'

'It would need a Director to supervise it—who could well be an Oxford or Cambridge Fellow since he would not be required to be in Thurchester very often as he would have one or more assistants working here. You are one of the three or four best qualified scholars in this field, and since it was largely by your efforts that the manuscript was found, you are the obvious choice. It would not be my decision alone, of course. And it's possible to conceive of circumstances in which the decision would be taken out of my hands by the Dean and the rest of the Chapter.'

'Circumstances?' I ventured.

He gazed at me thoughtfully. 'I will speak frankly. Everything depends on the trial of Perkins and its implications for the bequest to the Foundation.'

'Has anything further transpired?'

'A woman claiming to be Stonex's sister has telegraphed to Thorrold from Yorkshire.'

'Is it certain that she is who she claims to be?'

'That will, of course, be looked into, but it seems so. She has worked as a housekeeper in Harrogate for many years but has recently suffered a stroke which has incapacitated her.'

'So the Foundation will lose the bequest?'

'Unless it can be proved that the will was destroyed against the wishes of the testator. Your testimony that he was searching for it is crucial, Dr Courtine. Thorrold assures me that all that is required is evidence that Mr Stonex mentioned the will in a way which gave no impression that he intended to cancel it. In that case, it could be reinstituted from the draft which he has fortunately located.'

'Fickling will continue to deny that the incident with the clock-case occurred.'

'After his performance this afternoon, he is discredited as a witness.'

'He was certainly lying about his own involvement. The persons responsible must be brought to justice.'

'Your theory about a brother . . .'

'I realize I was wrong. He never existed.'

He looked at me in surprise. 'Then you accept that Perkins was paid by the sister to murder the old man and find the will?'

'In that case,' I replied, avoiding his question, 'who hired him on her behalf if she is in Yorkshire?'

'Never mind about that,' he said abruptly. He seemed to realize how rudely he had spoken and said, choosing his words with care: 'What I mean is that the investigation of that issue should be left to the proper authorities who are Thorrold and the police. They may be relied upon to do what is required. It would be most injudicious of you to involve yourself in it any further, Dr Courtine. If you begin to make accusations against Fickling there is certain to be some disagreeableness and everyone will suffer. You in particular as a friend of his.'

'Our friendship is over. He is not the man he was when I knew him at Cambridge. Then he was upright and decent. Except that he used to go on what he called his 'rantipoles'—drinking sessions that lasted several days—which I suppose have led him to his present condition.'

'He has fallen under a bad influence. He is notorious in the town. He has been picked up from the gutter and carried home many times. And his friendship with Slattery has occasioned gossip of a deeply unpleasant nature.' He hesitated and then said: 'They have had several drunken quarrels in public and on one occasion he apparently tried to kill Slattery. Let us say no more on that topic.'

At that moment there was a knock at the door and the servant-girl reappeared. 'The mistress says dinner is ready, sir. She is waiting for you in the dining-room.'

'Gracious heavens! Is it as late as that!' He turned to me: 'I do apologize. How very discourteous of me. I meant to take you into the drawing-room to meet my wife.'

As we left the room I reminded him that I had already had the pleasure of meeting Mrs Locard. He led the way to the dining-room—a spacious room at the front of the house—and we found his wife waiting for us there.

'Robert has been so busy in the last few days that I've seen very little of him,' she said to me with a smile as we shook hands.

'Ah yes,' I said. 'On top of everything else, there has been the business of the body in the memorial.'

'And what do you think is the truth of that matter?' she asked.

Dr Locard was talking to the maid about the serving of the first course. 'Your husband has very ingeniously explained that the body must be that of Canon Burgoyne who was killed by the Cathedral Mason, Gambrill, because he was about to denounce him for murder.'

'I don't believe that,' her husband said, turning from his discussion of soup and its temperature.

I flushed. 'I thought you said so this morning when we discussed it.'

'I evidently failed to make myself entirely clear,' he said with a careful courtesy that I found more offensive than bluntness would have been. 'I said I believed that Gambrill thought that Burgoyne was about to make a public exposure of his murder of Limbrick's father. But I don't believe that that was really what Burgoyne was about to denounce.'

'How complicated,' Mrs Locard murmured, smiling at me.

'But the inscription on the wall of the New Deanery,' I began, 'suggests that Gambrill . . .'

'The inscription!' he exclaimed. 'The inscription has nothing to do with the murder of Burgoyne. It was not put there until 1660 and it refers to the murder of Freeth.'

'Does it? It's very hard to understand what it does refer to.'

Dr Locard said: 'It is ambiguously worded because it was erected at a time when the Burgoynes were still powerful. It was put there by the canons, principally Champniss, the Sacrist.'

'He was the eyewitness whose evidence Pepperdine heard more than twenty years later. I didn't realize he was the Sacrist. But you can't mean that he was the man who was humiliated by Burgoyne and Gambrill and had a nervous collapse? He must have been long dead by then?'

'Indeed I do mean him. Rather surprisingly, he survived most of the other canons. He had been a loyal friend of Freeth and was bitterly upset by his death and so the inscription was, in effect, an accusation of murder against the Burgoyne family.'

'And was he right?'

'After the Siege the officer who was in command of the town and therefore in some sense responsible for Freeth's death . . .'

'Forgive me for interrupting,' I said, 'but I know this story.'

'Then you know that the officer was Willoughby Burgoyne, the Treasurer's nephew, and you will understand why the canons held him responsible.'

I nodded. But of course I was astounded at that piece of information. In that case the explanation I had heard yesterday afternoon was untrue: the officer in charge had not acted in cold blood to save the town but to avenge a family wrong. I remembered how close Champniss had come, in Pepperdine's account, to accusing the officer of having murdered Freeth. Even after the defeat of the Roundheads, it would have been dangerous to have denounced a family as powerful as the Burgoynes. It was plausible, then, that the canons might have made the veiled accusation contained in the ambiguous words of the inscription.

There was a momentary silence while the servant cleared away the soup-plates.

'Then who was Burgoyne about to denounce if it was not Gambrill?' I asked.

The Librarian smiled enigmatically. 'Do you remember that one of the singing-boys died during the Great Storm?' I nodded. 'He was Gambrill's nephew.'

'Was that a coincidence?' I remembered that Dr Locard had hinted that the boy was murdered. 'Are you suggesting that he was murdered by Burgoyne?'

'How can I know what happened that night? I can only conjecture and you can do that as well as I. Probably better.'

If Burgoyne had killed the boy he must have had a motive. A powerful one. What could it have been? Suddenly I realized what Locard had been hinting at.

I glanced at Mrs Locard who was arranging something with the servant. 'I think I understand whom it was that Burgoyne was about to denounce.'

He nodded. At that moment his wife turned back to us and said: 'I beg your pardon, Dr Courtine. You were saying that the poor Canon was murdered by the Mason. But in that case, who killed *him*?'

'A very good question,' I said.

'Limbrick,' Dr Locard said. 'The Mason's Deputy.' Seeing my sceptical expression he demanded: 'If there was no second man with him, how did Gambrill lift the slab into place that sealed Burgoyne into his living tomb?'

I shrugged my shoulders: 'Could even two men have done that?'

'With the aid of the pulley that was waiting on the scaffolding for that purpose, it was perfectly possible. The slab was balanced by lead weights so that they could let it slowly descend while guiding it into the right position.'

'Even two men would have had difficulty,' I murmured.

'Have you a better explanation, Dr Courtine?' he said with a thin smile.

'I can do no more than venture a hypothesis. I believe I can imagine what happened that night . . .'

'We should invent nothing beyond the given facts,' the Librarian interrupted. 'On the evidence we have it must have happened like this: when Burgoyne collected the key and went into the Cathedral that night, Gambrill and Limbrick followed him. They attacked him, knocked him unconscious and perhaps thought they had killed him. They then lifted him up onto the scaffold, pushed him into the memorial, and sealed it with the slab.'

'A task which five or six men would have found difficult,' I interpolated. His hypothesis seemed far more fanciful than my own.

Dr Locard nodded to acknowledge that he had heard, but was paying no attention to, my objection. 'Limbrick then murdered Gambrill by bringing the scaffold down on top of him.'

'Why did they remove Burgoyne's outer garments and why did Gambrill put them on?'

'That is a minor detail.'

'A truly convincing account would explain everything.'

As he rose to carve the roast beef which the servant had laid on the table, my host said: 'That is an unrealistic hope and, if I may say so, a strange one to be expressed by a historian.'

I smarted at the remark but reflected that my revenge would lie in finding evidence that he was wrong. His logic-chopping failed to take account of the element of the unknown and for that one needed imagination.

I managed a smile. 'There we have two quite opposite approaches. In my view, the true test of a hypothesis is that it explains even the anomalies. It's not difficult to produce one that roughly accounts for the main features of any given mystery. But if that is at the expense of ignoring the recalcitrant elements, then such a hypothesis cannot be regarded as a sufficient explanation.'

'Then what would satisfy your requirements, Dr Courtine?'

'A narrative which—though bizarre in some of its elements— accounts for every anomaly. And the creation of such a narrative often requires the exercise of the imagination.'

Dr Locard pursed his lips in distaste. 'That is not the role of a historian.'

'But the alternative is an act of destruction which is just as crucial. Where there are conflicts or absurdities they are dismissed as the products of misunderstanding or dishonesty. But it must frequently be the case that there is some circumstance or motive which is missing from the historical record and which would account for the apparent inconsistencies. All I am arguing is that the historian should try to find the missing piece of the puzzle.'

'I can't agree. The historian has an obligation to stay with the known facts rather than dream up phantasms from his own imagination. In the case we are discussing, we know that Limbrick had a reason to hate Gambrill and that he later married his widow. That is enough to accept the simple and obvious explanation that the two men killed Burgoyne and then Limbrick murdered his employer. It would be illogical—if not absolutely perverse—not to accept it.'

I turned to Mrs Locard. 'I am in a minority on this point. The Coroner said virtually the same thing this afternoon when he warned the jury against giving credence to a theory of my own.'

The servant handed me the plate of beef that her master had just carved. 'While I concede that there are some trivial anomalies,' Dr

Locard said, 'in the explanation of the old gentleman's murder that the Coroner recommended to the jury . . .'

I could not forbear interrupting: 'The time of death? The fiend-like destruction of the victim's face? Trivial?'

The Librarian continued as if I had not spoken: 'The essential truth is very simple. Perkins was put up to the murder. He was paid to kill the old gentleman and secure his will.'

'You don't accept that, Dr Courtine?' Mrs Locard asked.

'I am convinced the young man is innocent.'

'I'm frankly astonished that you should say that,' her husband said. 'However, I am in hopes that by the time of his trial a link will have been proven between him and the sister.'

'Then the will has not come to light?' his wife asked. 'And she will inherit?'

'Perkins must have received money as payment for the murder,' Dr Locard said. 'I expect proof of that to be discovered.'

'No,' I answered Mrs Locard. 'The will has not been found.' I was surprised that her husband had not told her.

'It never will be now,' Dr Locard said. 'Perkins took it when he ransacked the house. That fact must emerge. And that's why, Courtine, when you are in the witness-box at his trial it would be advisable not to blur the issue by saying that the house had already been searched. It will only confuse the jury.'

'It's an unimportant anomaly?' I suggested.

He glanced at me sharply. 'Precisely. And try to avoid other matters which will muddy the waters like the old man rubbing out the message on the slate which you suddenly brought up, although you had not mentioned it to the police.'

'My memory was jogged and I literally recalled it only at that moment.'

Dr Locard said very carefully: 'You've remembered so much that I am hopeful you might remember more.'

'It's perfectly conceivable,' I said. 'The memory is a strange thing.'

We had just begun to eat, but now he laid down his knife and fork and said: 'Very little would be required. Thorrold assures me that a sworn affidavit from yourself would be sufficient to allow Mr Stonex's will to be probated. He has reconstructed it from the draft.'

'Thorrold? The executor of the Stonex estate?'

'He also acts for the Dean and Chapter.' I was astonished. Was I absurdly fastidious to think that the lawyer had an obvious conflict of interest? 'Such a move would, of course, be contested by the sister but Thorrold believes it has a fair chance of being upheld. Especially if Perkins is convicted.'

'What would I need to remember?'

'Nothing more than Mr Stonex mentioning that he had found the will in the clockcase and saying that he intended to lodge it somewhere for safekeeping—perhaps with his solicitor or at the bank.'

'Fickling would contest that. He would accuse me of lying.'

He pushed his plate away. 'Let me speak with complete frankness. This affair has ramifications involving Fickling, Slattery, at least one of my fellow canons and other individuals, of which I am sure you, as an outsider, are unaware. If Thorrold's reconstruction of the will is accepted and probated, nothing of these larger complications need become public, for the sister of the deceased—or whoever it was who hired Perkins—would have nothing to gain from either his conviction or his acquittal. The estate would be disposed of in accordance with the terms of the will, regardless of who Mr Stonex's heir is. If, on the other hand, the reconstructed will is not accepted, then certain facts will inevitably emerge during the trial of Perkins. I dearly hope that can be avoided because it will be enormously damaging to many people, but if that is the price that has to be paid, then so be it.'

There was a silence. I glanced from the face of my host to that of his wife who crimsoned slightly and looked away. I carefully phrased my next remark: 'I'm reluctant to swear such an affidavit given that a man is on trial for his life.'

Dr Locard said in a low, intense voice: 'If you swear this affidavit and allow the will to be executed, you can say what you like at the trial. It would then be a matter of complete indifference whether Perkins was convicted or not.'

'But if I don't swear it, then the trial would turn out to be a very disagreeable experience?'

'Inescapably. For Fickling would have to be discredited by letting certain circumstances become known and that would be most unpleasant for you.'

I made no response. It occurred to me that by delivering to the Dean the package of photographic plates stolen from Sheldrick, I had put into his hands a weapon which could, under certain circumstances, effectively bring about the death of Perkins. And I regretted my impulsive naivety in having done so.

Dr Locard went on: 'Cruel rumour would spare nobody. Do you understand me, Dr Courtine?' I gazed back at him without making any response. 'One consequence would be that I would be unable to persuade my fellow canons to entrust publication of the manuscript to you, for every past acquaintance of Fickling would be under suspicion. You are unmarried, I believe?'

'I have no wife.'

He glanced at his wife and then turned back to me: 'An unmarried friend of Fickling would, to speak quite bluntly, be peculiarly vulnerable to gossip of the most malicious kind.'

Mrs Locard lowered her gaze.

'I have nothing to hide.'

'I have no doubt of that, Dr Courtine. You may be prepared to accept the risk for yourself, but can you inflict this on your family and friends?'

'I have no family.'

'None at all!' Mrs Locard exclaimed, trying to turn the conversation. 'How very sad. No brothers and sisters?'

Dr Locard turned away with an expression of irritation.

'I had one sibling only—a sister who died four years ago. My only living relative is her daughter. I am on my way to stay with her and her husband for the festive season.'

'Do they have children?'

'Two little girls. My bag is filled with gifts for them.'

'I can see you are a devoted uncle—and great-uncle. But you have no children yourself?'

'As I just said, I have no wife.'

I had spoken more abruptly than I had intended and I saw that she was dismayed.

At that moment the servant came in and handed a note to her employer. With an apology to me, he opened and read it. 'I am terribly sorry, but I am summoned to the Deanery.'

'At this hour?' his wife exclaimed.

'Something has occurred which the Dean wishes to discuss with me.'

'And, Robert, you've hardly eaten a thing.'

'I do beg you to forgive me,' Dr Locard said to me. 'Please continue with your dessert and I hope to rejoin you very soon in the drawing-room.'

As soon as he had left us, I said: 'I must request your pardon for my rudeness just now. I don't know why I spoke so curtly.'

'I should not have asked you such a question,' she said.

'Not at all. It is I who was in the wrong. I'm still upset because of everything that has occurred in the last two days.'

'I'm so sorry you were involved in the dreadful business with poor Mr Stonex. It must have been deeply upsetting for you.'

'And in addition to that, I've just had one of the most disagreeable experiences of my life. To discover that an old friend . . . is not a friend.'

I glanced up and found her grey eyes upon me. 'I had the most terrifying nightmare last night. This morning, I should say. I woke with a black sense of despair that has stayed with me all day. How strange that the thing that has shaken me most is not something that actually happened.'

'I'm not surprised you should have a nightmare. You've been so close to death—to violent death—in the last two days.'

'And yet the dream seemed to have nothing to do with that. I believe it was occasioned by the memory of a story I recently read—a foolish thing that upset me, though I can't imagine why. I believe it's not death that frightens me for when I looked at the body of Burgoyne this morning I found it merely sad and moving. Even Mr Stonex. He died hideously but he is at peace. What has disturbed me is the sense of evil.'

'Because both of them were murdered?'

'Murder is part of it. But evil does not manifest itself merely in murder. And, heaven knows, not all murder results from evil.' Seeing that she looked puzzled, I said: 'For example, if Perkins had killed Mr Stonex it would have been the result of greed and stupidity rather than evil.'

'But you don't believe he did?'

'No. I'm sure that he was killed from real malevolence and that's what has upset me.' I had no intention of describing to her the brutally battered face of the old man. 'The conviction that I have been in the presence of evil.'

'People mean such different things by that word.'

'For me it means pleasure in inflicting pain on others or seeing others suffer.'

'Are any of us entirely innocent of that?' Coming from her those words astonished me.

Perhaps because I was taken by surprise I found myself saying: 'I've certainly had to acknowledge it in myself today and I think that is what has frightened me most.'

Apparently unperturbed by my admission, she said: 'If we are honest, we will all recognize it in ourselves. Our religion teaches us to return good for evil. But that is hard.'

I had no desire to tell her that her religion was not mine. And had I cast off Christian superstition if I could still talk of evil?

'It's particularly hard when the person who is being cruel has been a friend,' I said, 'and therefore knows how best to wound.'

'And yet, don't you think that only people who are themselves very unhappy want to inflict pain on others?'

'I suppose so. But I'm shocked by the malevolence he showed towards me, his anger and the strength of his desire to hurt me. And that was what had terrified me in my nightmare—the feeling of evil.'

'Would you like to tell me about it? I find that it often helps to dispel the effect of a nightmare if you narrate it to someone.'

'It seems ungenerous to inflict it on you.'

'I am truly interested. I should like to hear it, Dr Courtine. But let us move to the drawing-room and have our coffee there.'

A few minutes later we were sitting on the large sofa in the brightly lit room with a cheerful fire blazing before us. My hostess prompted me to keep my promise.

'Well, it was very strange,' I began. 'I had my arms locked around some creature—something that was reeking with the most appalling smell. My eyes were closed. I seemed to be fighting it. I was high up somewhere. I think I was lying on a bed. There were birds crying outside the window. What was so upsetting was my conviction that the monstrous thing had some kind of claim upon me. It was almost a part of myself. In desperation and in order to save myself, I tore off an arm—or, rather, a thing like an arm which was more like a wing or a tentacle—and I felt pain in my left arm.

Then I woke up—in my dream, I mean, though I believed I had really awoken—and found that I was lying on the sofa in my rooms in College. I felt such a terrible, black sense of despair. There was a period in my life when I slept on that sofa. It was not the happiest of my existence. Then I really awoke and found what seemed to be my own severed arm beneath me. I had been sleeping on it and it had lost all sensation.'

She shuddered sympathetically. 'Nightmares are like vultures that emerge to prey upon us in our moments of vulnerability.'

'I have been sleeping badly ever since I arrived. I will be glad to leave the town.' Tomorrow I would be making a long journey by train, travelling from one place where I was not wanted to another. 'I'm sorry. That was rather rude of me.'

'Of course not. You must be looking forward to Christmas and the children will be excited at the prospect of seeing their uncle.'

'The truth is that I am dreading it.'

If she was surprised she concealed it and waited for me to go on with an expression in which sympathy was so evident and was so different from mere curiosity that I continued: 'They are so happy with their new baby and so much in love that I know they don't want me there. They ask me each year because they feel sorry for me being alone at Christmas.'

'I'm sure they want you there. I'm sure of it.'

'Why should they want me?'

'You seem to me to be a very kind person. Well-intentioned and honourable. Forgive me for being so presumptuous but I can't believe that you don't have friends who love you.'

I smiled. 'A few old College chums, as dusty and as dull as myself. I don't think "love" would be at all the appropriate word for our feelings for each other. I should have stayed in College with them as usual and not thought of inflicting myself on my niece. It's a terrible thing when the happiness of others makes one feel sad. And then one feels so guilty for resenting their happiness.'

'It would be unnatural not to feel that,' she said. 'But that's not the same as wishing them harm.'

'No, no. I don't wish anyone harm. I just wish myself a little more good. I could never have guessed when I was young that at nearly fifty I would have so little. I thought that everything I wanted would just happen. I threw away my single chance.'

I regretted the confession as soon as I had made it and perhaps because she sensed that, she said: 'I believe you can be more lonely when you're not alone.'

I was surprised by the frankness of her admission. I had seen enough of her husband's manner towards her to have formed some conception of their life together. In that moment I had a vivid and unbidden image of what I had glimpsed in the front-parlour two hours earlier and it seemed to me suddenly that I had lived a life devoid of courage or daring. At least Burgoyne and Fickling had not done that.

'Especially,' she added, 'when there are no children.'

'That is my great regret,' I said, recalling what Dr Sisterson had said about her loss of a child. 'I feel it more and more as I grow older.'

She gave me a sad smile: 'I have known gentlemen considerably older than you marry and have children.'

'As far as marriage is concerned, I've had my single chance.'

'But I understood you to say you have no wife.'

'I can't marry. I wasn't merely rude a little while ago. I was also somewhat dishonest. I told you I have no wife. The truth is . . .' I stopped.

'You don't need to say anything,' she said gently.

'She left me. I was devastated. I was completely destroyed by it. It's easier to give the impression that she is dead. I used to try to think of her as dead. But I now know that is wrong. It's not she who has been dead all these years. It is I.'

'I understand. When you love, you entrust to that person your sense of your own worth, and if that person throws you aside, you believe profoundly and utterly that it is because you are worthless. That is a kind of death.'

'That describes my experience precisely. May I tell you the whole story?'

'Are you really sure you want to?'

'Yes, though I've never spoken of it to anyone. There has been enough lying and concealment and I would like to tell the truth now. That is, if you don't mind hearing a common enough tale?'

'Every such story is unique.'

'Twenty years ago I married a woman—a girl, for she was ten years younger than I. She was the daughter of the Master of an Oxford college. She was very beautiful. Very sweet and very beautiful. I loved her and I believed, I still believe, that she loved me—to begin with. And we were happy at first. At first! But it all happened so quickly. Our time together was so brief—just a few months. I first saw her when she was fifteen. But then she was sent abroad to be educated and I did not see her again until one Christmas—just after I had been elected to a Fellowship at my old College, Colchester. I proposed that January and we were married in April. After the honeymoon—which we spent in a Scottish castle owned by relatives of my wife—we moved into a house my College owned. We were happy then.

'I had a friend. An old friend from my days as an undergraduate. He had been disappointed in the degree he had hoped to obtain and had had to abandon his expectations of a Fellowship but he had stayed on and was teaching at one of the choir-schools. He was witty and charming and he made my wife laugh, and moreover he sang and played the flute and she sang and played the piano, so they made music for whole evenings together. And I was grateful, for I feared that our life was rather dull for her. She must have been lonely for she knew very few young women in Cambridge. I was deeply preoccupied with my duties—for I was now Junior Dean of my College—and my historical studies and spent all day at the College and most evenings working in my library. Then my friend began to bring a friend of his. I was a fool. A complacent, conceited fool. I hardly need to go on.'

'Go on if you wish,' she said very gently.

'I both knew and did not know—or did not want to know—what my friend was doing. Many years later I forgave him. Or, rather, I thought I had forgiven him because I allowed myself to believe that he did not play a malign role in what happened. I have recently discovered that he did indeed do exactly what I accused him of. He must have resented me. I suppose he envied my happiness. I had embarked on a career as a scholar and was happily married. He was in neither of those fortunate situations. So he envied me, but I think that he was even a little jealous of me. And perhaps he wanted to do a favour to his friend, even though it was at my expense. The friend was a man he was fond of. Particularly fond. The story is banal—like an incident from a French novel.

'As I have said, my wife was young, beautiful and she was even rich. I didn't mention that, did I? Her mother had been a great heiress. So my wife was a wonderful prize. I was a very lucky man. And in some ways I knew it and yet at the same time I did not. My friend, the schoolmaster, stopped coming so often and on those occasions his friend—who never became a friend of mine for there was something in him I never cared for—came alone. He was handsome, charming and knew how to make himself very amusing. He had lived in exotic places and done extraordinary things. He had a little money of his own. Enough to indulge some of his tastes but not enough to live the kind of life he desired. He wrote poetry and travel sketches, and must have dazzled a young woman who had known only dusty university men. But he was unworthy of her. I felt so humiliated by her preferring him to me.'

I had to break off for a few moments.

'The worst time, I think, the worst time of all the bad times was when I suspected but did not know. It was in the last weeks of Trinity term just before the summer vacation. There was an occasion when I came home unexpectedly and happened to pass an open window and saw them in the drawing-room. They were simply looking at each other, not smiling or speaking but sitting at opposite ends of a sofa and gazing at each other with such an intensity of emotion between them that it was palpable. She seemed so sweet and innocent, and yet I believed she was planning to betray me. I started to follow her. I'm so ashamed of myself now. When she believed me to be in College I skulked about the streets near our house like a thief, waiting to see where she was going and whom she was meeting. The strangest thing was that I became frightened of her.'

'Frightened?'

'Yes, I mean literally afraid. She could do me so much harm. I felt I had mistaken her nature. She was not what I had fallen in love with. The innocent, sweet young girl I had loved could not have done such a cruel thing to me. By a horrible perversity, I believe my suspicions drove her into what she did. I believe I suspected the truth before there was anything to suspect, at least, before the situation had become irretrievable. But I said nothing. I found I could not speak to her about it. When at last I found out . . . When I knew the truth . . . For everybody in Cambridge knew the truth before I did. I was so humiliated. No, I believe I can guess what you are thinking. But it wasn't the public shame that I can't forgive her for. After all, I stayed on in Cambridge afterwards when I might have resigned my post and left. I found I couldn't stay in the house, though. It frightened me. I started sleeping on a sofa in my rooms in College. After a year I gave up the house.' Again, I had to break off for a moment or two before I was able to continue. 'I'm sorry, I've forgotten what I was going to tell you.'

'You were telling me about how you found out. But please don't say any more if it would distress you.'

'It came to a head in the summer vacation. The three of us—my wife and I, together with my friend, the schoolmaster—went to the coast, to Great Yarmouth in fact. She was very quiet, very sad. I feared she was missing her lover but I still was not sure of her feelings about him or what had passed between them. I kept trying to talk to her about it but I couldn't. Then on the night before we were to return to Cambridge, I managed at last to raise the subject. To my horror—and, I suppose, my relief—she confessed. She told me the whole story. How she had believed she had been in love with me but when she had met this man she understood what passion really was. And he had returned her feelings, she said, with an intensity that she had never found in me. Though, God knows, I adored her. I suppose I lacked her new friend's facility in expressing those feelings. She told me that our friend, the schoolmaster, seemed to have guessed from the beginning and she said that he even seemed to be encouraging them.' I looked down at the floor. I felt there had been enough evasions. I said: 'They had become lovers, she told me.'

I broke off and covered my face for a moment. 'She was not the person I had fallen in love with and married. She was not the innocent young girl I loved. That was the real deception.'

I felt a touch on my arm and lowered my hands. Mrs Locard was looking at me solicitously. 'Forgive me, Dr Courtine, but perhaps that was the cause of the misunderstanding between you. You believed you were married to an innocent young girl and it may be that she felt that she was no longer that—if she ever had been even when you first knew her.'

I thought of Fickling's cruel words about why she had married me.

'Do you mean that she married me under false pretences?'

'Not exactly, no. Or not deliberately. It may be that she came to feel more and more that you did not understand her true nature, that you did not see the whole of her. You wanted her to remain a sweet young girl but she was growing and learning and changing.'

'And I was too immersed in my work to see that? Yes, there may be some truth in that.'

'But more than that, you wanted her to stay as you imagined her to be when you first knew her. So when she told you what had happened you believed that she had betrayed you by hiding her real nature from you, and that's quite understandable because what she did hurt you dreadfully. You think she acted simply from selfish motives but don't you think it's possible that she felt she was deceiving you—I mean, before she actually deceived you? She felt guilty and came to believe that it would end in unhappiness for both of you.'

'Someone said something rather like that to me very recently. Is it possible that in some perverse way I wanted her to betray me in order to feel superior? To feel like a heroic martyr?'

'There are people who invite betrayal. They are demanding towards themselves and don't realize how hard they are on other people. They make it difficult for others not to fail them. And in some cases they even take a grim pleasure from being let down. But that's not the same as saying they want to be betrayed.'

'I believed I was being kind and fatherly to her. I was so much older than she.'

'But if I'm right, Dr Courtine, that was part of the difficulty. You did not treat her in the way she wanted. And perhaps the other man did because he talked to her as an adult woman and an equal. And so she felt that her true self was engaged with him and only a false self with you.'

I was not sure I was understanding her. Seeing my perplexity, Mrs Locard said: 'May I ask if, when she made that admission that night in Great Yarmouth, she was asking you for a separation?'

'No. She said she knew that what she had done was wrong. She had broken off relations with her lover. She wanted us to remain husband and wife. She wanted it to be as it had been before.'

'Then did you refuse?'

'I neither refused nor agreed. I found that I was unable to give her an answer. I knew that despite what she said, everything was changed utterly. I could never trust her again. She was not the innocent, guileless girl I had married. If she could inflict such misery on me, she could not love me. And it was worse than that. I now doubted that she had ever loved me. I asked myself if she had only pretended to love me. Had she always found me dull and plain? The situation continued like that and, hardly speaking, we returned to Cambridge. Her lover was sending messages to her every day. Several times a day. He was urging her to go abroad with him. This was now the middle of August.'

When I stopped Mrs Locard said mildly: 'And then?'

'Then nothing. I was in a turmoil of emotions and yet I could not express anything to her. I recoiled from her when she tried to touch me. We haunted the house like two ghosts. After ten days she went to her lover. I have not seen or heard from her since then. For some years I've been letting people assume that I am a widower. It's not entirely a lie for she is dead to me, but she is alive and is still my wife. They are living in Florence—or were when I last heard news of them.'

'Yet you are not divorced?'

I shook my head. 'A private separation was arranged through our lawyers. She has her fortune back in her own hands. I wanted no part of it. Her lover is now able to live the kind of life he has always wanted.'

'She has not asked for a divorce so that they can marry?'

'Yes, but I have refused because I am not prepared to legitimize a relationship founded on betrayal.' My voice quavered on those last words. How pompous I sounded now that I had actually uttered the phrase I had used so often to myself.

'I can see how painful it still is for you. It was wrong of me to question you.'

'No, no, on the contrary. It's a relief to tell someone about it at last. I'm not usually like this. Everything that's happened in the last few days . . . And something I didn't know.' I turned away from her and said: 'They have a daughter. I have just learnt that and it has brought it all back. She is now fifteen. She was the child we should have had. I had no notion that such a child existed. Fickling told me because he wanted to wound me.' As soon as the words were out of my mouth I realized that I had revealed that it was Fickling who had been the intermediary, but I imagined she had already guessed that.

'It's understandable that that should have upset you. Poor Mr Fickling has many reasons for being unhappy and wanting to make others the same. But I'm sure you don't believe that they had the child just to inflict pain on you.'

'Oh no, I'm not as self-obsessed as that.'

She hesitated for a moment. 'It might be easier for you if I say something which sounds cruel. I wonder if I should say it?'

'Please do.'

'When someone has wounded us by rejecting us, we think they have acted from a desire to hurt us and that they are continuing to do us harm. And that is painful. But we find the thought of their malice is strangely reassuring because it at least implies that they are still interested in us. But the truth is nearly always that the harm was not the main point but an incidental effect. The truth is often that the other person soon feels nothing towards us. The pain we believe they are inflicting on us is something we are creating ourselves because mingled with it is a certain gratification.'

It was difficult to accept and yet I felt the truth of it. I had gripped the memory of her like a thorn which hurt because that was preferable to losing her altogether. And then it came to me that inflicting pain on myself in that way had allowed me to continue to feel morally superior to them.

'Then you think I should let them have the divorce?'

'I think you should let yourself have it.' Seeing my bewilderment she went on: 'Wouldn't it be best for yourself to put it all behind you? To end the difficulties for both them and you?'

'For me? The fact that we are still married in the eyes of the law makes no difference to me.'

'Does it not? Isn't it rather like delaying the funeral after a death? It's only when the burial is over that the process of grieving can begin.'

'Begin? I've been grieving for twenty years.'

'But grieving lets you eventually put the past behind you,' she said with a smile that softened the reproach. 'And you haven't done that.'

'You can't leave the past behind,' I said. 'You are your past. As a historian, I'm bound to believe that.'

She seemed to be searching for the right words. 'But not granting a divorce has legal as well as emotional consequences. While it prevents them from marrying, it means that you can't either.'

I smiled in surprise. What an extraordinary conversation this was.

She smiled back: 'Why not? Gentlemen are so much more fortunate than we in being able to marry and, indeed, have children at an age when a woman's active and useful life is judged to be over.'

'That would mean forgiving them and why should they have everything and I have nothing when it is they who are guilty?'

'They behaved badly—your wife and her lover and your friend—and you have every right to feel that. But I know from my own experience that we are usually harder on ourselves than on others, and so if you feel like that about them, I suspect that you blame yourself even more.'

'Blame myself? Do you mean, for not being more on my guard?'

She looked at me appraisingly.

'I'm sure I wasn't blameless. I was naive and trusting and I suppose that was because I was conceited enough to think my wife's affection for me would remain.'

Mrs Locard said nothing and after a moment I asked: 'Do you think I should have forgiven her and taken her back?'

'Dr Courtine, I would not dream of making that kind of judgement. But from the way you described that time, it seems you had no choice. You said you simply could not speak to her.'

'I was in such a turmoil of emotions.'

As I uttered the words I felt their inadequacy. I wanted to say more, to explain myself, to say that I could not speak because I could not reconcile the girl I loved with the woman I believed had deliberately injured me, but at that moment the door opened and Dr Locard entered. He had taken off his overcoat and hat but was carrying a wooden box the best part of a foot in length. He carefully put it down on a side-table. When he turned round he looked at us curiously and I was afraid that it was obvious that I had been upset. He poured himself some coffee while he apologized for having been away for so long.

'Has anything happened, Robert?' his wife asked.

He made himself comfortable in front of the fire before he spoke. 'There is very grave as well as some rather good news. The grave is that the Dean has just told me that the unfortunate Perkins was found dead early this evening.'

His wife gasped and covered her face with her hands.

Dr Locard gave us an account of how the young man had managed to hang himself in his cell, during which I was able to collect myself. Dr Locard made it clear that there was no suggestion that the death was anything but self-inflicted.

'How could the police be so negligent?' I exclaimed.

'He leaves a wife and children, I believe. How many children does his poor widow have to bring up on her own?' Mrs Locard asked.

'The authorities have conducted themselves with a most reprehensible lack of diligence throughout this case,' Dr Locard agreed.

'I believe he had four children,' I said to Mrs Locard.

'A subscription must be got up for them,' she said.

'Yes, most certainly.' I turned back to her husband: 'So now we will never know the truth.' I was aware of a feeling of guilty relief that I was spared some difficult consequences. And it occurred to me that my putting into the Dean's hands the evidence of Sheldrick's wrongdoing and of Slattery's and Fickling's blackmailing of him had not, after all, worked against poor Perkins.

'There will be no trial,' he agreed, looking at me meaningfully. 'Though this proves Perkins's guilt since an innocent man does not commit suicide. I hope, however, that the truth will come out about the destruction of the will even though he is dead.'

'I don't see how.'

'It depends on you, Courtine. Now more than ever. The people behind this affair must not be permitted to get away with it simply because Perkins was not man enough to take his medicine. If you will swear an affidavit in the terms we discussed earlier, justice may yet be done.'

I said nothing and he went on: 'You need not worry any longer about Fickling, Dr Courtine, if that is what you are concerned about. For my second piece of news is that he and Slattery have been dismissed.'

'The dismissal of Fickling surprises me not at all. But I'm curious about Slattery. Is it thought that he played some role in recent events?'

Dr Locard looked at me shrewdly. 'What part might he have played?'

'I'm not sure but I feel he must have.'

When he saw that I was not going to say any more, he went on: 'In strict confidence, Courtine, their dismissal is not directly related to the murder of Stonex but, rather, to an undertaking one of the canons has given the Dean this evening that he will resign on grounds of health within the next month.'

His wife looked up. 'Canon Sheldrick?'

Dr Locard winced. 'I'm sure I can rely on your discretion,' he said to me. His wife flushed. 'Something occurred this evening which allowed the Dean to put an end to a difficult situation without unpleasant consequences.'

'I won't press you for more,' I said with a secret feeling of pleasure at his surprise at my lack of curiosity. I wondered if he knew as much about this as I did. Did he even guess the role I had played in destroying the power that Fickling and Slattery had exercised over Sheldrick and therefore the rest of the Cathedral community?

'Thorrold has sketched out what you need to say in your affidavit,' Dr Locard said, reaching into his pocket.

'Thorrold? You have seen him?'

'He was, of course, consulting with the Dean in the light of this new development.' He handed me a piece of paper. 'This is merely an outline of the main points you would need to make. Thorrold advises that it would be better to do it with your own lawyer in Cambridge in order to avoid any appearance of collusion.'

'Heaven forbid,' I said, glancing at the document. I saw that Thorrold had written out precisely the form of words that I would need to swear to having heard old Mr Stonex utter: *I intend to deposit this copy of my will with my lawyer.*

'Please think over the various matters that we have discussed,' Dr Locard said.

'May I have until tomorrow to decide?'

'To decide?'

'I mean, to decide whether I can remember Mr Stonex making that remark.'

'By all means.'

There was a brief silence. 'I fear that Dr Sheldrick's resignation will mean a great deal more work for you, Robert,' Mrs Locard said.

'Certainly I will have responsibility for overseeing the Choir School until a new Chancellor is instituted,' he said, and I looked at him in surprise.

'The Librarian acts as a kind of under-study to the Chancellor in case of incapacity,' he explained.

'I see. Is each office supported in that way?'

'Yes. For example, the Treasurer is shadowed—as it were—by the Sub-Dean.'

'And the Sacrist by the Precentor?'

'Yes.' He looked at me curiously.

'I was thinking of the story of Burgoyne's death. I assume the system hasn't changed.'

'Nothing is changed until it very conspicuously fails to work,' he said, getting to his feet. 'That is the great strength of the Church of England.' He crossed to the side-table and opened the box he had left there. 'And while we are speaking of Burgoyne, this will interest you, Courtine. The Dean has just given them into my custody. They will be displayed in the Library.'

'What are they, Robert?' Mrs Locard asked from the sofa as I got up and went over to look.

Her husband took from the box and laid out on the table two sets of keys, each on a short chain. One of them held just two keys—both large—and the other had six smaller ones of different sizes. Dr Locard picked up the latter. 'This, I assume, is Burgoyne's own set of keys to his office, his house, his chests, and so on.'

'I imagine so,' I said. I turned to Mrs Locard: 'They were taken from the body found in the Cathedral this morning.' I turned to her husband: 'I recall from Dr Sheldrick's account that Burgoyne's keys were not found on the corpse that was taken to be his, and so Freeth and Limbrick had to break into his office.'

'What I am baffled by is the provenance of these two,' he said, pointing to the other ring.

'They are large, are they not?' I agreed. 'Too large for a private house.' In fact, I guessed what at least one of them was. 'As it happens I have my own keys with me and one of them is just as large since my rooms date from the early seventeenth century and the locks are original.'

I took my keys from my pocket and laid them alongside the other set. 'Burgoyne's are even bigger.'

'I wonder why he should have been carrying another set of keys,' Dr Locard said as he crossed to the sideboard where the coffee-jug stood.

There was a moment's silence. I had a sudden impulse to act boldly and decisively for once in my life, and my heart started pounding.

'Have you solved the mystery, Robert?' Mrs Locard enquired from her chair by the fire where she was working on a piece of lace.

Glancing round and seeing that her husband was pouring the coffee, I picked up a set of keys.

'Will you take another cup, Dr Courtine?' Dr Locard asked.

I turned to my host and hostess. 'Thank you, but I won't. This has been a very pleasant evening but it is late and I imagine you have much to do in the morning. I myself have a long journey to make.'

'Do please come and find me before you leave,' Dr Locard said. 'I am very anxious to know what you decide. I will be in the Library all morning from about half-past eight. I want to do some more work on the manuscript.'

'I'm sure there is much more to be learnt from it.'

He smiled: 'I hope we might discuss the arrangements for its publication tomorrow.'

I bowed my head without speaking.

'Goodbye, Dr Courtine,' Mrs Locard said.

'Thank you so much for this evening,' I replied.

As she took my hand, she said with a smile: 'I don't suppose you will come to Thurchester in the near future, Dr Courtine?'

'Now that there will be no trial, I think it highly improbable. But I hope I might have the pleasure of receiving you and Dr Locard in Cambridge one day.'

'I would like that very much. Robert visits Cambridge occasionally and might be persuaded to take me.'

Her husband said: 'I will see you out, Courtine.'

'I do very much hope that things go well with you, Dr Courtine,' she said in a low voice as he passed into the hall.

'I have profited greatly from our conversation,' I said. 'I will always remember it.'

At the front-door Dr Locard took my hand and, holding on to it, said: 'I look forward to learning of your decision.'

'One way or another, you will know it tomorrow without fail.'

He released my hand and I plunged into the darkness of the Close.

Friday Night

❖

SO FICKLING WAS OUT OF WORK AFTER ALL. I felt no sense of triumph, even though it was a consequence of my actions. Anyway, it was very probable that he would not be in want of money. The decision about that was, strangely, also in my hands. I had no need to feel guilty over what had happened to him, for I understood at last how he had lured me to the town with the promise of reconciliation only in order to make use of me. He had not expected that I would meet Dr Locard and learn anything of the politics of the Chapter because he had assumed I would be spending my time on Woodbury Downs.

I thought about what Mrs Locard had said. The possibility of marrying if I were free to do so had occurred to me once or twice and I had thought several times of the widow of a colleague—a woman some ten or fifteen years younger than myself—whose husband had died a year ago leaving her with two small children. She was a kind, sweet-natured woman and I believed she liked me. It would be difficult on my emoluments to take on so much responsibility. Although the salary of a professor would make it possible, I knew that I would have no chance of the Chair if the manuscript were given to Scuttard to edit. By one means or another, Dr Locard would ensure that I lost even the credit for having found it.

I paused beside the Old Gatehouse, just where the wall of the garden behind Gambrill's house must have been. I could see the tall, black figure of Canon Burgoyne standing here as he had done night after night all those years ago brooding on the 'secret offence' which led to his death. I knew now that he had no interest in the Mason. It was not his murder of Robert Limbrick that he was threatening to reveal, if he even knew of it. No, it was a dark, loathsome offence that he himself had committed—or had desired to commit—that he was trying to find the courage to denounce. I remembered the words of his sermon: *He alone knows how he has wandered out of his way into the foul and strange path that leads to the sty of pestilential filth.*

Burgoyne must have been in torment during those weeks and days, steeling himself to escape the wicked course he was embarked upon. He had discovered how close you are to hating the person you love because of the power your love gives to the beloved.

For many years I had been enslaved like that. Now I realized that I was free. My feelings about my wife had become a habit, an outer shell whose inside had gradually withered without my realizing it. I had idealized and sentimentalized her, partly to save myself the trouble of starting a new life. Mrs Locard had helped me to see that, but what had made me certain was that remark of Fickling's which he had intended to wound me. By repeating my wife's cruel words—that she only married me to get away from her mother—he had made me aware of her small-mindedness. I had built her up in my imagination but now I knew she was smaller and more mean-minded than I had remembered. The ghost had been laid.

The hardest thing now would be to admit that I had been child-ish and sentimental by writing to my wife telling her she could have a divorce. And then to start a new chapter in my life. Burgoyne had taken a different means to get free. In his case it was not so much the beloved person that he hated as the very fact of that love—which he knew was shameful and repugnant. *He alone . . .*

knows what darkness he nourishes in the privy mansions of his being. For two weeks he had forced himself to speak of it in public, though in veiled terms. His conscience demanded no less. On the next day he was committed to revealing the whole truth before the assembled townspeople. Unless there was some other way of escape. And then he saw a solution. During the storm in the middle of that night, he came here to the Old Gatehouse which housed the college and entered with his key. The key he had been given by the Precentor so that he could come and go at night—as I assume he had done many times before.

He had crept up the stairs unheard amid the crashing thunder and lashing rain, and for a moment—just a few minutes or even a few seconds—he had believed that he could set himself free by a single decisive act. Gambrill had shown him how a roof might be made to collapse, and under cover of the storm he was able to make use of that knowledge. He had committed a deed more terrible than any he had committed before, although to his anguished conscience it had seemed a lesser offence. And what had he done after that?

I would retrace his steps and in doing so try to imagine what must have passed through his mind. It occurred to me how much Dr Locard would despise this way of proceeding. What would I see if I were able to go back to that night and hide myself in the Cathedral? I entered the darkened building—unlocked because the workmen were still labouring to repair the damage they had inflicted. There they were, just as I had seen them on my first night, although now in a different place: hacking at the bowels of the ancient construction with a couple of lanterns to light them. Old Gazzard was, as always, hovering in the shadows and showed no surprise—and, equally, no pleasure—at seeing me.

I greeted him and asked without prevarication: 'Do you remember how I came here late on Wednesday night and found you with the workmen trying to find the source of the smell?' He nodded.

'Did anyone else come here that night? I mean, very much later, at about two o'clock?'

He frowned. 'Why, yes. That Mr Slattery. He had heard somehow about the trouble here and he came to ask how it would affect the organ. The foreman told him it would have to be shut down for several weeks. He didn't look none too pleased.'

I thanked him. He had merely confirmed what I had guessed: having heard from Fickling my piece of news about the calamity in the Cathedral, Slattery had been anxious to know if he would be able to perform on the organ on Friday afternoon—the original date of the tea-party—because that had been intended to provide him with an alibi. Because of what he had learnt from the foreman, the conspirators had decided that night at his house in Orchard Street to bring forward the conspiracy to the following day.

When the old verger was not watching, I picked up one of the lanterns that was standing on a tomb and went to the tower door. I had a theory about what I would find up there which I was anxious to put to the proof. I tried one of the keys which I had taken from Dr Locard, picking them up as if in mistake for my own keys which I had left in their place. It occurred to me that I was becoming an accomplished thief: the photographs, the keys and now the lantern. The second key engaged and turned. I had expected that for there would have been no reason to have changed the lock in the last couple of centuries.

Burgoyne had come here on that thrice fatal night still wearing *the outward garb of sanctimony* and had used this very key to pass through this door. (From Dr Locard's explanation of how the canons substituted for each other, I had realized that when Burgoyne had borrowed the keys to the College, the key to the tower was also on the chain since the Sacrist's duties had devolved to the Precentor during his illness.)

I went a little way up the narrow stairs. On my right was a locked door which I knew led to the organ-loft. I had guessed that

Slattery used it while his usual way out was blocked and that that was how he had left the Cathedral unobserved by myself on Thursday morning. I had taken him for a supernatural apparition. I smiled at my own credulousness.

I went on again round the twisting stair. I tried to imagine Burgoyne's feelings as he ascended the tower that night. The storm was raging—tiles crashing, thunder roaring and the wind howling like a demented bassoon. And he was in turmoil. He had just crossed a line that divided him decisively from his past, from other people, from everything he had known in his life. Killing the boy had not saved him but damned him and he must have realized that within a few minutes of the murder. He knew he was damned—literally damned. I had seen that knowledge in another face in the last few days, and I understood what it meant for someone who accepted completely the reality of salvation and perdition.

Now I was at the top of the stairs at the summit of the tower just beneath the spire. I rounded the last turn and there it was—just as I had expected: a big wooden wheel more than twice the height of a man, now a skeletal ruin with struts and spokes missing. It had been here so long that everybody had forgotten what it was. But I knew: it was a treadwheel-windlass built to the clasp-arm design with two felloe-rims. A man walked inside it and by turning it transferred to the windlass axle running through it enough force to raise nearly two tons.

It was built here while the Cathedral was being constructed and its function was to raise materials to this level. Gambrill had used it to repair the spire in secret, using funds which he would later be accused of having embezzled for his own profit. After his master's death, Limbrick had his own reasons for letting people believe that Gambrill had been guilty of embezzlement. Or, to be more accurate, I thought bitterly, malversation.

I had worked out what must have happened using the evidence of the inscription and the Chancery record: Gambrill had been using the treadwheel-windlass on the day many years before when he had lost an eye. He was being lowered with a heavy load while the elder Limbrick was inside the treadwheel, 'walking' the load down as the rope slowly unwound. (As the inscription had put it: *All things revolve and Man who is born to Labour revolves with them.*) About fifteen feet above the ground the rope had parted and the load fell so that the windlass wound back at great speed, making the treadwheel spin very fast and killing the man inside it. And so he had been, in the words of the inscription, *shattered into pieces.* Gambrill himself had fallen and been seriously injured—more seriously than he had anticipated, for I was sure that he had cut the rope.

Dr Locard was wrong. The inscription was not put up by the canons to denounce the Burgoyne family for the murder of their dean, but by the younger Limbrick to make it clear that Gambrill had murdered his father and had been punished for it.

I peered down through the rafters to the top of the vault, just as Burgoyne had done that night. In his time there had been gaps in the brickwork wide enough for the loads of material to pass through. Or a man's body. Burgoyne had announced the previous Sunday that in one week he himself would make manifest the sinner in that very place. His body would plunge through the vault and be found a hundred and twenty feet below at the foot of the chancel steps. Just as he had himself predicted: *Yet shall his wickedness be laid bare before the eyes of men. Yea, even in the dark places shall his sins be blazoned forth.*

I turned to peer out through the louvres, leaning on the ledge. The huge bells loomed above me. On this quiet night, the town was sleeping peacefully below me, its higgledy-piggledy roofs and gables resembling the dark waves of a frozen sea. At my feet was the maze of little streets around the Cathedral, then the river with the moonlight glinting on it, and the hill up which I had hastened in terror only two nights before. I smiled to think of my superstitious fears on that occasion. There was no evil power abroad in the universe. People did wicked things because, as Mrs Locard had said, their own unhappiness led them to find a bitter pleasure in the pain of others.

I would write to my wife's lawyers telling them I would do all that was in my power to expedite the divorce. Fickling was right. I had made it only too easy for her to betray me. In this moment I understood what Mrs Locard had been implying. Some of the blame for what had happened was mine. And yet 'blame' did not seem to be the right word for I felt no guilt. Rather, I was now able to take responsibility for what I had done or failed to do.

I had taken another decision and a much easier one. The bargain that Dr Locard had offered me that evening had tempted me. If nothing else, that had had the effect of bringing home to me that my contempt for worldly success was in some degree an affectation.

That night nearly two hundred and forty years ago, Burgoyne had been standing exactly where I was now—perhaps trying to find the courage to hurl himself down—when Gambrill came quietly up the stairs behind him. Did anything pass between them? Did Burgoyne confess to killing the boy, Gambrill's nephew? Did Burgoyne realize that the other man was about to kill him? If so, did he welcome it since it would forestall his own suicide?

However that might be, Gambrill strangled him. And then he lowered what he believed was the lifeless corpse to the ground, walking it down using the treadwheel-windlass.

I descended the steps of the tower, locked the door at the bottom and walked across to the Burgoyne memorial. Once he had got the body to the ground Gambrill had, for some reason, stripped off the Canon's outer garments. Then he had put his hated enemy in the space high up in the wall made ready for the slab.

In order to lift that huge piece of carved marble into place he had required neither supernatural aid nor the help of Thomas Lim-brick. He had used the pulley on top of the scaffolding in combination with the treadwheel-windlass to take most of the weight. He must have gone up and down the tower stairs a dozen times, on each occasion cranking the windlass a few steps further and using the ratchets and pawl to hold it in place while he hurried down to clamber onto the scaffolding and manoeuvre the great slab into position. That must have taken him a couple of hours. Then he had sealed it up with mortar.

But why had he then put on Burgoyne's garments? And taken from the body the key which Burgoyne had borrowed from Claggett and should have returned to him? *Should* have returned to him! For the truth suddenly came to me. The old verger was dying and earlier that evening Burgoyne was given the key by his young serving-maid 'who was too timid to look into the face of a gentleman'. Gambrill put on Burgoyne's clothes because he intended to impersonate him when he took back the key! If Burgoyne was believed to have returned the key in the early hours of the morning before disappearing and Gambrill was seen by witnesses from that moment onwards, he would have an unanswerable alibi. I understood exactly how the murderous design was intended to work. How could I—of all people—not understand it?

Ingenious. But then had he really made a foolish mistake and precipitated the collapse of the scaffolding on himself? It seemed hard to believe. What had brought it down was this: there were leads balancing the slab on the pulley and once it was in place in the wall he should have lowered them to the ground, using the ratchet on the pulley. By neglecting to do so he had put such a strain on the rope that it had parted so that the full weight of the leads had borne against the pulley and brought the whole construction crashing down upon him in his moment of triumph.

His moment of triumph! Of course. *Then shall the Guilty be shat-*

tered into pieces like unto the Innocent, by their own Engin brought to Destruction even in the Moment of Triumph. Limbrick had silently entered the unlocked Cathedral and watched the man he believed had murdered his father. He had brooded all his life about revenge and now he saw his opportunity. Severing a rope would kill Gambrill just as it had killed Robert Limbrick. So *Engin* in the inscription alluded to all three senses of the word: Gambrill had been intellectually destroyed by his own ingenuity, politically caught in his own plotting and physically crushed under his own machine.

I had made another decision. I would contest the Chair whether or not Scuttard was also in for it and regardless of whether he was given responsibility for publishing the manuscript. I would try for it, not because I expected to obtain it, but to show that I believed myself a worthy candidate and to prove to myself that I was not afraid to fail. I was now able to admit to myself with no trace of guilt that I earnestly desired the Chair with all the respect, the power and, indeed, the material benefits accompanying it.

I reached the inn at half-past one and had to hammer at the door to wake the night-porter who was slumbering before the fire in the hall. I left instructions with him that I was to be woken at six to catch the mail-train. I slept very little that night. While I was breakfasting alone in the dining-room the next morning a message was brought to me. It was, as I expected, a package containing my own keys with a note from Dr Locard: 'I hope these reach you before you leave. Would you be good enough to return the set you took from me by mistake when you come to the Library this morning. I shall, as I mentioned, be working on our manuscript and look forward to discussing it with you again.'

I sent the keys back with an apology for my stupidity and a brief letter of thanks for his and his wife's hospitality. I wrote that I had to deny myself the pleasure of another discussion of the manuscript because I had decided to take the first train to avoid arriving late at my destination, and I added that he would be disappointed to learn that after considerable reflection, I had decided that I could recollect nothing worth affirming in an affidavit. I enclosed a cheque for Mrs Locard's subscription for the family of the unfortunate Perkins.

This last duty discharged, I packed, settled my bill and, with an enormous sense of relief, boarded the cab which was waiting for me.

I have spent the time since I arrived at my niece's in writing this account. I realize that I have strayed far from the murder itself but it has seemed impossible to disentangle the different threads. I must have been an unsatisfactory guest for my mind has been preoccupied by my anguished debate which I could not reveal to those around me: Should I tell the authorities what I suspect? How could I prove it? Since the Coroner declined to believe my theory about a mysterious half-brother—a hypothesis which was mistaken but contained much of the truth—it is hardly likely that my even more extraordinary theory would be believed, even though it accounts satisfactorily for the most puzzling anomalies. There is a point at which you have to go beyond the mere evidence by using your imagination or you will not discover the 'truth'.

Since the unfortunate Perkins is dead, I can see nothing to be gained by making allegations against people which would not lead to their prosecution. Yet I want some record of the truth to survive—if only so that the children of Perkins should understand the miscarriage of justice and the blackening of their father's name. His only offence was to have lied to the police—an act which was foolish and wrong, but understandable since he saw immediately how convincing a case could be made against him.

As for the question of what I will do with this Account, I have not decided. Self-evidently, it cannot be published while those responsible for the murder are still alive. That consideration allows me a great deal of time to contemplate its eventual disposition.

EDWARD COURTINE

Exeter and Cambridge, January 1882

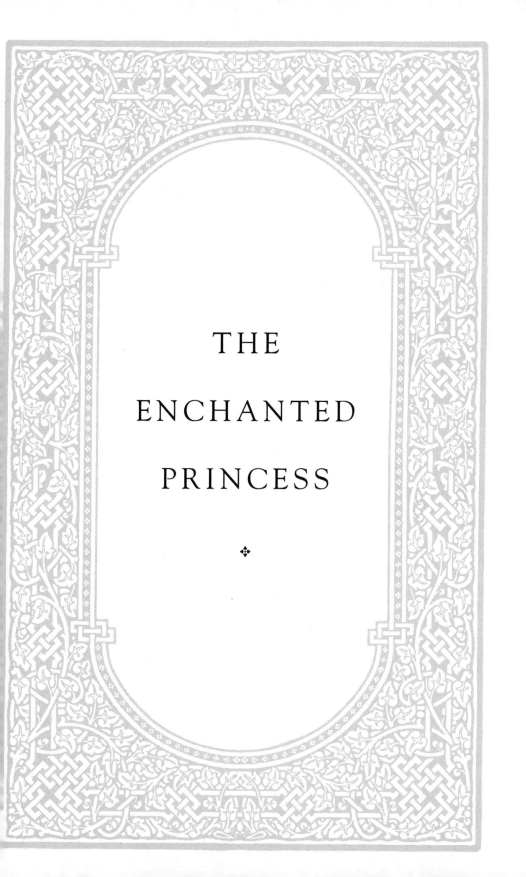

THE

ENCHANTED

PRINCESS

❖

I N A FARAWAY KINGDOM and long ago there lived a fair
young prince who, in addition to being handsome, was clever
and good-natured, and was therefore loved and admired by
everybody who knew him. His father and mother, who were the
king and queen of that country, doted upon him, but since he was
the youngest of three brothers he knew that he would not inherit
the crown but would have to make his own way in the world. And
so one day he would have to leave the kingdom and set off on his
adventures, and he looked forward to that day and yet at the same
time regretted that he would have to part from those he loved.
Knowing this, he always listened to the tales of travellers newly arrived in the country from other lands. And meanwhile, he dili-
gently pursued the studies and pastimes appropriate to a young
prince. He read old books with his tutors and he learnt from older
warriors in his father's retinue how to fight with sword, shield and
lance both on foot and on horseback. But most of all, in the company of his brothers and other young men of the court, he hunted
in the wild forests around the castle with his stallion, his hawk and
his hound. These three beautiful creatures had been given him by

Editor's Note: This is the story which Courtine read late on Wednesday night.

his father and he was prouder of them than of anything else he possessed.

And then one day a traveller, who had come from across the oceans and through the mountains and over the rivers, told him a story. Many days' journey from that kingdom was a land whose king lived in a high, grim castle surrounded by a great, dark, trackless forest. The castle stood on the edge of a wide river and was reached by boat, for the forest was too dangerous for travellers to venture into. The king had only one child, a beautiful daughter, and when he died she would be queen of the country. The princess had no husband, for a witch had placed her under an enchantment so that only the suitor who could reach the castle by passing through the forest would be given her hand in marriage. The king had decreed that whoever succeeded in this task would become king when he died. The kingdom was rich and powerful, and many princes had tried to reach the castle in that way but all of them had perished while passing through the forest, for many were the dangers that dwelt therein. Of all of these, the greatest danger was a monster which lay in wait for travellers and killed them and then ate their corpses.

When he heard this story the prince felt a thrill of excitement mingled with terror and he resolved that he would be the man who would win the hand of the princess. His father and mother and his two elder brothers heard his decision with much sorrow, but they knew that it was the fate of youngest sons to brave great perils in order to make their fortune and so they did not try to dissuade him. Instead they gave him gifts that would help him in his task. The king gave him the sword which he himself had wielded as a young man—a finely tempered weapon with ancient spells chased on the blade. His mother gave him a beautifully intricate suit of chain-mail that was light and yet was proof against all but the most savage sword-thrust. His eldest brother gave him a dagger of the finest steel with the sharpest blade and point that any smith had ever forged, and his elder brother gave him a shield that weighed very little and yet was extremely strong. His old nurse wept more than anyone else and while she was weeping she made up baskets of provisions: loaves of bread, cheeses, cured meat, dried fruit and flasks of wine. And so one fine morning in the early summer the prince donned his armour, took up his weapons, strapped the provisions onto his stallion and, bidding farewell to all those who loved him, rode off with his hawk on his wrist and his hound trotting beside him.

He journeyed for many days and many nights and at last entered the great dark forest in the middle of which lay the castle with the beautiful princess. When the lofty trees closed high over his head he found himself in darkness and since there were no paths and he could not see the stars at night and could scarcely see the sun by day, he had great difficulty in steering his course. And so he travelled round in circles for three days and three nights and used up all the food and drink that his old nurse had provided for him. Although he constantly heard the sound of running water around him, he was unable to find a stream or a spring. And so by the end of the third day, as dusk was approaching, he was hungry and very very thirsty. Then it was that he saw his first sign of a living creature: an old woman was coming towards him and she was carrying a big basket.

'Mother,' he said. 'I am hungry and thirsty. If you have food and drink in your basket, please spare me some of them.'

'I have food and drink aplenty,' she replied. 'But I will not give them to you.'

'Then let me buy them from you. I have gold.' And he pulled from his saddle-pouch a handful of gold coins.

'Put away your money,' she said. 'It is of no use to me here in the forest.'

'Then is there anything I can say or do to make you give me some of what you have?' he asked.

She eyed him strangely and after a moment she said: 'Give me all that you have: your sword, your suit of chain-mail, your dagger, your shield, your hawk, your hound and your stallion. And then I will give you everything I have in my basket.'

'If I give you all my means to defend myself,' the prince replied, 'I will have no chance against the many perils of the forest and in particular against the monster that kills men and eats their corpses.'

The old woman smiled and said: 'You will lose nothing by giving me everything you have, since your horse and your weapons will not save you from the monster.'

She spoke with such certainty that the prince believed her. And so he got down from his stallion and gave it to her, and took off his chain-mail and gave it to her, and likewise gave her his sword, his dagger, his shield, his hawk and his hound.

The old woman handed him her basket and he opened it and found that it was full of meat and drink. He ate and drank enough to satisfy his immediate need and put the rest away for the remainder of his journey.

Then the old woman said: 'I have met many young princes in the forest before you and all of them have taken from me by threats the provisions that I carried. You are the first who has not offered me violence but has peacefully surrendered all that he had. In return, therefore, I am going to tell you what those other princes did not know. I am going to tell you how to save yourself from the monster when you meet it—as you most assuredly will.'

The prince thanked her and she went on: 'All the other princes perished because they trusted in their weapons and in their own strength. The only things that will overcome the creature are truth and courage, and you have displayed those qualities in your dealings with me. I will therefore tell you this secret which will show you how to defeat the monster. You must know that it paralyses those who look upon its face and that is why no man who gazes upon it can hope to live.'

'Is it so ugly and terrifying?' exclaimed the prince.

'I have told you,' the old woman said, 'that all men who look into its eyes are lost. Be satisfied with that. You must therefore close your eyes when you glimpse it from afar or when you scent it. When you have closed your eyes you will know where it is by its loathsome smell. It will come rushing at you with a fearful roar but you must neither open your eyes nor try to run away. If you cannot trust yourself to keep your eyes closed, blindfold yourself as soon as you know it is at hand. Then you must let the monster seize you and clasp you to it as it will do in order to strangle you. And at that moment you must overcome your fear and brave the stench and you must kiss it on its bare flesh.'

The prince shuddered and the old woman said: 'I see you look doubtful, but I promise you that your kiss will burn the monster and inflict more pain upon it than any weapon could.'

The prince thanked the old woman and bade her farewell, and strode on deeper into the forest.

Some hours later, at about midnight, he suddenly found himself in a great clearing and now that the light of the moon and stars shone down without hindrance, he found he could see almost as if by day. He smelt a hideous stench and at that moment he saw that the ground was strewn with dismembered human bodies. Every one of the princes who had entered the forest before him lay here scattered about: arms, legs and heads. And to his dismay he perceived that the limbs and bones were half-chewed. Then he noticed that at the far edge of the clearing there was something moving. It was a creature with its back to him which, as he drew nearer, he saw was gnawing on a shinbone. He instantly plucked his scarf from around his neck and tied it tightly around his eyes. As he stood there with his heart thumping, he became aware that the horrible stench—the odour of blood and rotting corpses and some ancient uncleanliness—was growing stronger and knew that the monster was approaching.

He heard its tread and then its rasping breath which stank unendurably and in a moment he was seized by arms that seemed to him cold and scaly. He felt its hands around his neck and he found himself pushed to the ground with the creature on top of him as its grip began to tighten. Remembering what the old woman had said, however, he forced himself to thrust his face towards it and, as his lips touched cold flesh, to plant a kiss.

Instantly the monster uttered a howl of grief and agony, and let go of him. The prince heard it moving further off and the dreadful smell grew less. He lifted the blindfold and was just in time to see the monster at the edge of the clearing as it dragged itself with a hobbling movement into the darkness of the surrounding forest.

With a last horrified glance around the clearing, the prince hastened into the forest again to continue his journey. By now it was nearly dawn and as the sun rose he sighted a glint of water and a moment later saw the castle standing high on its rock above the glittering river with the town below it.

He announced himself at the gate and was immediately welcomed as a hero since he was the first prince who had ever managed to pass through the forest. He was ushered into the presence of the king, who threw himself upon his neck and wept with gratitude at the deliverance of his daughter from the enchantment. The king was overjoyed to find that his daughter's bridegroom, and his own heir, was such a handsome and gracious young prince as well as a courageous one.

The princess was sent for, and when she entered the chamber, the prince saw that she was young and lovely even beyond his dreams. Her eyes were astonishingly beautiful and as soon as he looked into them he was utterly lost in his love for her and could not stop looking at her. She was graceful and modest, and she smiled with charming shyness and in every way he was delighted with her. The king feasted him and meanwhile summoned the whole of his court and then, to the prince's joy, announced that the marriage would be celebrated that very evening.

The proclamation was made in the castle and in the town, and a great banquet was ordained and all the lords and ladies came hurrying there in their best finery. The king, whose queen had died of grief when the princess was placed under the enchantment all those many years ago, gave away his daughter in marriage to the prince and all the ladies of the court wept in the way that was expected and appropriate. The feasting began, and while it was at its height, the prince and his bride stole away to the bedchamber appointed for them at the top of one of the towers high over the river.

The princess had a maidservant who, she explained, had served her faithfully since she was a baby, and while the prince waited in the great bed with the curtains drawn back, the woman undressed her mistress before the window through which the moonlight flooded. First the maidservant removed her necklaces and bracelets, then she plucked off her shoes, then she let down her golden tresses, then she unfastened her girdle and let her bodice float to the ground, and all the while the prince gazed in mounting excitement at the beauties that were being revealed. Then finally the maidservant pulled the shift over the head of the young princess and she stood before her new husband in all her unadorned beauty. Imagine his feelings as his gaze travelled slowly and longingly down her body from her slender neck to her plump breasts to her smooth belly until, low on her body, he found the burn-mark in the shape of his own lips.

He sprang from the bed and stood with his back against the door, more frightened now than he had been even when he waited blindfolded in the clearing for the monster to approach him.

Distressed by his alarm, the princess explained that she had been put under an enchantment by a wicked witch and condemned to haunt the forest, killing and devouring those who came in quest of her hand. By overcoming her with a burning kiss, the prince had broken the spell. She loved him, she insisted, because he had rescued her and because he was young and handsome and brave.

The prince stood speechless with horror and surprise and so now the maidservant spoke and revealed to him that she had been the old woman whom he had met on the way through the forest. Her task had been to encounter all the suitors as they approached the clearing and find out if they were worthy of being given assistance. All of them, with the exception of the prince himself, had proved themselves undeserving by seizing the food and drink from her with threats of violence. All of them had trusted to their youth and strength and weapons against the monster, and all of them had been defeated. To him alone had she confided the secret of how to overcome the enchantment and he had possessed enough courage to follow her advice. By blindfolding himself he had avoided being rendered immobile by the loveliness of the princess, and above all by the beauty of her eyes, as she came towards him naked and reeking of corpses.

The maidservant concluded by saying that by his honesty and his courage he had lifted the enchantment placed upon the princess and he should now accept her as his bride. The prince remained horrified and at last managed to say that he could not. He could not accept as his wife someone who had killed and eaten men. Opening the door behind him, the prince said he was going to raise the alarm and tell everyone in the castle that their princess had been the monster who had haunted the forest for so long.

The maidservant laughed and told him that no purpose would be served by his action since everyone in the castle knew the truth. They were now celebrating the lifting of the hideous curse under which the whole kingdom had suffered for so long.

The prince stopped, unable to decide what to do. And at that moment the princess, who had been gazing at him longingly all this while, told him that the maidservant had lied to him. She was none other than the witch who had enchanted her and forced her to kill her suitors. The prince had not yet broken the enchantment fully but if he would truly accept her as his wife knowing what she had done, the last traces of the enchantment would be overcome. If he rejected her, she would fall under the power of the witch once again and go back to haunting the forest. As she spoke those last words, and still with nothing to cover her but her long golden tresses, she began to advance slowly towards the prince.

He raised one hand to ward her away. The maidservant smiled and said that the princess was telling the truth. 'I am the witch who enchanted her,' she said. 'And the reason why your kiss inflicted such pain was that it was a reminder of the human love that the princess was denied while she dwelt in the forest and fed on dead men's bodies. You must decide now whether you are going to accept the princess as your bride or reject her.'

The prince found he still could not speak but he shook his head.

The witch laughed and said: 'Then do you wish me to give you back the weapons I made you give me in the forest?'

'Yes,' the prince cried.

Instantly he heard a peal of laughter from the maidservant and in that instant the women and the room began to fade away. As the castle disappeared he felt himself fall through the air until he landed on a soft floor of leaves and found that he was back in the forest. In the moonlight he saw that he was wearing his suit of chain-mail and that his sword and his dagger were restored to him and that his shield was lying beside him. And when he looked round he saw his hawk and hound nearby and his horse standing a few paces away, tossing its head and blowing nervously through its nostrils. For then the young prince noticed the smell that was frightening his steed and realized that he was in the great clearing that was strewn with parts of bodies, and at that moment, as he peered towards the distant line of trees in the faint moonlight, he saw that something was approaching from the forest.

Editor's *Afterword*

❖

I WAS BORN IN HYDERABAD where my father was an officer in
the Indian Army. When I had just turned twelve my parents
decided to send me back to England to board at school, not
merely because the climate was healthier and the education supposed to be better, but also because of certain difficulties at home.
One of the consequences of these circumstances was that they were
not well off and because I had some—though, as it turned out, not
much—musical ability, and because of the financial advantages of
my tuition and board being paid for, it was decided that I should
become a chorister.

The usual age for entry to the school was seven or eight and so
by the time boys had reached twelve, alliances and friendships had
formed from which I, as a late arrival, was necessarily excluded.
With my Indian ways and the premature habit of introspection
which the domestic problems had encouraged, I suppose I was an
odd little boy. I had been an only child—at least since the death
from yellow fever of a younger sister of three, which occurred when
I was eight. I had adored her, and her loss and the other family difficulties which I had experienced had added to my melancholy cast
of mind a precocious solemnity, with the result that I found it hard

to join in and care about the childish concerns of my fellows. Arriving halfway through Trinity term I found that cricket was the great issue of the day and I had neither aptitude for nor interest in the game. Perhaps because I was shunned, unhappy and shy, I developed a severe stammer. (At least, I don't know whether I had it before and if I did nobody remarked upon it in India where I chattered away to my ayah in Hindustani.) Since this fuelled the contempt of the other boys, I retreated increasingly into silence and spent as much time as I was able to on my own. It became something of a pastime when there were no flies to torment or cats to chase, to hunt me down and goad me into a fury when my stammer made my attempts to defend myself highly amusing.

Disliked by the other boys, I was the object of disapproval on the part of the Headmaster even though I never tried to be naughty or to break the rules. But I seemed to get into trouble more often than any other boy and I suppose that was because I lived in a day-dream which meant that I didn't notice that I was late or forgot things. The world I was imagining was more pleasant and more interesting than the one I was required to live in and I believe it enraged the Headmaster to see me lost in an invented realm.

The Headmaster—as he was called, rather grandly since there were only two other full-time masters in addition to the assistant-organist who taught music—would fly into sudden rages during which he would hit us savagely and repeatedly. This was usually done without the ceremony of a cane on the hand or buttocks, but with the flat of his hand across our heads. The punishment for a serious offence, however, was to be formally caned by him on the buttocks. At that time his rages were inexplicable and no more to be investigated than the reason why it rained one day and the sun shone the next. When I was an adult I understood his bitterness, his frustration at his ambitions and hopes ending in the headship of a small and very undistinguished choir school in a distant provincial town. I later realized, too, that there were many occasions when his irascibility and unpredictability were due to his having taken intoxicating spirits.

We learnt very little, partly because we were worked so hard as choristers. We had Evensong every day—except for Saturdays when there were no sung services. And we had Practice every day for an hour before breakfast and again for half an hour before Evensong. I was not gifted musically and so I was terrified of the choirmaster, a young man who was determined to raise the reputation of the choir and who had a particularly harsh way of dealing with us. Music at the Cathedral had fallen into a decline because of the prolonged ill-health of the elderly organist who for many years had had sole responsibility for the singing. (The Precentor was also old and had taken little interest for a long time.) And so in the hope of improving things, the Foundation had, some seven or eight years before my arrival, appointed an assistant-organist—a man who seemed quite old to us but was not forty at the time I am writing of. The appointment was temporary but had been periodically renewed because of the continued incapacity of the organist—at least, that was the reason that was given out. As well as playing for services and teaching us music, he was supposed to take over most of the old man's responsibility for the choir, but he was lazy and preferred to spend his time slovening in the town's taverns. Though he never hit us or did anything else, there was something about him with his queer slouching gait, his dishevelled dress, his crooked smile, and his sarcastic remarks that made us recoil from him and fear him more than we feared even the choirmaster.

This more recent addition to the staff of the Cathedral had been employed only at about the time I myself began at the school, at the moment when the canons had finally acknowledged that the appointment of the assistant-organist had done nothing to raise the standard of singing. The choirmaster had therefore not selected me to be in the choir. He told me several times that I was not good enough to be a chorister. I did not disagree with him on that point, but although I disliked everything to do with the choir, at least there was the consolation that I did not stammer when I sang. That was not enough to save me, and the choirmaster used to humiliate and occasionally beat me at Evensong if he believed I had sung off-key or had sung softly in the hope that he would not hear. He did this to the other boys, too, but I believed he made a particular butt of me, singling me out because of my poor musicianship and my stammer. And that was why I used sometimes to cut Evensong even though I knew the punishment that would follow. The choirmaster would report my absence to the Headmaster and he would hunt me down and cane me. But at least I would have respite for a few hours and the bruises from a flogging gave me a certain status among my fellows. A beating was sometimes preferable to being shown up and laughed at.

I might mention that while the beatings by the Headmaster were bad enough, most of all we dreaded being invited to tea by the Chancellor to cheer us up afterwards.

Our life was altogether fairly miserable. We were lodged in a dark old building—a former gatehouse—in the shadow of the Cathedral in the Upper Close. We slept in narrow truckle beds almost at the top of the ancient edifice. We were locked in at nine o'clock and were usually left all night to our own devices—which were unpleasant enough, for the bigger boys tormented and humiliated the smaller ones—and though I was among the oldest, I counted as one of the bullied.

Although this happened less than forty years ago, it seems to me that that was another age. No school would be allowed these days to treat children in the way we were treated. The dormitory was completely unheated in the winter and, winter and summer, infested by rats. There were eighteen of us in this one big room whose windows we sealed as tight, during the bitter winter nights, as their rattling frames permitted. At half-past six we had to rise and dress in order to attend Early Practice, after which we had our meagre breakfast and then assembled in a big schoolroom on the ground floor—a room which was poorly heated by a single coal-fire and was always filled with the stench of the cheapest tallow-candles.

Saturdays were my favourite time—at least until it was dark, for then my favourite day turned into the night I most feared; Saturday was the only night of the week when I was alone in the Old Gate-house. Although my family had at one time had a connection with the town, I had no living relatives there. And so on Saturdays, after Practice and breakfast, when the other boys went to visit their families until the morning service the following day, I would find myself alone and completely without any adult taking an interest in what I was doing since the cook and housemaid had the day off. Or, I should say, taking an interest that I welcomed. I would spend a solitary day mooching about the town, returning for the bread and cheese left out for me by the servants. And on Saturday nights, rather than sleep by myself in the big room, I would carry my bedding up to the little top room under the roof—though that did not save me.

It was because of this solitariness that I made the friendship as a result of which I became involved in the case.

Of course I don't mean to say that I was unhappy all the time. There were some moments when I enjoyed myself—lying with a book on the grass of the Lower Close in the summer or roasting chestnuts on the schoolroom fire in the autumn. Once or twice one of the younger canons, Dr Sisterson, invited us to his house where we were well treated by his friendly wife and his own children, and there were occasions when I joined in the games and it was forgotten that I was different and queer. Later—after the time I am now speaking of—I even made a friend, a quiet, timid boy of whom I had taken very little notice at first, except occasionally to wonder enviously how he managed to avoid being singled out and ridiculed for not enjoying rough games, loud noises, and so on. (He had a brother—much older than he—who worked in the Library.) Another consolation was that I found I enjoyed Latin and Greek which were taught by an old man who passionately loved the ancient literature and took a kindly and unselfish interest in us.

But when I started again in the Michaelmas term after my arrival—after a dreadfully dull and lonely summer with an elderly uncle and aunt in a remote village in Cumberland—I became more and more unhappy. I passed whole hours in imagining how I might be set free. My parents might both die and since the fees would not be paid, I would be sent out into the world to earn my living. Or somebody might adopt me. And if neither of these things happened, then one day I would just run away. I had good reasons for wanting to.

Not only was I bullied by my fellows, but all of us choristers suffered from the fact that there was another school in the Close. We choirboys were scholars, recipients of charity, and the fact that the school occupied the Old Gatehouse was used to insult us. The Courtenay boys were rich—at least, richer than most of us—and self-assured. They swaggered about the town in their distinctive garb—dark blue gown, blue knee-breeches and buckled shoes—secure in the possession of their own territory, the Lower Close, so that if one of us ventured into it they would beat us. On the other hand, they strutted freely around our territory—the Upper Close—and we were required to get smartly out of their way or take our punishment in kicks and blows.

One Saturday, towards the end of September, I was crossing the Upper Close when I saw an old gentleman whom I knew by sight walking ahead of me, carrying a couple of things—a large object that looked like a book and a package—under his left arm, his right being occupied by the leather case which he always bore. He let the package fall and walked on without noticing. I picked it up, ran after him and handed it back. He was grateful and appeared to be very struck by the fact that I stammered so badly and by my sallow complexion and slightly exotic manners. He was intrigued to learn that I had been born in India and told me he had a passion for far-away places and showed me the book under his arm. It was a beautifully illustrated collection of maps, printed in Leiden, he told me, two hundred years ago. He explained that he collected maps and atlases and said that one day he hoped he would have the opportunity to show me his collection. I knew him only as the old man who lived in the big ancient house at one end of the Upper Close.

I met him again now and then, and during October and November I talked to him perhaps five or six times—always outside his back-door. I happened to meet him on a Saturday when the Close was deserted and mentioned my solitariness on that day and it was then that he invited me to tea the following Saturday, telling me to mention it to nobody for it was to be our secret and he would not even inform his housekeeper but would buy the bread and cakes himself. I believed I knew what to expect for I had twice been invited to have tea with Dr Sheldrick who occasionally invited boys to his house in the afternoon. (The Headmaster either did not know or did not care about these visits—probably the latter for he and the Chancellor, both staunch members of the Low Church tendency, were allies in the convoluted politics of the Chapter.)

I was by nature suspicious and already good at keeping secrets for, because of the difficulties in my family which I have mentioned and which very soon after this led my parents to live apart, I had been introduced at an early age to habits of secrecy and instinctive suspicion of the motives of others. My involvement in the so-called Stonex Case had a fearful effect upon me—all the greater because nobody ever knew of it. At the time I vowed to myself never to reveal what I had learnt in such an accidental manner. (In truth, there was nobody I trusted to whom I dared reveal it.) I had to nurse my secret and the burden of guilt that accompanied it without the relief of confiding it to another. I said nothing at all of what I knew and avoided all discussion of the matter until a few years ago when I was moved to write to a newspaper to correct errors of fact which had appeared in a grotesque article on the case. It was that letter which, in a way I had not foreseen or intended, drew me into the case again and which indirectly explains why I am writing this 'Afterword' now. Apart from poor Perkins's wretched children, I suppose I am the last surviving victim.

So one Saturday at the beginning of December I went into the house for the first time—the first of only two occasions, for I have entered it only once since then. (After the old gentleman's death it was sold by his sister who turned all the assets she inherited—principally, of course, the bank but also various properties in and around the town—into cash within a few months of probate and went to live abroad. The house later became the office of the solicitors, Gollop and Knaggs—as it has remained to this day.)

Tea with the old gentleman went off very well. He seated me at the table opposite him and talked to me as if I were an adult. He did not use the babyish language that the Chancellor employed and, above all, he did not bring up the question of beatings.

He asked me about my studies. I told him I enjoyed Greek and Latin because I liked the master who taught Classics, and he confessed that he had hated those languages when he was a boy and had been a complete dunce at them. (I might remark here that it was because I enjoyed my studies under that kind old gentleman that I continued with them when I passed on to my public school and later went up to Cambridge to read for the Classical Tripos.) He told me that he, too, had attended the Choir School. We found that—despite the difference of some sixty years—the existence he had led was not very different from mine. There was another link between us for he told me that he himself had stammered when he was my age. We talked about the teachers. Mr Stonex asked me about the assistant-organist and seemed intrigued by the little I was able to tell him.

It was almost time for me to go when he remembered that he had not shown me his atlases as he had promised to do. He wasted more time—as it seemed to me—in telling me how he had wanted to be a sailor or an explorer when he was a boy and that was how he had acquired his love of maps. He told me he had had to sacrifice his dreams of travel because he had had to take on onerous family responsibilities at an early age because of the premature death of his father. Then he talked, somewhat obscurely in my view, of how ironic it was that he had wanted to be a hero and had dreamed of returning to his native town feted and lionized as a great warrior or bold navigator, and had, in fact, become a kind of hero but a secret one. He became quite upset as he described how, far from being thanked and adored, the reward for his heroism was to be despised and shunned. None of that meant anything to me then, of course, and it was only three years ago that I came to understand what he meant. (Little as I understood then, I remembered his words because only a short time later I found myself similarly nursing a terrible secret.) The old gentleman became so absorbed in his story that he forgot the time. The chiming of the grandfather clock—fortunately rather ahead of itself—reminded us of the lateness of the hour and when I had to take my leave without having been shown the famous atlases, my host promised me that I should come again soon and look at them properly.

And yet, kind though he was to me, I don't believe he was a very nice man. Certainly not a very good one. For he treated his sister badly when she was very young and in difficult circumstances. I remember that when I learnt that the entire fortune had gone to Mr Stonex's sister who had turned out to be living in Harrogate in sadly reduced circumstances, I felt—as did many in the town—that some kind of justice had at least emerged from the horror of the old gentleman's brutal murder. It was learnt that the sister had lived in a tiny cottage for some years and had recently had a stroke and become bedbound. There was something profoundly romantic in the idea of the forgotten relative being raised suddenly from illness and poverty to vast wealth.

Some years after the murder an article appeared about it in the *Daily Mail* in February 1903. The journalist revealed that Mr Stonex's sister had always believed that her brother had cheated her of her share of their father's estate. The article recounted this story: her father had always preferred her above her elder brother and the animosity this created between the siblings had been enhanced by the fact that they were temperamentally opposite: he was cautious, unsociable and shy. She was flamboyant, extravagant and easily bored. Their father died when the girl was fourteen and her brother, some seven years older than she, had treated her badly to get revenge.

At sixteen she had been one of the greatest heiresses in the district, but her brother had refused her a dowry, and by doing so had discouraged the interest of young men from distinguished families in the county. As a result of his ill-treatment of her, she had been seduced by a much older man—an actor visiting the town with a theatrical company—who had taken her away. She tried to earn her living on the stage herself but, apart from a few early triumphs, failed in this career. She was a brilliant, passionate, compelling and daring actress but she would wilfully depart from the text and improvise her lines in the heat of the moment, with the consequence that other performers refused to go on stage with her and managers declined to employ her. During the years that followed, her brother succeeded, she maintained, in stealing her share of their inheritance. When she reached twenty-one and tried to claim it and failed, her lover abandoned her and their young child. The writer of the article claimed that the seducer was himself closely related to an aristocratic Irish family and had some expectation, therefore, of making a good marriage despite his somewhat dubious manner of earning his living.

All of that, of course, happened some thirty or forty years before the time I am speaking of—the afternoon when I sat opposite Mr Stonex at that big table in the houseplace and he talked to me about the sacrifice of the hopes that he had had as a boy. It occurred to me some years later that he felt guilt at what he had done to his sibling and even that he had seen me as the child of his sister whom he had more recently turned away penniless from his door. I sympathized with him for I know how oppressive and corroding a sense of guilt can be, since if any living person is responsible for the unjust and cruel death featured in the foregoing account, it is I. Much later again, however, I realized how wrong I was about the old man's feelings.

After our tea-party I spoke to him only twice more—and since the first of these occasions was about a week after I had been to tea, it must have been only a week or ten days before he died. I met him in the Close and he asked me where I would be during the Christmas holiday and I told him I would have to stay at the school for my aunt and uncle had decided they were too old and frail to take responsibility for me again. He said nothing but looked thoughtful. I did not speak to him again until the day of his death.

I have been obsessed by the Stonex Case all my life but until a few months ago I never expected to learn more about it or, indeed, to make public what I knew. The article in the *Daily Mail* started a chain of events which eventually brought the truth to light, though it was itself no more than a tissue of lies about the case. It was published on the occasion of the death of Professor Courtine and the journalist took advantage of the fact that you cannot libel the dead to make grave allegations against him. Ever since the murder, the most outrageous stories had been told and grave calumnies made against a number of unlikely people. A strange feature of the article is that, because the writer was not sure if Austin Fickling was still alive, he simply omitted him entirely—in a most cowardly and dishonest fashion—from his speculative account of events on the fatal afternoon.

The article was called 'The Thurchester Conspiracy Unmasked'. The author began by asserting that there were rumours from the very first that Dr Courtine—as he then was—had been involved himself in some way. Nobody had ever seriously suggested until then that Dr Courtine had lied—though many believed he was deceived about certain matters. The journalist argued that the theory about a mysterious brother of the victim propounded by Dr Courtine when he gave evidence at the inquest was a calculated distortion of the truth. His grotesque claim was that Dr Courtine had himself battered Mr Stonex to death when he arrived for tea, and then spent several hours ransacking the house for money and securities. So, the writer insisted, the young doctor was right when he asserted that the old gentleman had been dead for several hours by the time he saw the body.

Although I knew how completely absurd this was, I resisted the temptation to reveal the information I possessed. I could not, however, forbear writing a brief letter to the Editor of the newspaper saying that I had been at school there at the time and had even known Mr Stonex slightly, and pointing out a circumstance which destroyed the article's argument completely. This was the fact that Austin Fickling had been at the New Deanery with Dr Courtine on the afternoon of the murder and that the two men had contradicted each other at the inquest about what had happened there. That made the idea that Dr Courtine had been involved in a conspiracy virtually impossible. The letter was published and some correspondence followed on the topic. It was because of that letter that a few years later Miss Napier, the author of the book that was eventually published as *The Thurchester Mystery*, wrote to ask me for my help.

❖

The old gentleman's kindness helped me more than he could have known to endure the next few weeks when every misery seemed to worsen. I had never known an English winter and this was a harsh one with a hard frost that gripped for weeks and a thick, choking fog. In our big room in the Old Gatehouse, we had to break the ice in the buckets to wash in the mornings. And during the night, under our thin blankets, with the windows leaking what heat there was despite the rags we stuffed into the cracks, we were often too cold to sleep. I suffered from chilblains and had a cough and a constantly running nose.

As Christmas approached I became more and more unhappy at the prospect of spending it alone in the ancient building. We boys used to terrify each other with tales of the ghosts that haunted it and certainly there were often creaks at night as if someone was on the stair, perhaps creeping up to the empty attic-room under the roof. There was a story which had been handed down from generation to generation of schoolboys about a ghost—a canon of the Cathedral in the old times—who used to sneak up the stairs to the attic at night for some mysterious purpose. Many a time I would be lying awake in the middle of the night and would hear him on the stair. This was frightening enough while surrounded by my sleeping companions. The prospect of facing this by myself for the ten days of the Christmas vacation was terrifying. Particularly since I suspected that sometimes there really would be someone creeping up the stairs. On Christmas Day—which fell on a Sunday that year—all the other choristers would go home after the second service in the morning and I would be alone. The Headmaster and his wife would keep an eye on me but it would be an ungenerous—as well as an unsteady—one. I dreaded that Dr Sheldrick might have me to spend the day with him—though at least it would be too cold for photography.

And so my friendship with Mr Stonex was important to me. The fact that there was an adult who seemed to like me for myself, without wanting anything from me, gave me reason to believe that I was of some worth. And the fact that it was a secret made me feel powerful. In bed at night I hugged it to myself like a magic talisman. I knew something the other boys did not. Something even the masters did not know. (I've remained good at keeping secrets, perhaps too good. The habit of reticence has become deeply engrained.) I allowed myself to imagine that the old man would adopt me as his grandson and take me away from the school to live with him. More realistically, I hoped he would ask me to have Christmas dinner with him.

On the Thursday before Christmas Day I was coming back from Early Practice in the company of another chorister. It had snowed overnight, which was extraordinary to me for I had never seen the stuff before. I didn't notice the old gentleman—who must have been on his way to the bank—until he was close upon me because I was lost in my thoughts, for I had been plunged into a state of horror during Practice that morning by something the choirmaster had announced. Mr Stonex suddenly addressed me by my name. The other boy went on ahead, turning round curiously to look at us, and it happened that at that moment young Mr Quitregard came past on his way to open up the Library as he always did at that hour on Thursdays.

Mr Stonex asked me if I would care to come to him for Christmas dinner. Then he said: 'You still haven't seen my maps, have you? Well, I expect to receive a fine old atlas this afternoon which I will show you if you come.'

'I should like that very much, sir,' I said. 'When?'

'This afternoon,' he said. His words were ambiguous and I so much wanted him to ask me to come to his house that very afternoon in order that I might avoid Late Practice that I persuaded myself that he was asking me to visit him that day. I half knew that he meant that the atlas was arriving that afternoon and he would show it to me on Christmas Day, and also that visiting him was not merely not a justification for missing Practice, but was to compound the offence. But I was desperate and was clutching at straws.

❖

Miss Napier wrote to me four years ago, just as the dark shadow was beginning to fall across Europe which has only just been lifted, asking for help with her book. I declined. My reason was not a lack of interest—on the contrary, I call myself the last victim for not a day passes but I think, with considerable anguish, of poor Perkins. The famous set of keys from Mr Stonex's house, about which so much to-do was made at the time, sat for many years on my desk where I saw them every day. Those keys went to the heart of the mystery of how the murderer got out of the house leaving it locked and were therefore crucial to Perkins's guilt or innocence.

I did not explain any of that to Miss Napier but merely said that I had taken a resolution many years before to divulge nothing about the case that was not already public knowledge. But because I liked the straightforward and friendly tone of her letter, I offered to read the manuscript in order to save her from errors of fact of the kind that had rendered the article so nonsensical. I made it absolutely clear that I would offer no advice on any speculation contained in the manuscript. The author thanked me and accepted those terms. And so some months later I received the manuscript of *The Thurchester Mystery* and corrected a few facts and was thanked in the 'Acknowledgements'.

That reference to myself, and my earlier letter to the newspaper, led in a roundabout way to my editing the foregoing Account. For it was because my name appeared in the book and I was described as a master at the Choir School and its Archivist that the Librarian of Colchester College wrote to me about a year ago. (I should explain that immediately after gaining my degree I had returned to Thurchester where—strangely, perhaps—I became a schoolteacher at the school where I had been so unhappy. Whether I had some idea of making up for my own unhappiness by helping others or was drawn back to the place simply because of how much I had endured there, like a ghost haunting the scene of its misery, I do not know. By that time, of course, which was nine years after the death of Mr Stonex, most of the people mentioned by Dr Courtine were long gone. But this is not an account of my life—which cannot be interesting to anyone else and is less and less so even to myself—and therefore I shall say no more.)

The theory propounded in *The Thurchester Mystery*, which was widely discussed and generally accepted, was of little interest to me since I knew it was wrong. I derived much amusement from listening to the heated arguments about it that took place in many of the houses and bars of the town. I would shake my head gravely when appealed to as someone who might have firsthand knowledge of what happened that afternoon inside the New Deanery. It would have been more truthful to have made it clear that I chose not to divulge what I knew. Although Miss Napier's book disclosed no facts about the murder which I did not know already, I found I was fascinated by the material which she had discovered about the early life of the victim and his relations with his sister and his extraordinary father, and also the subsequent life of those involved.

Miss Napier confirmed that as soon as their father died Mr Stonex brought to an abrupt end the many indulgences he had lavished on his daughter—the costly dresses, the lady's-maid, the succession of governesses whom she bullied, and the pony-cart which was at her sole disposal. It must have seemed to the headstrong, spoilt teenager that he was getting his revenge for years of humiliation and contempt at the hands of their father. It was true that for the next two years he refused to promise her even a share of their joint inheritance, and that he so neglected her that she was able to meet the actor with whom she eloped. And Miss Napier confirmed that five years later, when the sister reached her majority and demanded her share of what she imagined to be a large inheritance, he gave her nothing. They had fought a fierce legal battle and it may well be that he used underhand means to thwart her claim, though Miss Napier revealed that he had a good reason for what he did. When the father of her child realized that she was never going to be wealthy, he deserted her.

Left entirely without resources and having failed on the stage, she found a position as a housekeeper in Harrogate, and that is how she earned her living for the next twenty-five years. It was there and in those difficult circumstances that she brought up her son. He grew up deeply embittered towards both his father—for deserting his mother and himself—and his uncle, for refusing to surrender his mother's share of their inheritance. His mother called herself Mrs Stonex and gave the impression that she was the widow of a member of the well-known West Country family of that name. Perhaps she hoped that her son would eventually be recognized by her unmarried brother as his heir. Yet in giving in to her hatred she defeated her own purpose by poisoning her son against the brother she believed had wronged them both. She constantly reminded him that if they had had what was due to them in both morality and law, she would not be drudging for her living and he would be facing a glittering future. As a consequence the boy, who turned out to be wild and rebellious, so hated his uncle for what he had done that when he was eighteen he repudiated that side of his ancestry and adopted his father's name.

He tried to find his father and went to Ireland where he attempted to claim kinship with the grand families of Ormonde and de Burgh to which his father had always insisted he was related. But they unceremoniously rejected him and denied that he or his father had any legitimate connection with themselves. He had then hunted down his father and found him to be a hopeless drunkard who was deeply in debt and burdened with another young and illegitimate family. He now turned violently against him and blamed him for all his misfortunes, including the fact that he walked with a limp—though the truth is that that was not due to an accident caused by his father but to a congenital defect. Baffled in that direction, he then developed a passionate interest in his mother's family and her stolen inheritance. But while he had been dazzled by his father's aristocratic pretensions and had suffered a severe disappointment in discovering the reality, he had no feelings towards his uncle, except resentment and the desire for retribution.

I was particularly interested by what Miss Napier had discovered of the later destiny of the victim's sister after she inherited the estate. That was related to the matter about which the Librarian wrote to me when he informed me that Professor Courtine, who on his retirement had returned to Cambridge as an Emeritus Fellow, had left in the Governing Body's trust a sealed Account. This, it was assumed, would shed new light on the Stonex Case. In a covering letter written some years before he died, he had stipulated that the Account had to remain unopened until fifteen years after his death (a period which, the Librarian explained, had just expired) and could only be opened then if certain conditions had been met. It was in order to fulfil these requirements that the Librarian was soliciting my help.

I wrote back saying I would give him what assistance I was able to. And so in his next letter he enclosed a copy of Dr Courtine's covering letter. I need hardly say that I was astonished that an account by somebody so closely implicated in those events should come to light so many years later and was very anxious that the conditions should be met. I had never expected that my version of events—that of a child of twelve—would be believed. Now I knew that there was testimony which would confirm my own. It was that of someone else who had been in the New Deanery on the fateful afternoon and had had reasons for holding back some of his evidence.

Although I had not at the time been aware of the existence of Dr Courtine, he, as I eventually discovered when I read his Account, had noticed the incident involving myself which took place early that morning when Mr Stonex invited me to spend Christmas Day with him. (A day which, in the event, turned out to be the most miserable Christmas of my life.) I was so pleased by the prospect that had opened so suddenly before me that my concentration lapsed and as I was crossing the Upper Close I did not get out of the way of a bigger Courtenay boy quickly enough. He taunted me with a remark about the Gatehouse and when I tried to answer him I stammered badly and he jeered at me and seized from me the sheet of music which I was holding and dropped it into the muddy snow. Then he punched me and put his foot on the music and twisted it so that it became torn and dirtied.

All that day I was in a state of mounting terror about what would happen at Practice in the afternoon.

Miss Napier had managed to find the sister and discovered that she then lived in an enormous villa on the outskirts of Geneva. She had not answered Miss Napier's requests for an interview, but the indefatigable author had managed to find some of the servants who had worked for her. She had learnt that she had no friends and that the only people she received were those conducting her financial affairs. As far as her servants knew, she had no living relatives. And despite prolonged enquiries which, in the later stages of her research, were made even more difficult by wartime conditions, Miss Napier had been unable to discover anything about her son, who was, she assumed, sole heir to the enormous fortune which the old lady would presumably leave.

A little less than a year ago I received from the Librarian of

Colchester College the covering letter written by Dr Courtine. The letter said: 'Fifteen years having passed since my death, this account may be unsealed—provided the conditions below have been satisfied. When it has been opened and read by the Librarian, the President and the Fellows of the College, any use may be made of it which they think appropriate. The conditions require that both the individuals named below be certified as dead and if either of them is alive then the account can only be opened on that person's death.'

The Librarian said that one of them was known to be still living but asked for help with the other. In fact, I had corresponded about exactly that issue with Miss Napier without our coming to any conclusion. My interview in Geneva failed to resolve the matter, but the idea that had occurred to me on the journey back turned out to bear fruit. At the end of several months, therefore, I was able to produce proof, which satisfied the Librarian and the President of the College, that the other person on the list was dead.

The Librarian also sent me a copy he had made of a note which Dr Courtine had written on the outside of the package containing his Account. I was intrigued because I knew precisely when and why he had added it. It was because of me—because of something I had told him.

As I grew up, and in the years that followed, I tried to find out as much as I could about the people involved in the case. One day, while I was an undergraduate at Cambridge, I learnt a piece of news about one of them and a few days later I took the train to Oxford where Dr Courtine—or Professor Courtine as he now was— had the Chair in Medieval History which he had held for three years since Scuttard, who had obtained the post in 1882, had dropped dead at the age of forty-four. Scuttard had supervised publication of the Thurchester manuscript but Professor Courtine had, in the interval, published his magisterial and absorbing *Life of Alfred the Great*. It was because of that biography that he had at last acquired his Chair, even though some of his colleagues considered his work to be more imaginative than scholarly. I attended a lecture he happened to be giving that afternoon. It was on the reign of Ethelred the Unready and he brought that enigmatic period and its main protagonists vividly to life—perhaps with more freedom of imagination than strictness of scholarship. After it was over I approached him and told him how much I had enjoyed it. When I mentioned that I had been a schoolboy in Thurchester, he immediately invited me to take tea in his study.

I brought the conversation round to the Stonex affair but he made it clear he would say nothing at all about it. And then I mentioned Austin Fickling, referring to him in the past tense. When he queried that, I said I had just seen some sad news about him and showed him the item which I had cut out of the *Thurchester Clarion*. It was a report of the death of Fickling in Rome after a long and painful illness. The journalist reprised at considerable length the Stonex Case and, in passing, mentioned that the Irish actor whose professional name was Valentine Butler, though he also called himself Valentine Ormonde, and who had eloped with Mr Stonex's younger sister, had died many years before the murder.

I could see that Professor Courtine was shocked by what he had read. I pretended to think it was the death of his old friend that had so upset him but I knew it was not just that. It must have been after this that he had written the note on the outside of the envelope saying that he had been wrong about the actor. For in the light of the newspaper's reference to his date of death, Professor Courtine must have realized that he had made a wrong assumption in supposing that the individual who had impersonated Mr Stonex at the tea-party was his brother-in-law. That relationship, he had believed, was the reason for the slip of the tongue in an otherwise faultless performance. After learning that that was impossible, he must have wondered who the impersonator was. He was correct, incidentally, that the impostor made a very revealing slip of the tongue, but he failed to understand its significance.

Professor Courtine was kind enough to say, as I was leaving, that one day I must come to tea at his house and meet his wife and children—more properly, he might have said, his step-children.

I was in a state of anxiety, on the day of the murder, because at Practice that morning the choirmaster had announced that the organ was going to be put out of commission from the next day for at least a couple of weeks, and that in order to make up for the lack of an organ-recital at the main Christmas service, we would have to sing unaccompanied anthems. I was to be one of the soloists! He had handed me the music which I would have to sing that afternoon at Practice—the music that the Courtenay boy had torn and muddied a few minutes later. The hated music had now got me into even worse trouble, for the choirmaster became furious if we lost or damaged scores, which had to be returned to him in perfect condition. I believed it was because he wanted to humiliate me that he had chosen me to sing a solo. How much more it would add to his pleasure when I had to show him the music in this condition and he would have a reason to beat me even harder than he usually did. I passed the rest of that day in school brooding on the shame and humiliation that lay ahead of me at Evensong.

Of course, I was not the only person plunged into a state of panic by the decision to shut down the organ from Thursday evening. As Dr Courtine's Account shows, the conspirators' plans were thrown into confusion by the postponement of the inauguration ceremony for the refurbished organ.

Although Miss Napier's book brought to light several startling facts relating to the identity of the murderers and the motive, and put forward a theory which was nothing less than brilliant, she was handicapped by legal constraints arising from her uncertainty as to whether all of those whom she was implicating were still living. By that time she knew, of course, that Austin Fickling was dead and that the old lady was still alive at nearly ninety. She was not sure, however, about the man she was unable to name but referred to as 'the Arch-Conspirator' and who, like Fickling, vanished immediately after the murder. It was this individual, she argued, who enticed Fickling into the plot. A suspect to take the blame for the murder was needed, and so Perkins was tricked by the message chalked on the slate into compromising himself in a crime he had no knowledge of. Also required was a highly respectable witness to give evidence against him, and she argued that Dr Courtine was lured into the affair as a completely innocent dupe.

Miss Napier had found a recent reference to the Arch-Conspirator that showed he was alive—now in his middle seventies. She had heard from someone who had known him years before that he had been seen in Naples recently.

It was immediately clear to me who was meant by the Arch-Conspirator and I found I was right when I received Dr Courtine's covering letter naming the two suspects. Anxious to read the Account, I therefore set out to discover whether or not this individual was still alive. The result of my efforts, following the death of the old lady six months after my frustrating though ultimately profitable visit to her, was that two months ago the President and the Fellows—with myself as the only outsider—assembled in the Combination Room of the College, and the Librarian broke the seal and read out Dr Courtine's account.

One mystery addressed by Miss Napier was the question of how the killer gained access to the house since Mr Stonex would open the door only to Mrs Bubbosh and the waiter, and only at times when he was expecting them. Miss Napier's brilliant suggestion that the murderer arrived just a minute or two before Perkins was due at half-past five and so the victim opened the door expecting the waiter would solve that problem.

Similarly, the puzzle as to how and when the murderer left the house would also be resolved by Miss Napier's astonishing hypothesis that he did so dressed as a woman and that he might have been the female whom the Headmaster, Appleton, met at the back of the house at about twenty minutes to six and who directed him round to the front in his search for myself.

In fact, both of those suggestions—ingenious though they are in their knitting together of known facts—are mistaken, although each of them comes close to the truth. The female seen by Appleton was certainly a real woman and Mr Stonex did not open the door to his killer at half-past five for he was dead by then. But Miss Napier had correctly guessed the means of entry to the house and was right that the figure seen by the Headmaster had impersonated the opposite sex.

Having brooded over my dilemma all day, I made a sudden decision as afternoon-school ended: not only would I mitch off Practice but I would also cut Evensong. I had never done that before and I could not imagine the consequences of such an offence, but they seemed less real than the certainty of the humiliation that would occur if I went.

I persuaded myself that Mr Stonex had, indeed, invited me to call on him that afternoon to look at the new atlas and so, without quite deciding to go there, I found myself outside the street-door of the New Deanery.

It was within a minute or two of ten minutes after four as I know for sure since school ended at a quarter to and I was thinking all the time of how the other boys were arriving for Practice and the choirmaster would be checking attendance, and I calculated the exact moment when he would realize that I was missing. Just as I reached Mr Stonex's front-door I saw the unfortunate Perkins leave the house to carry the dirty pans and dishes from the previous day across to the inn.

I went closer and noticed that there was a scrap of paper pinned to the door on which was written in small letters that would only be read from close to: 'Come in.' Although I guessed that this was addressed to the waiter, I permitted myself to believe that it was an invitation to myself and therefore, after knocking without result, I tried the door and, finding it unlocked, went in.

The houseplace was deserted and looked exactly as it had when I had last seen it—except that the table was not laid for tea but for dinner. The food left by Perkins was sitting there getting cold. Beside the plates and dishes was a large leatherbound volume which, greatly daring, I opened and found to be an old atlas with hand-coloured plates of the most fascinating nature. It was clearly the one the old gentleman had mentioned that morning and I was sure that he must be elsewhere in the house, and so I decided to wait until he came into the room for his dinner.

I must have looked at the atlas for about ten or fifteen minutes. Then I began to feel the awkwardness of my position. Perhaps Mr Stonex would not be pleased to find me waiting there. It began to seem increasingly odd that nobody came into the room, the food was sitting there uneaten, and the house was utterly silent. I dared not venture beyond the room I was in. I looked around and there on the sideboard I saw the slate with its chalked message exactly as the waiter later described it. I know that Perkins summarized it accurately for I recall thinking that if Mr Stonex was busy I should wait no longer, and so I walked out into the street.

Now I was in a dilemma. Until it was darker I could not wander around in the dress of a choir-school boy—a plain black jacket and salt and pepper breeches with a white stock—without attracting attention for it would be generally known that I should be at Practice at that hour. I had an idea. Very cautiously—because I could not allow myself to be seen by anyone who knew me—I went round to the side of the Cathedral where I could look in through a window of the Chapter House where Practice took place. I could see the choirmaster standing at the piano—he never sat because it would have been harder to hurry over to a boy and cuff him. The fact that he was playing the piano meant that Mr Slattery had not arrived and that did not surprise me for he was often late. A few minutes later I saw him come hurrying in—at about twenty minutes to five—looking as always defiant and yet lazy at the same time. The choirmaster glared at him but, with a vulpine smile, Mr Slattery pulled over the stool and seated himself at the keyboard. I should state that I noticed nothing untoward about his appearance. He was dishevelled—but then he always was. His pasty face seemed flushed—but that might have been with drink. In short, he looked as if he had spent the afternoon innocently enough in his custom-ary fashion—sitting in a public-house. For the next twenty minutes I watched the other boys and the men singers doing the things I should be doing with them and had a strange sense of no longer be-ing one of them, almost as if I had died. And the fears about the ru-ined sheet of music that had preoccupied me suddenly seemed absurdly petty.

Although I knew how frightened of the choirmaster I should have been if I had been inside, the scene looked cosy. The gas-lights were turned up, there was a stove burning brightly in the cor-ner, and I could faintly hear the music. Yet I knew that the charm was an illusion and I preferred the cold and darkness outside.

Shortly before five I saw Appleton arrive for Evensong just as Practice was ending, and I watched the choirmaster take him aside and the Headmaster's face darken, and I guessed that they were talking about me. Now my sense of detachment vanished, and when I saw Appleton stride towards the door I was sure that he was going to look for me. It suddenly occurred to me that the best way to avoid being found was to follow him.

For more than half an hour I trailed him around the darkening streets. I found that I was enjoying the game and yet I was possessed by a growing sense of dread as to the outcome, for eventually I would have to declare myself and accept a flogging. At about twenty past five, Appleton was walking along St Mary's Street when he met the friendly young man who worked at the Dean and Chapter's Library. I could not hear their conversation but I later guessed that Mr Quitregard mentioned—quite innocently—that he had seen me talking to Mr Stonex early that morning and that is why Appleton now hurriedly directed his steps towards the Close. At just after half-past five I found myself passing the back of the New Deanery about fifty feet behind the Headmaster. We must have missed seeing Dr Courtine and Austin Fickling leave by the back-door by no more than two or three minutes.

I was just level with the back-door when Appleton turned suddenly so that I had to press myself against the gates to avoid being seen. I was terrified that he was going to retrace his steps in which case he would find me, but he had heard footsteps behind him. It was an old woman. He accosted her and, as he said at the inquest, asked her if she had seen me. She said she thought I might be round at the front-door. I did not know what they were saying to each other, of course, but to my relief he cut through the alleyway where, as he said at the inquest, he found not me but the waiter, Perkins, knocking at the street-door. (I believe it was in order that he should see him that the woman had sent Appleton round there.)

What Appleton did not realize—but what I had perceived, being some yards behind him—was that the old woman had come from the back-gate of the New Deanery itself.

Miss Napier guessed that the old woman was crucial to the mystery and assembled much of the information required for the solution, but she put several of the pieces in the wrong place and failed to find others. For example, she did not understand why the victim's face was so hideously battered. Crucially, she left out of her account the doctor's conviction that the deceased died much earlier than seemed consistent with all the other evidence. And the departure from the house at twenty to six—when Appleton and I saw the woman leave—was impossible if the murderer's entry was as late as a mere ten minutes before that time, as Miss Napier assumes: the murderer would not have had time to batter the victim's face (somehow avoiding getting covered in blood) and ransack the house in the search for the will.

When I realized that the woman had just left the New Deanery, I was intrigued, because I knew how solitary and ordered a life the old gentleman led and that the house had been silent only an hour earlier. So I abandoned the pursuit of the Headmaster and followed her instead. She walked the few yards to the door into the Cloisters and disappeared. I advanced and watched from the doorway— hidden by the gathering darkness—and saw that she leaned over the stone wall that separated the Cloisters from the ancient well of St Wulflac and threw something towards it. Then she walked quickly towards the door into the Cathedral and passed through it. I hurried up to where she had stood. The well had—and still has to this day—a big stone conical basin surrounding it and the object had landed on its edge and was sliding towards the centre where it would fall hundreds of feet. I scrambled over the wall and, somewhat recklessly, reached down to save it just as it was about to slide out of reach for ever. It was a set of keys: two big old ones on a metal ring.

When I learnt from the Librarian that Dr Courtine's manuscript would remain sealed until and unless the second person on the list could be shown to be dead, I pondered deeply on my way forward.

And then it occurred to me that a passionate love of music was likely to endure. I persuaded a friend of mine, who is a composer of some note, to let me write a letter as if from him which I then sent to all the music-publishers and all the bookshops which specialized in sheet-music. This is the important part of the letter:

About eight years ago I met a gentleman who showed a profound knowledge and love of the organ and of the music written for it. When he learnt my name he was kind enough to tell me that he knew and admired my compositions—which, as you possibly know, have hitherto been exclusively for the pianoforte—and when I mentioned that I intended to write a piece for the organ he urged me to do so and asked me to send him a copy of it when I had finished it. It has taken all these years, but I am now close to completing a Fantaisie in A Major for the organ.

Unfortunately, I have mislaid the piece of paper on which I had written the gentleman's name and address which, to the best of my recollection, was in Rome or, perhaps, Naples. I am venturing to write to you because the gentleman mentioned that while he was living on the Continent he had sheet-music sent to him by your firm.

Absurdly, I am not even sure that I can remember his name precisely. To the best of my recollection his surname was something like Butler Ormonde or possibly Ormonde de Burgh. And his Christian name was, I think, Martin or perhaps Valentine.

The surnames were, of course, those of the families with whom 'Mrs Stonex's' lover claimed kinship. My little stratagem worked and one of the publishers wrote back saying:

We believe you must mean Mr Ormonde Martin, a gentleman who regularly purchased sheet-music for the organ over a long period of years. We are sorry to have to inform you that he died about three years ago, as was learnt when the last parcel

of music which was sent to him in Florence was returned—
after a considerable delay due to prevailing conditions—by a
lawyer dealing with his estate.

So he had been alive while Miss Napier was researching her book,
but dead for a couple of years by the time I made my visit to his
mother. Knowing the date and place of his death, obtaining from
the British consul in Florence the documentary evidence that I
needed was a mere formality. From him, incidentally, I learnt that
'Mr Ormonde Martin' had lived the life—the somewhat scandalous
life—of a rich idle man in Italy for the last thirty-five years of his
existence.

After retrieving the keys from the basin of the well, I went back to
the schoolroom, hid them in my box and waited for the summons
to punishment. It did not come that day, for the news of the old
gentleman's murder distracted the Headmaster's attention from my
offence, and the next day he had to attend the inquest. How ar-
dently I hoped that these shocking events had driven the memory
of my misdemeanour from his memory. All the rest of Thursday
and the next day I anguished about whether I should tell anyone
what I knew, but I was frightened to admit that I had befriended
Mr Stonex and gone to his house for tea and, above all, that I had
entered it again—and uninvited—that afternoon. Of course, I did
not understand the significance of the keys.

And then after breakfast on Saturday the Headmaster called me
to his study. He had not, after all, forgotten about me. I am certain
that if he had asked me then why I went to the New Deanery during Practice on Thursday afternoon, I would have told him everything I knew, so frightened and upset was I. But he had no curiosity
about my motives for absconding and simply set to in a workman-
like way, stinking of brandy and gasping as the blows fell. That af-

ternoon I learned of Perkins's death when I overheard two of the servants talking about it in shocked tones.

When I went to Cambridge a few months ago and laid before the President and Fellows of Colchester College the documents from Florence which were the proof that was required, I found that they were fascinated by the case—several of them revealing themselves to have what I would venture to call a scholarly knowledge of it— and were intrigued to learn that I had some undisclosed evidence of my own. With great solemnity the seals of Professor Courtine's Account were broken and it was read out by the Librarian. This took most of the day, with a break for luncheon. When the reading was completed, the President asked me to withdraw for a few minutes while he and the Fellows conferred as they were required to do by the terms of Professor Courtine's letter. He then called me back to ask if I would undertake responsibility for editing and publishing the Account and if I would write an 'Introduction' to it. I agreed immediately.

In taking on this task, I set out to explain as much as I could of the events of the crucial period covered by Professor Courtine's Account, creating a kind of scholarly edition with a commentary. For example, I was curious about the book of fairy-tales which Professor Courtine found in Fickling's house late on Wednesday night and from which he read a story while waiting for him to return. The book was borrowed from the library of Courtenay's and it was there that I found it some forty-five years later. (One might speculate as to why the story made such an impression on Dr Courtine.)

On that Friday night, as he makes clear in his Account, Dr Courtine realized the truth and understood how his old friend—I should say, his former friend—had made use of him. He had been lured to

Thurchester and tricked into playing the role of an unimpeachable witness—and yet the witness to a lie. On his first evening, the ghost-story was told him by Fickling merely to entice him into going to read the inscription so that he would meet the old gentleman— or, rather, the person whom he would take to be the old gentleman—and receive the invitation to tea. That meeting, of course, was a charade. The individual impersonating the old gentleman had merely taken up a position outside the back-gate at the time when Mr Stonex was sure to be eating his dinner. The intention was, as happened, that Dr Courtine would assume that the individual who gave him tea was Mr Stonex—though by the time he and Fickling arrived, the old gentleman was dead.

Miss Napier came close to the truth in suggesting that the murderer left the house disguised as the woman seen by Appleton, but in fact that individual *was* actually a woman. And it was the same woman whom Dr Courtine heard when he watched Fickling through the window of the house in Orchard Street in the early hours of the same day. But she had not acted alone at the New Deanery, of course, for a woman—even one in the prime of life, as this one was not, although she was healthy and active for her age and had certainly not suffered a stroke—would not have been strong enough to overpower Mr Stonex at his front-door, strangle him and drag his body across the houseplace.

And although Miss Napier was almost right when she guessed that the killer—in fact, the killers—gained entry to the house by knocking at the street-door just a few minutes before Mr Stonex was expecting the waiter, in fact that occurred at four o'clock and not at half-past five. By the time I arrived ten minutes later the old gentleman was dead.

I imagine he recognized his attackers. One of them he knew well but had not set eyes on for nearly forty years. He had probably only seen the other once at close quarters and that was eight years earlier when he came to demand a share of the money he believed he was entitled to. (It was after that that Mr Stonex started to take elaborate measures for his safety.)

The killers must have been filled with a sense of righteous vengeance, being convinced of the justice of their brutal act. It was too late for explanations but, ironically, Mr Stonex was very far from guilty of the offence for which they had condemned him. Miss Napier had spent weeks searching through the old records of the Thurchester and County Bank (which had been sold to the Somerset and Thurshire Bank and incorporated into it) and had found that the rumour handed down by Quitregard's grandfather was correct. When, at the age of twenty-two, Mr Stonex had inherited the bank on his father's death, he had made a terrible discovery: it was a sham. Although it had a note circulation of seventy-five thousand pounds, it had huge liabilities and no reserve funds so that it was teetering on the edge of collapse. His father had been pillaging it for years and his defalcations had robbed hundreds of people who had deposited their savings with the bank or mortgaged properties to it or accepted its notes. Their lives and those of their dependents could be destroyed by its collapse. Moreover, although he had been deeply injured by his father's treatment of him, he had loved him in a strange way, and he dreaded his memory being besmirched by the revelation of dishonesty. And therefore he had embarked on the endeavour to repair the bank's fortunes by performing an elaborate juggling act in which he had to balance monies received against liabilities without giving any sign of difficulty even to his senior clerk. Confidence was everything: so long as all seemed well, the bank's notes would continue to circulate. This was the long and secret act of heroism which he had mentioned to me in veiled terms.

He had not dared reveal the truth to his sister, for he could not trust a high-spirited young miss to keep the secret, and if it was suspected that the bank was in trouble, default would be inevitable. He had therefore had to impose upon her a penitential system of parsimony for which she could see no justification. Similarly, he dared not enter into negotiations on her behalf for a marriage-settlement, and because he could not explain, she never forgave him for ruining her life. Her elopement, though it brought disgrace, must almost have seemed a relief to him. And when he told his sister, on her reaching her majority, that there was no inheritance, he was telling the truth. In fact, it was only after thirty years of hard work, continuous worry and lacerating parsimony (which had become an engrained habit long after the need for it had gone) that he had succeeded in saving the bank and its depositors.

Unaware of this, his sister and his nephew—who had just strangled him with those strong hands that he stared at in fascination a few hours later when he met Dr Courtine—dragged the old man's body into the hall. It was then that they must have put the message on the street-door and written the one on the slate in order to lure Perkins into the trap and make him incriminate himself. He took the bait and left, bearing with him the package which—as he realized on Friday night alone and terrified in his cell—would surely have hanged him within a few months.

I believe that at the moment when I arrived at the street-door and read the message which they had not yet removed, the murderers were stripping the old man of his top clothes. When they heard my knock they must have been dismayed for they were at the most vulnerable and incriminating point of the whole undertaking. They probably looked through the door-jamb into the houseplace from the hall and, seeing that it was only a boy, decided to wait until I had gone.

By the time I left, I had made them nearly fifteen minutes late so that they didn't have time to drag the body along the passage into the dining-room as had been planned. They therefore decided to leave it where it was. (That was why Fickling was so horrified at the idea of going into that room when Dr Courtine expressed a desire to see it.) During this time he had approached the house with Dr Courtine but, failing to see the signal that all was ready, had led him back to his own dwelling.

As soon as I had gone Mrs Slattery, now dressed in her brother's clothes, cleared the dinner away, dirtying the plates as if Mr Stonex had used them and packing the food into a parcel so that she could take it away with her. Then she set the tea, laying out the cakes she had baked in the early hours of that day—the smell of which had led Dr Courtine to the conspirators' house. While she was doing this, her son was in the study removing his own outer clothes in order to smash his uncle's face without getting blood on them.

They must have been alarmed at the delay I had caused because Slattery could not be too late for choir Practice since that occasion, and then Evensong, were to provide him with his unimpeachable alibi. My unwitting intervention also meant that they had only a few minutes to find the will, which was crucial if their crime was not to benefit the Choir School rather than themselves, and it was now that they ransacked the houseplace. Failing to find it, the resourceful actress hit upon the idea of a lost account of the murder of Freeth in order to continue the search right under the nose of Dr Courtine. In their haste they made one small mistake in forgetting to rub out the chalk message and hide the slate.

A minute or two after I had gone, Slattery hurried out of the New Deanery, probably visited a public-house to down a quick glass of beer, and arrived for Practice—as I happened to notice since I was looking in through the window—just a little later than he should have. Only now did his mother light the candle in the window of the dining-room to signal to Fickling that he could arrive with Dr Courtine.

At the end of the charade, Fickling's guess—based on the poor time-keeping of the clock—that old Mr Stonex might use the same ingenious hiding-place as himself saved the day for the conspirators. As a consequence, the will was safely destroyed and the victim's sister inherited the estate. There is a curious post-script on that topic. A Swiss newspaper reported that the old lady, having outlived the rest of her wealthy family—and, presumably, having inherited from her son the money they had divided between them—and therefore leaving no heir, had died intestate and her estate had gone to the Swiss Treasury.

By late on Saturday morning the other boys had gone. I was alone and, in the excitement, Appleton and his wife had forgotten that I existed. I was in too much pain from my flogging to be able to spend the afternoon wandering around the town according to my usual custom. I passed it instead gazing out of the schoolroom window, thinking about the events of the previous day. The news of Perkins's suicide had added mental anguish to my physical suffering. Lying in the little top room under the bed-coverings to try to keep warm, since I was not allowed a fire all to myself, I thought of the miserable Christmas Day I would have alone tomorrow instead of looking at Mr Stonex's maps and eating his dinner. I was sorry for the old man but most of all I was sorry for Perkins and his widow and children and asked myself over and over again if he would still be alive if I had had the courage to tell someone what I had seen, and shown them the keys. Not everybody had forgotten me. Towards midnight I heard a familiar creaking and knew that Dr Sheldrick was creeping up the stairs to rub embrocation on my bruises.

PHILIP BARTHRAM
Thurchester, 17 August 1919

List of Characters

The names of characters in historical periods earlier than the late nineteenth century are in italics.

ADAMS: the Police-Sergeant.

ALFRED: King of Wessex in the ninth century.

ANTROBUS, MAJOR: the Police Superintendent.

APPLETON: the Headmaster of the Cathedral Choir School.

ATTARD: the Coroner.

BARTHRAM, PHILIP: the Editor of the Courtine Account.

BEORGHTNOTH: the nephew of Alfred, according to *De Vita Gestibusque Alfredi Regis*.

BUBBOSH, MRS: Mr Stonex's servant.

BULLIVANT, GILES: the correspondent of the antiquarian, Ralph Pepperdine.

BULMER: the Surveyor of the Fabric.

BURGOYNE, WILLIAM: the Canon-Treasurer.

BURGOYNE, WILLOUGHBY: the Parliamentary officer who is the canon's nephew.

CARPENTER, DR: the physician.

CHAMPNISS: the Sacrist.

CINNAMON: the Precentor.

CLAGGETT: the head-verger.

COURTINE, EDWARD: the author of the Account.

FICKLING, AUSTIN: the Schoolmaster at Courtenay's Academy who was at Cambridge with Courtine.

FREETH, LAUNCELOT: the Sub-Dean who becomes Dean and is murdered.

GAMBRILL, JOHN: the Cathedral Mason.

GAZZARD: the head-verger.

GRIMBALD: the assumed author of *De Vita Gestibusque Alfredi Regis* (*Life of Alfred the Great*).

HOLLINGRAKE: the Librarian who becomes Treasurer.

LEOFRANC: the Bishop of Thurchester in the early twelfth century.

LIMBRICK, ALICE: the mother of Thomas.

LIMBRICK, ROBERT: the father of Thomas who was the Deputy Cathedral Mason.

LIMBRICK, THOMAS: Gambrill's foreman.

LOCARD, MRS: the wife of the Librarian.

LOCARD, ROBERT: the Librarian.

NAPIER, MISS: the author of *The Thurchester Mystery*.

PEPPERDINE, RALPH: the antiquarian who finds in the Library in 1663 the document Courtine is looking for.

PERKINS, EDDY: the waiter at the Angel Inn.

POMERANCE: the second assistant-librarian.

QUITREGARD: the first assistant-librarian.

SCUTTARD: Courtine's competitor for Chair of History at Oxford.

SHELDRICK: the Chancellor.

SISTERSON, FREDERICK: the Sacrist.

SLATTERY, MARTIN: assistant-organist and teacher at the Choir School.

STONEX, JAMES: the old banker who is murdered.

STONEX, MRS: the mother of Slattery.

THORROLD: Stonex's and the Cathedral Foundation's solicitor.

WATTAM, ALFRED: the senior-clerk from Stonex's bank.

WULFLAC: according to *De Vita Gestibusque Alfredi Regis*, the martyred Bishop of Thurchester in Alfred's time.

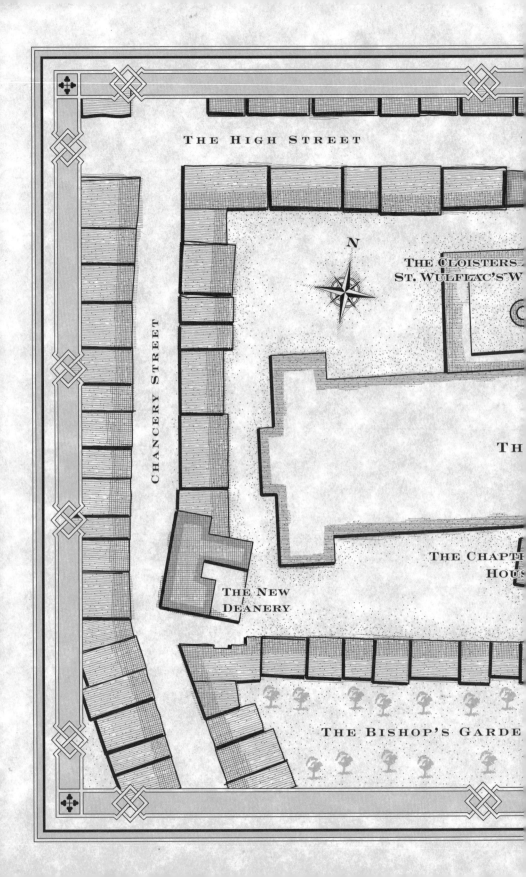

THE HIGH STREET

CHANCERY STREET

N

THE CLOISTERS
ST. WULFLAC'S W

TH

THE CHAPT
HOUS

THE NEW
DEANERY

THE BISHOP'S GARDE